♥ 62 likes

m_agarwal_69 she. is. my. everything. 🤍🖤😍😍

**VOLUME
THREE**

NO M

VOLUME THREE

NO MERCY, VOL. 3. First printing. May 2017. Published by Image Comics, Inc. Office of publication: 2701 NW Vaughn St., Suite 780, Portland, OR 97210. Copyright © 2017 Alex de Campi, Carla Speed McNeil, & Jenn Manley Lee. All rights reserved. Contains material originally published in single magazine form as NO MERCY #10-14. "No Mercy," its logos, and the likenesses of all characters herein are trademarks of Alex de Campi, Carla Speed McNeil, & Jenn Manley Lee, unless otherwise noted. "Image" and the Image Comics logos are registered trademarks of Image Comics, Inc. No part of this publication may be reproduced or transmitted, in any form or by any means (except for short excerpts for journalistic or review purposes), without the express written permission of Alex de Campi, Carla Speed McNeil, Jenn Manley Lee, or Image Comics, Inc. All names, characters, events, and locales in this publication are entirely fictional. Any resemblance to actual persons (living or dead), events, or places, without satiric intent, is coincidental. Printed in the USA. For information regarding the CPSIA on this printed material call: 203-595-3636 and provide reference #RICH–736904. For international rights, contact: foreignlicensing@imagecomics.com. ISBN: 978-1-63215-893-2.

IMAGE COMICS, INC.
Robert Kirkman—Chief Operating Officer
Erik Larsen—Chief Financial Officer
Todd McFarlane—President
Marc Silvestri—Chief Executive Officer
Jim Valentino—Vice-President

Eric Stephenson—Publisher
Corey Murphy—Director of Sales
Jeff Boison—Director of Publishing Planning & Book Trade Sales
Chris Ross—Director of Digital Sales
Jeff Stang—Director of Specialty Sales
Kat Salazar—Director of PR & Marketing
Branwyn Bigglestone—Controller
Sue Korpela—Accounts Manager
Drew Gill—Art Director
Brett Warnock—Production Manager
Meredith Wallace—Print Manager
Tricia Ramos—Traffic Manager
Briah Skelly—Publicist
Aly Hoffman—Events & Conventions Coordinator
Sasha Head—Sales & Marketing Production Designer
David Brothers—Branding Manager
Melissa Gifford—Content Manager
Drew Fitzgerald—Publicity Assistant
Vincent Kukua—Production Artist
Erika Schnatz—Production Artist
Ryan Brewer—Production Artist
Shanna Matuszak—Production Artist
Carey Hall—Production Artist
Esther Kim—Direct Market Sales Representative
Emilio Bautista—Digital Sales Representative
Leanna Caunter—Accounting Assistant
Chloe Ramos-Peterson—Library Market Sales Representative
Maria Eizik—Administrative Assistant
IMAGECOMICS.COM

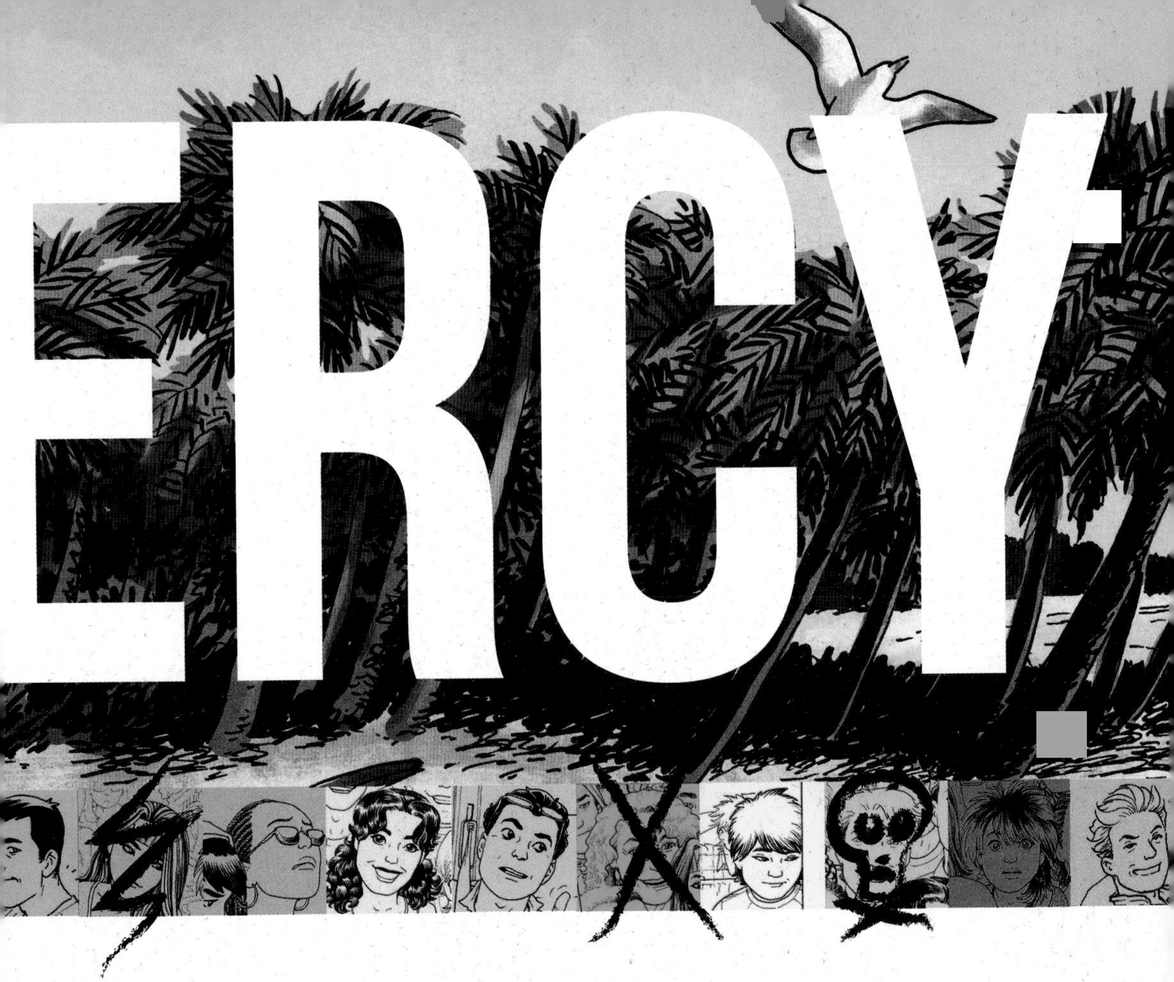
ERCY

ALEX DE CAMPI

CARLA SPEED MCNEIL

JENN MANLEY LEE

AND FELIPE SOBREIRO

CHAPTER ONE

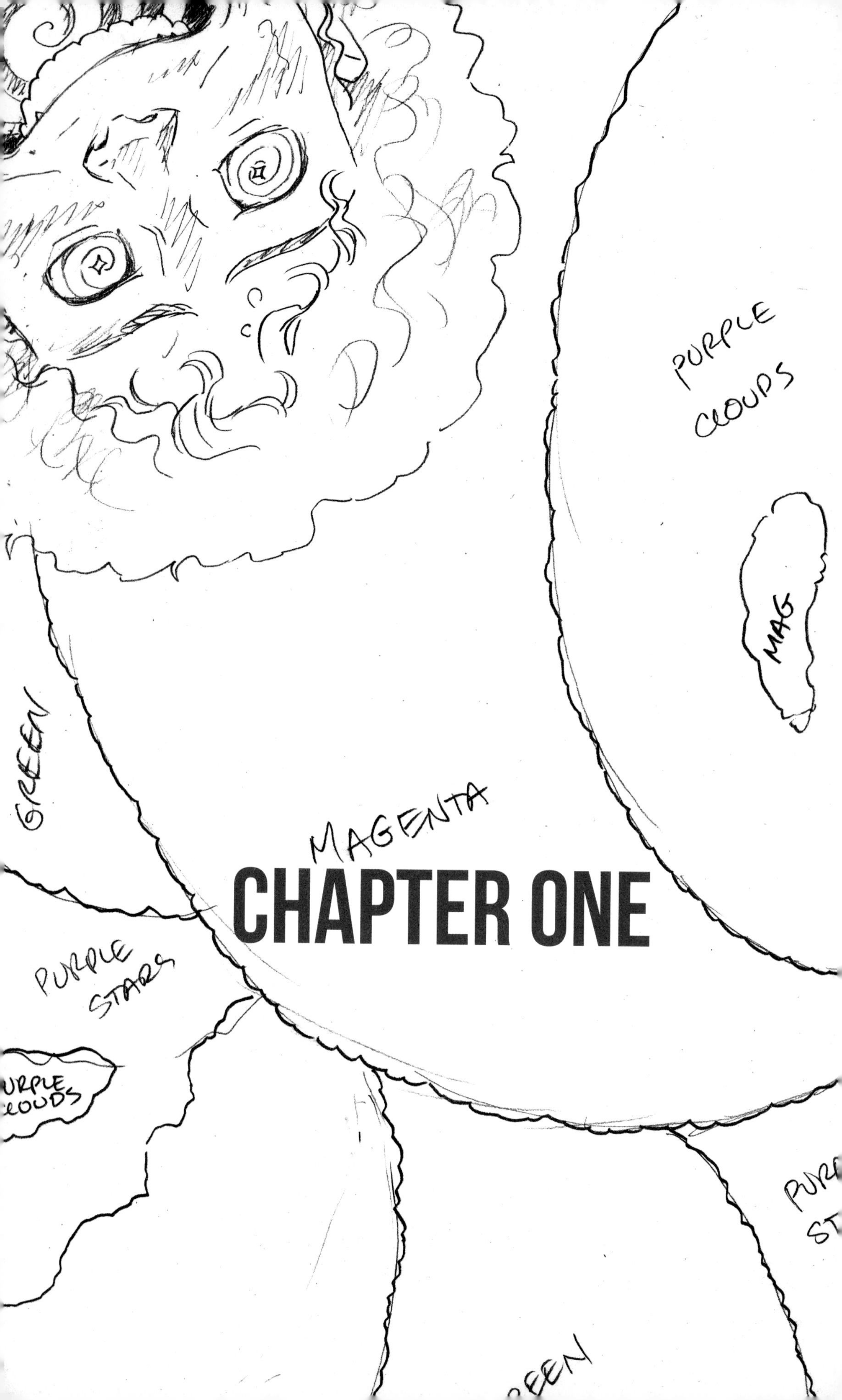
PURPLE CLOUDS
MAG
GREEN
MAGENTA
PURPLE STARS

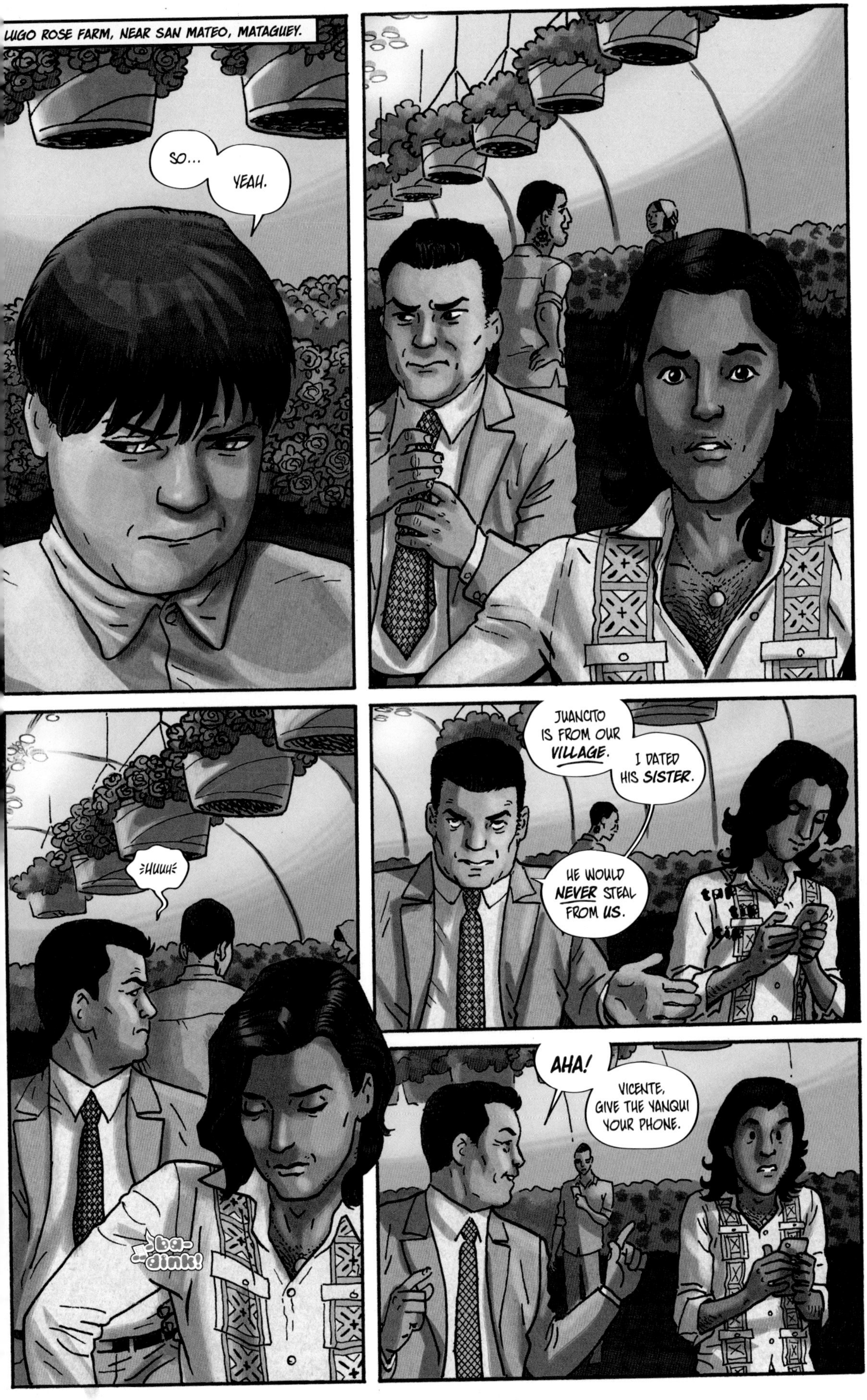
LUGO ROSE FARM, NEAR SAN MATEO, MATAGUEY.
SO...
YEAH.
HUUUH
JUANCITO IS FROM OUR VILLAGE.
I DATED HIS SISTER.
HE WOULD NEVER STEAL FROM US.
ba-dink!
AHA!
VICENTE, GIVE THE YANQUI YOUR PHONE.

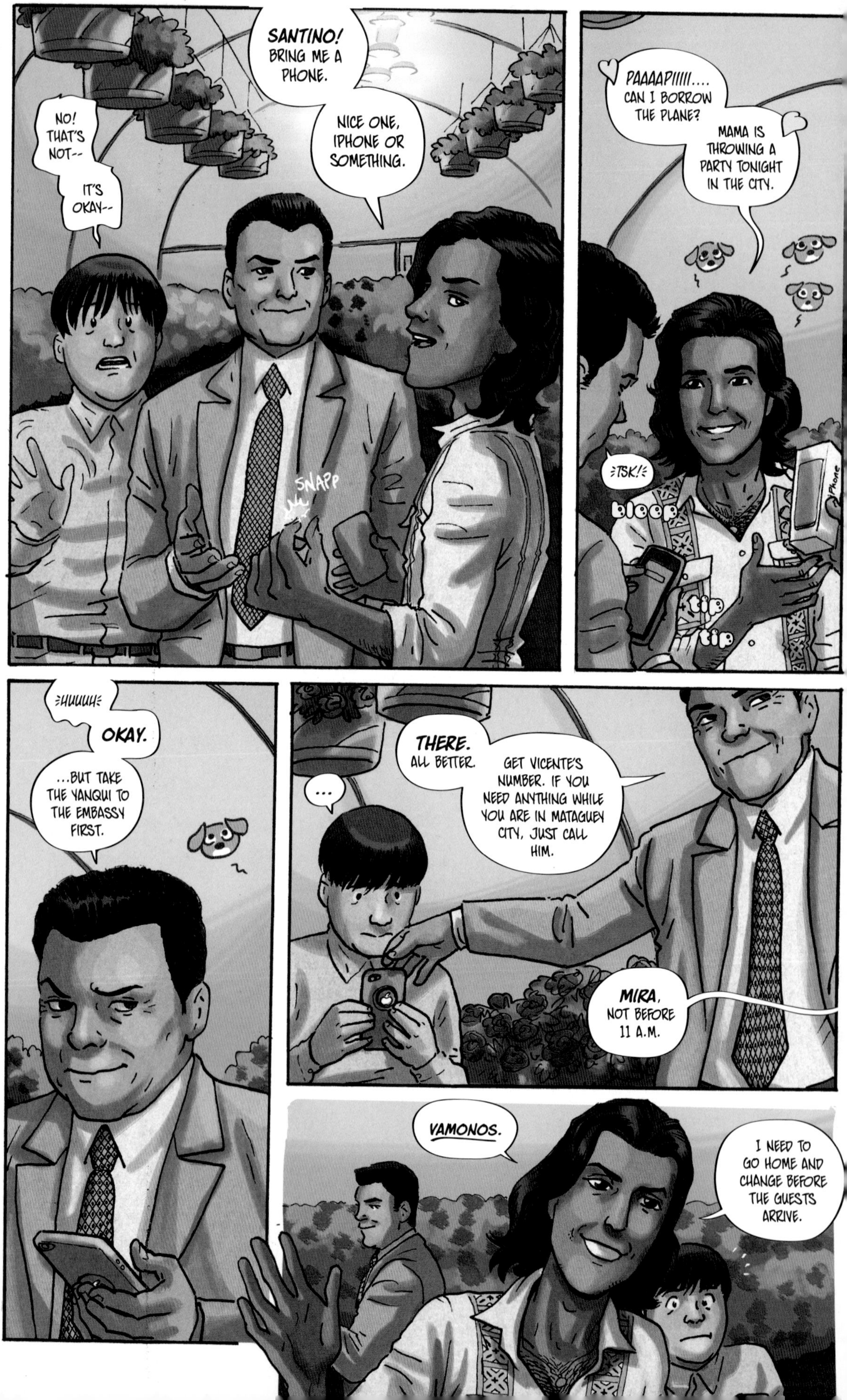
SANTINO! BRING ME A PHONE.
NO! THAT'S NOT--
IT'S OKAY--
NICE ONE, IPHONE OR SOMETHING.
SNAPP
PAAAAPIIIII.... CAN I BORROW THE PLANE?
MAMA IS THROWING A PARTY TONIGHT IN THE CITY.
TSK!
bleep
tip
tip
iPhone
HUUUH
OKAY.
...BUT TAKE THE YANQUI TO THE EMBASSY FIRST.
...
THERE. ALL BETTER.
GET VICENTE'S NUMBER. IF YOU NEED ANYTHING WHILE YOU ARE IN MATAGUEY CITY, JUST CALL HIM.
MIRA, NOT BEFORE 11 A.M.
VAMONOS.
I NEED TO GO HOME AND CHANGE BEFORE THE GUESTS ARRIVE.

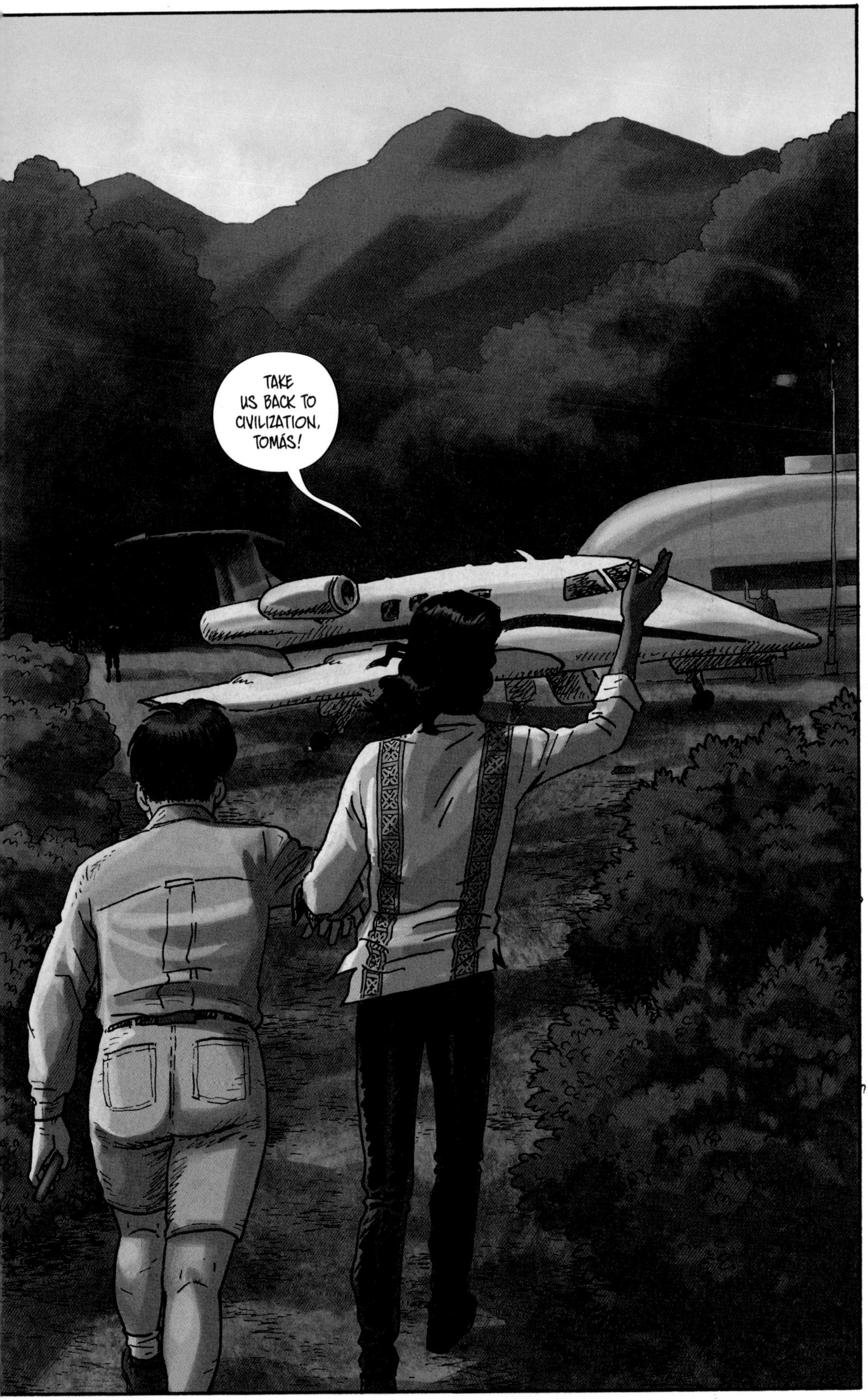
TAKE US BACK TO CIVILIZATION, TOMÁS!

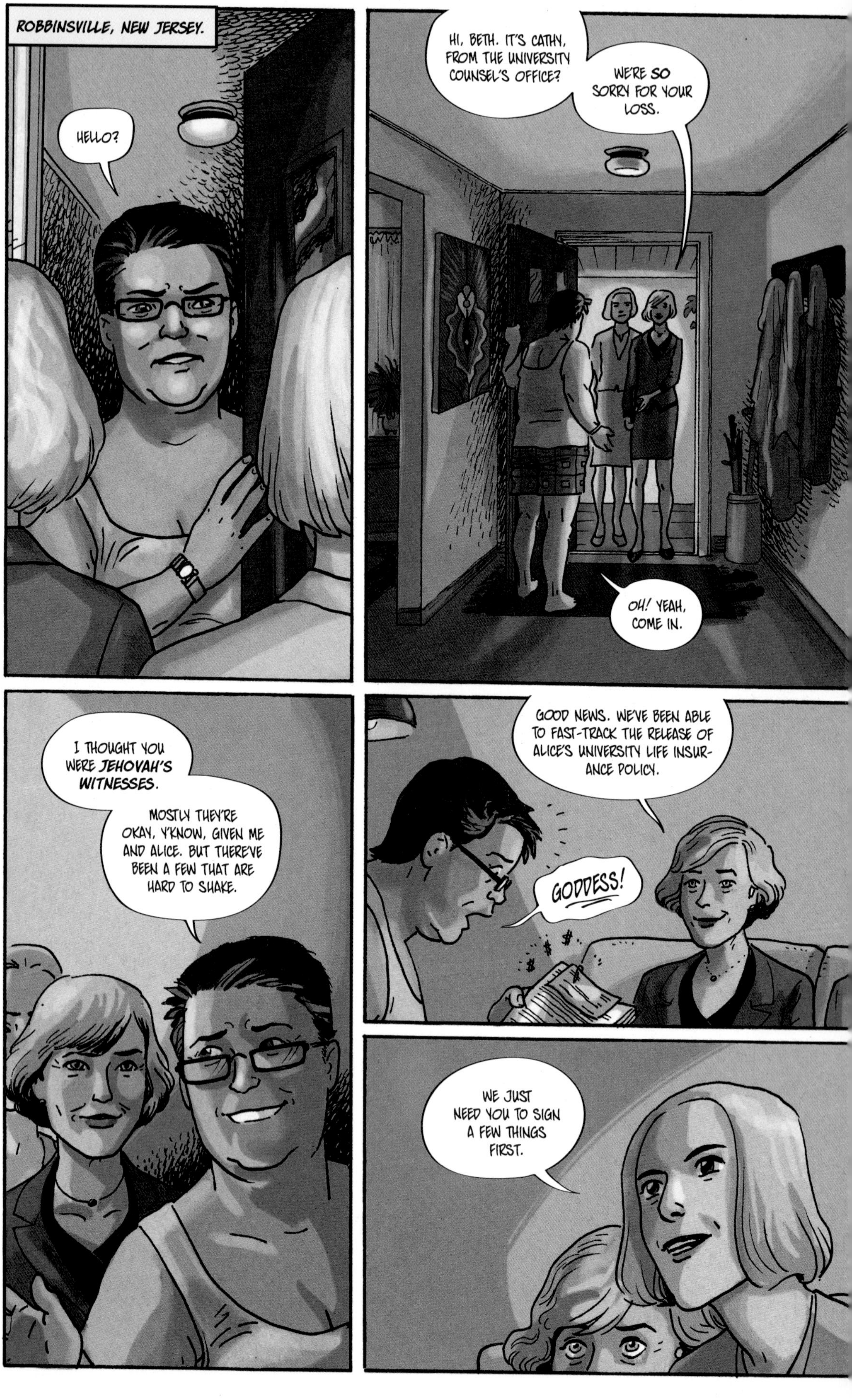
ROBBINSVILLE, NEW JERSEY.
HELLO?
HI, BETH. IT'S CATHY, FROM THE UNIVERSITY COUNSEL'S OFFICE?
WE'RE SO SORRY FOR YOUR LOSS.
OH! YEAH, COME IN.
I THOUGHT YOU WERE JEHOVAH'S WITNESSES.
MOSTLY THEY'RE OKAY, Y'KNOW, GIVEN ME AND ALICE. BUT THERE'VE BEEN A FEW THAT ARE HARD TO SHAKE.
GOOD NEWS. WE'VE BEEN ABLE TO FAST-TRACK THE RELEASE OF ALICE'S UNIVERSITY LIFE INSURANCE POLICY.
GODDESS!
WE JUST NEED YOU TO SIGN A FEW THINGS FIRST.

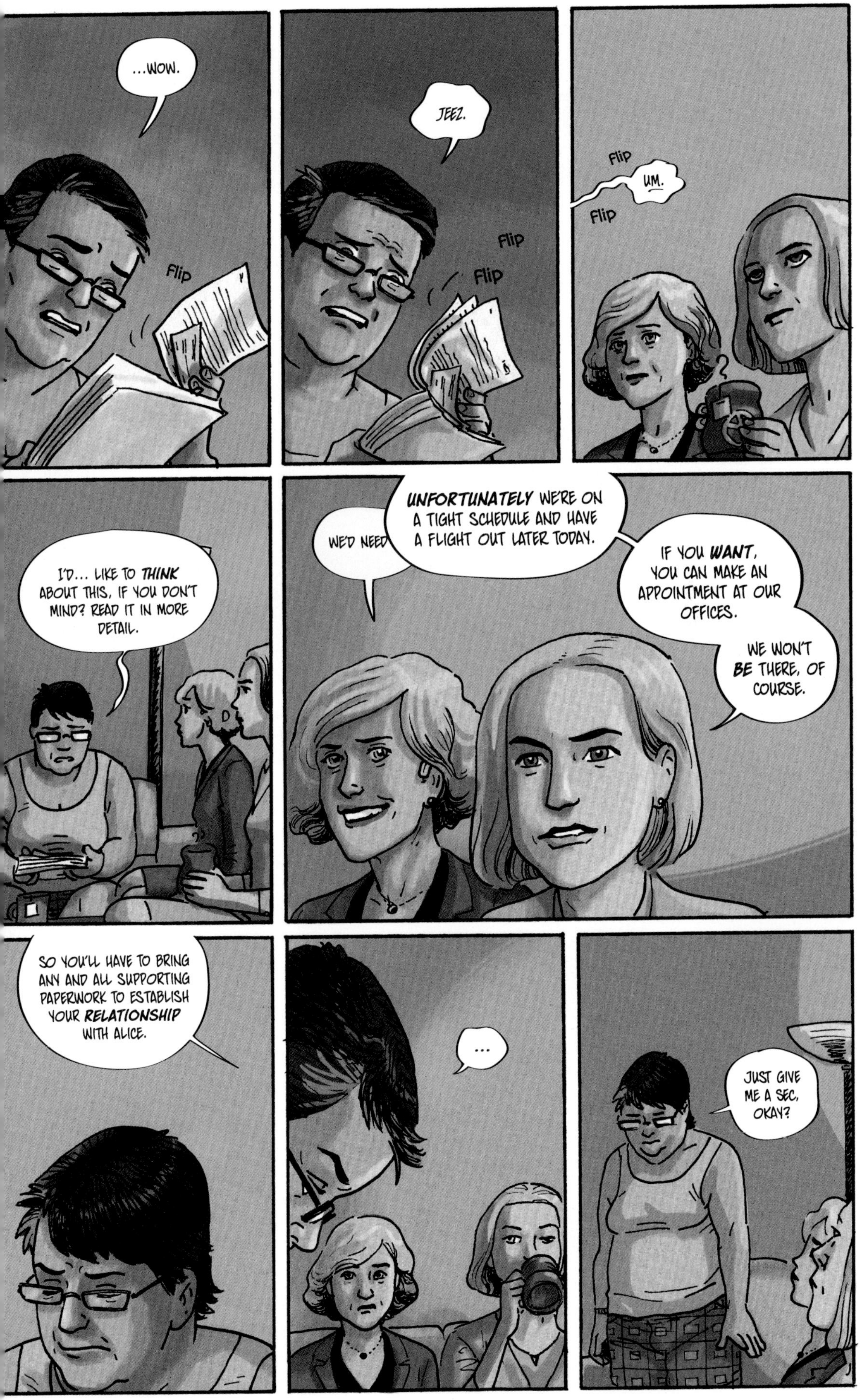
...WOW.
Flip
JEEZ.
Flip
Flip
Flip
UM.
Flip
I'D... LIKE TO THINK ABOUT THIS, IF YOU DON'T MIND? READ IT IN MORE DETAIL.
WE'D NEED
UNFORTUNATELY WE'RE ON A TIGHT SCHEDULE AND HAVE A FLIGHT OUT LATER TODAY.
IF YOU WANT, YOU CAN MAKE AN APPOINTMENT AT OUR OFFICES.
WE WON'T BE THERE, OF COURSE.
SO YOU'LL HAVE TO BRING ANY AND ALL SUPPORTING PAPERWORK TO ESTABLISH YOUR RELATIONSHIP WITH ALICE.
...
JUST GIVE ME A SEC, OKAY?

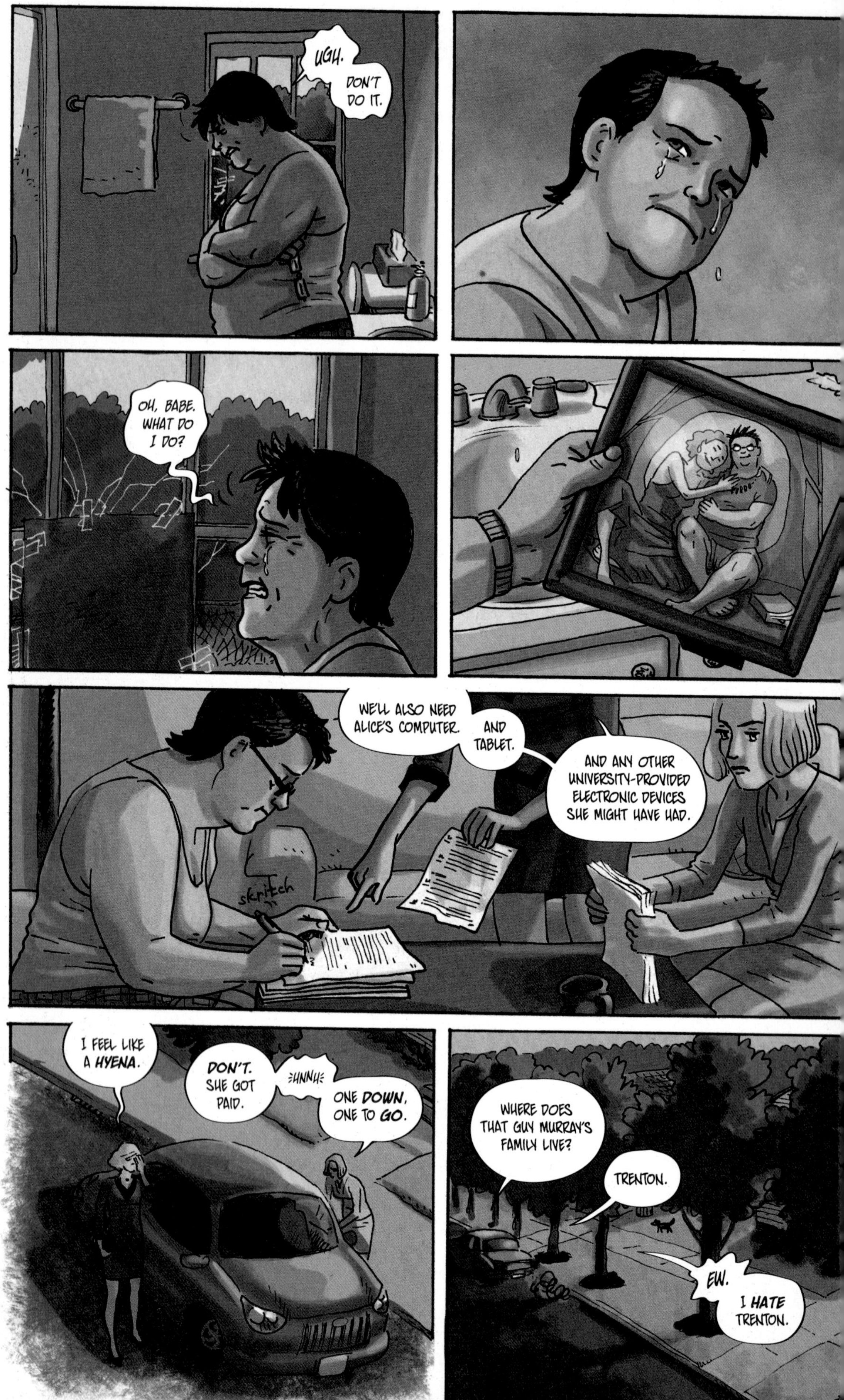

UGH.
DON'T DO IT.
OH, BABE. WHAT DO I DO?
WE'LL ALSO NEED ALICE'S COMPUTER.
AND TABLET.
AND ANY OTHER UNIVERSITY-PROVIDED ELECTRONIC DEVICES SHE MIGHT HAVE HAD.
skritch
I FEEL LIKE A **HYENA**.
DON'T. SHE GOT PAID.
HNNH
ONE **DOWN**, ONE TO **GO**.
WHERE DOES THAT GUY MURRAY'S FAMILY LIVE?
TRENTON.
EW.
I **HATE** TRENTON.

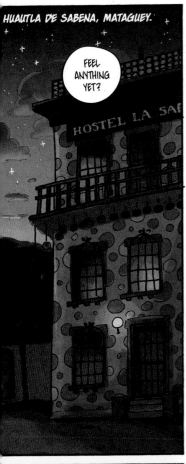

HUAUTLA DE SABENA, MATAGUEY.
FEEL ANYTHING YET?
HOSTEL LA SA
NOPE.
LITTLE FLOATY.
EDDIE, YOU SURE YOU DON'T WANT ANY?
NAH. I'M GOOD.
OOOOH.
SIIIGH
THIS IS BULLSHIT.

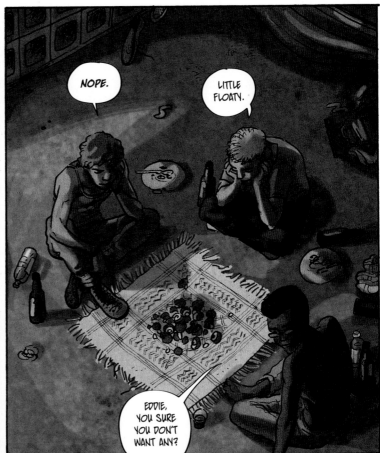

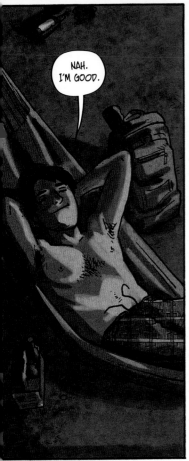

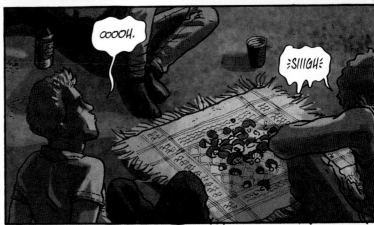

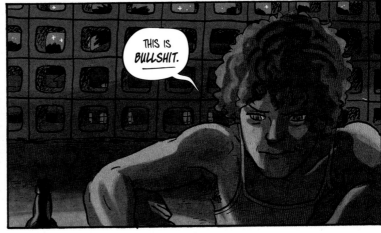

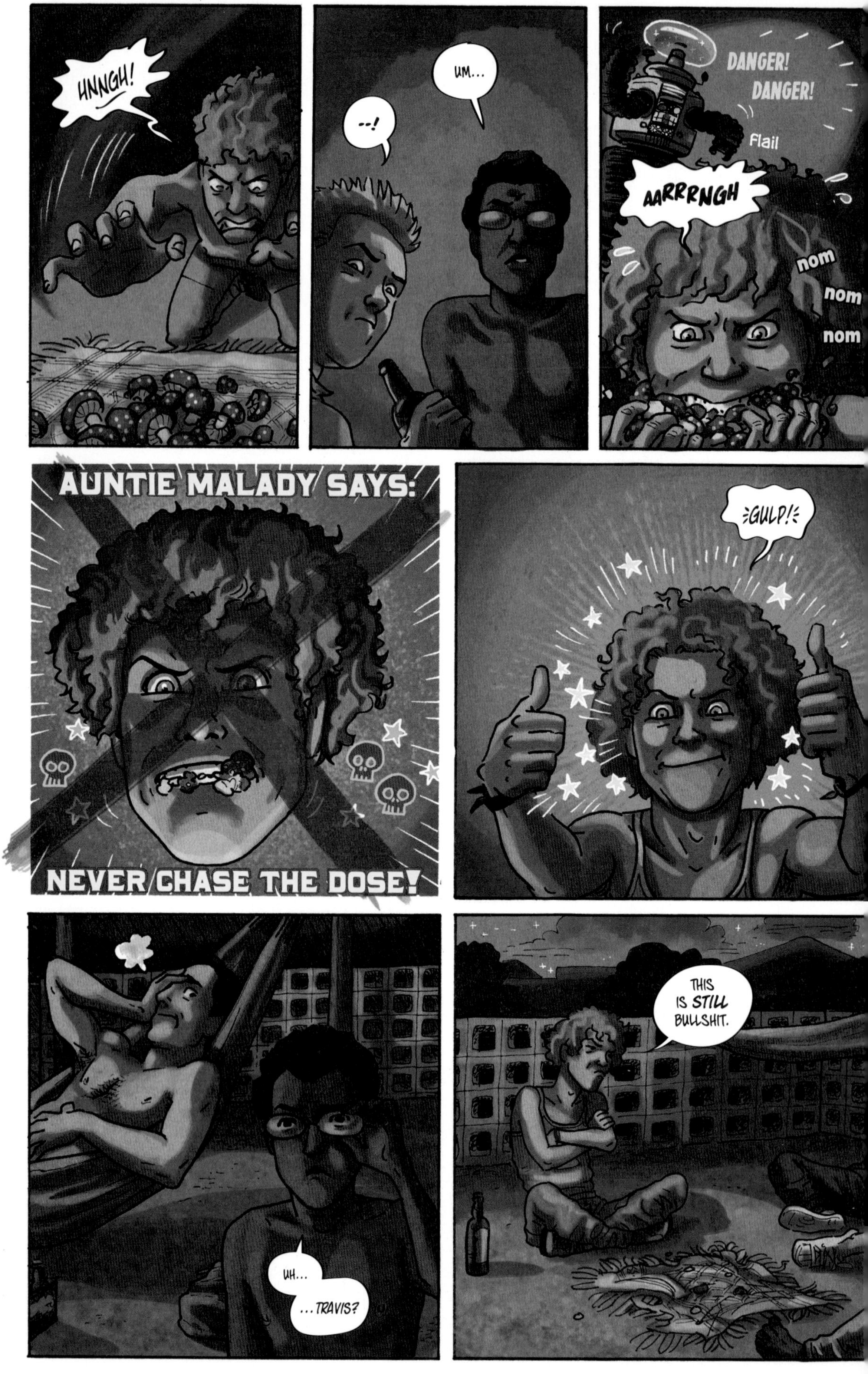

HNNGH!
--!
UM...
DANGER!
DANGER!
Flail
AARRRNGH
nom
nom
nom
AUNTIE MALADY SAYS:
NEVER CHASE THE DOSE!
GULP!
UH...
...TRAVIS?
THIS IS STILL BULLSHIT.

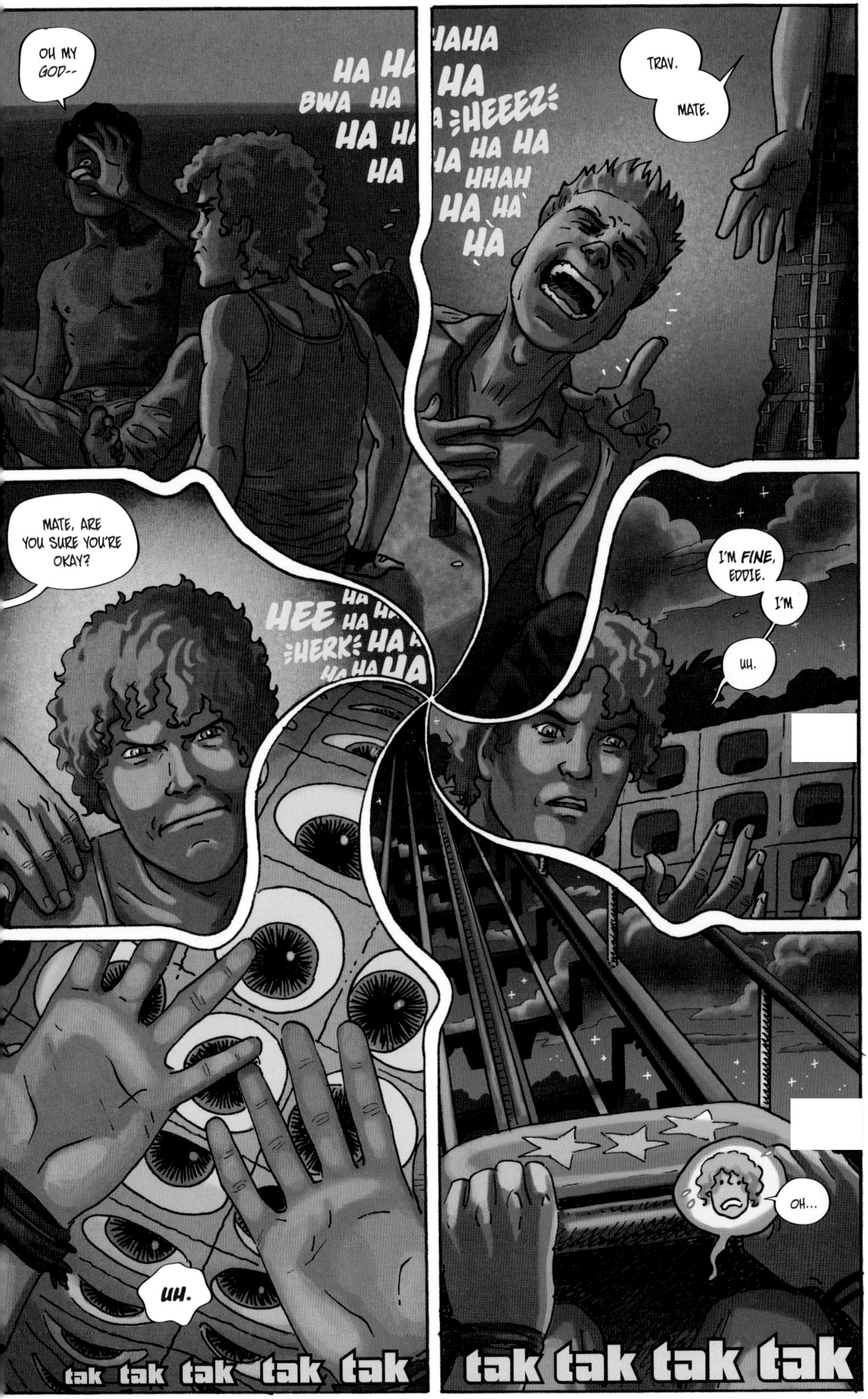
OH MY GOD--
HAHA
HA HA
BWA HA
HA HA
HA
HA
HA
HEEEZ
HA HA
HA HA
HHAH
HA HA
HA
TRAV.
MATE.
MATE, ARE YOU SURE YOU'RE OKAY?
HEE
HERK
HA HA
HA
I'M *FINE*, EDDIE.
I'M
UH.
UH.
tak tak tak tak tak
OH...
tak tak tak tak

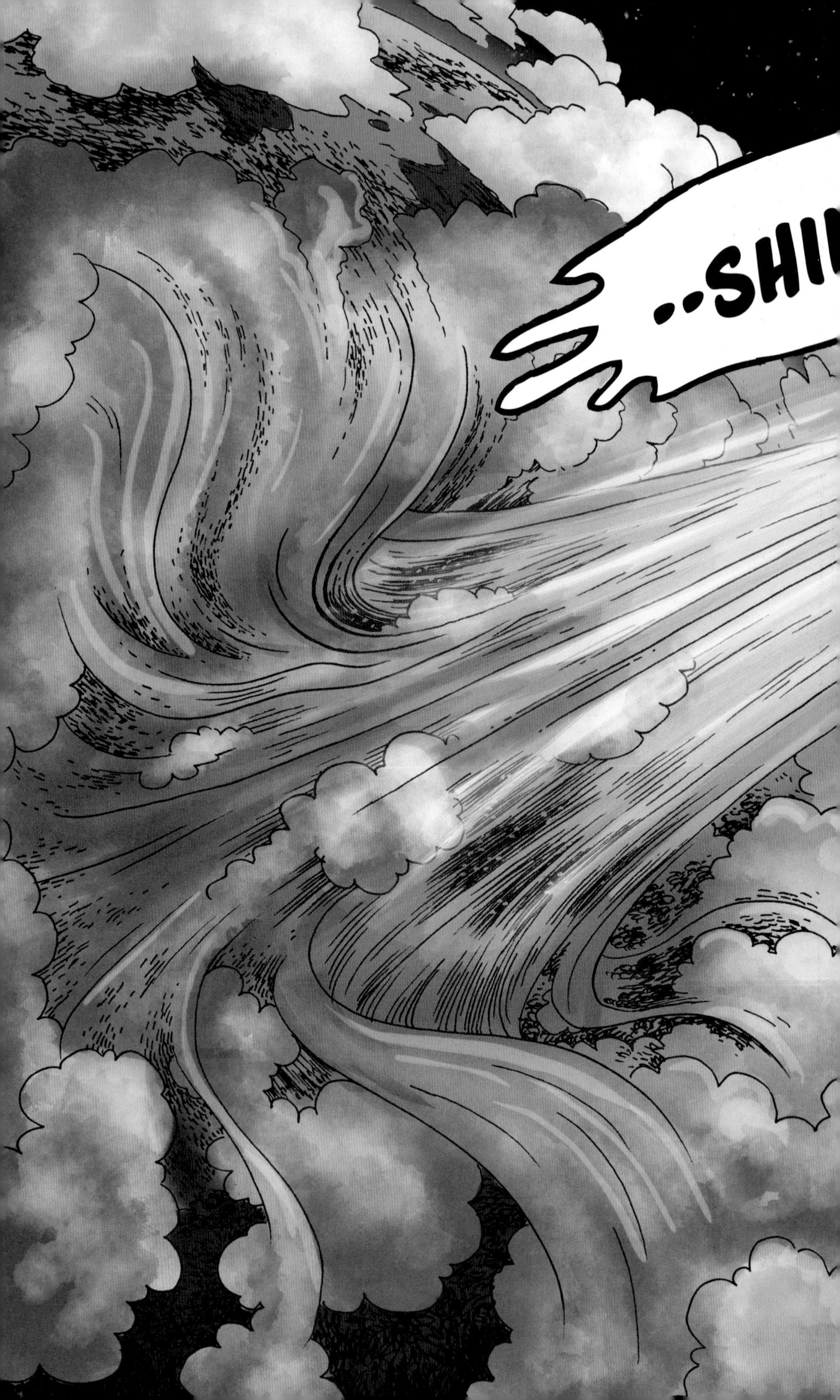
..SHI

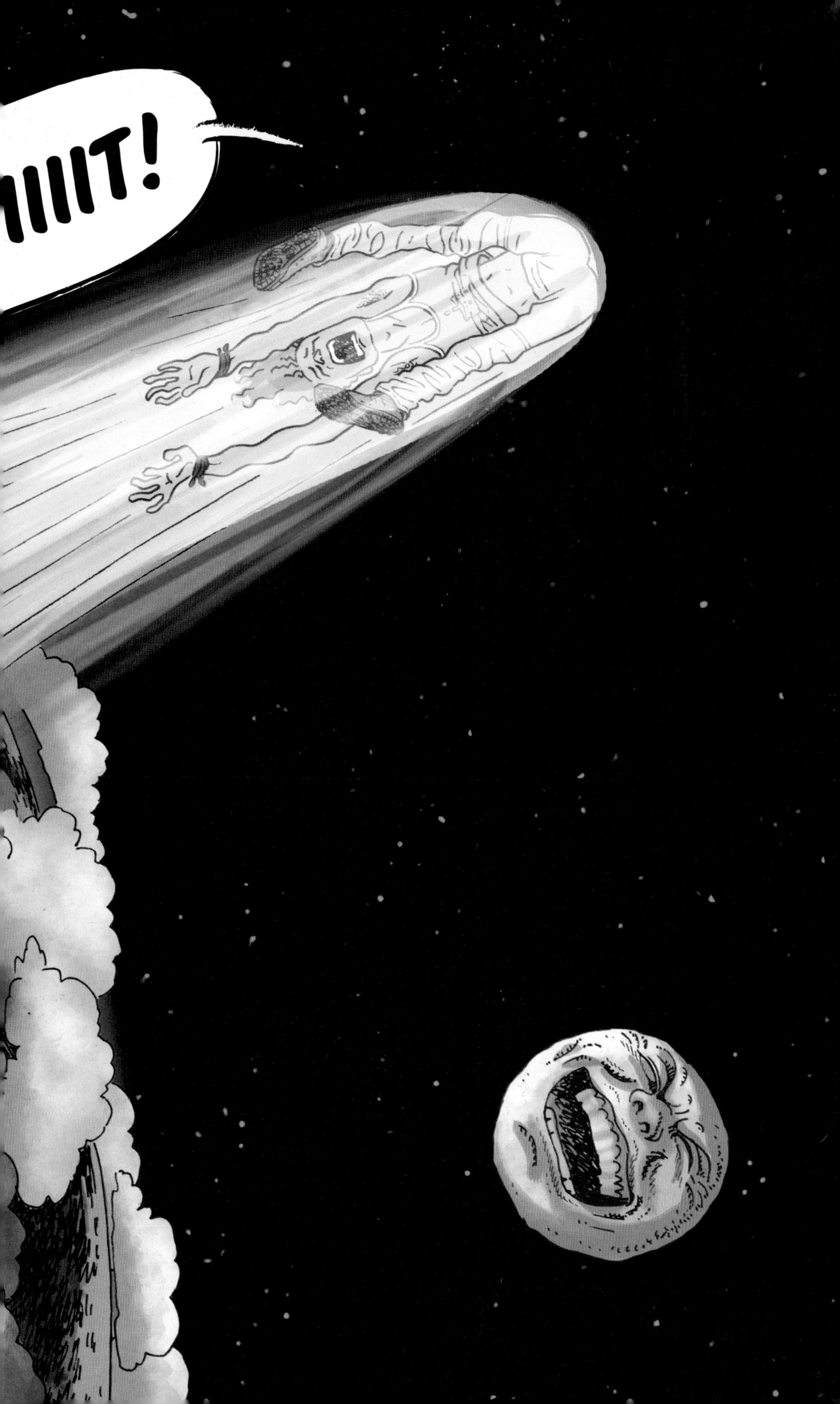
IIIIT!

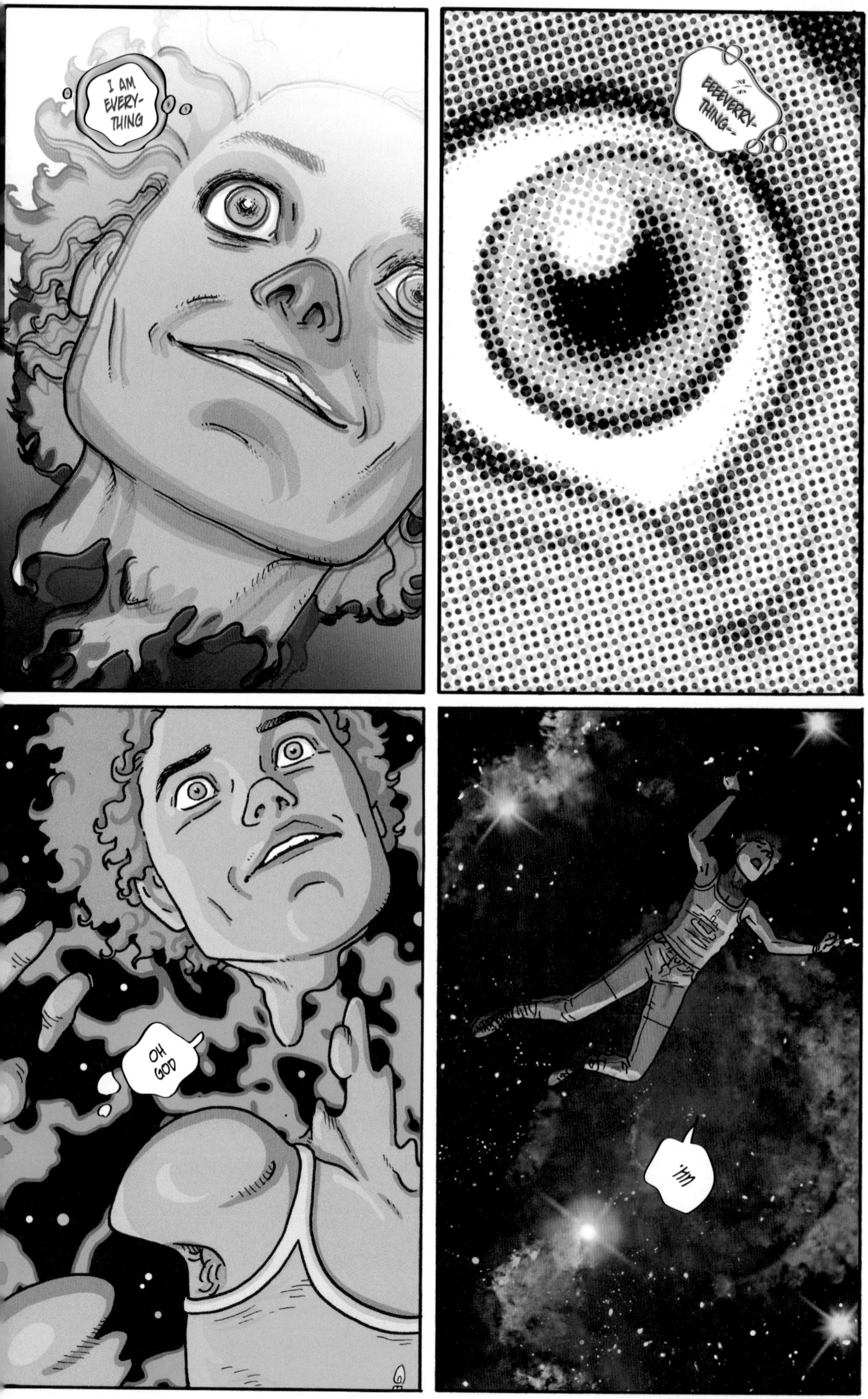
I AM EVERY-THING
EEEEVERRY-THING--
OH GOD
...hm

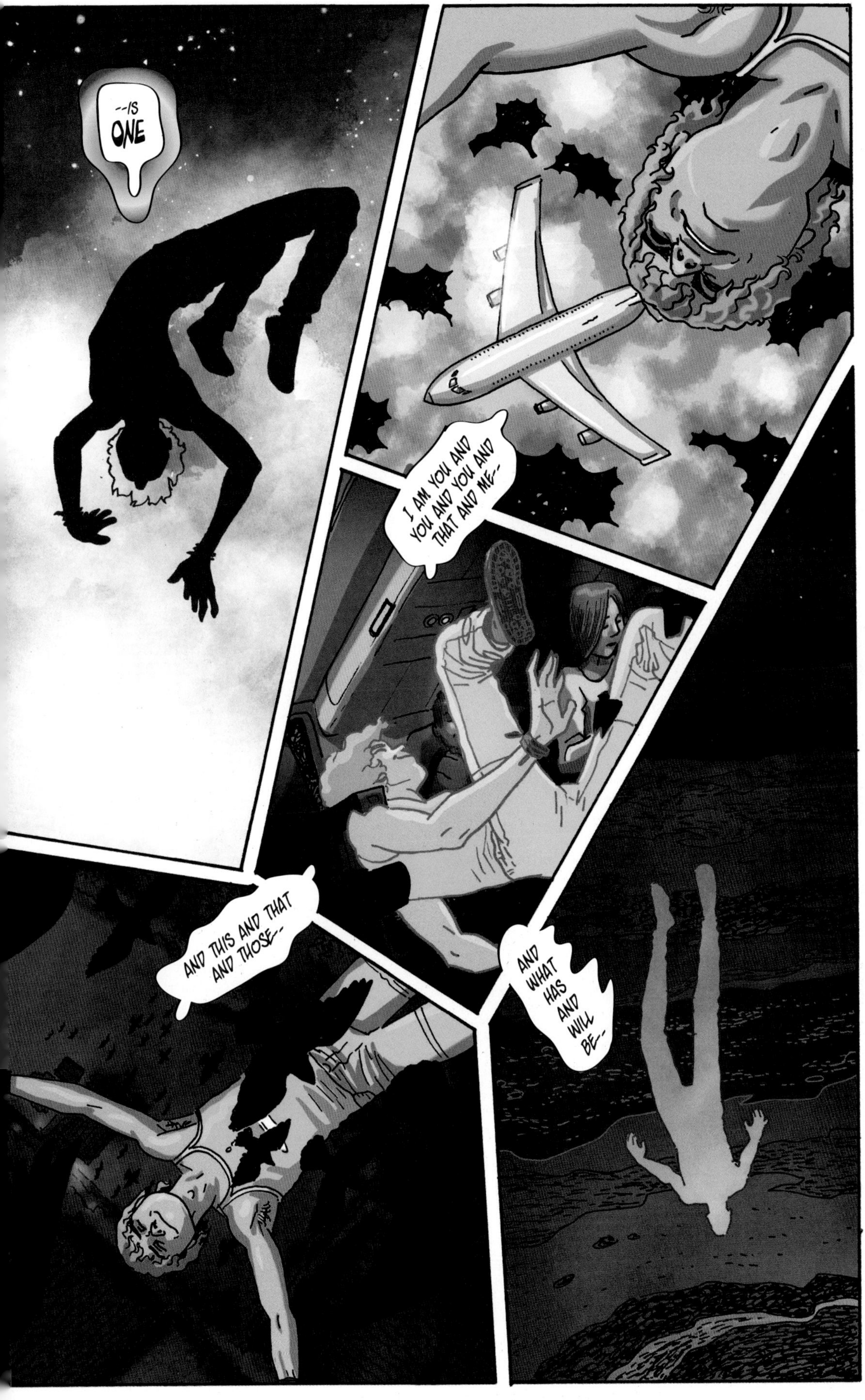
--IS ONE
I AM YOU AND YOU AND YOU AND THAT AND ME--
AND THIS AND THAT AND THOSE--
AND WHAT HAS AND WILL BE--

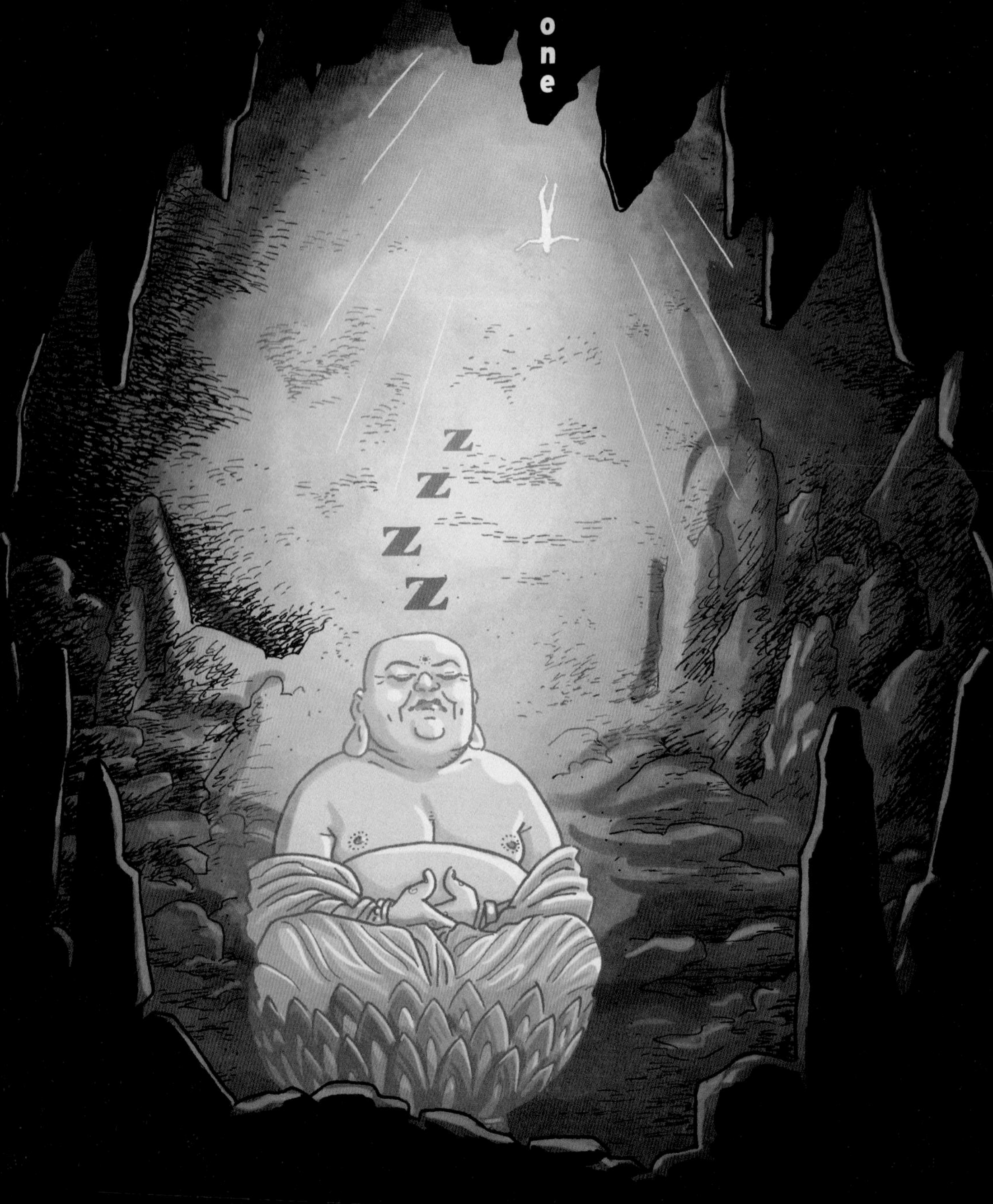
one
Z
Z
Z
Z

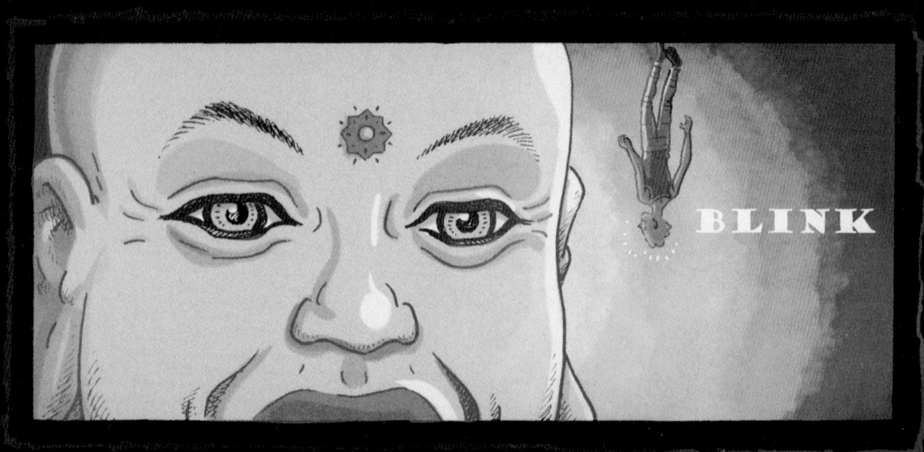
BLINK

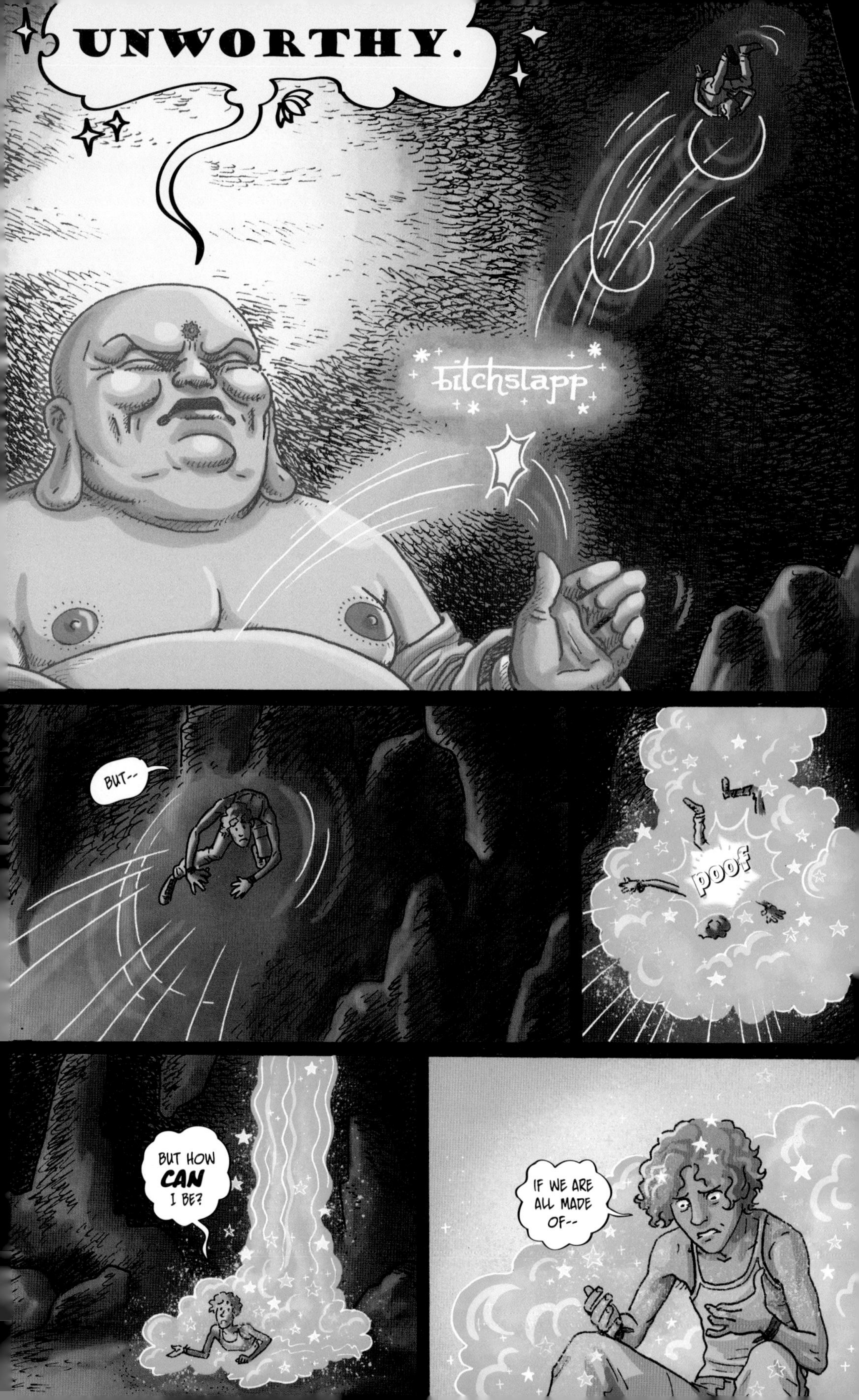
UNWORTHY.
bitchslapp
BUT--
poof
BUT HOW CAN I BE?
IF WE ARE ALL MADE OF--

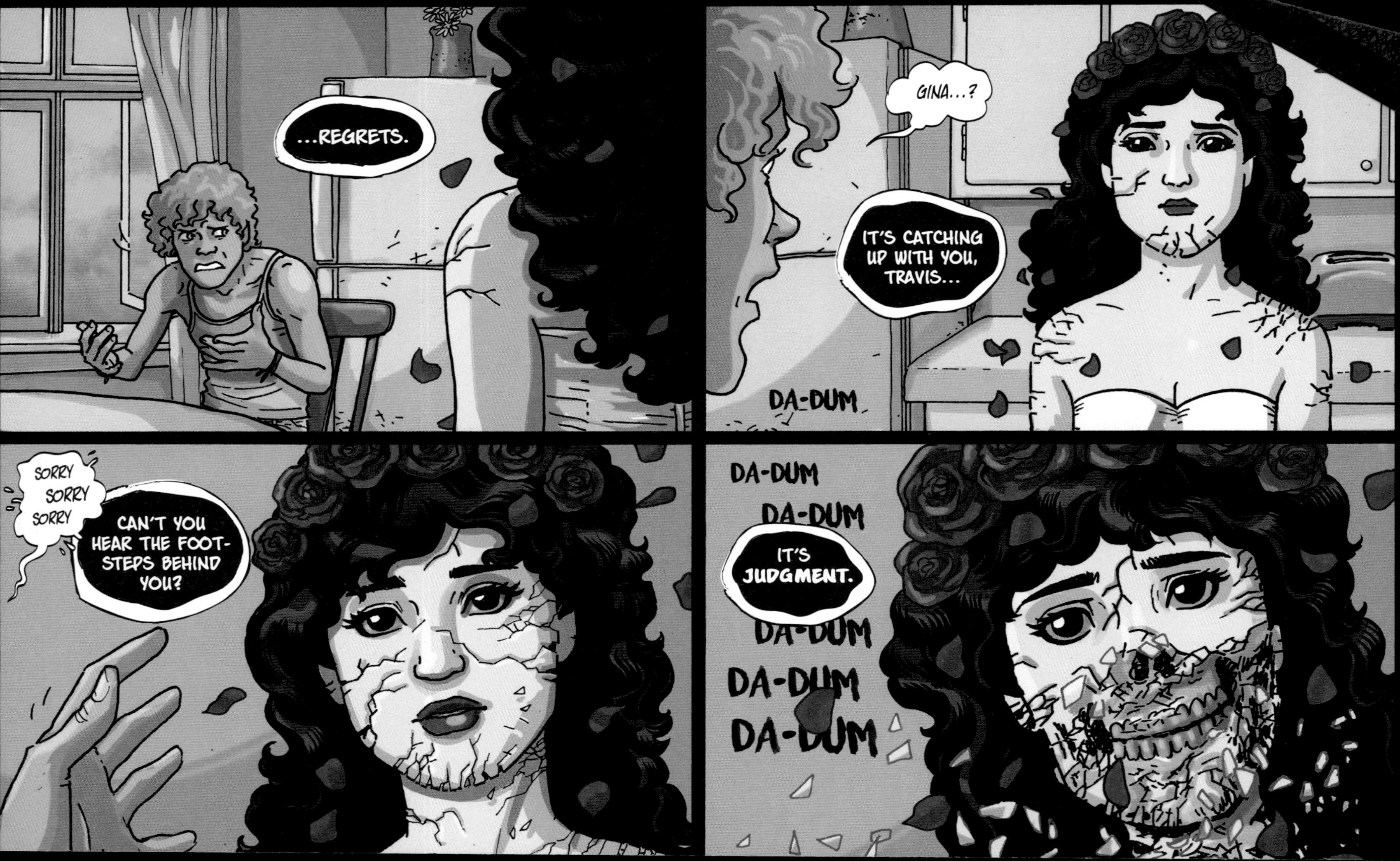
...REGRETS.
GINA...?
IT'S CATCHING UP WITH YOU, TRAVIS...
DA-DUM
SORRY SORRY SORRY
CAN'T YOU HEAR THE FOOT-STEPS BEHIND YOU?
DA-DUM
DA-DUM
IT'S JUDGMENT.
DA-DUM
DA-DUM
DA-DUM

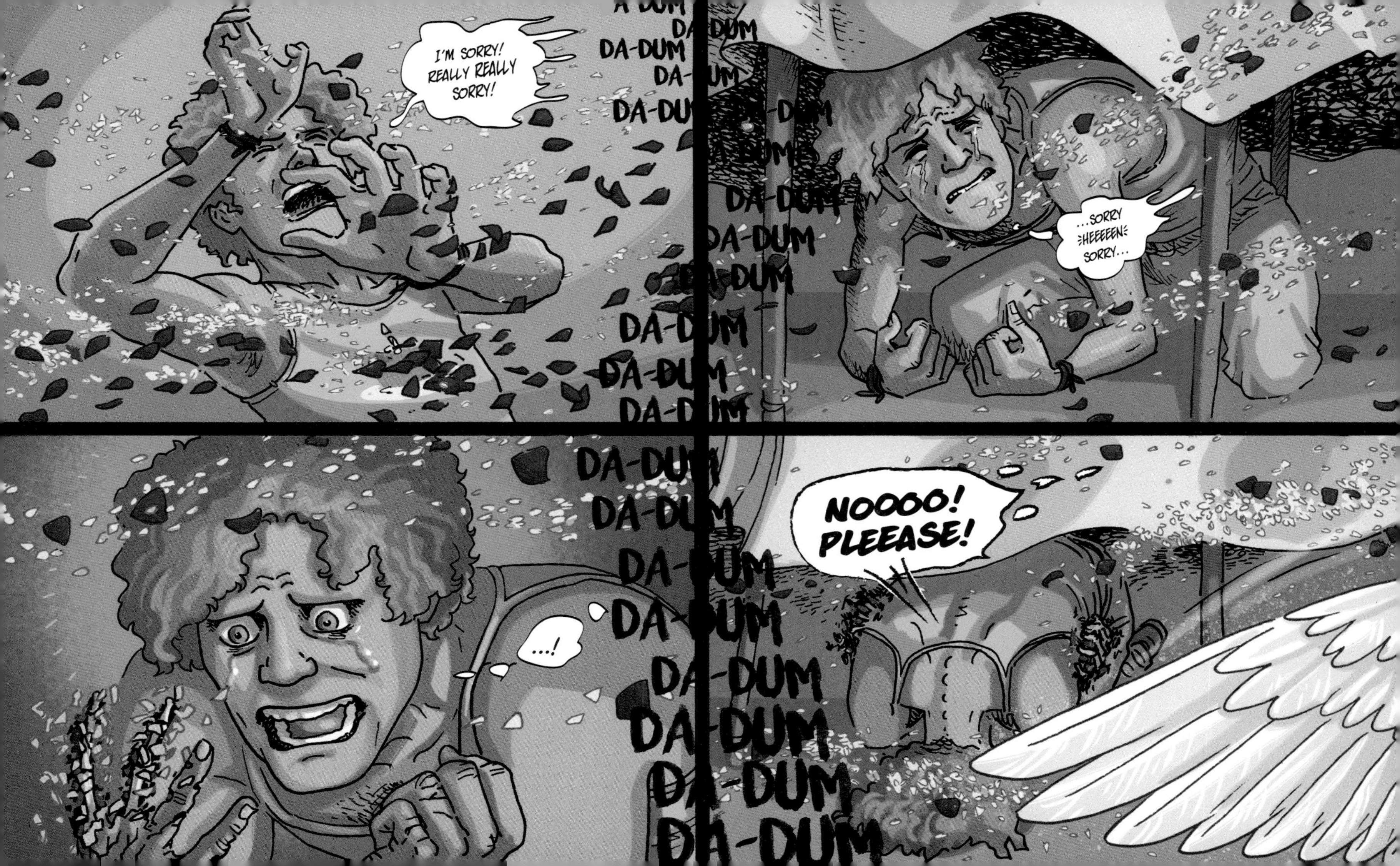
I'M SORRY! REALLY REALLY SORRY!
DA-DUM
DA-DUM
DA-DUM
DA-DUM
...SORRY ≡HEEEEEN≡ SORRY...
DA-DUM
DA-DUM
DA-DUM
DA-DUM
DA-DUM
...!
NOOOO! PLEEASE!
DA-DUM
DA-DUM
DA-DUM
DA-DUM
DA-DUM
DA-DUM

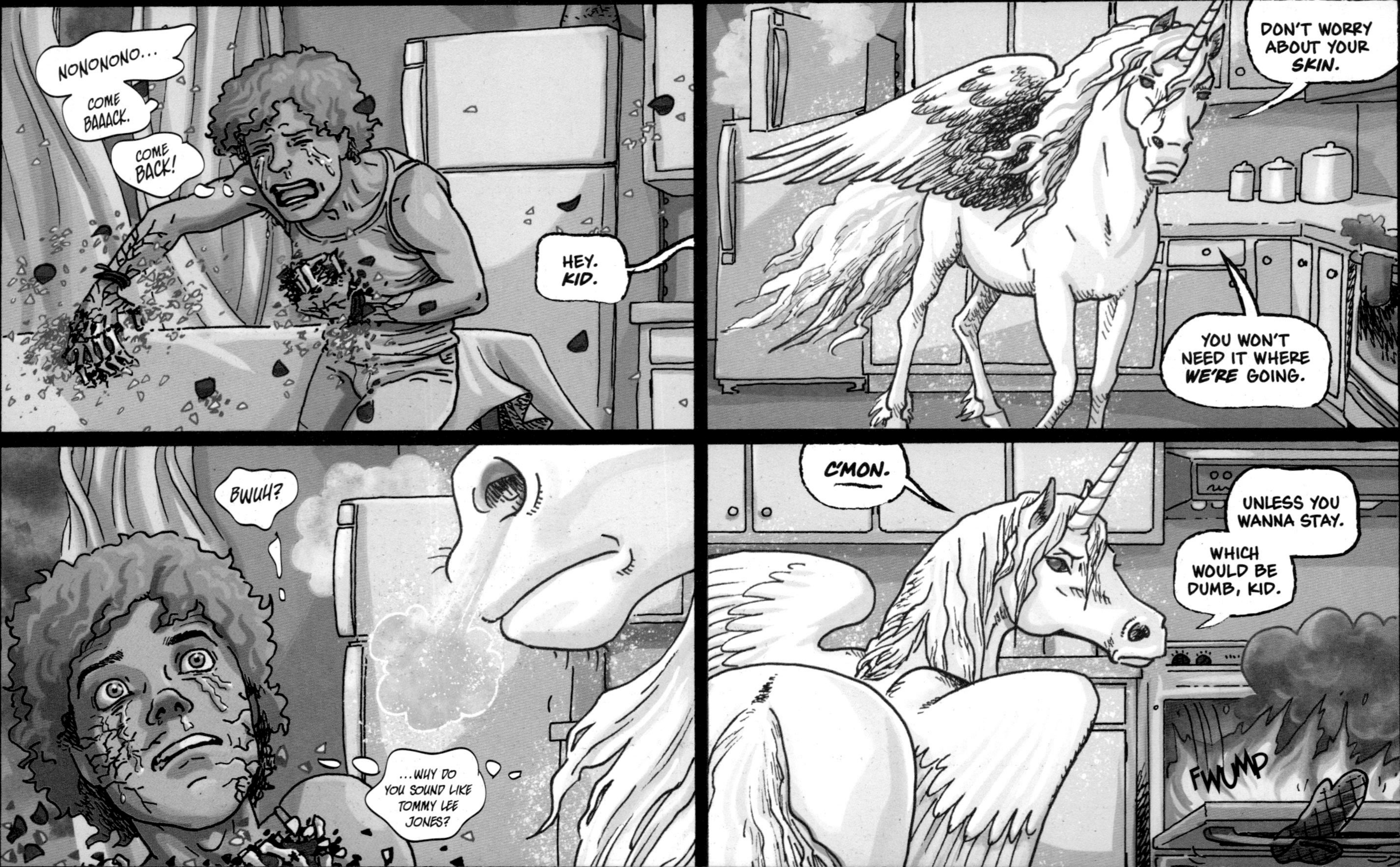
NONONONO...
COME BAAACK.
COME BACK!
HEY. KID.
DON'T WORRY ABOUT YOUR SKIN.
YOU WON'T NEED IT WHERE WE'RE GOING.
BWUH?
...WHY DO YOU SOUND LIKE TOMMY LEE JONES?
C'MON.
UNLESS YOU WANNA STAY.
WHICH WOULD BE DUMB, KID.
FWUMP

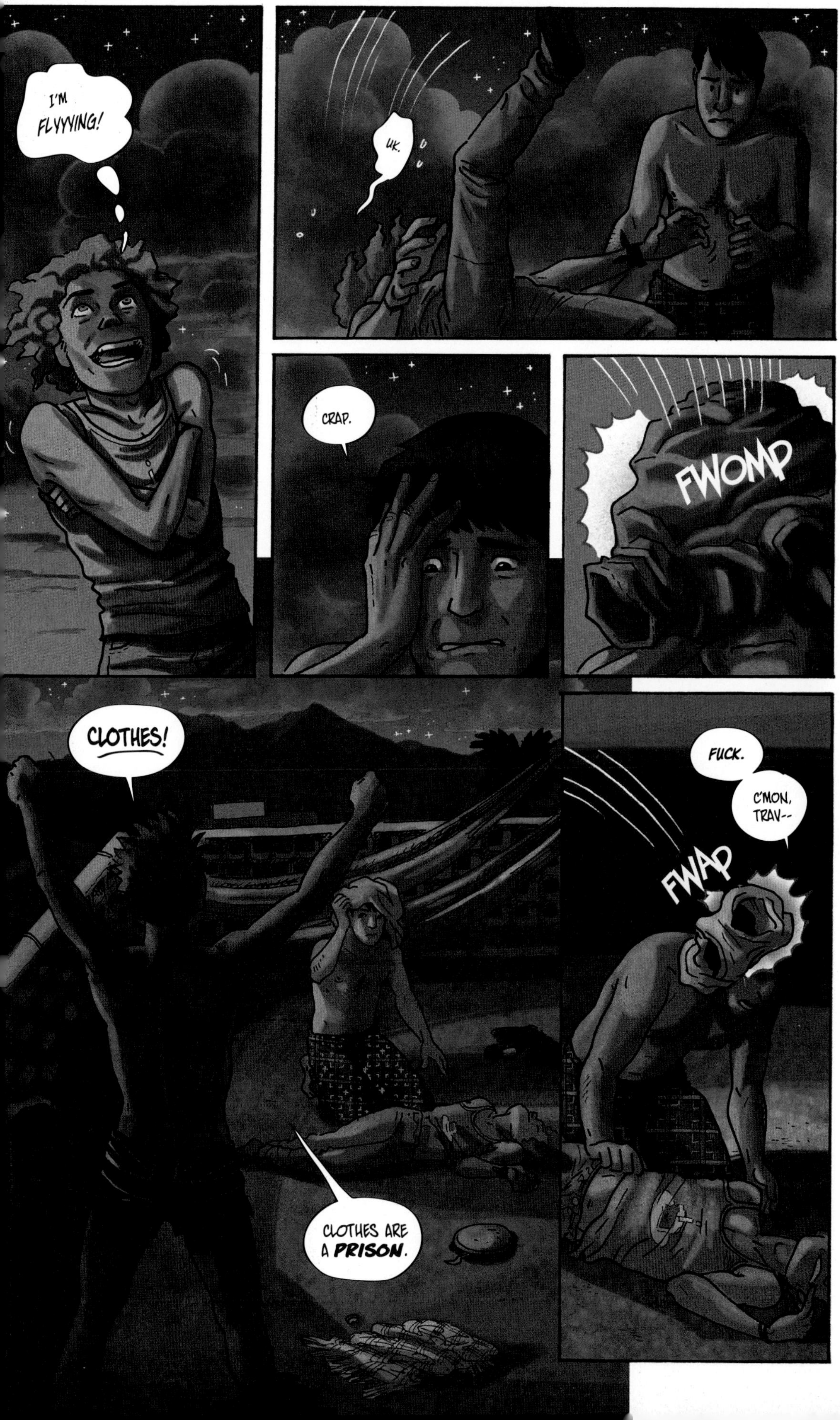
I'M FLYYYING!
UK.
CRAP.
FWOMP
CLOTHES!
CLOTHES ARE A **PRISON**.
FUCK.
C'MON, TRAV--
FWAP

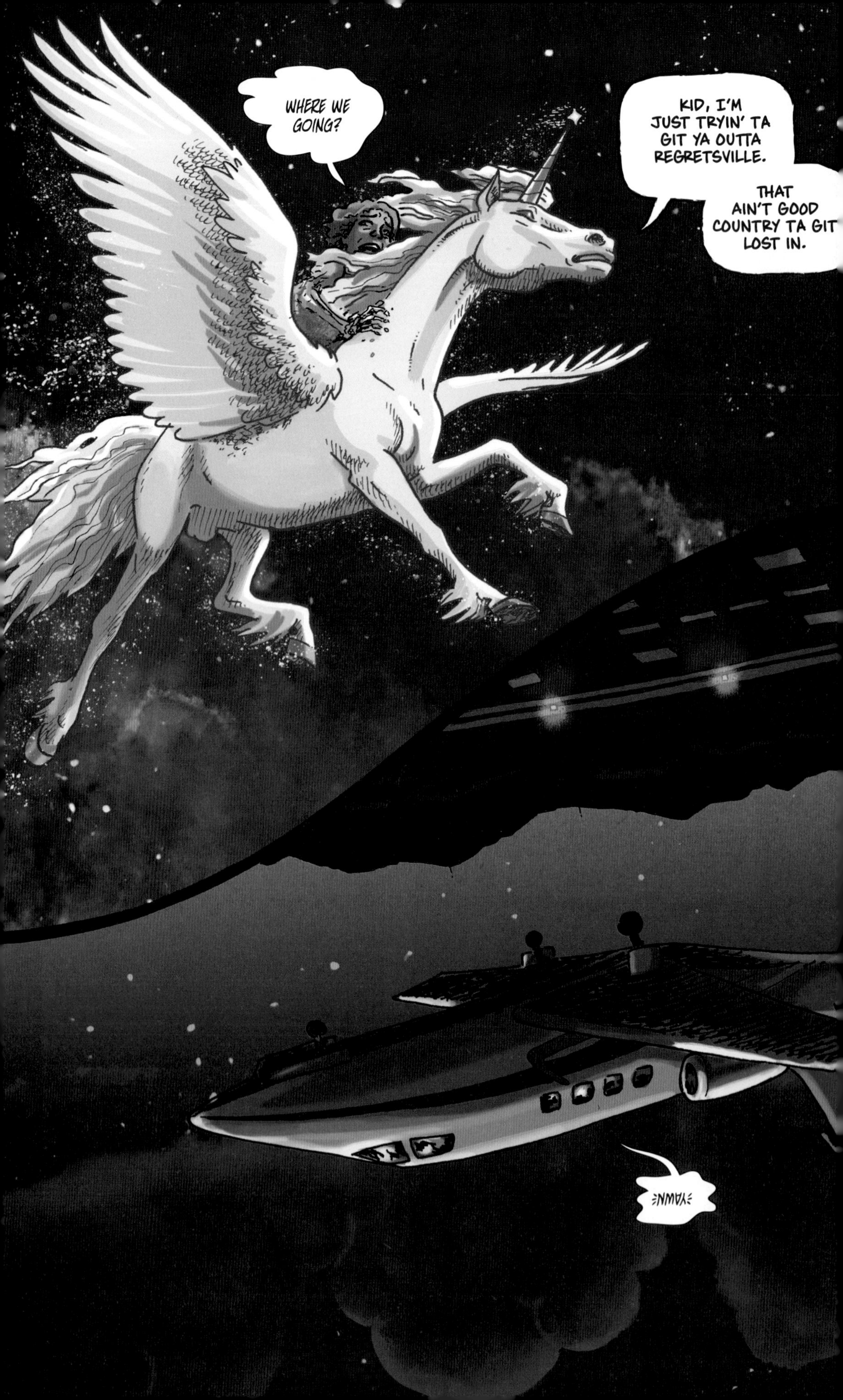
WHERE WE GOING?
KID, I'M JUST TRYIN' TA GIT YA OUTTA REGRETSVILLE.
THAT AIN'T GOOD COUNTRY TA GIT LOST IN.
YAWN

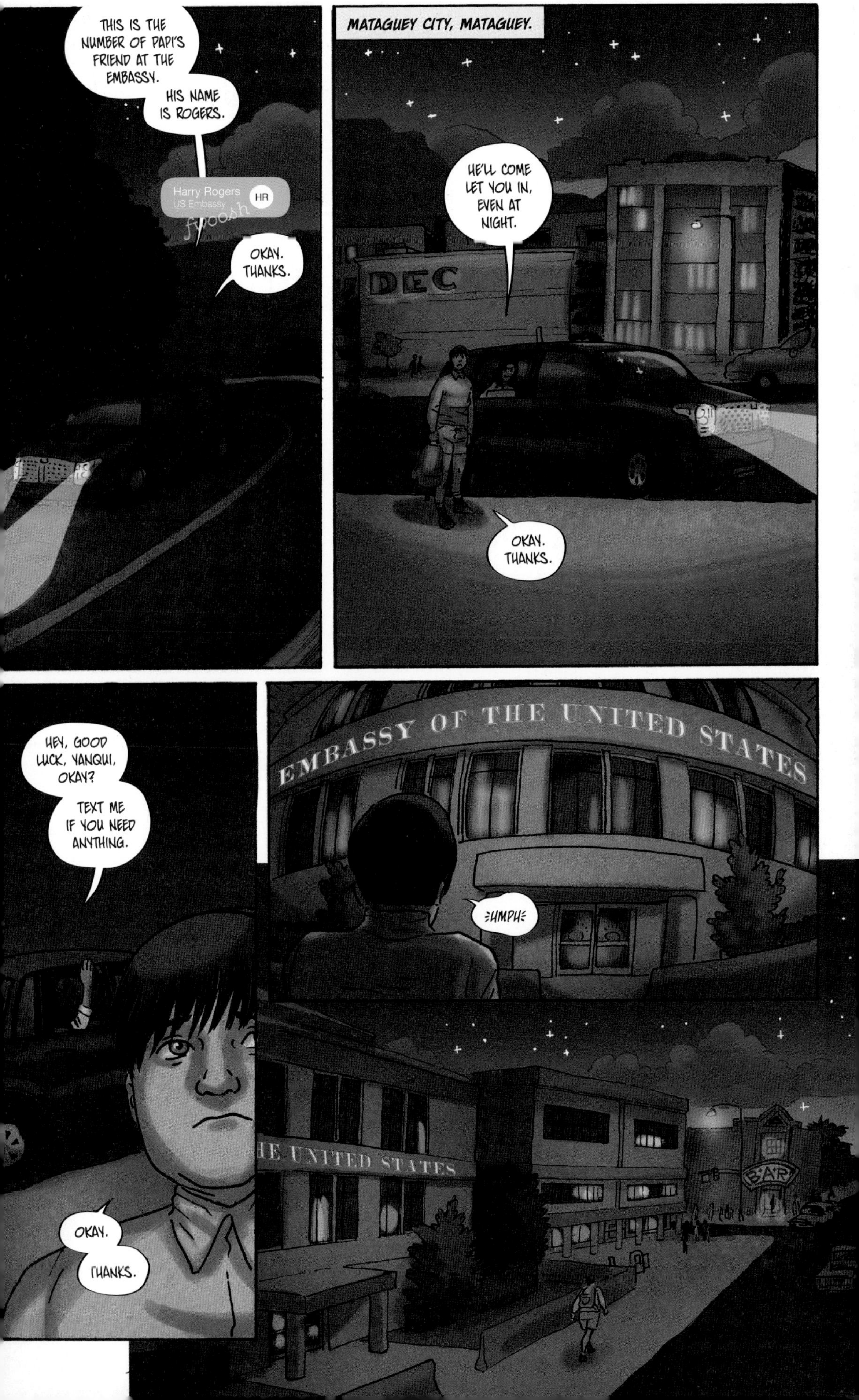
THIS IS THE NUMBER OF PAPI'S FRIEND AT THE EMBASSY.
HIS NAME IS ROGERS.
Harry Rogers
US Embassy
HR
fwoosh
OKAY. THANKS.
MATAGUEY CITY, MATAGUEY.
HE'LL COME LET YOU IN, EVEN AT NIGHT.
DEC
OKAY. THANKS.
HEY, GOOD LUCK, YANQUI, OKAY?
TEXT ME IF YOU NEED ANYTHING.
EMBASSY OF THE UNITED STATES
HUMPH
OKAY.
THANKS.
HE UNITED STATES
BAR

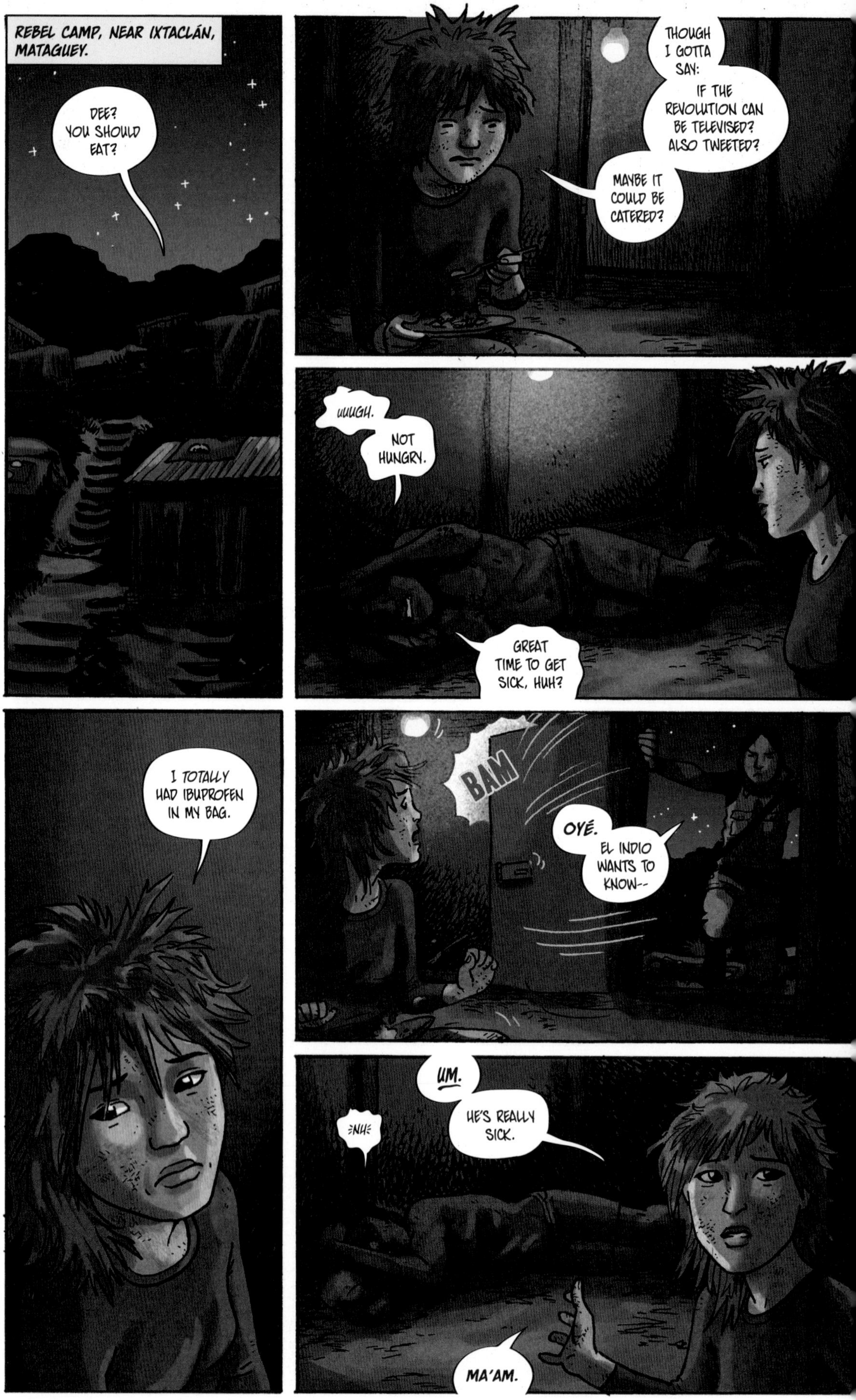
REBEL CAMP, NEAR IXTACLÁN, MATAGUEY.
DEE? YOU SHOULD EAT?
THOUGH I GOTTA SAY:
IF THE REVOLUTION CAN BE TELEVISED? ALSO TWEETED?
MAYBE IT COULD BE CATERED?
uuugh.
NOT HUNGRY.
GREAT TIME TO GET SICK, HUH?
I TOTALLY HAD IBUPROFEN IN MY BAG.
BAM
OYÉ.
EL INDIO WANTS TO KNOW--
UM.
HE'S REALLY SICK.
NU
MA'AM.

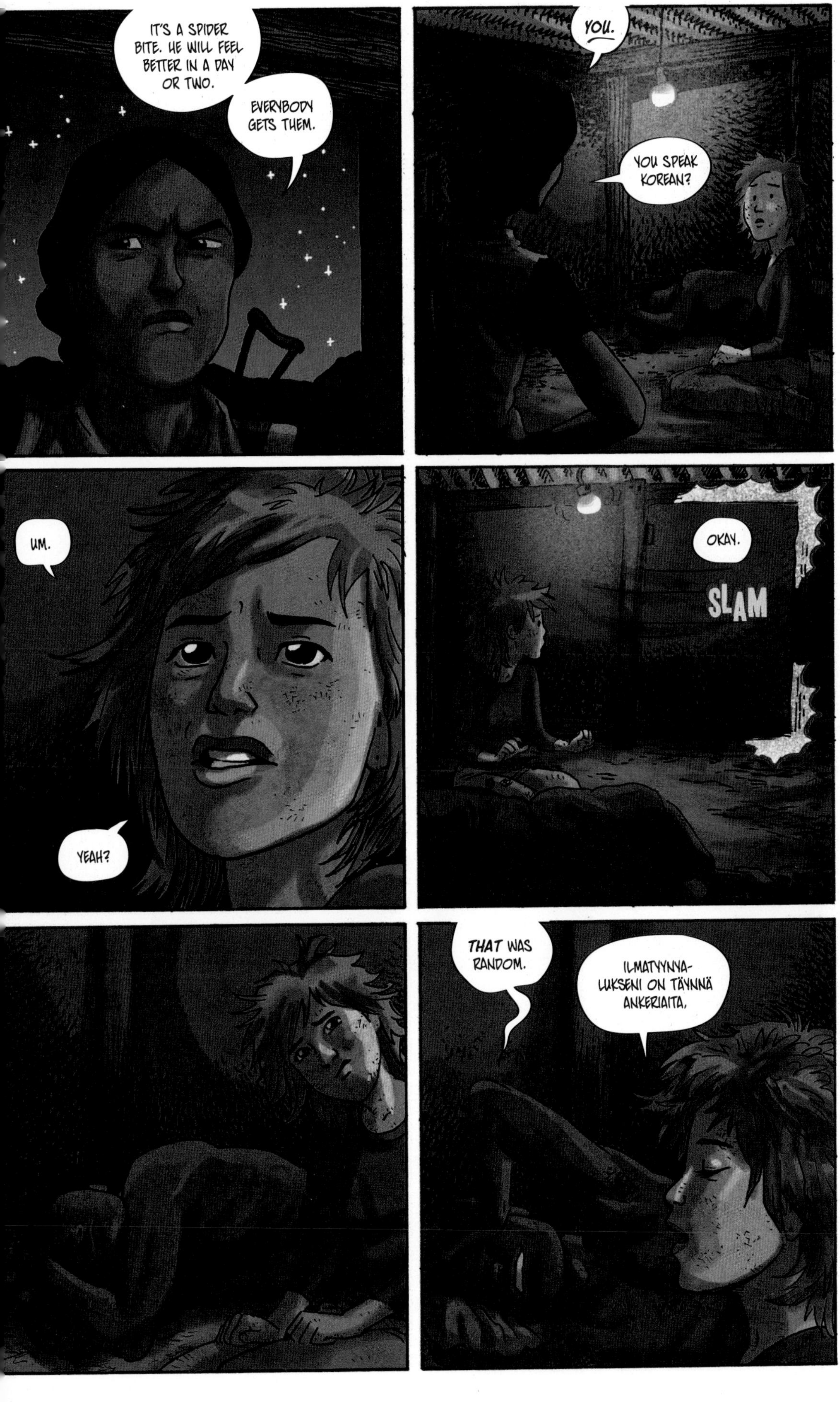

IT'S A SPIDER BITE. HE WILL FEEL BETTER IN A DAY OR TWO.
EVERYBODY GETS THEM.
YOU.
YOU SPEAK KOREAN?
UM.
YEAH?
OKAY.
SLAM
THAT WAS RANDOM.
ILMATYYNYA-LUKSENI ON TÄYNNÄ ANKERIAITA,

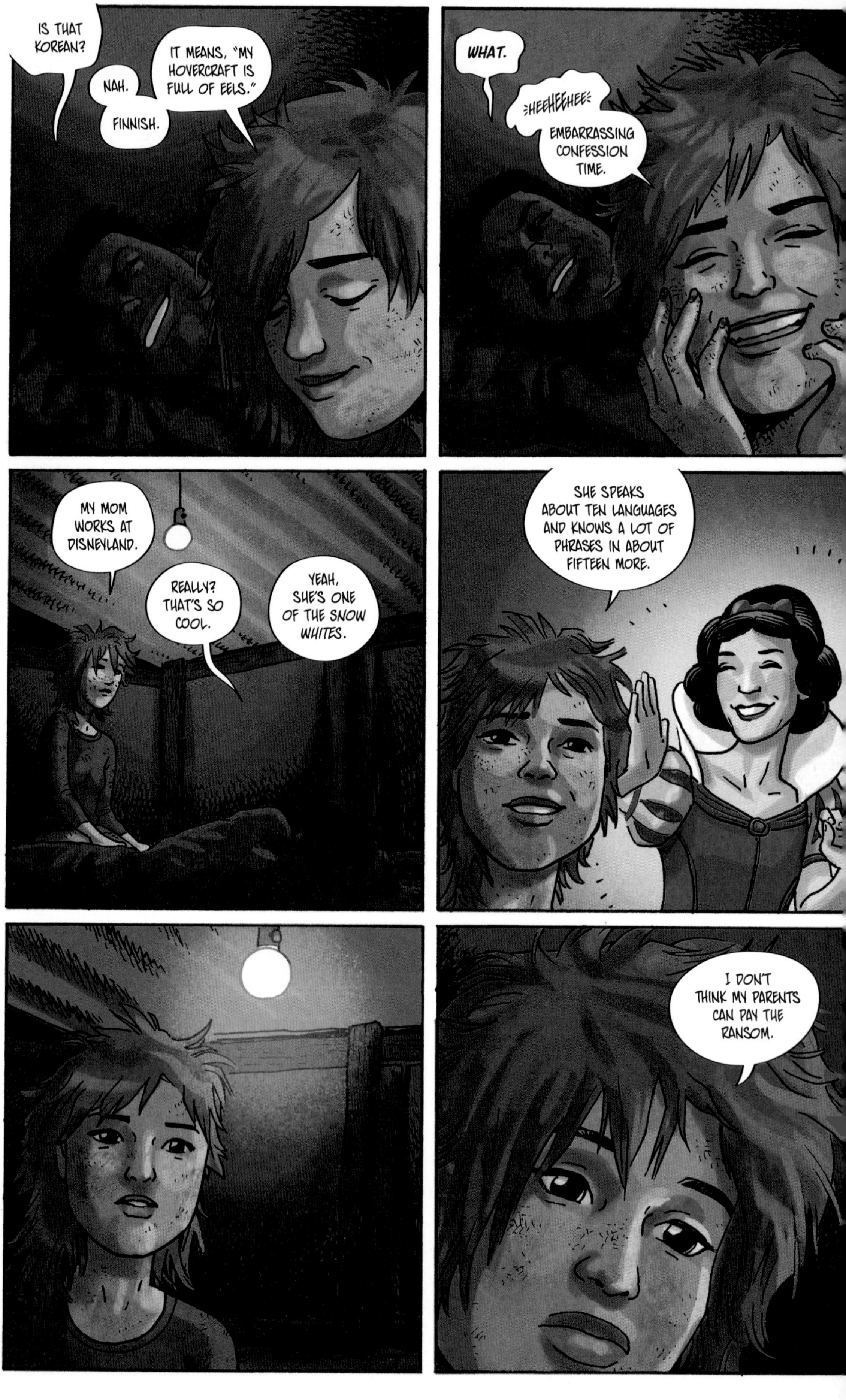
IS THAT KOREAN?
NAH.
FINNISH.
IT MEANS, "MY HOVERCRAFT IS FULL OF EELS."
WHAT.
HEEHEEHEE
EMBARRASSING CONFESSION TIME.
MY MOM WORKS AT DISNEYLAND.
REALLY? THAT'S SO COOL.
YEAH, SHE'S ONE OF THE SNOW WHITES.
SHE SPEAKS ABOUT TEN LANGUAGES AND KNOWS A LOT OF PHRASES IN ABOUT FIFTEEN MORE.
I DON'T THINK MY PARENTS CAN PAY THE RANSOM.

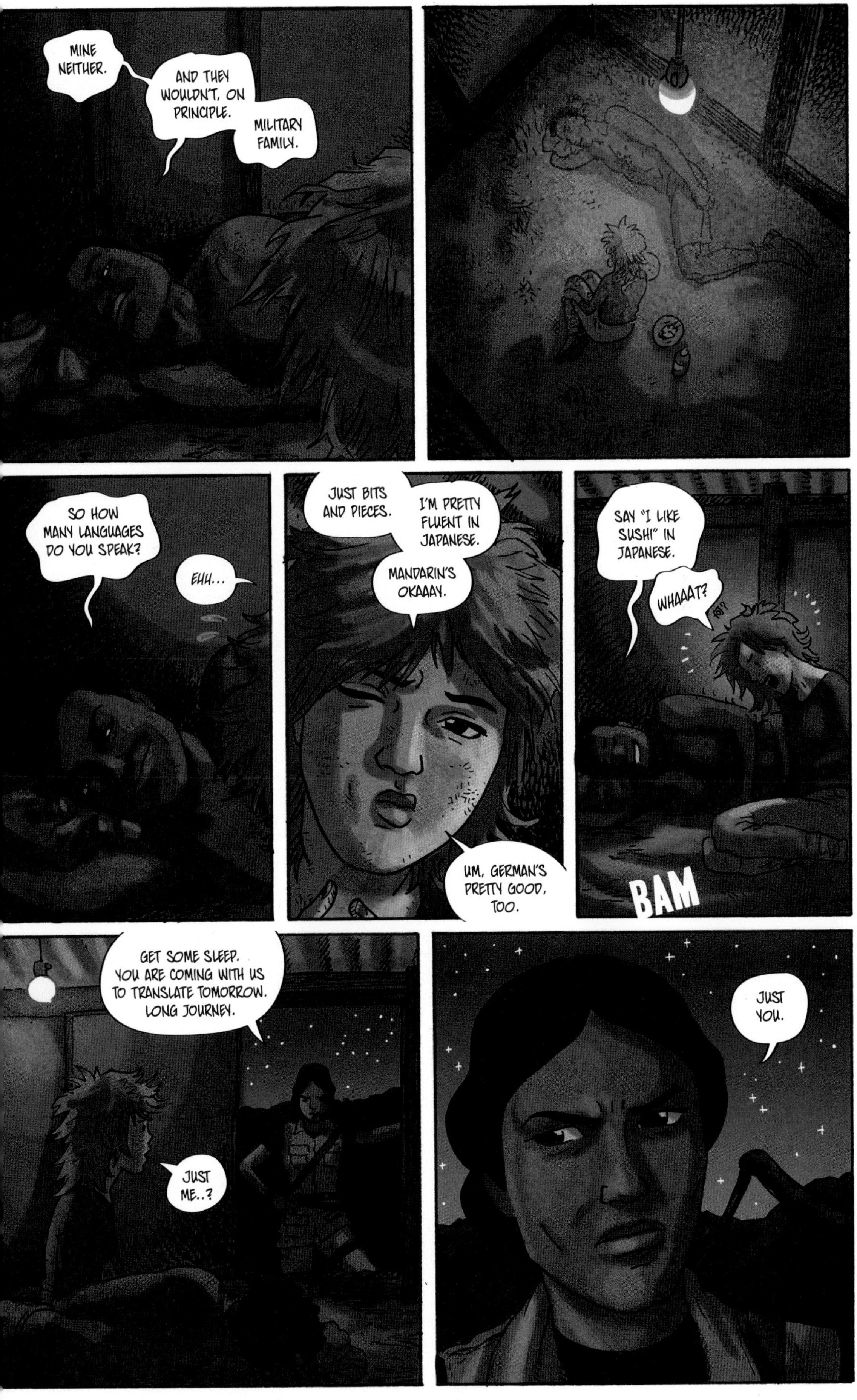
MINE NEITHER.
AND THEY WOULDN'T, ON PRINCIPLE.
MILITARY FAMILY.
SO HOW MANY LANGUAGES DO YOU SPEAK?
EHH...
JUST BITS AND PIECES.
I'M PRETTY FLUENT IN JAPANESE.
MANDARIN'S OKAAAY.
UM, GERMAN'S PRETTY GOOD, TOO.
SAY "I LIKE SUSHI" IN JAPANESE.
WHAAAT?
BAM
GET SOME SLEEP. YOU ARE COMING WITH US TO TRANSLATE TOMORROW. LONG JOURNEY.
JUST ME..?
JUST YOU.

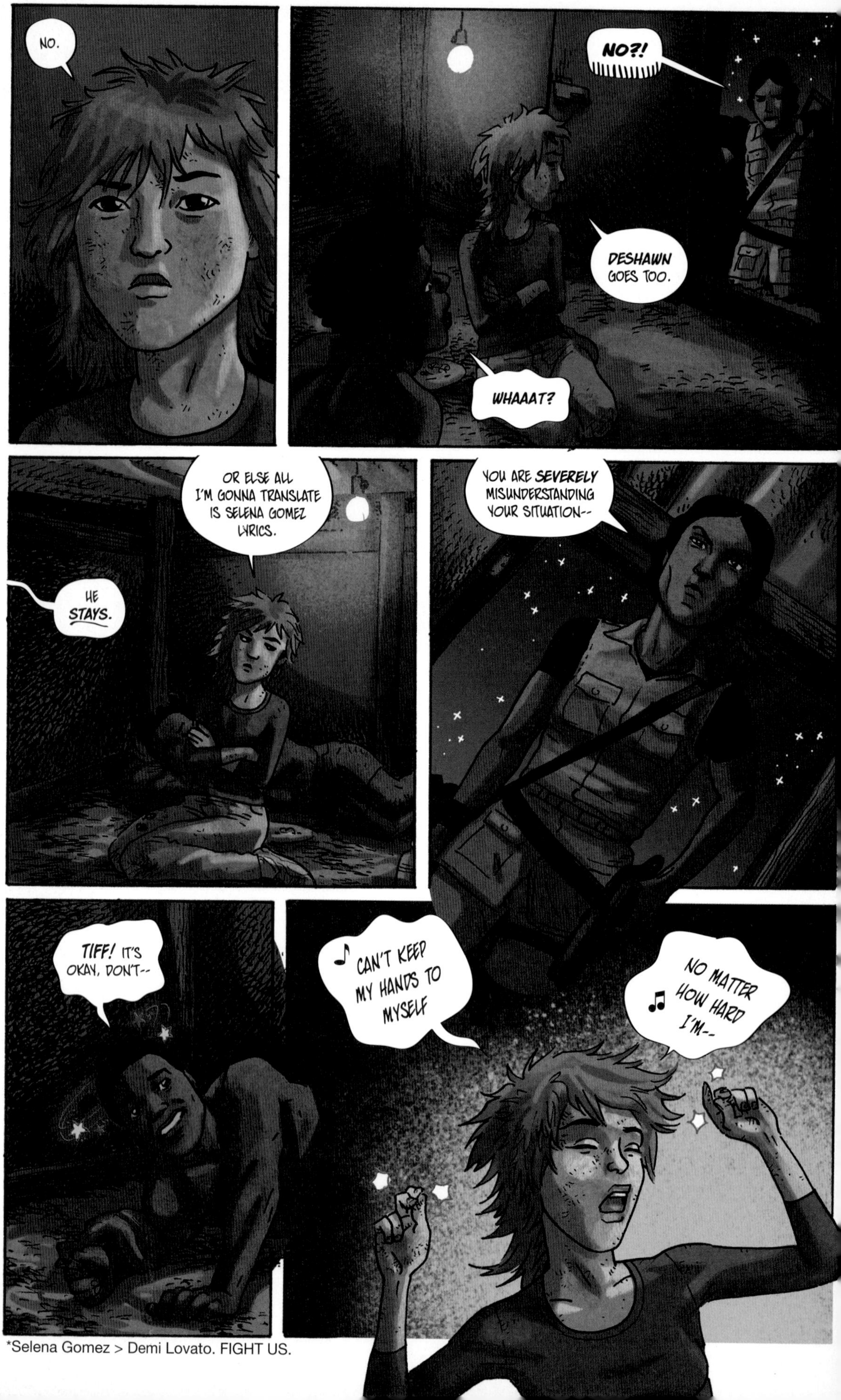
NO.
NO?!
DESHAWN GOES TOO.
WHAAAT?
OR ELSE ALL I'M GONNA TRANSLATE IS SELENA GOMEZ LYRICS.
HE STAYS.
YOU ARE SEVERELY MISUNDERSTANDING YOUR SITUATION--
TIFF! IT'S OKAY, DON'T--
♪ CAN'T KEEP MY HANDS TO MYSELF
♫ NO MATTER HOW HARD I'M--

*Selena Gomez > Demi Lovato. FIGHT US.

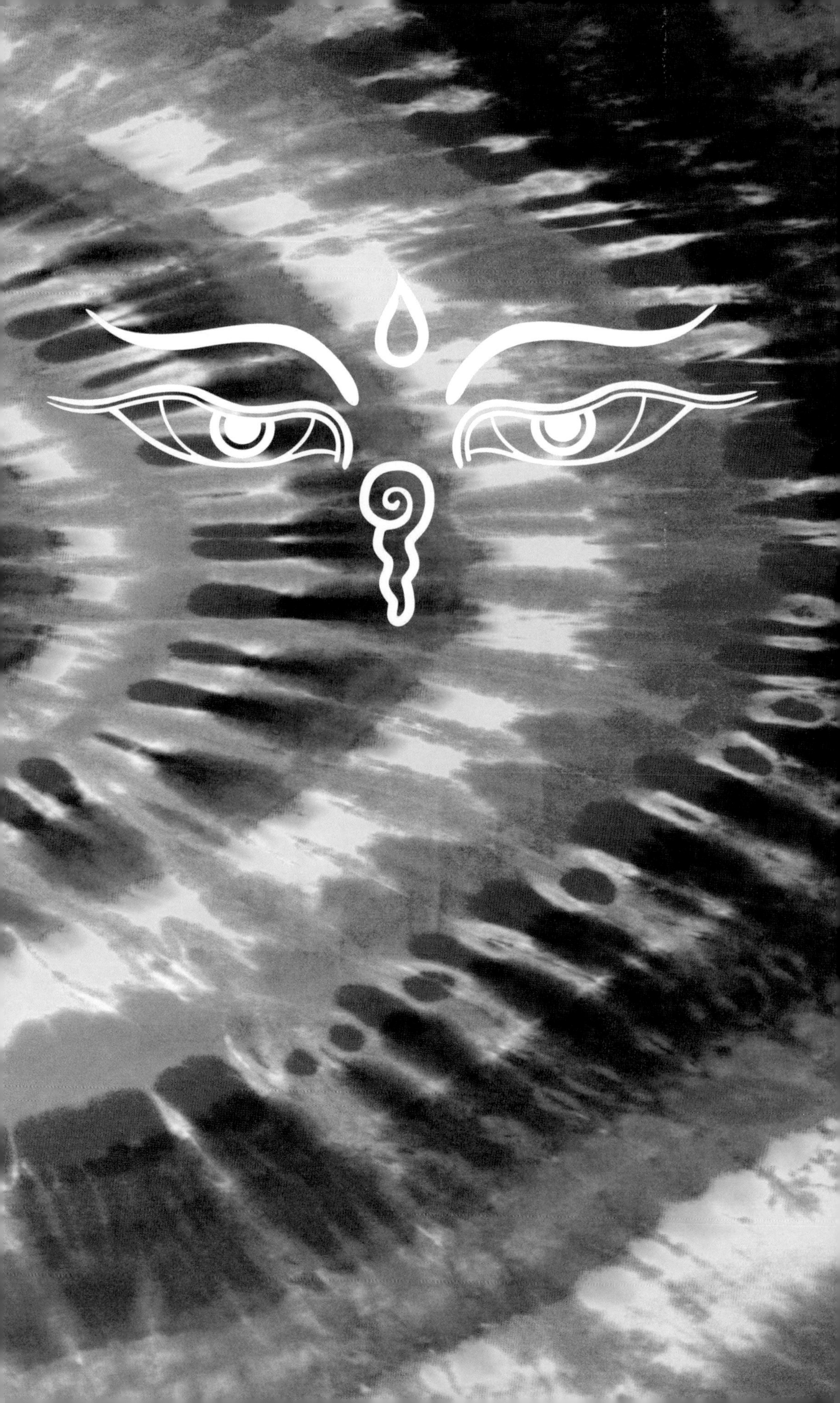

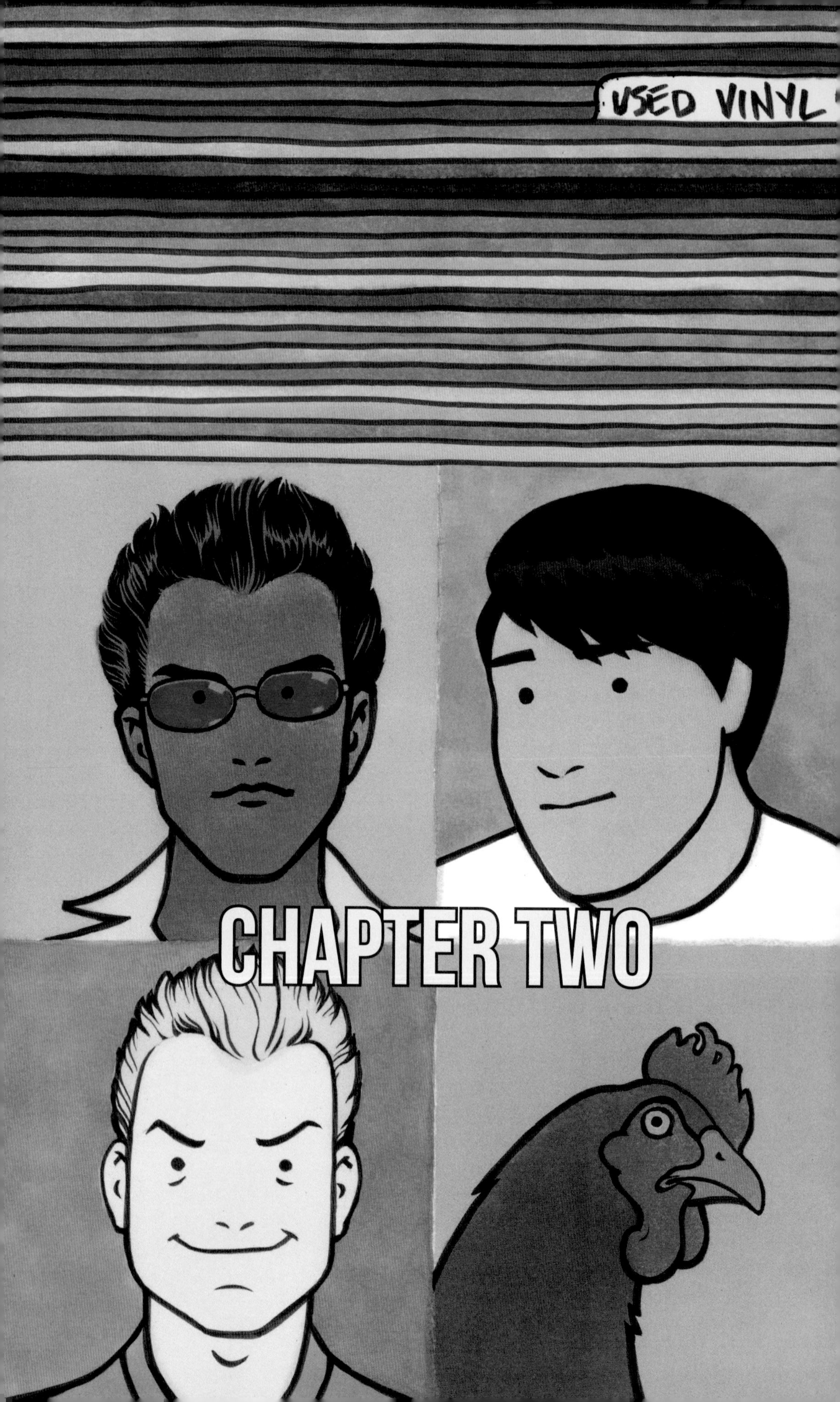
USED VINYL
CHAPTER TWO

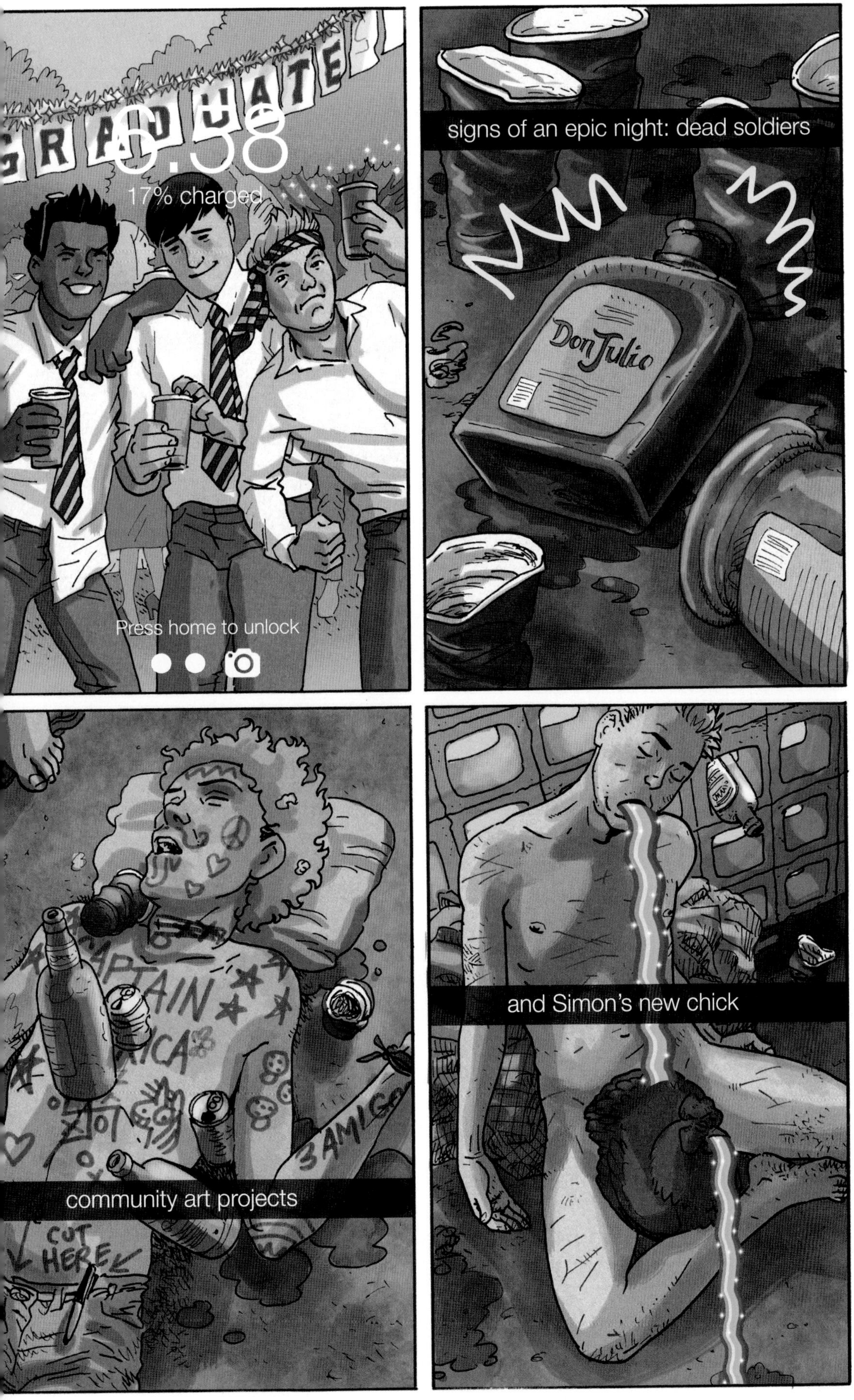
GRADUATE
6:58
17% charged
Press home to unlock
signs of an epic night: dead soldiers
Don Julio
APTAIN
ICA
3 AMIGO
community art projects
CUT HERE
and Simon's new chick

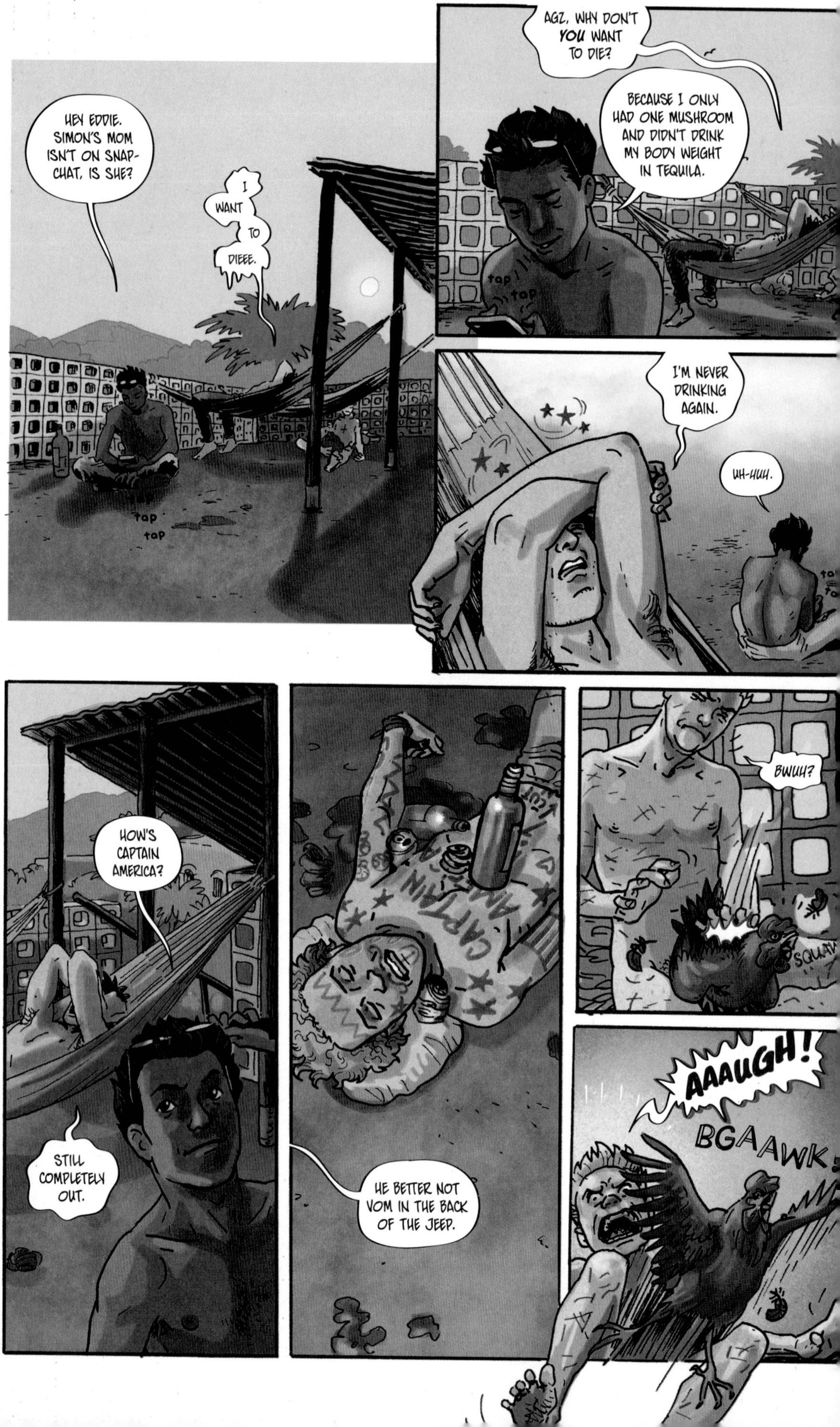
HEY EDDIE. SIMON'S MOM ISN'T ON SNAP-CHAT, IS SHE?
I WANT TO DIEEE.
tap tap
AGZ, WHY DON'T YOU WANT TO DIE?
BECAUSE I ONLY HAD ONE MUSHROOM AND DIDN'T DRINK MY BODY WEIGHT IN TEQUILA.
tap tap
I'M NEVER DRINKING AGAIN.
UH-HUH.
HOW'S CAPTAIN AMERICA?
STILL COMPLETELY OUT.
CAPTAIN AMERICA
HE BETTER NOT VOM IN THE BACK OF THE JEEP.
BWUH?
AAAUGH!
BGAAAWK

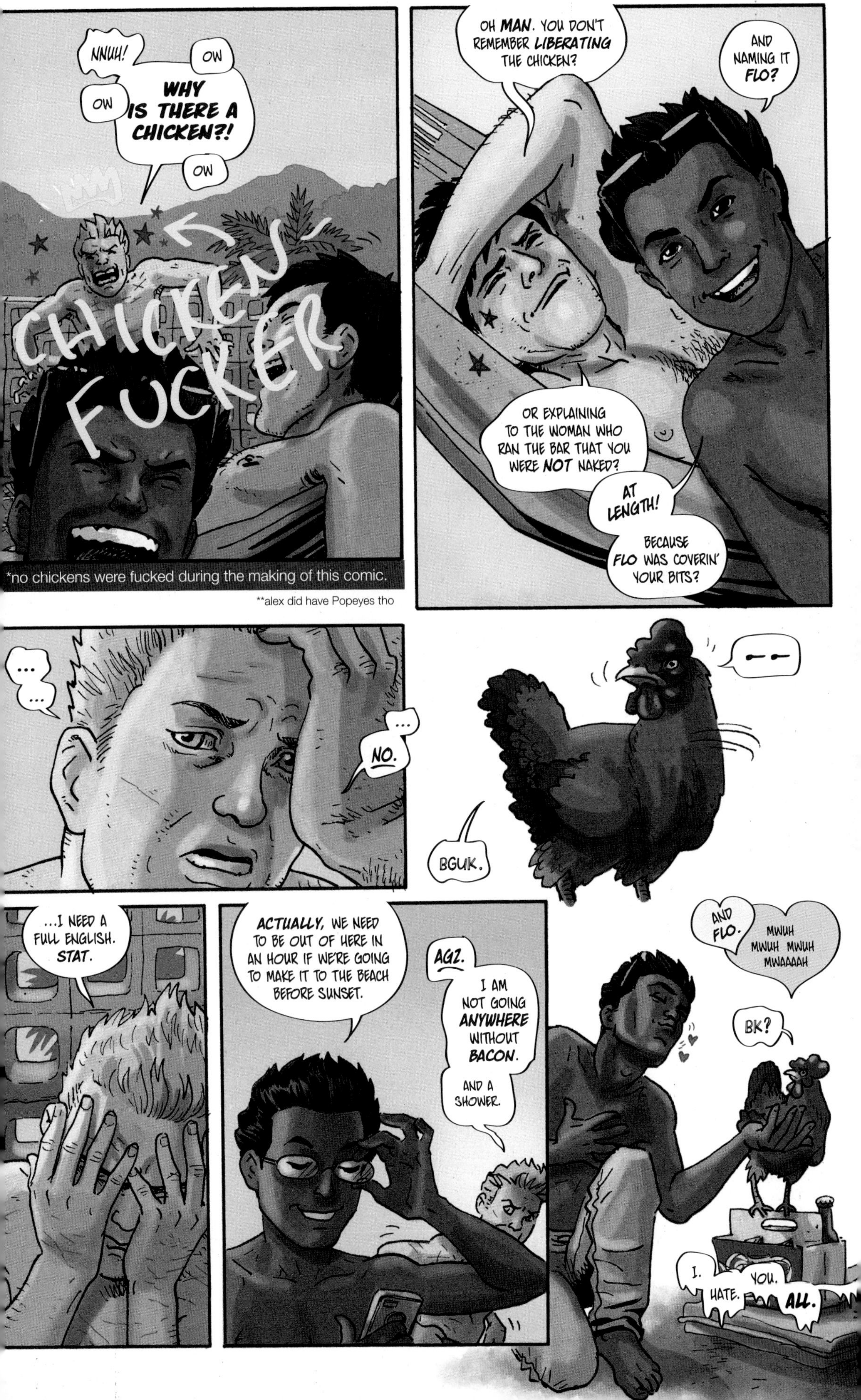
NNUH!
OW
OW
WHY IS THERE A CHICKEN?!
OW
CHICKEN-FUCKER
*no chickens were fucked during the making of this comic.
**alex did have Popeyes tho
OH MAN. YOU DON'T REMEMBER LIBERATING THE CHICKEN?
AND NAMING IT FLO?
OR EXPLAINING TO THE WOMAN WHO RAN THE BAR THAT YOU WERE NOT NAKED?
AT LENGTH!
BECAUSE FLO WAS COVERIN' YOUR BITS?
...
...
...
NO.
BGUK.
...I NEED A FULL ENGLISH. STAT.
ACTUALLY, WE NEED TO BE OUT OF HERE IN AN HOUR IF WE'RE GOING TO MAKE IT TO THE BEACH BEFORE SUNSET.
AGZ.
I AM NOT GOING ANYWHERE WITHOUT BACON.
AND A SHOWER.
AND FLO.
MWUH MWUH MWUH MWAAAAH
BK?
I.
HATE.
YOU.
ALL.

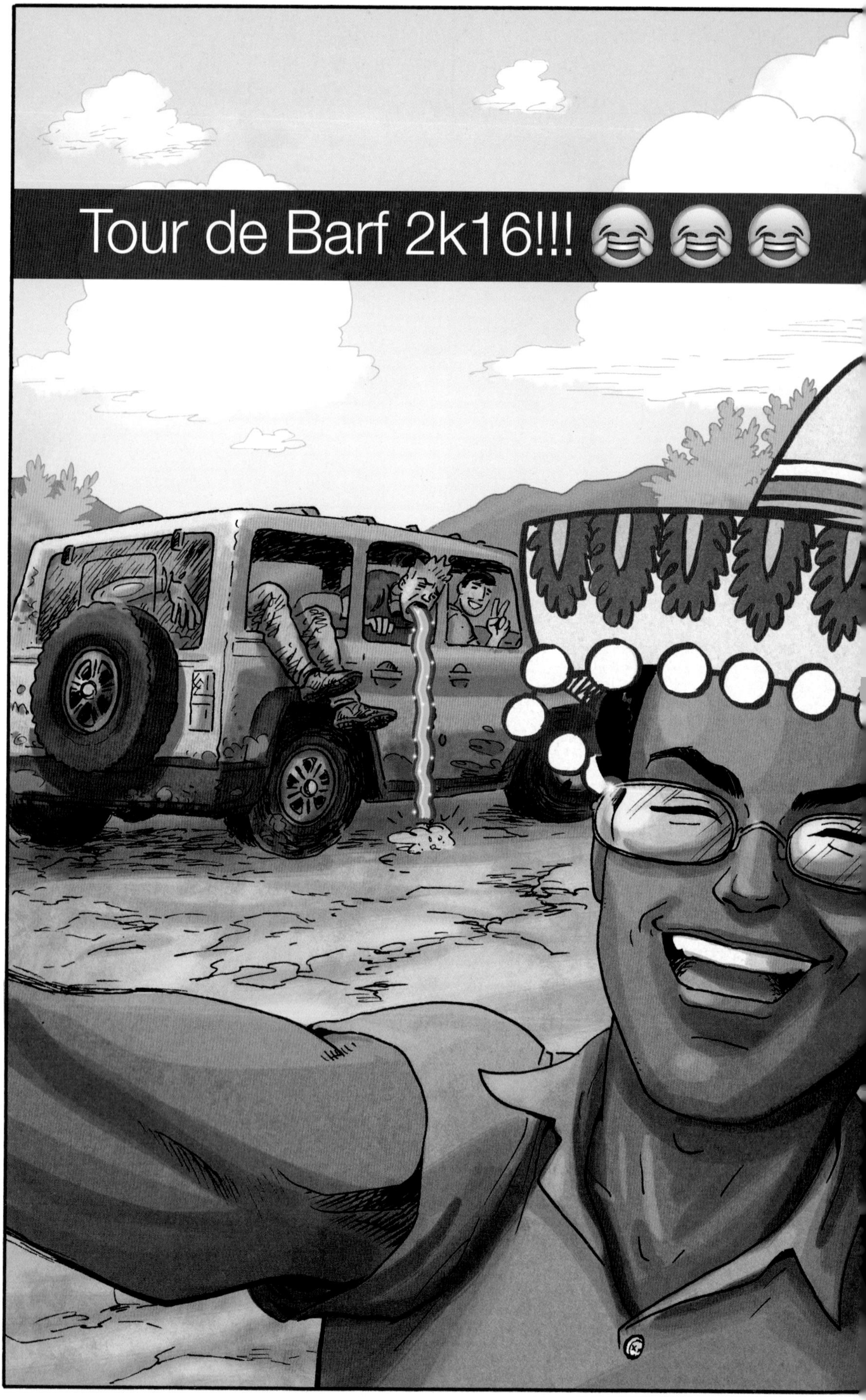
Tour de Barf 2k16!!! 😂😂😂

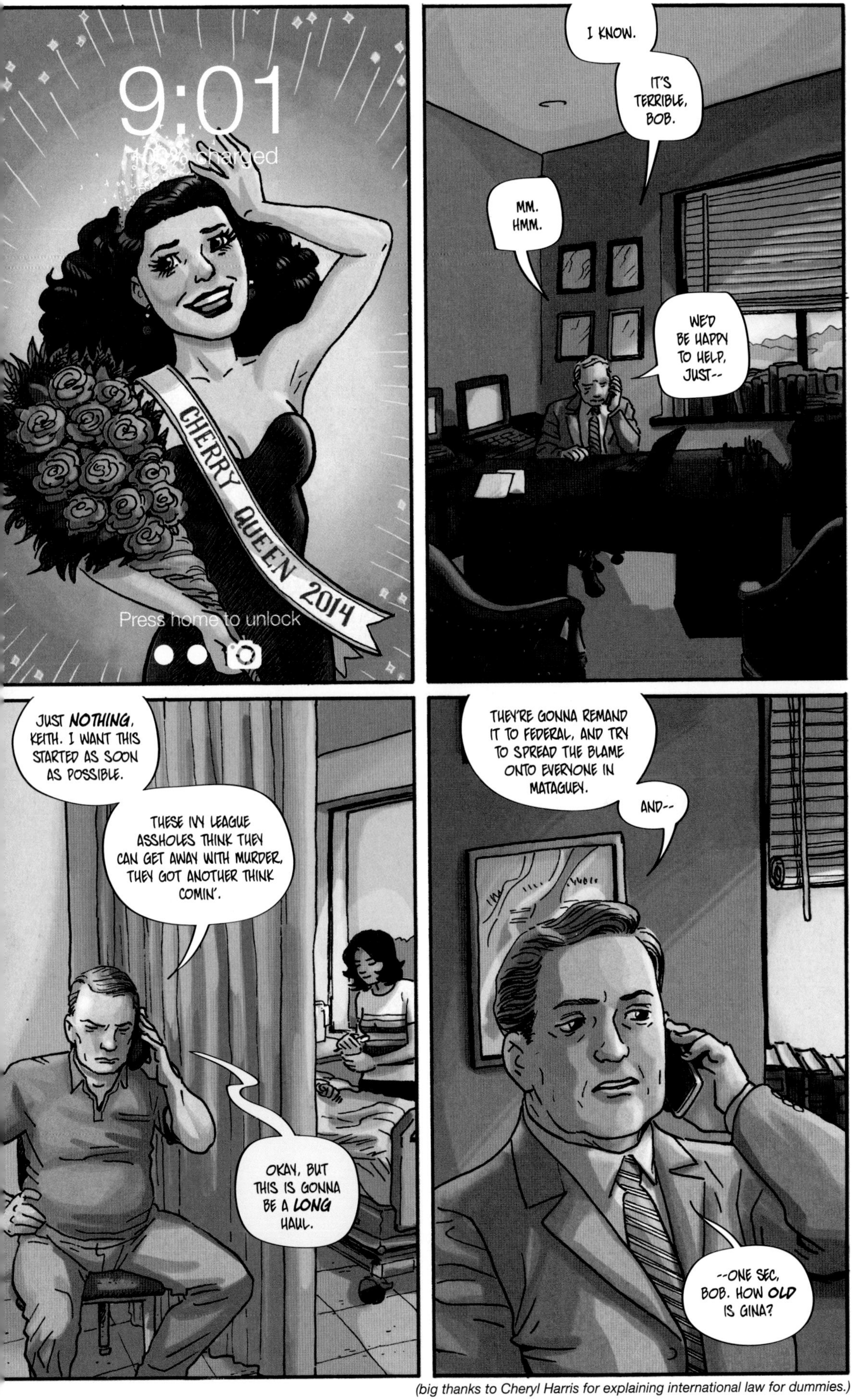
9:01
Press home to unlock
CHERRY QUEEN 2014
I KNOW.
IT'S TERRIBLE, BOB.
MM. HMM.
WE'D BE HAPPY TO HELP, JUST--
JUST **NOTHING**, KEITH. I WANT THIS STARTED AS SOON AS POSSIBLE.
THESE IVY LEAGUE ASSHOLES THINK THEY CAN GET AWAY WITH MURDER, THEY GOT ANOTHER THINK COMIN'.
OKAY, BUT THIS IS GONNA BE A **LONG** HAUL.
THEY'RE GONNA REMAND IT TO FEDERAL, AND TRY TO SPREAD THE BLAME ONTO EVERYONE IN MATAGUEY.
AND--
--ONE SEC, BOB. HOW **OLD** IS GINA?

(big thanks to Cheryl Harris for explaining international law for dummies.)

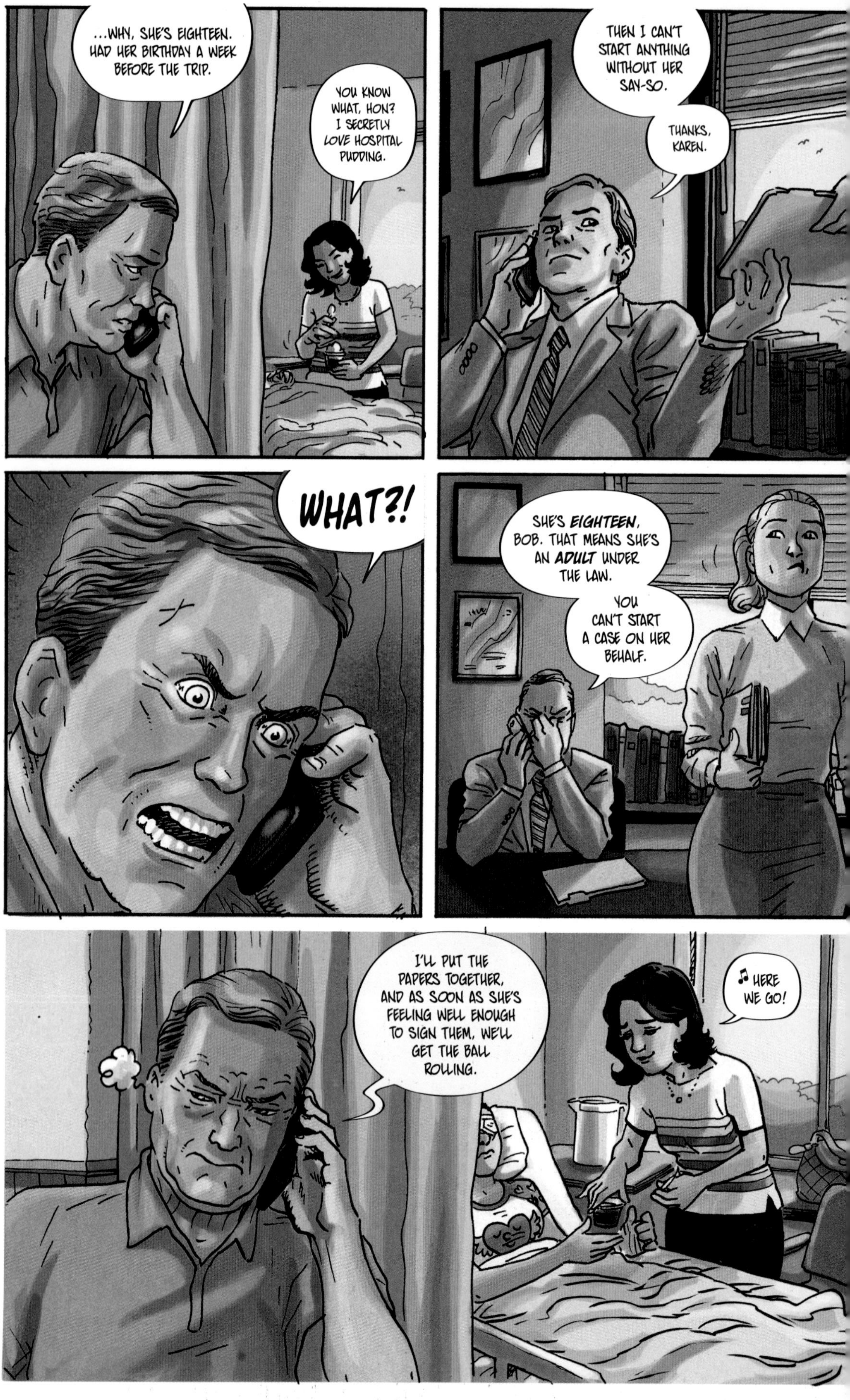

...WHY, SHE'S EIGHTEEN. HAD HER BIRTHDAY A WEEK BEFORE THE TRIP.
YOU KNOW WHAT, HON? I SECRETLY LOVE HOSPITAL PUDDING.
THEN I CAN'T START ANYTHING WITHOUT HER SAY-SO.
THANKS, KAREN.
WHAT?!
SHE'S EIGHTEEN, BOB. THAT MEANS SHE'S AN ADULT UNDER THE LAW.
YOU CAN'T START A CASE ON HER BEHALF.
I'LL PUT THE PAPERS TOGETHER, AND AS SOON AS SHE'S FEELING WELL ENOUGH TO SIGN THEM, WE'LL GET THE BALL ROLLING.
♫ HERE WE GO!

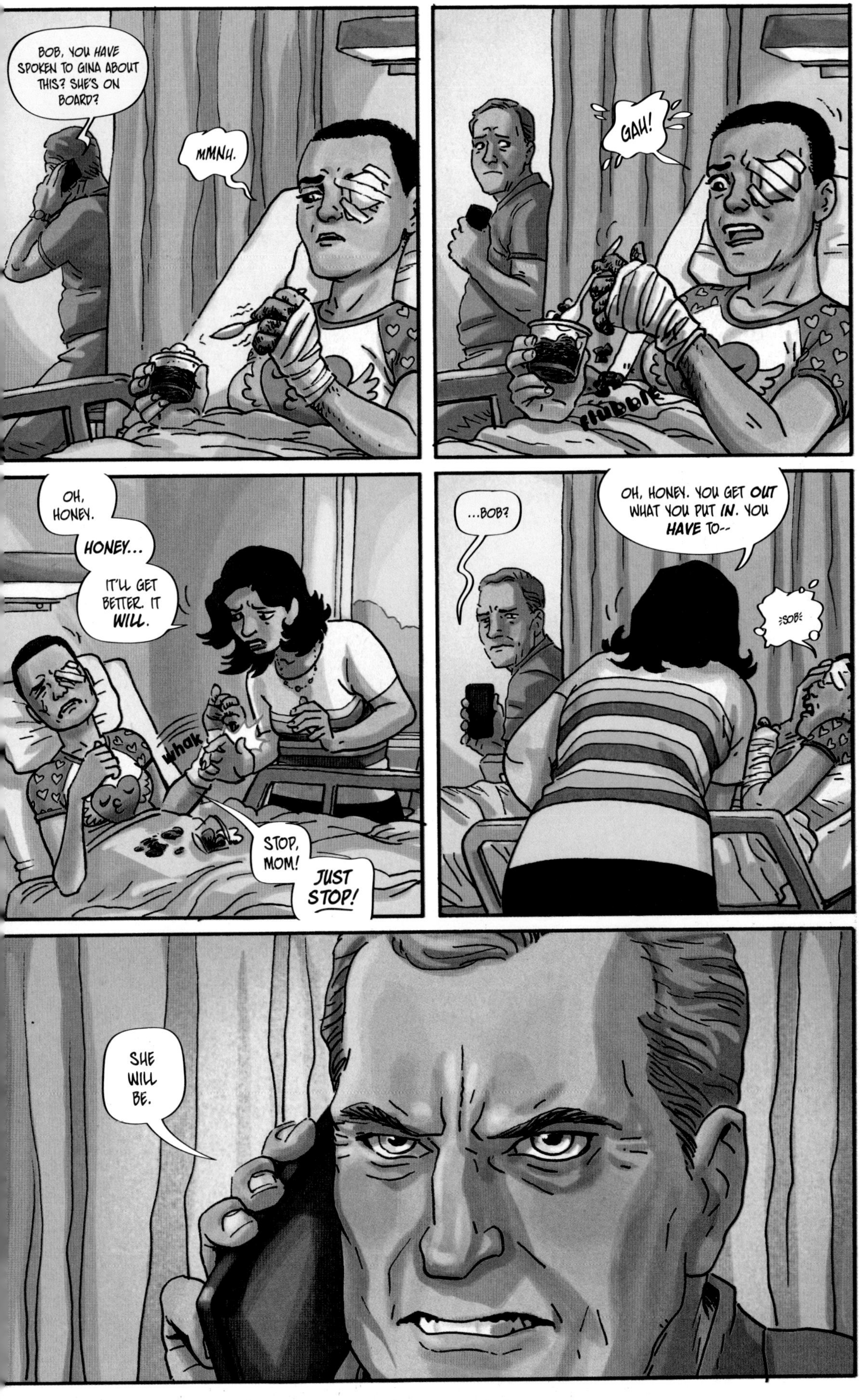
BOB, YOU HAVE SPOKEN TO GINA ABOUT THIS? SHE'S ON BOARD?
MMNH.
GAH!
flubble
OH, HONEY.
HONEY...
IT'LL GET BETTER. IT WILL.
whak
STOP, MOM!
JUST STOP!
...BOB?
OH, HONEY. YOU GET OUT WHAT YOU PUT IN. YOU HAVE TO--
SOB
SHE WILL BE.

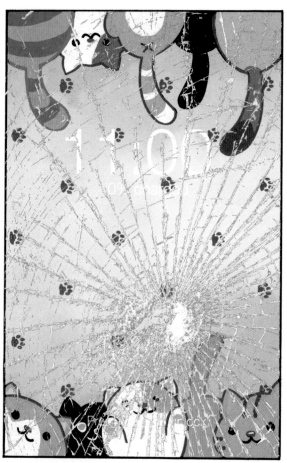

UM, 'SCUSE ME, BUT DESHAWN IS *REALLY SICK?* AND THIS IS *NOTHING* LIKE A SPIDER BITE!

GUH

LEAVE IT, TIFF!

YEAH BUT YOU CAN'T GET *RANSOMS* FOR *DEAD PEOPLE!*

≡HNNH≡

NA'GUNNA GET ONE ANYWAY...

WHEN WE RETURN TOMORROW WE WILL CALL FOR THE LOCAL *DOCTOR.*

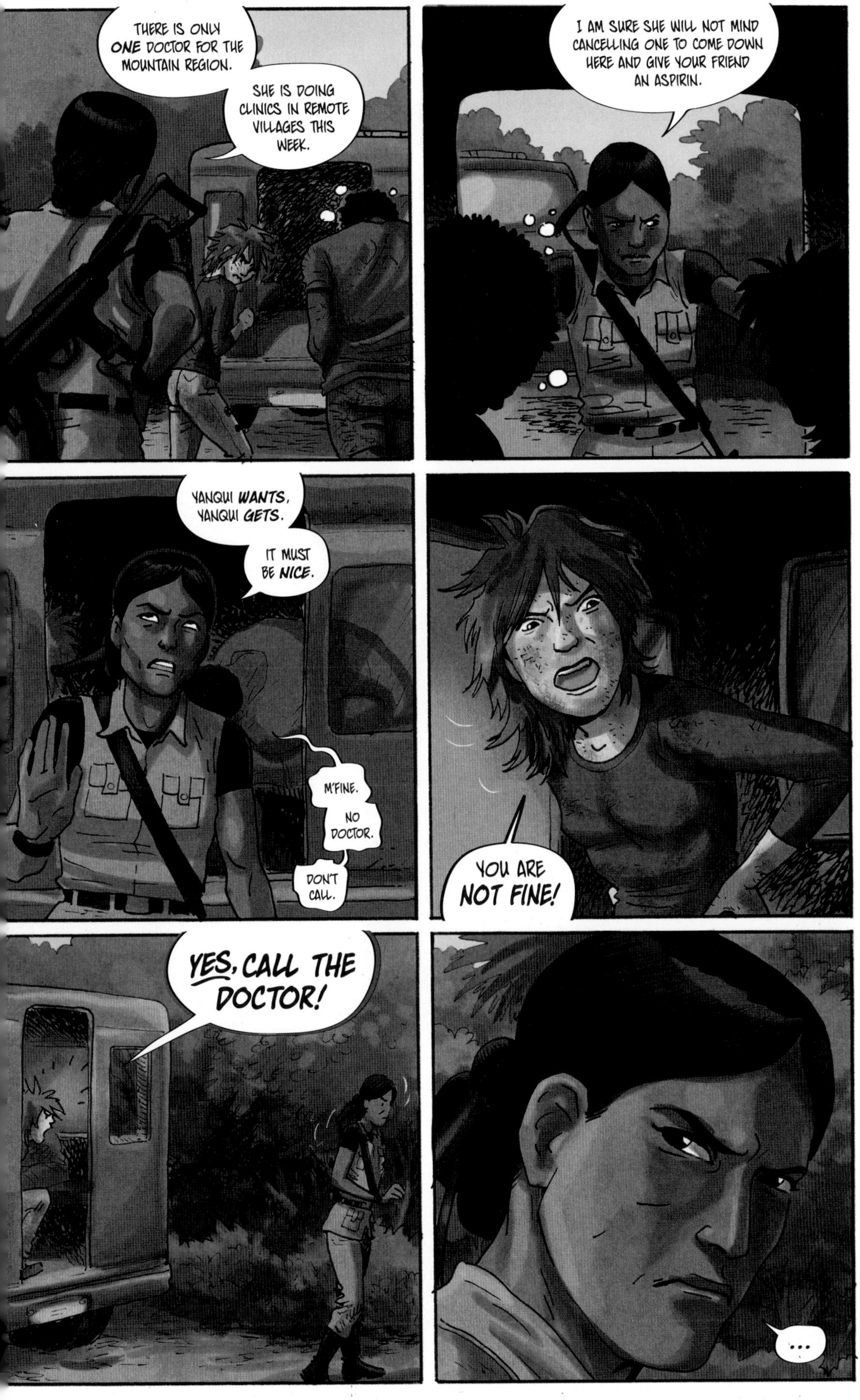
THERE IS ONLY ONE DOCTOR FOR THE MOUNTAIN REGION.
SHE IS DOING CLINICS IN REMOTE VILLAGES THIS WEEK.
I AM SURE SHE WILL NOT MIND CANCELLING ONE TO COME DOWN HERE AND GIVE YOUR FRIEND AN ASPIRIN.
YANQUI WANTS, YANQUI GETS.
IT MUST BE NICE.
M'FINE.
NO DOCTOR.
DON'T CALL.
YOU ARE NOT FINE!
YES, CALL THE DOCTOR!
...

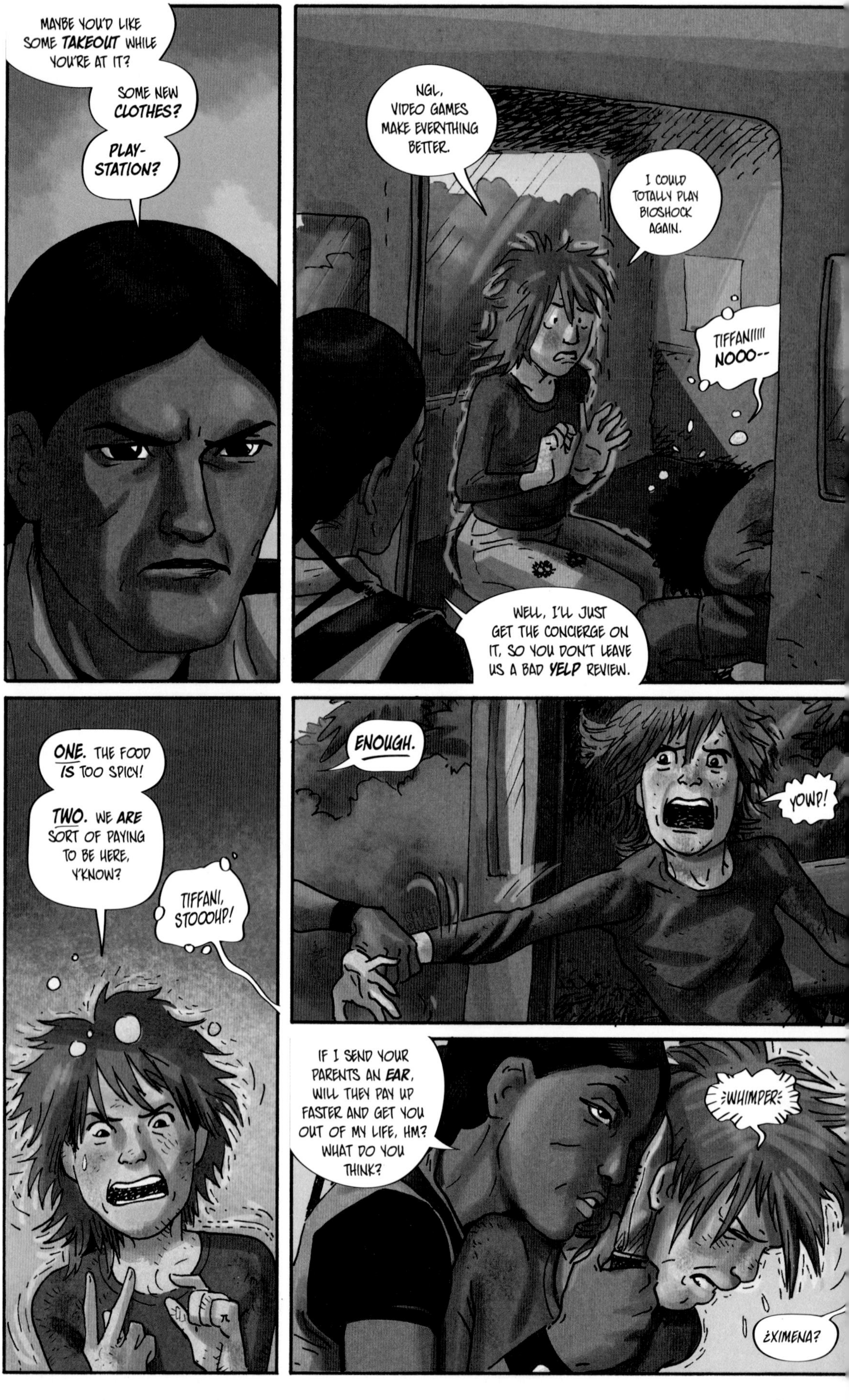
MAYBE YOU'D LIKE SOME TAKEOUT WHILE YOU'RE AT IT?
SOME NEW CLOTHES?
PLAY-STATION?
NGL, VIDEO GAMES MAKE EVERYTHING BETTER.
I COULD TOTALLY PLAY BIOSHOCK AGAIN.
TIFFANI!!!!! NOOO--
WELL, I'LL JUST GET THE CONCIERGE ON IT, SO YOU DON'T LEAVE US A BAD YELP REVIEW.
ONE. THE FOOD IS TOO SPICY!
TWO. WE ARE SORT OF PAYING TO BE HERE, Y'KNOW?
TIFFANI, STOOOHP!
ENOUGH.
YOWP!
IF I SEND YOUR PARENTS AN EAR, WILL THEY PAY UP FASTER AND GET YOU OUT OF MY LIFE, HM? WHAT DO YOU THINK?
WHIMPER
¿XIMENA?

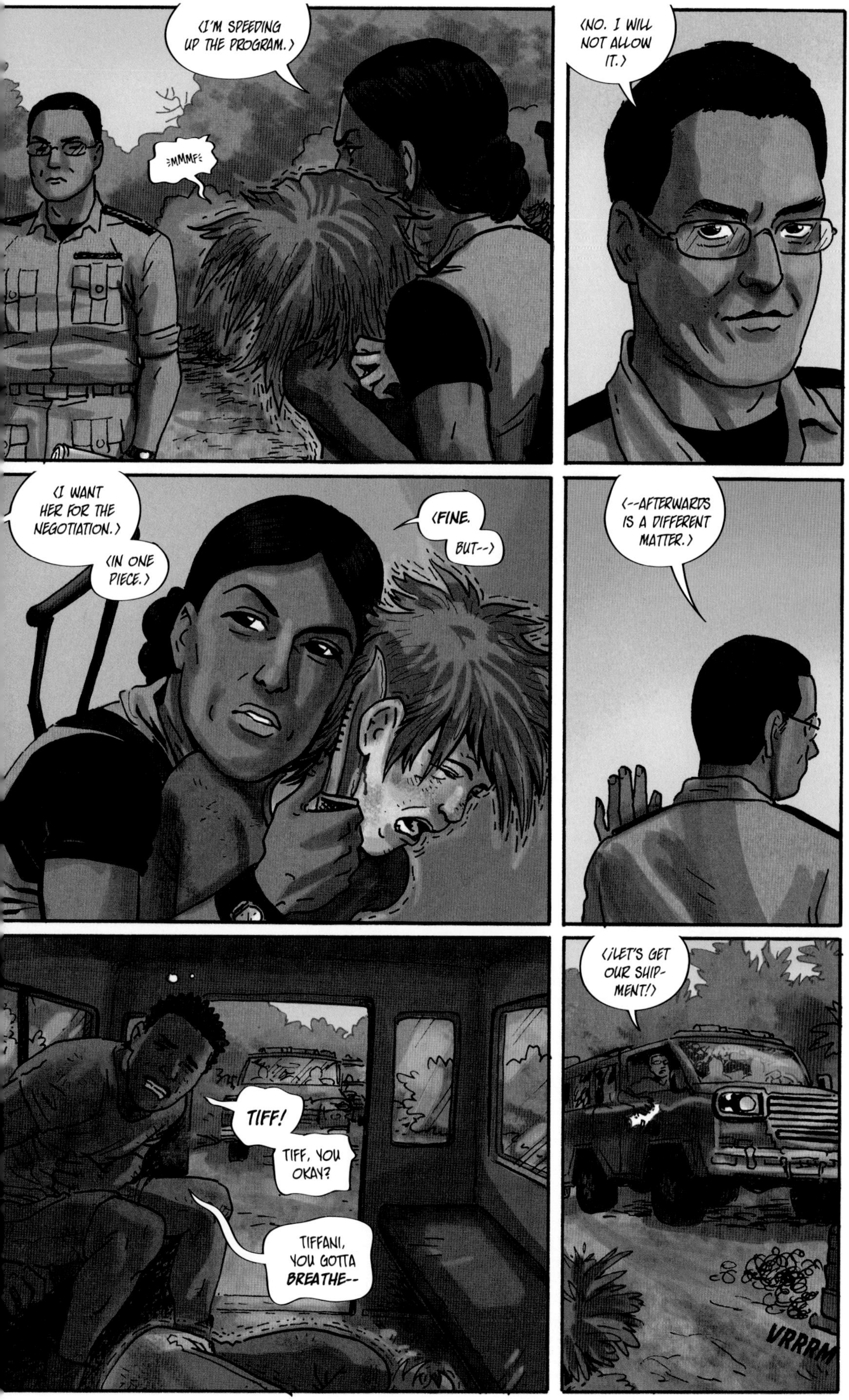

‹I'M SPEEDING UP THE PROGRAM.›
MMMF
‹NO. I WILL NOT ALLOW IT.›
‹I WANT HER FOR THE NEGOTIATION.›
‹IN ONE PIECE.›
‹FINE.
BUT--›
‹--AFTERWARDS IS A DIFFERENT MATTER.›
TIFF!
TIFF, YOU OKAY?
TIFFANI, YOU GOTTA BREATHE--
‹¡LET'S GET OUR SHIP-MENT!›
VRRRM

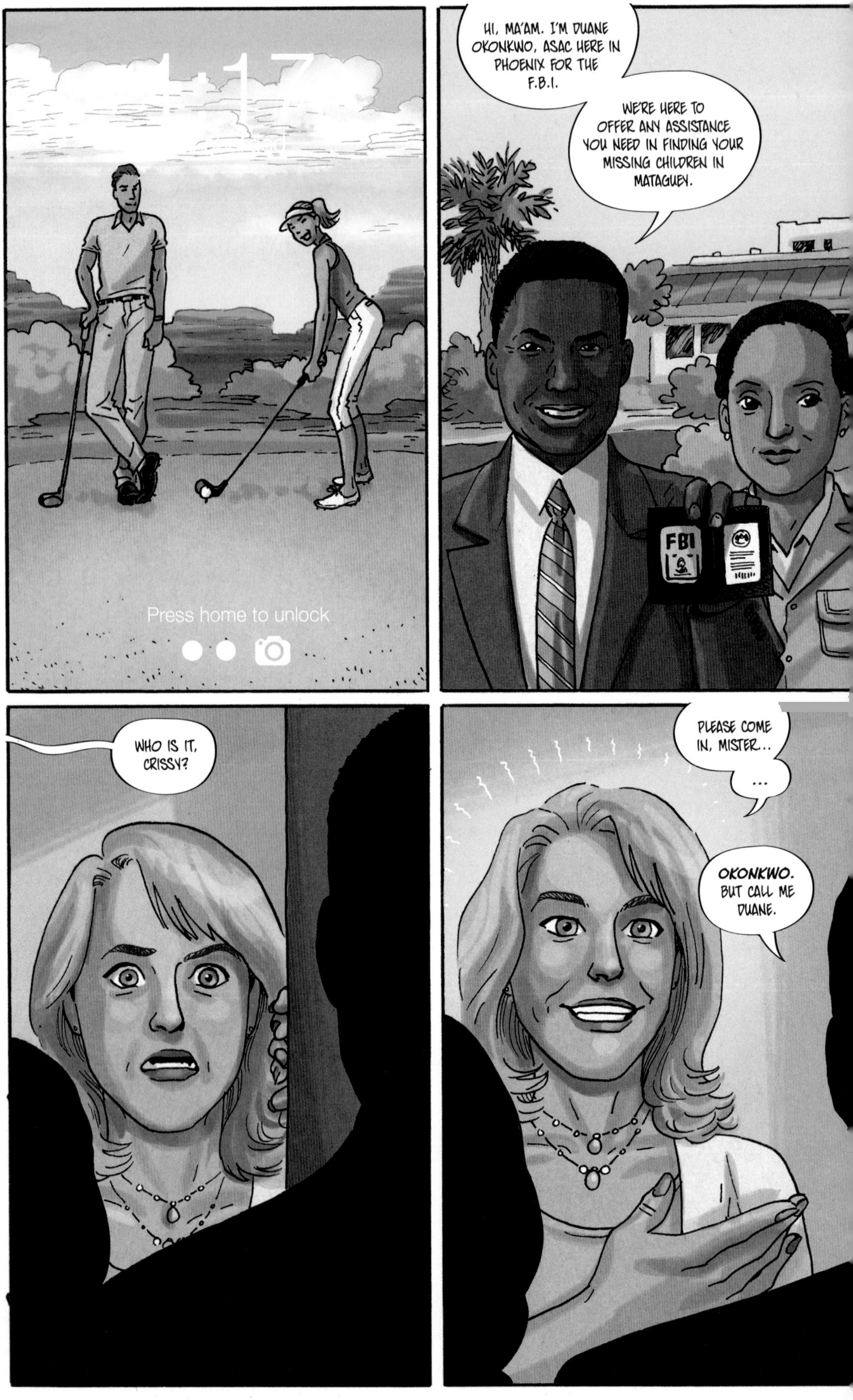
Press home to unlock
HI, MA'AM. I'M DUANE OKONKWO, ASAC HERE IN PHOENIX FOR THE F.B.I.
WE'RE HERE TO OFFER ANY ASSISTANCE YOU NEED IN FINDING YOUR MISSING CHILDREN IN MATAGUEY.
FBI
WHO IS IT, CRISSY?
PLEASE COME IN, MISTER...
...
OKONKWO. BUT CALL ME DUANE.

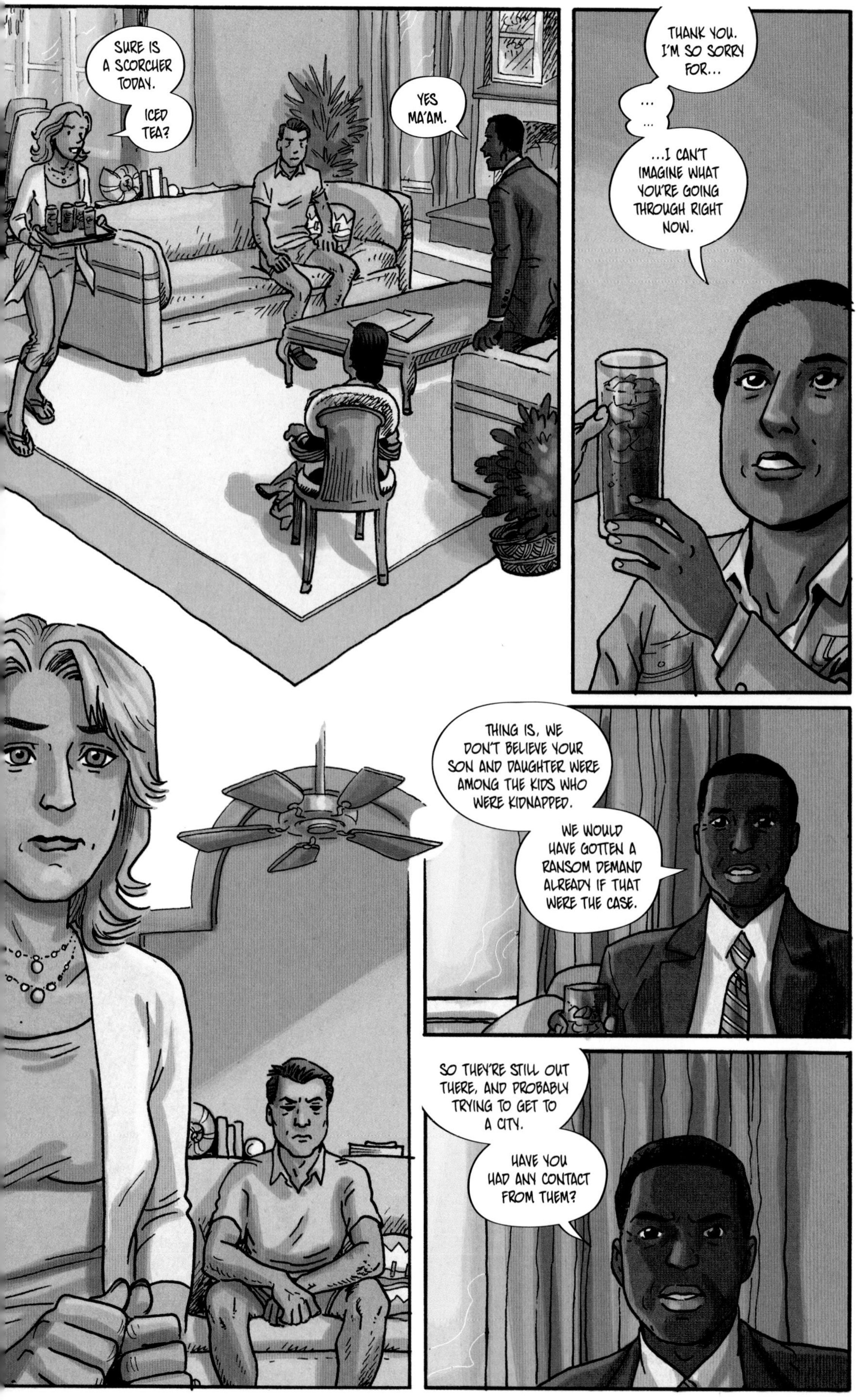
SURE IS A SCORCHER TODAY.
ICED TEA?
YES MA'AM.
THANK YOU. I'M SO SORRY FOR...
...
...
...I CAN'T IMAGINE WHAT YOU'RE GOING THROUGH RIGHT NOW.
THING IS, WE DON'T BELIEVE YOUR SON AND DAUGHTER WERE AMONG THE KIDS WHO WERE KIDNAPPED.
WE WOULD HAVE GOTTEN A RANSOM DEMAND ALREADY IF THAT WERE THE CASE.
SO THEY'RE STILL OUT THERE, AND PROBABLY TRYING TO GET TO A CITY.
HAVE YOU HAD ANY CONTACT FROM THEM?

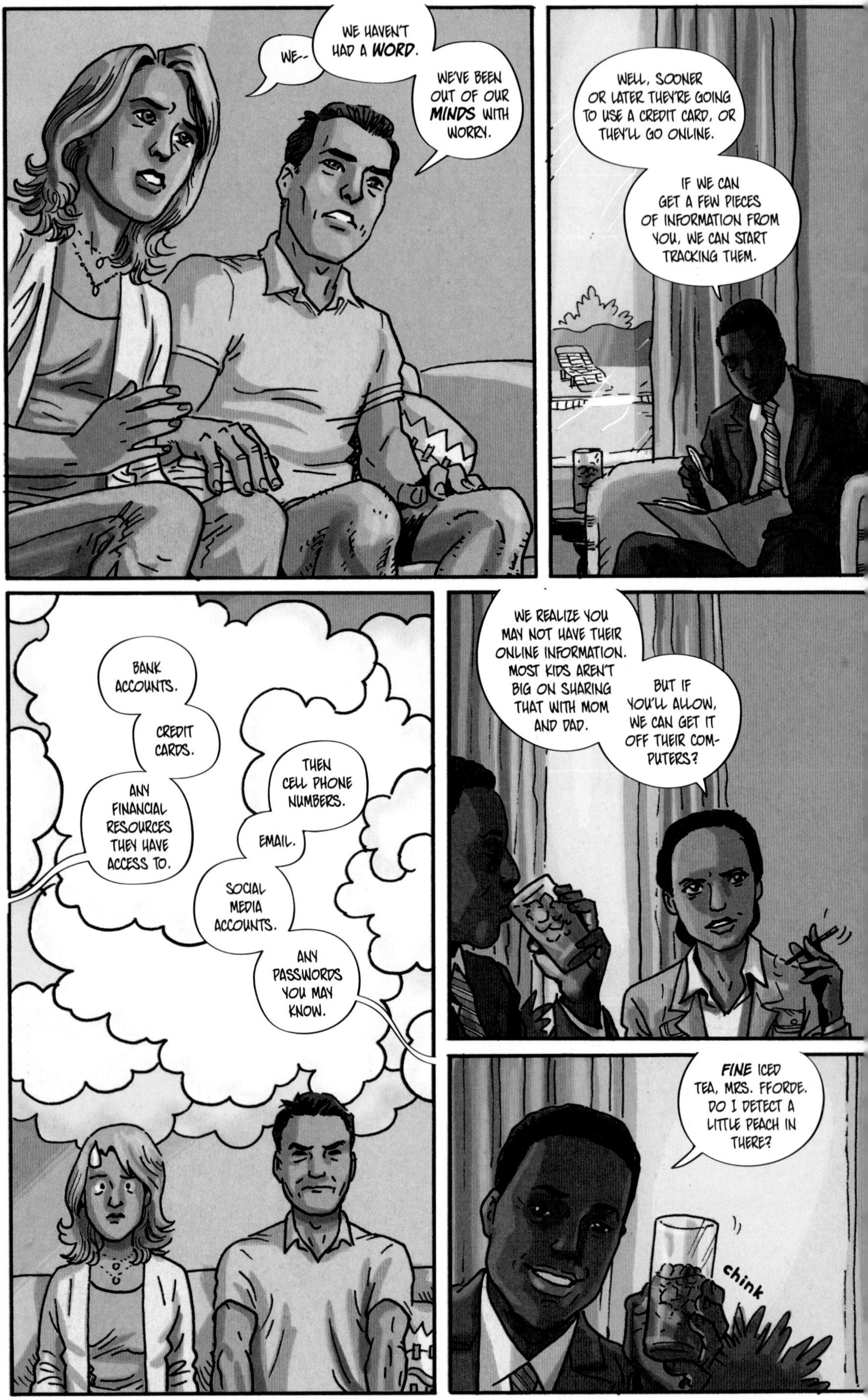
WE--
WE HAVEN'T HAD A **WORD**.
WE'VE BEEN OUT OF OUR **MINDS** WITH WORRY.
WELL, SOONER OR LATER THEY'RE GOING TO USE A CREDIT CARD, OR THEY'LL GO ONLINE.
IF WE CAN GET A FEW PIECES OF INFORMATION FROM YOU, WE CAN START TRACKING THEM.
BANK ACCOUNTS.
CREDIT CARDS.
ANY FINANCIAL RESOURCES THEY HAVE ACCESS TO.
THEN CELL PHONE NUMBERS.
EMAIL.
SOCIAL MEDIA ACCOUNTS.
ANY PASSWORDS YOU MAY KNOW.
WE REALIZE YOU MAY NOT HAVE THEIR ONLINE INFORMATION. MOST KIDS AREN'T BIG ON SHARING THAT WITH MOM AND DAD.
BUT IF YOU'LL ALLOW, WE CAN GET IT OFF THEIR COMPUTERS?
FINE ICED TEA, MRS. FFORDE. DO I DETECT A LITTLE PEACH IN THERE?
chink

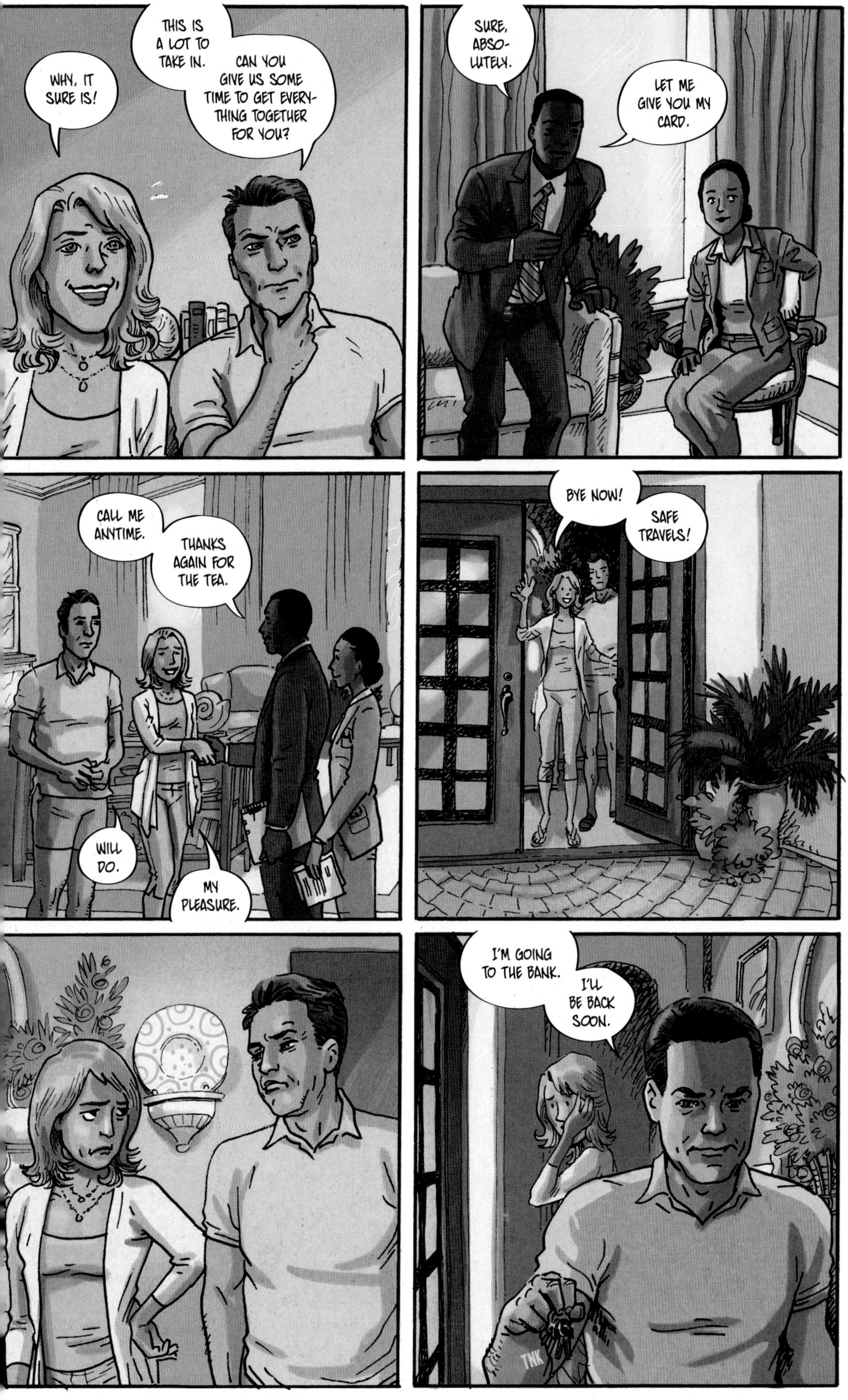
WHY, IT SURE IS!
THIS IS A LOT TO TAKE IN.
CAN YOU GIVE US SOME TIME TO GET EVERYTHING TOGETHER FOR YOU?
SURE, ABSOLUTELY.
LET ME GIVE YOU MY CARD.
CALL ME ANYTIME.
THANKS AGAIN FOR THE TEA.
WILL DO.
MY PLEASURE.
BYE NOW!
SAFE TRAVELS!
I'M GOING TO THE BANK.
I'LL BE BACK SOON.
TNK

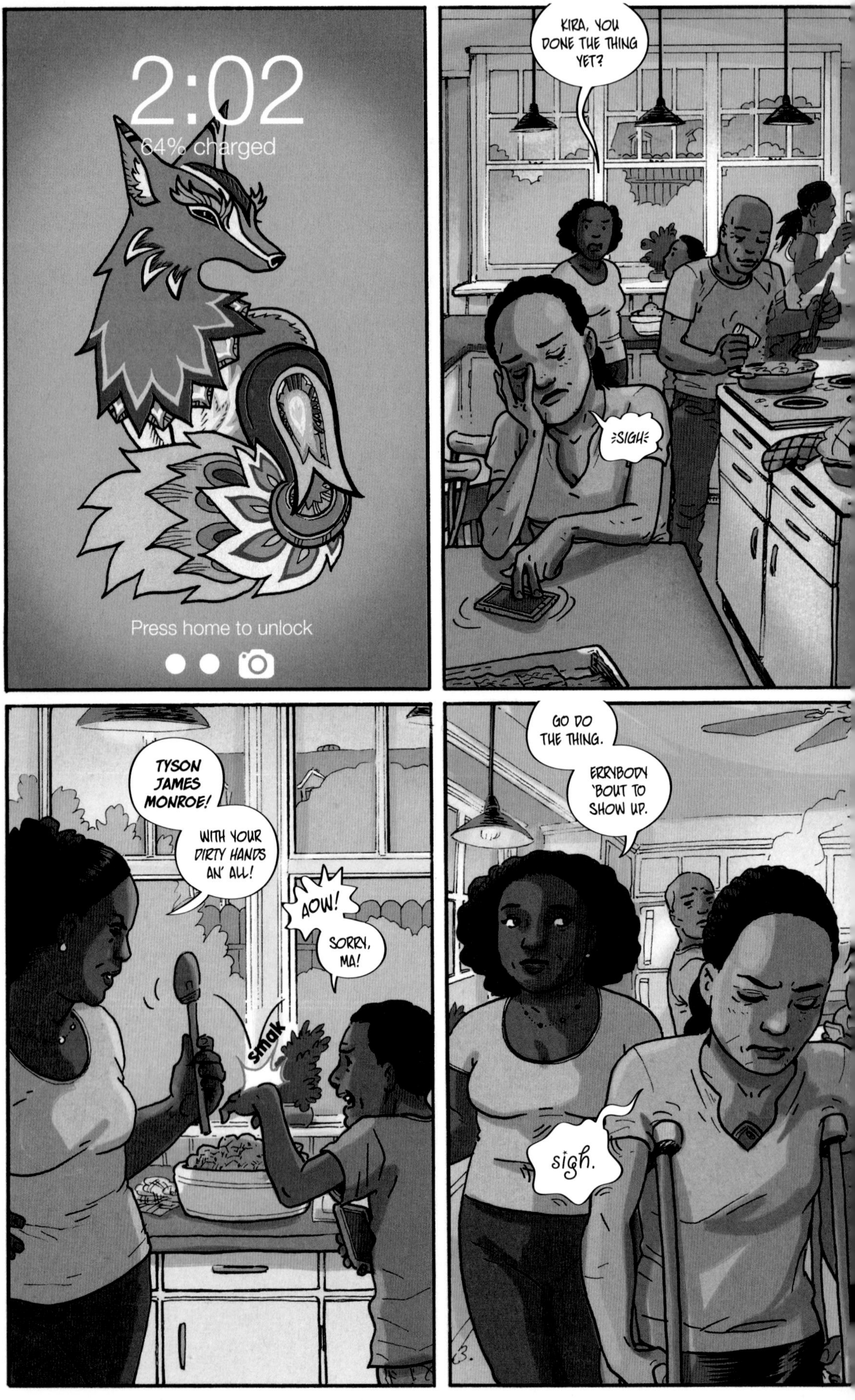
2:02
64% charged
Press home to unlock
KIRA, YOU DONE THE THING YET?
SIGH
TYSON JAMES MONROE!
WITH YOUR DIRTY HANDS AN' ALL!
AOW!
SORRY, MA!
SMAK
GO DO THE THING.
ERRYBODY 'BOUT TO SHOW UP.
sigh.

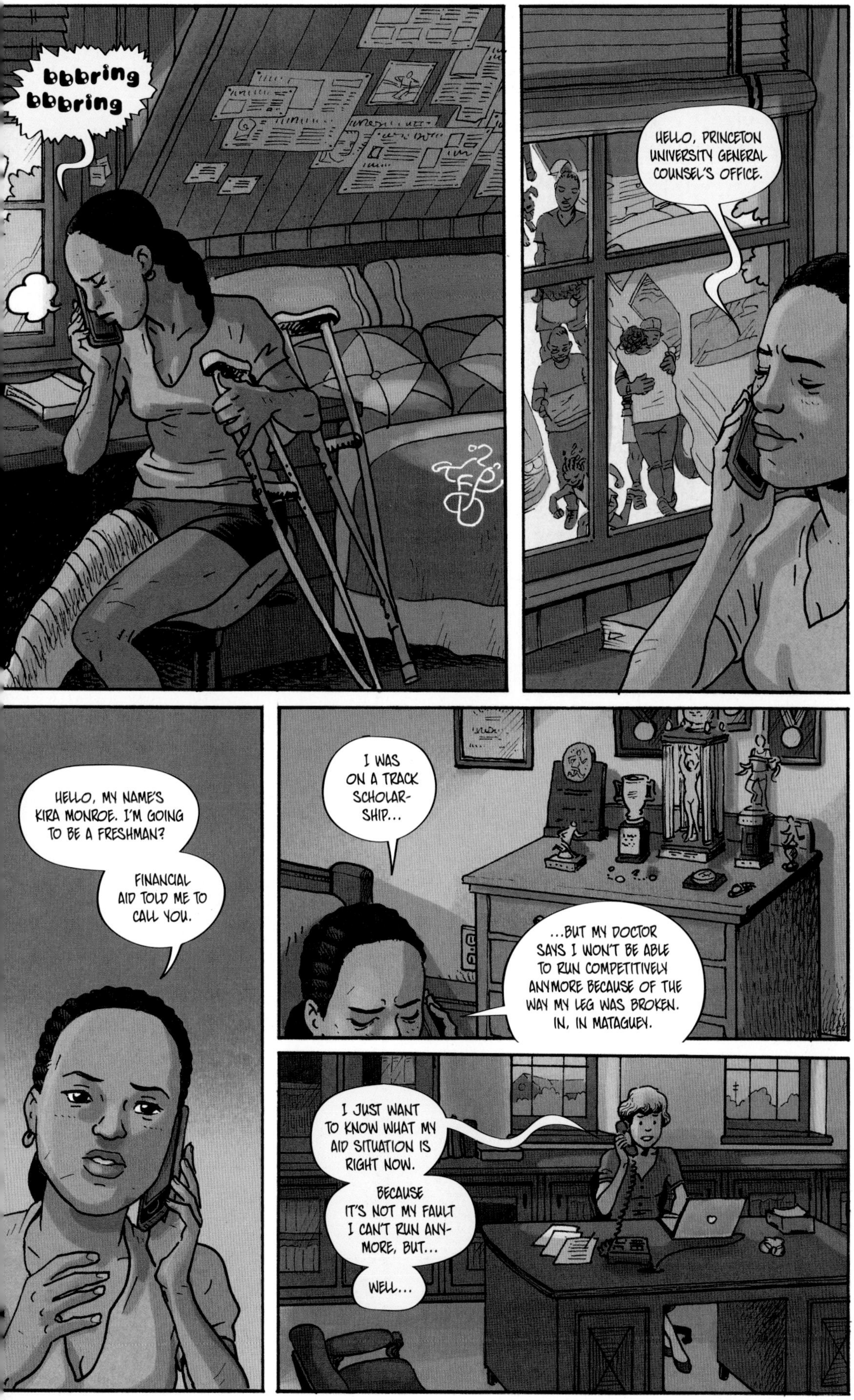

bbbring bbbring
HELLO, PRINCETON UNIVERSITY GENERAL COUNSEL'S OFFICE.
HELLO, MY NAME'S KIRA MONROE. I'M GOING TO BE A FRESHMAN?
FINANCIAL AID TOLD ME TO CALL YOU.
I WAS ON A TRACK SCHOLAR-SHIP...
...BUT MY DOCTOR SAYS I WON'T BE ABLE TO RUN COMPETITIVELY ANYMORE BECAUSE OF THE WAY MY LEG WAS BROKEN. IN, IN MATAGUEY.
I JUST WANT TO KNOW WHAT MY AID SITUATION IS RIGHT NOW.
BECAUSE IT'S NOT MY FAULT I CAN'T RUN ANY-MORE, BUT...
WELL...

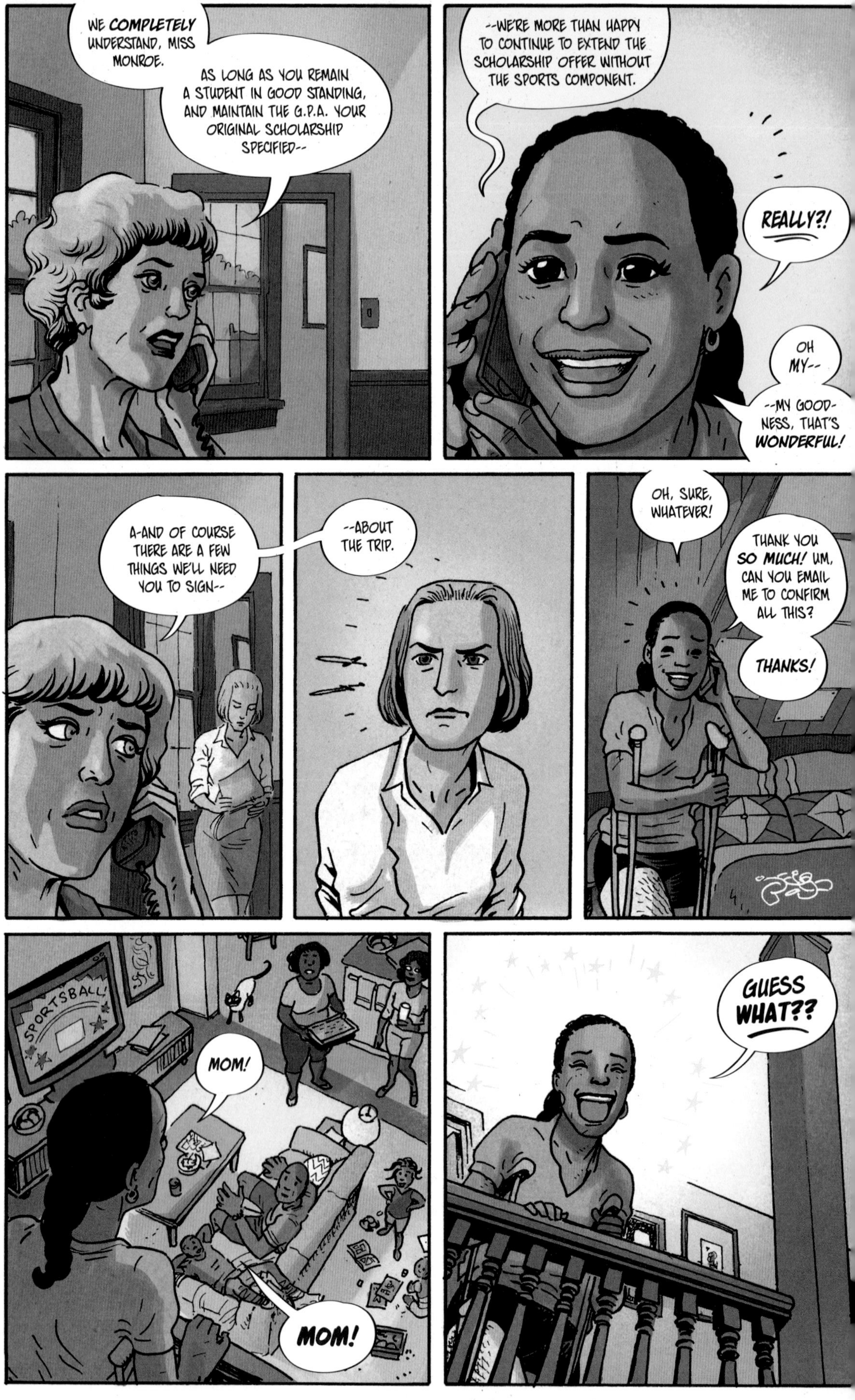
WE **COMPLETELY** UNDERSTAND, MISS MONROE.
AS LONG AS YOU REMAIN A STUDENT IN GOOD STANDING, AND MAINTAIN THE G.P.A. YOUR ORIGINAL SCHOLARSHIP SPECIFIED--
--WE'RE MORE THAN HAPPY TO CONTINUE TO EXTEND THE SCHOLARSHIP OFFER WITHOUT THE SPORTS COMPONENT.
REALLY?!
OH MY--
--MY GOOD-NESS, THAT'S **WONDERFUL!**
A-AND OF COURSE THERE ARE A FEW THINGS WE'LL NEED YOU TO SIGN--
--ABOUT THE TRIP.
OH, SURE, WHATEVER!
THANK YOU **SO MUCH!** UM, CAN YOU EMAIL ME TO CONFIRM ALL THIS?
THANKS!
SPORTSBALL!
MOM!
MOM!
GUESS WHAT??

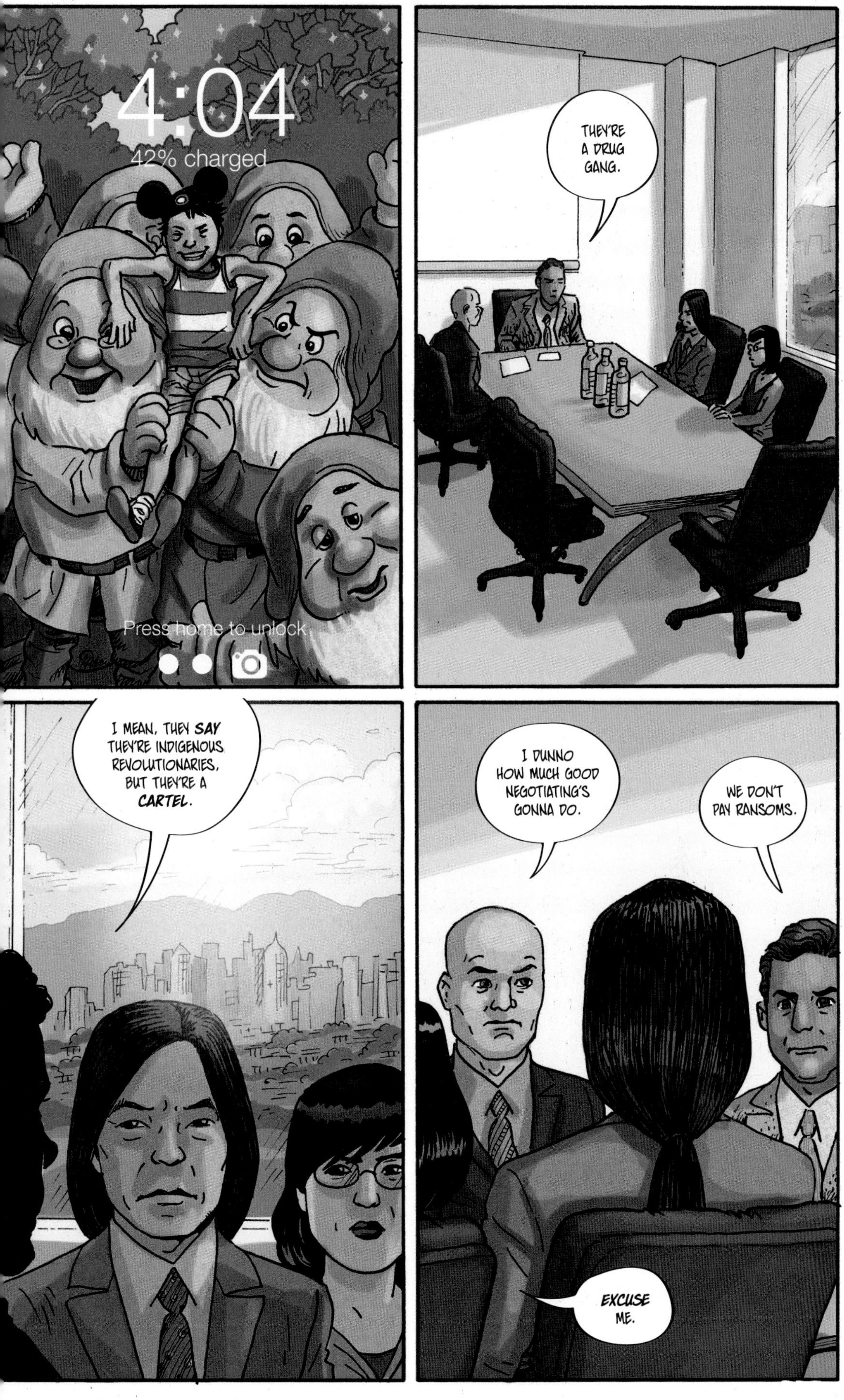
4:04
42% charged
Press home to unlock
THEY'RE A DRUG GANG.
I MEAN, THEY SAY THEY'RE INDIGENOUS REVOLUTIONARIES, BUT THEY'RE A CARTEL.
I DUNNO HOW MUCH GOOD NEGOTIATING'S GONNA DO.
WE DON'T PAY RANSOMS.
EXCUSE ME.

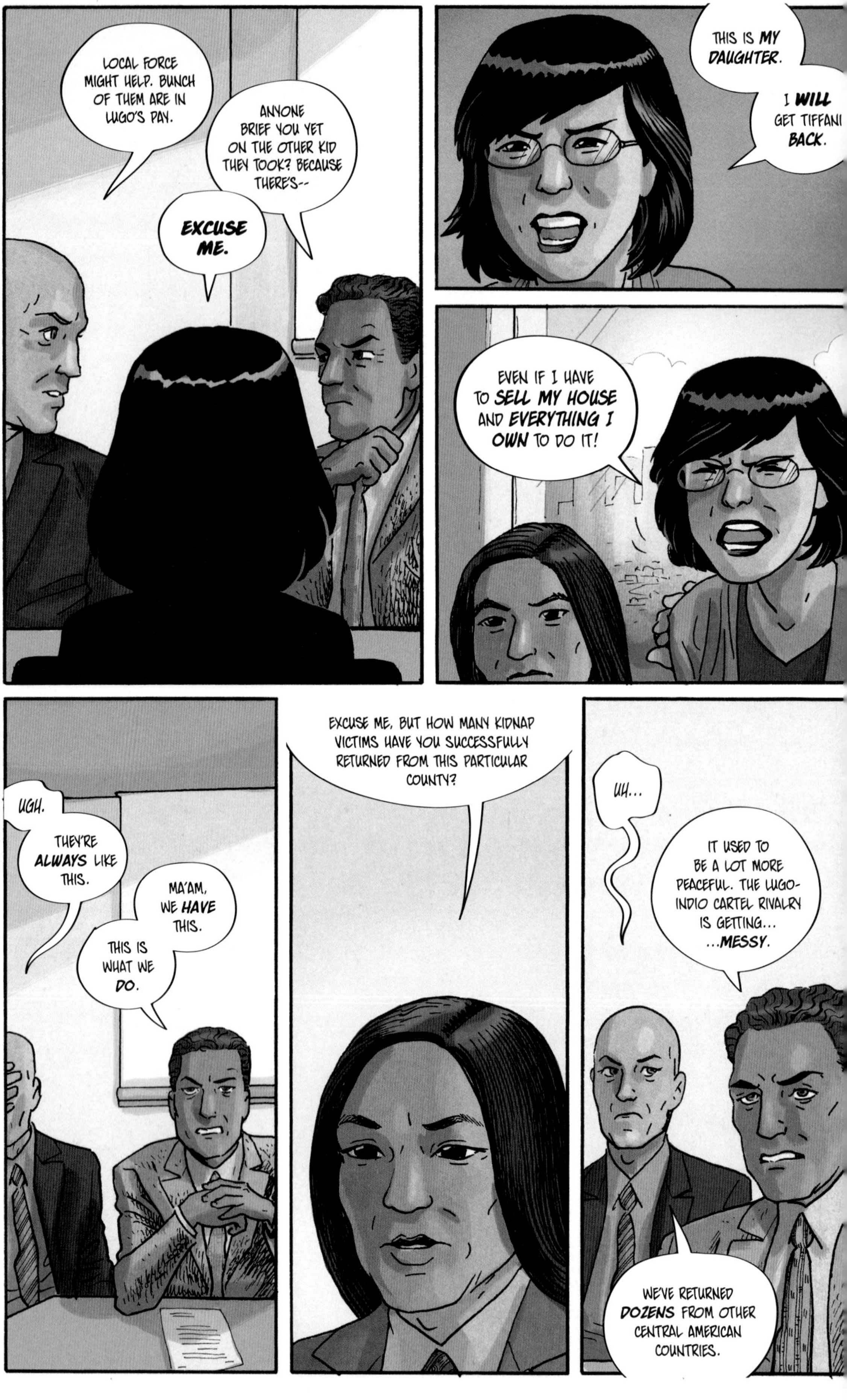

LOCAL FORCE MIGHT HELP. BUNCH OF THEM ARE IN LUGO'S PAY.
ANYONE BRIEF YOU YET ON THE OTHER KID THEY TOOK? BECAUSE THERE'S--
EXCUSE ME.
THIS IS MY DAUGHTER.
I WILL GET TIFFANI BACK.
EVEN IF I HAVE TO SELL MY HOUSE AND EVERYTHING I OWN TO DO IT!
UGH.
THEY'RE ALWAYS LIKE THIS.
MA'AM, WE HAVE THIS.
THIS IS WHAT WE DO.
EXCUSE ME, BUT HOW MANY KIDNAP VICTIMS HAVE YOU SUCCESSFULLY RETURNED FROM THIS PARTICULAR COUNTY?
UH...
IT USED TO BE A LOT MORE PEACEFUL. THE LUGO-INDIO CARTEL RIVALRY IS GETTING... ...MESSY.
WE'VE RETURNED DOZENS FROM OTHER CENTRAL AMERICAN COUNTRIES.

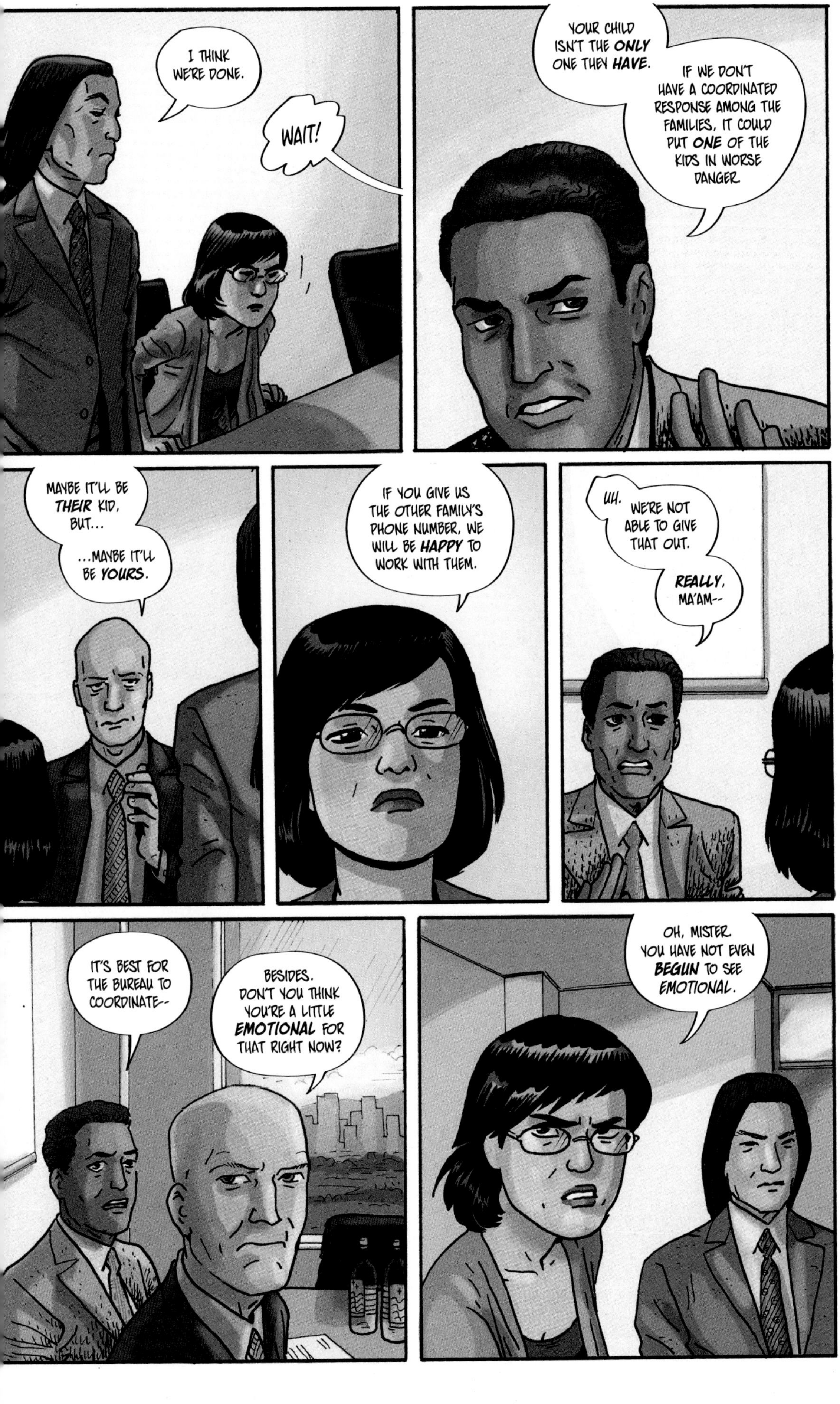

I THINK WE'RE DONE.
WAIT!
YOUR CHILD ISN'T THE ONLY ONE THEY HAVE.
IF WE DON'T HAVE A COORDINATED RESPONSE AMONG THE FAMILIES, IT COULD PUT ONE OF THE KIDS IN WORSE DANGER.
MAYBE IT'LL BE THEIR KID, BUT...
...MAYBE IT'LL BE YOURS.
IF YOU GIVE US THE OTHER FAMILY'S PHONE NUMBER, WE WILL BE HAPPY TO WORK WITH THEM.
UH.
WE'RE NOT ABLE TO GIVE THAT OUT.
REALLY, MA'AM--
IT'S BEST FOR THE BUREAU TO COORDINATE--
BESIDES. DON'T YOU THINK YOU'RE A LITTLE EMOTIONAL FOR THAT RIGHT NOW?
OH, MISTER. YOU HAVE NOT EVEN BEGUN TO SEE EMOTIONAL.

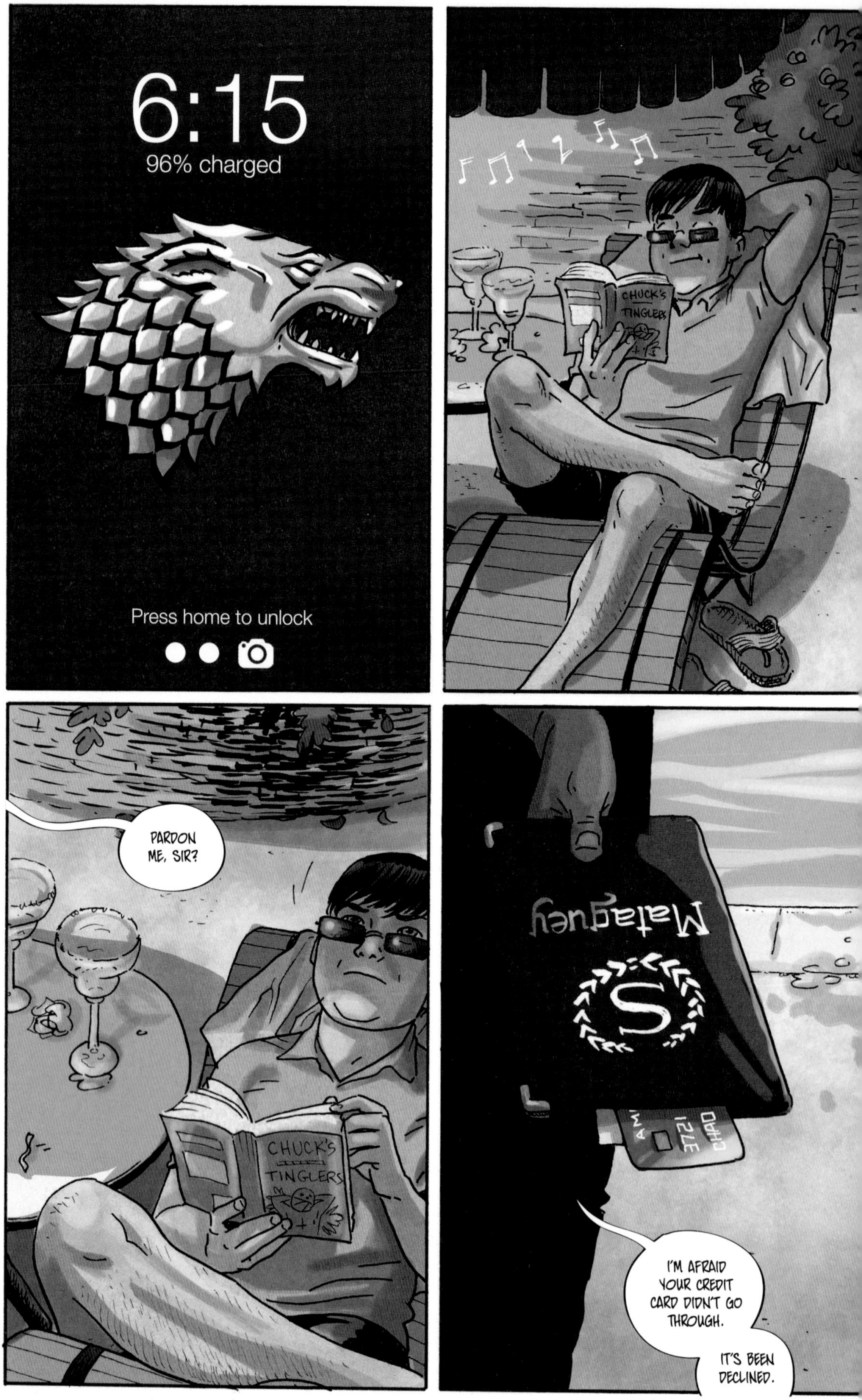
6:15
96% charged
Press home to unlock
CHUCK'S TINGLERS
PARDON ME, SIR?
CHUCK'S TINGLERS
I'M AFRAID YOUR CREDIT CARD DIDN'T GO THROUGH.
IT'S BEEN DECLINED.

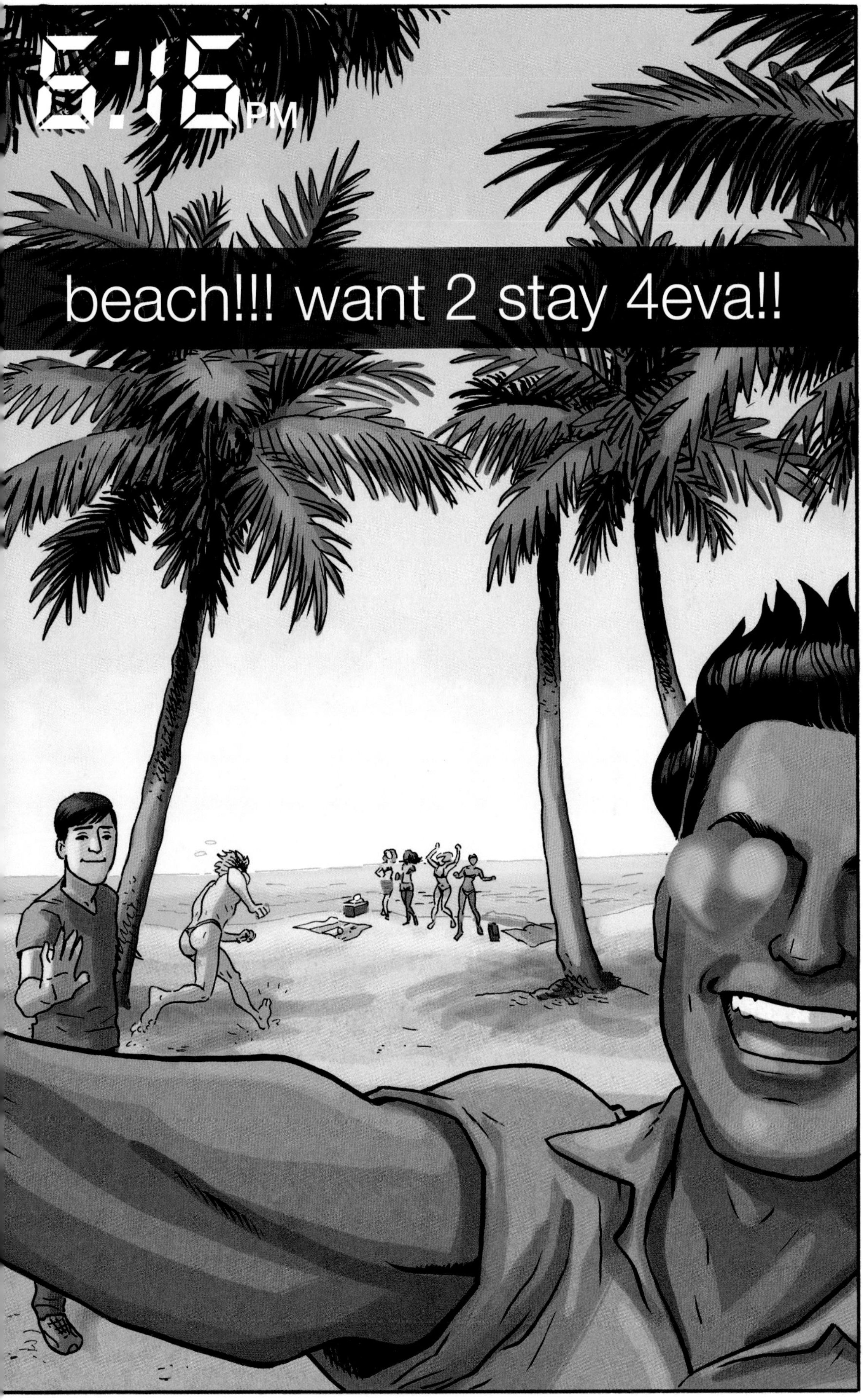

6:16 PM
beach!!! want 2 stay 4eva!!

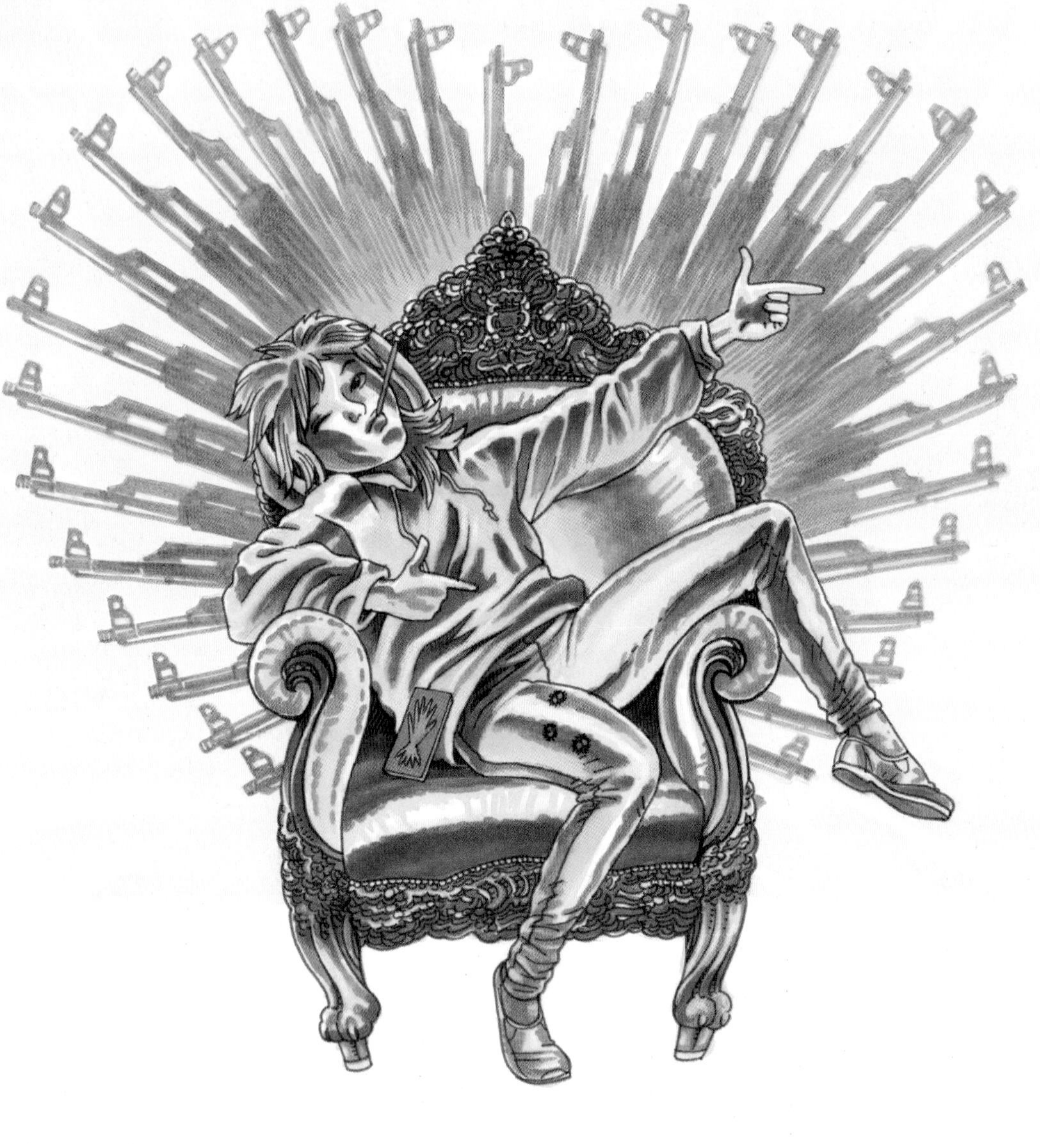

CHAPTER THREE

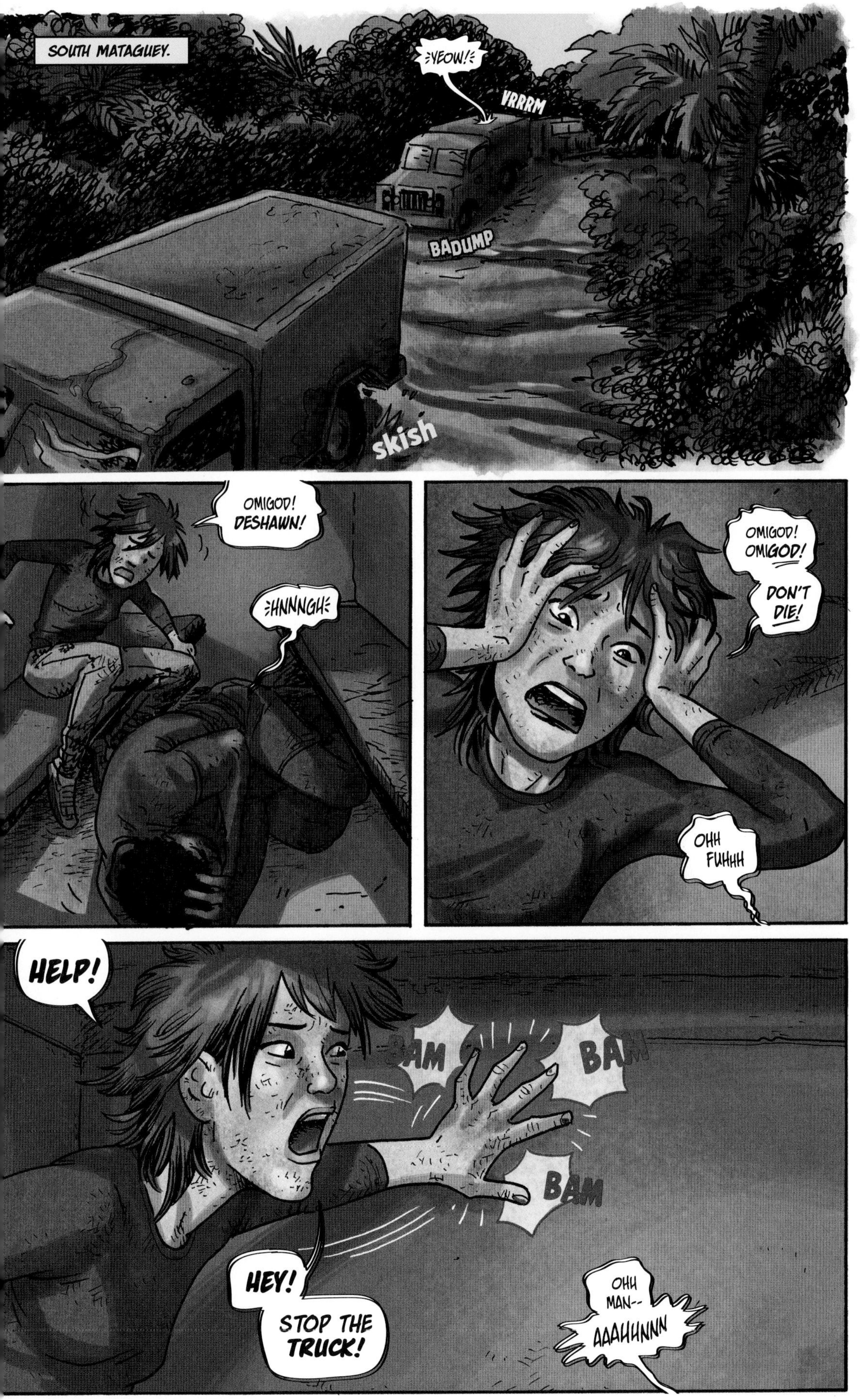
SOUTH MATAGUEY.
YEOW!
VRRRM
BADUMP
skish
OMIGOD! DESHAWN!
HNNNGH
OMIGOD! OMIGOD!
DON'T DIE!
OHH FUHHH
HELP!
BAM
BAM
BAM
HEY!
STOP THE TRUCK!
OHH MAN--
AAAHHNNN

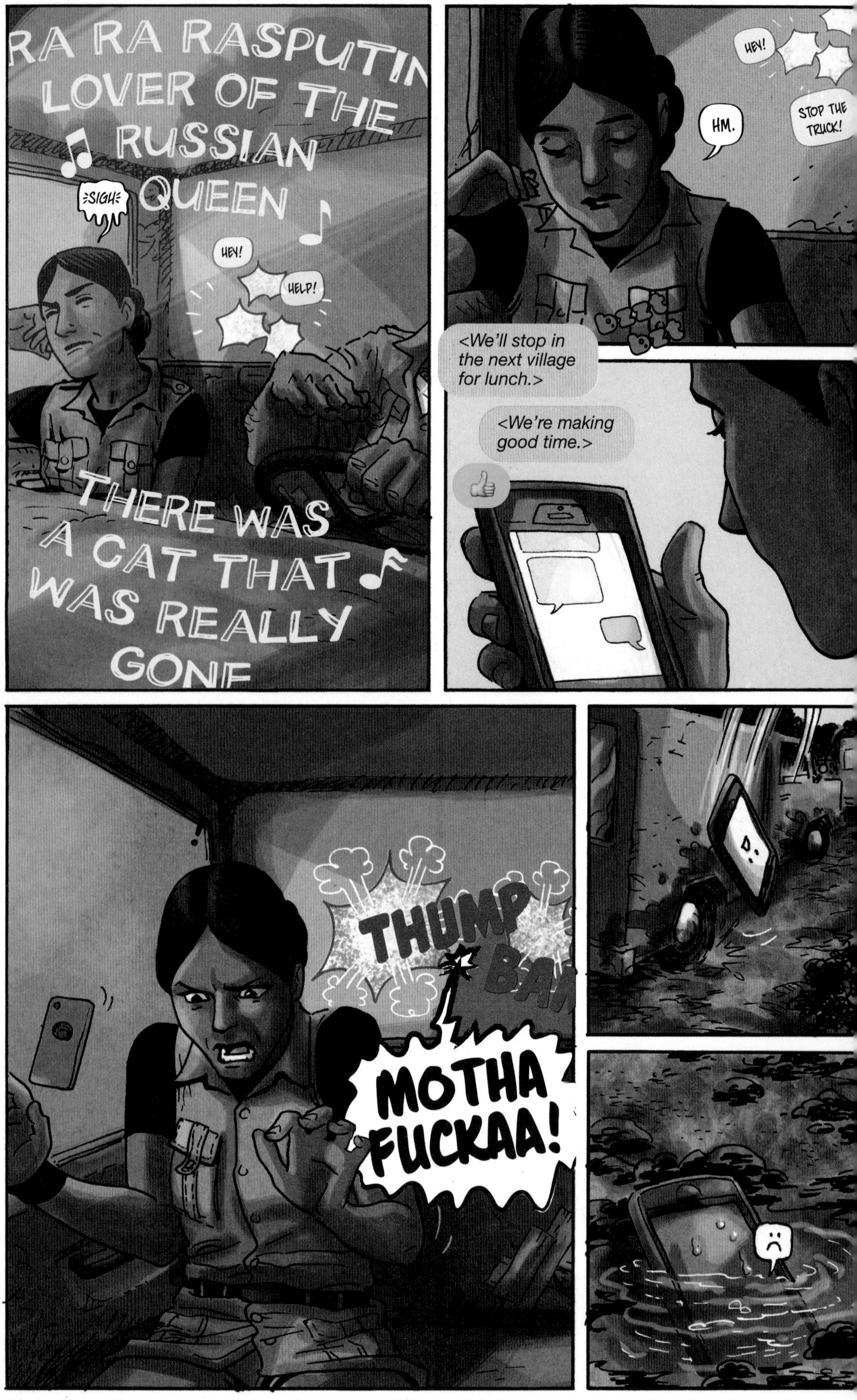

RA RA RASPUTIN LOVER OF THE RUSSIAN QUEEN
SIGH
HEY!
HELP!
THERE WAS A CAT THAT WAS REALLY GONE
HEY!
HM.
STOP THE TRUCK!
<We'll stop in the next village for lunch.>
<We're making good time.>
THUMP
MOTHA FUCKAA!

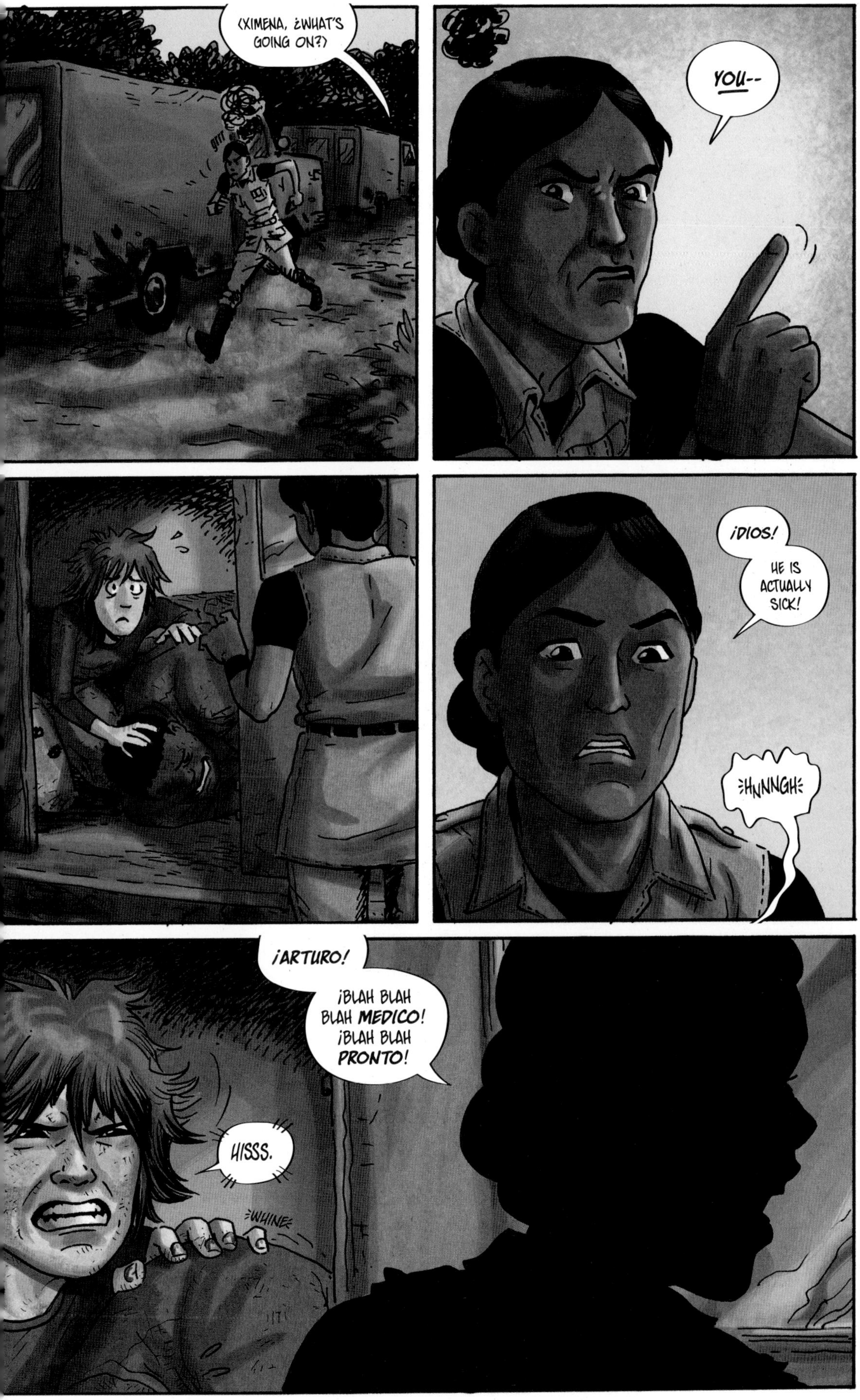
‹XIMENA, ¿WHAT'S GOING ON?›
YOU--
¡DIOS!
HE IS ACTUALLY SICK!
HNNNGH
¡ARTURO!
¡BLAH BLAH BLAH MEDICO! ¡BLAH BLAH PRONTO!
HISSS.
WHINE

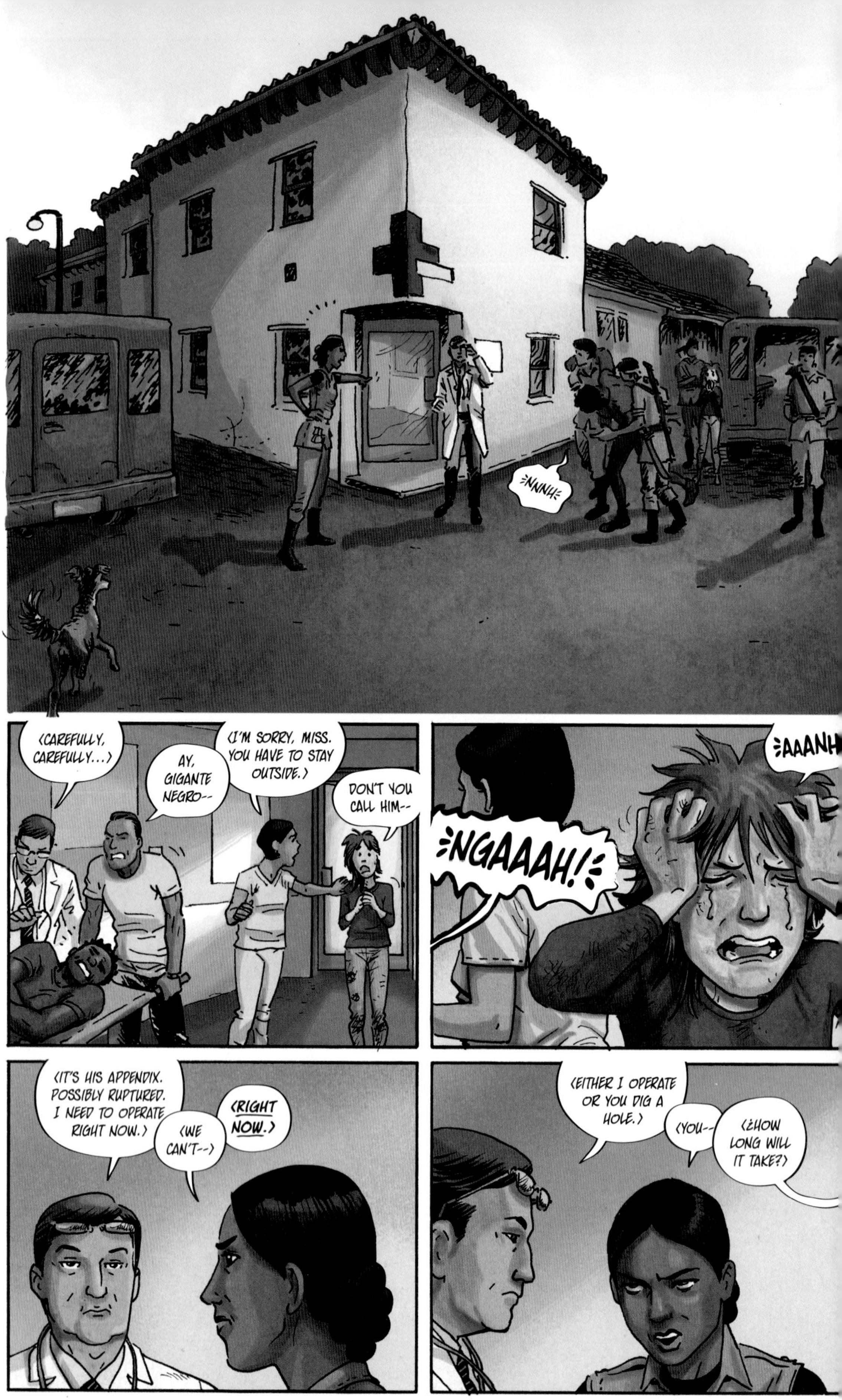
NNNH
‹CAREFULLY, CAREFULLY...›
AY, GIGANTE NEGRO--
‹I'M SORRY, MISS. YOU HAVE TO STAY OUTSIDE.›
DON'T YOU CALL HIM--
AAANH
NGAAAH!
‹IT'S HIS APPENDIX. POSSIBLY RUPTURED. I NEED TO OPERATE RIGHT NOW.›
‹WE CAN'T--›
‹RIGHT NOW.›
‹EITHER I OPERATE OR YOU DIG A HOLE.›
‹YOU--
‹¿HOW LONG WILL IT TAKE?›

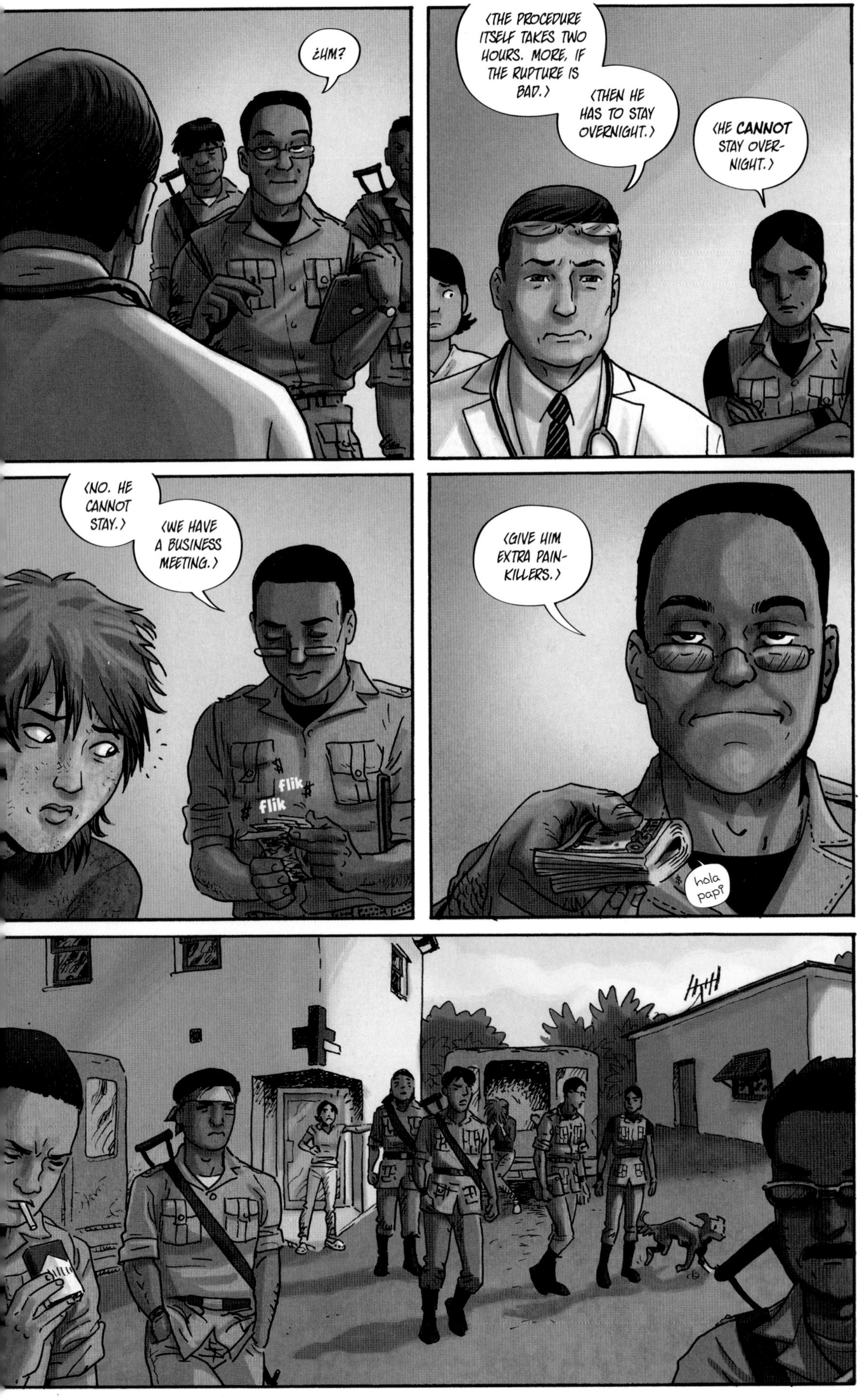
¿HM?
‹THE PROCEDURE ITSELF TAKES TWO HOURS. MORE, IF THE RUPTURE IS BAD.›
‹THEN HE HAS TO STAY OVERNIGHT.›
‹HE **CANNOT** STAY OVER-NIGHT.›
‹NO. HE CANNOT STAY.›
‹WE HAVE A BUSINESS MEETING.›
flik
flik
‹GIVE HIM EXTRA PAIN-KILLERS.›
hola papi

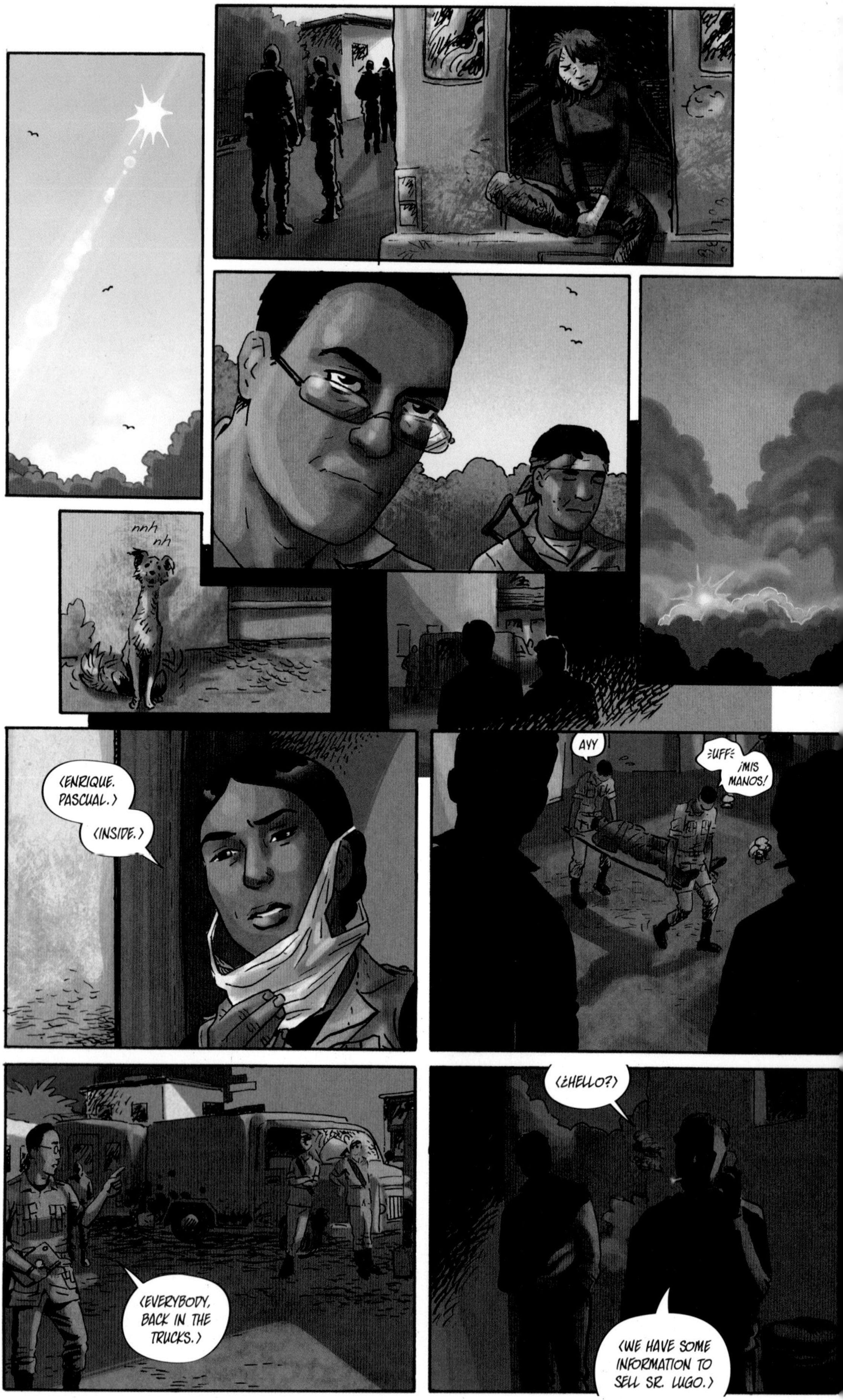
nnh
nh
‹ENRIQUE. PASCUAL.›
‹INSIDE.›
AYY
¡UFF!
¡MIS MANOS!
‹EVERYBODY, BACK IN THE TRUCKS.›
‹¿HELLO?›
‹WE HAVE SOME INFORMATION TO SELL SR. LUGO.›

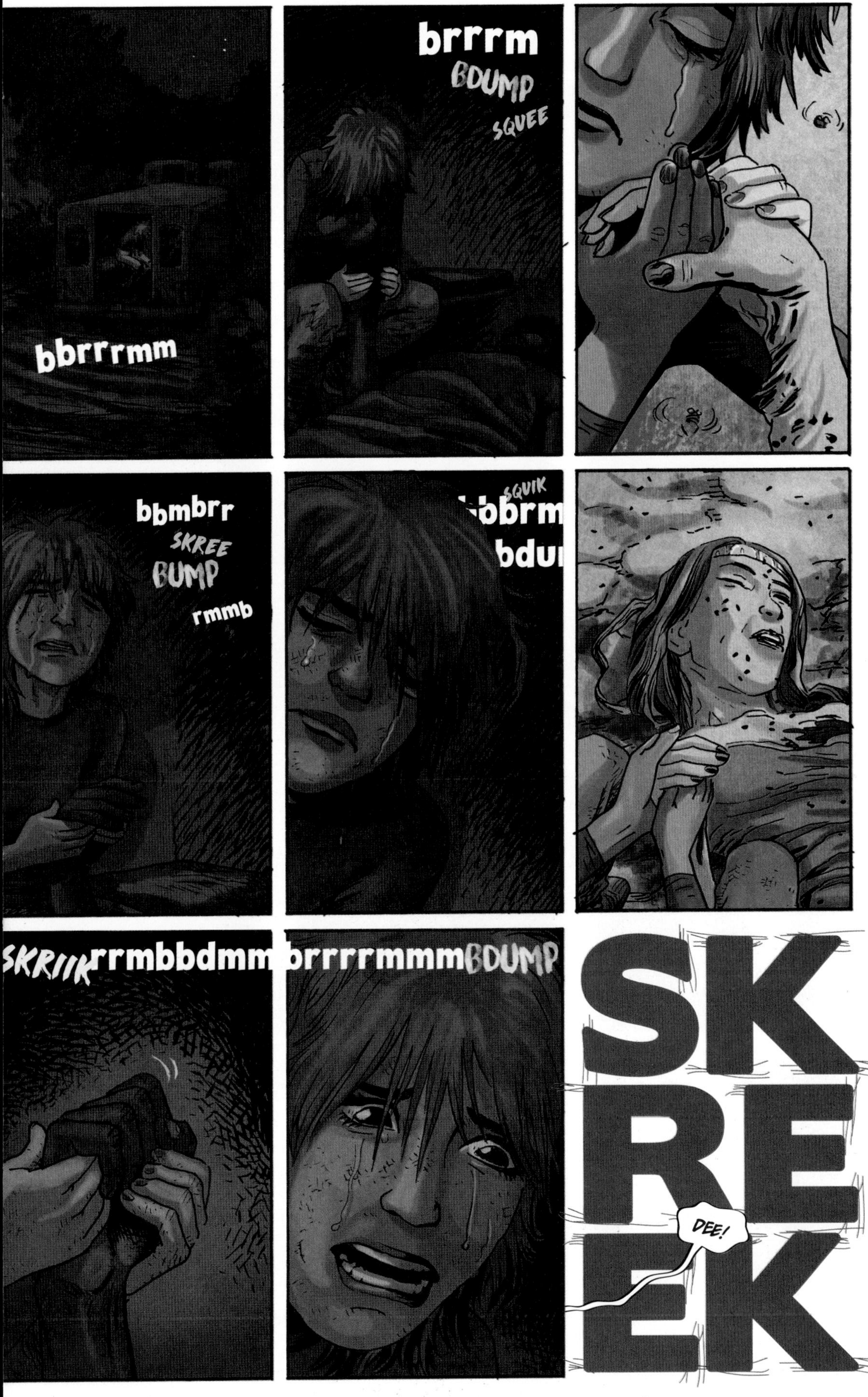
bbrrrmm
brrrm
BDUMP
SQUEE
bbmbrr
SKREE
BUMP
rmmb
SQUIK
bbrm
bdu
SKRIIK
rrmbbdmm
brrrrmmmBDUMP
SK
RE
EK
DEE!

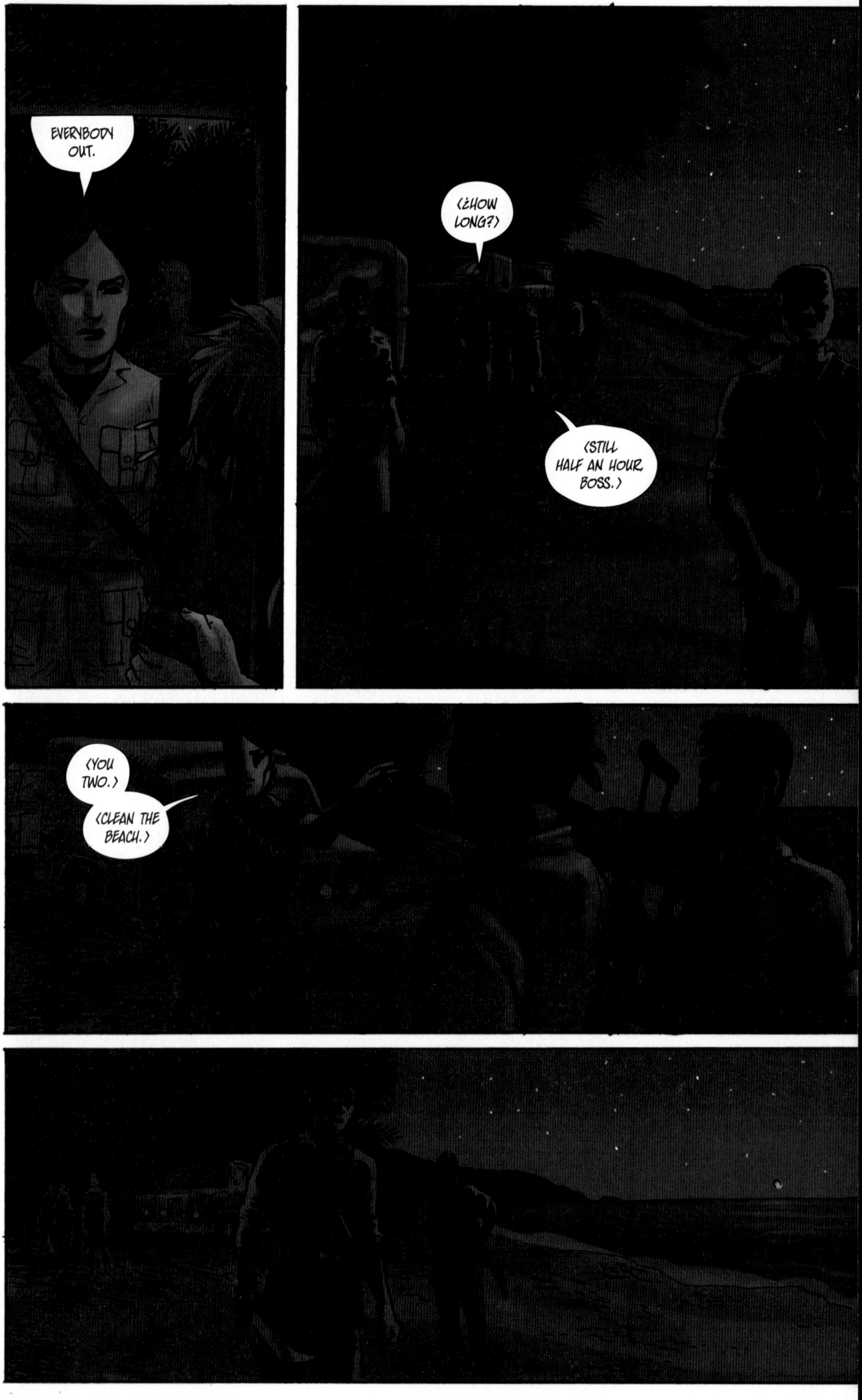
EVERYBODY OUT.
‹¿HOW LONG?›
‹STILL HALF AN HOUR, BOSS.›
‹YOU TWO.›
‹CLEAN THE BEACH.›

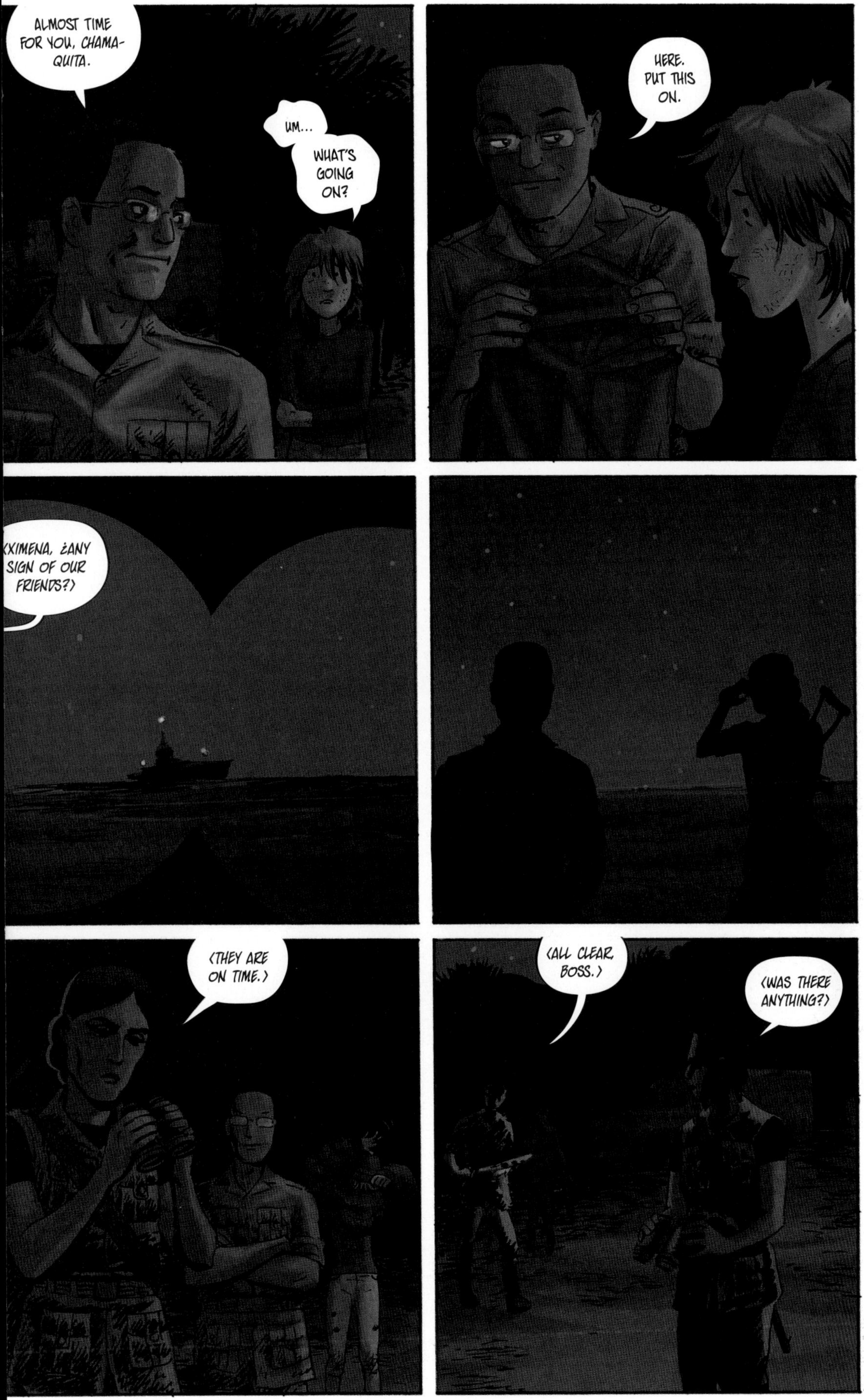
ALMOST TIME FOR YOU, CHAMA-QUITA.
UM...
WHAT'S GOING ON?
HERE. PUT THIS ON.
‹XIMENA, ¿ANY SIGN OF OUR FRIENDS?›
‹THEY ARE ON TIME.›
‹ALL CLEAR, BOSS.›
‹WAS THERE ANYTHING?›

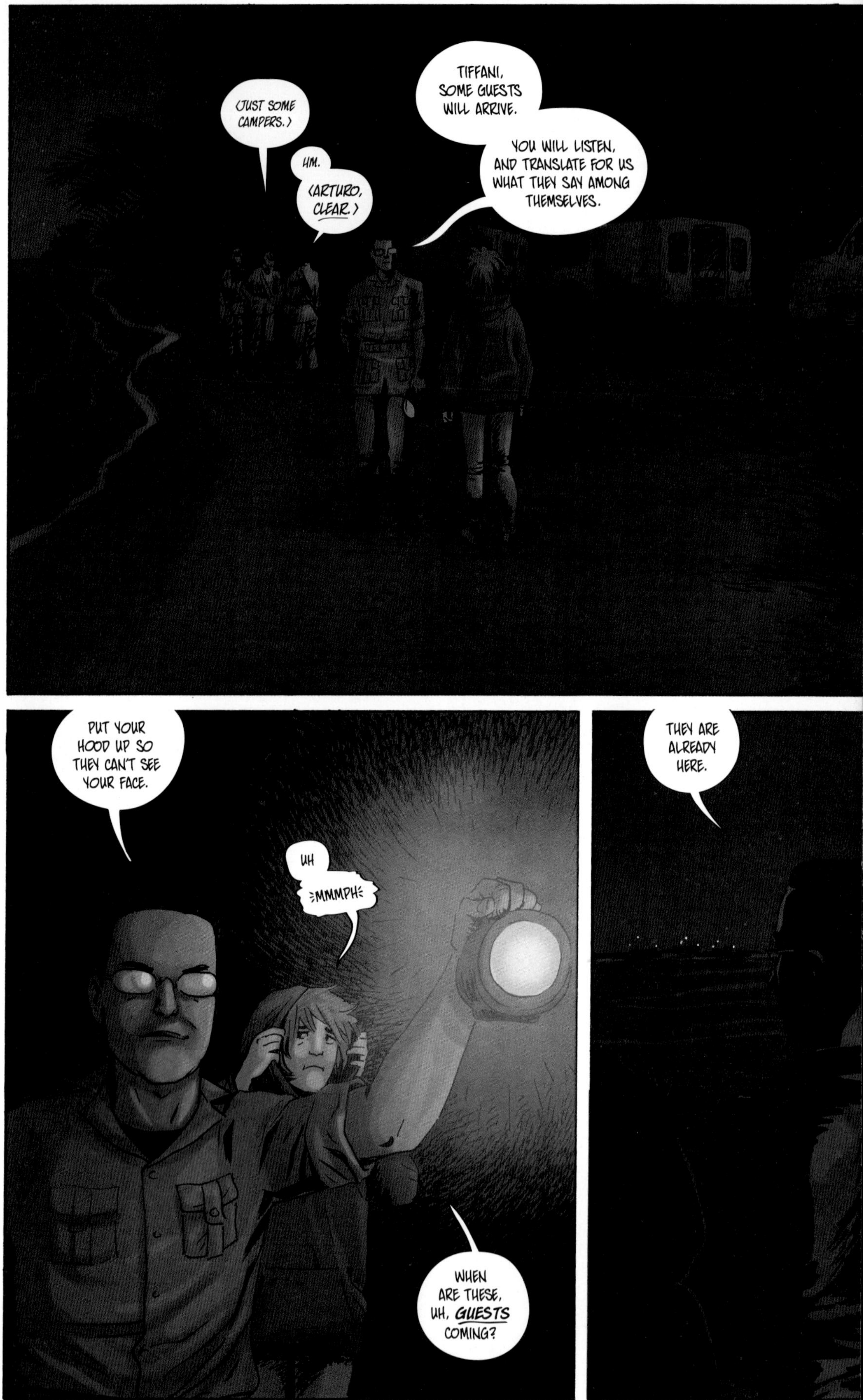

<JUST SOME CAMPERS.>
UM.
<ARTURO, CLEAR.>
TIFFANI, SOME GUESTS WILL ARRIVE.
YOU WILL LISTEN, AND TRANSLATE FOR US WHAT THEY SAY AMONG THEMSELVES.
PUT YOUR HOOD UP SO THEY CAN'T SEE YOUR FACE.
UH
MMMPH
WHEN ARE THESE, UH, GUESTS COMING?
THEY ARE ALREADY HERE.

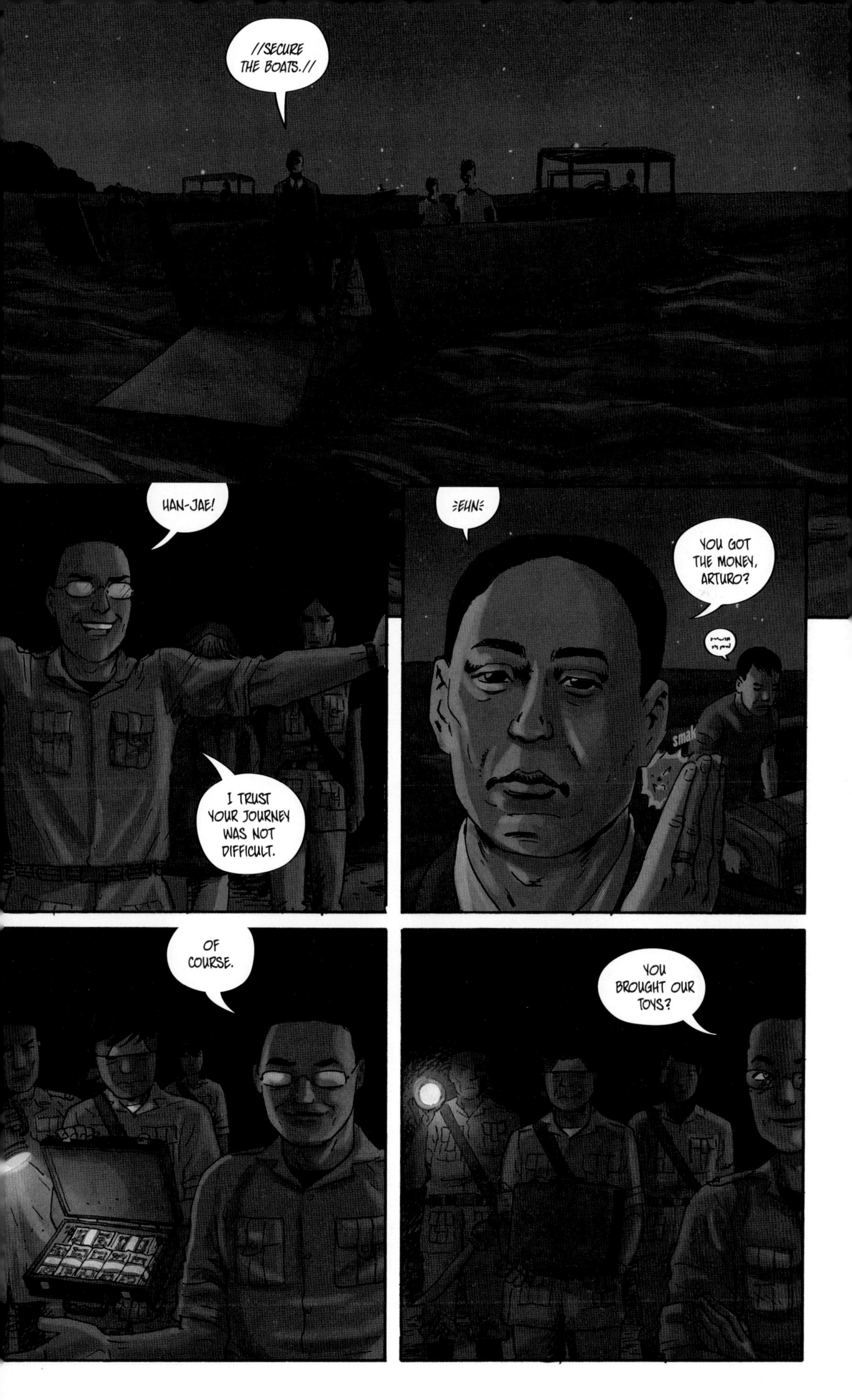
//SECURE THE BOATS.//
HAN-JAE!
I TRUST YOUR JOURNEY WAS NOT DIFFICULT.
EUN
YOU GOT THE MONEY, ARTURO?
smak
OF COURSE.
YOU BROUGHT OUR TOYS?

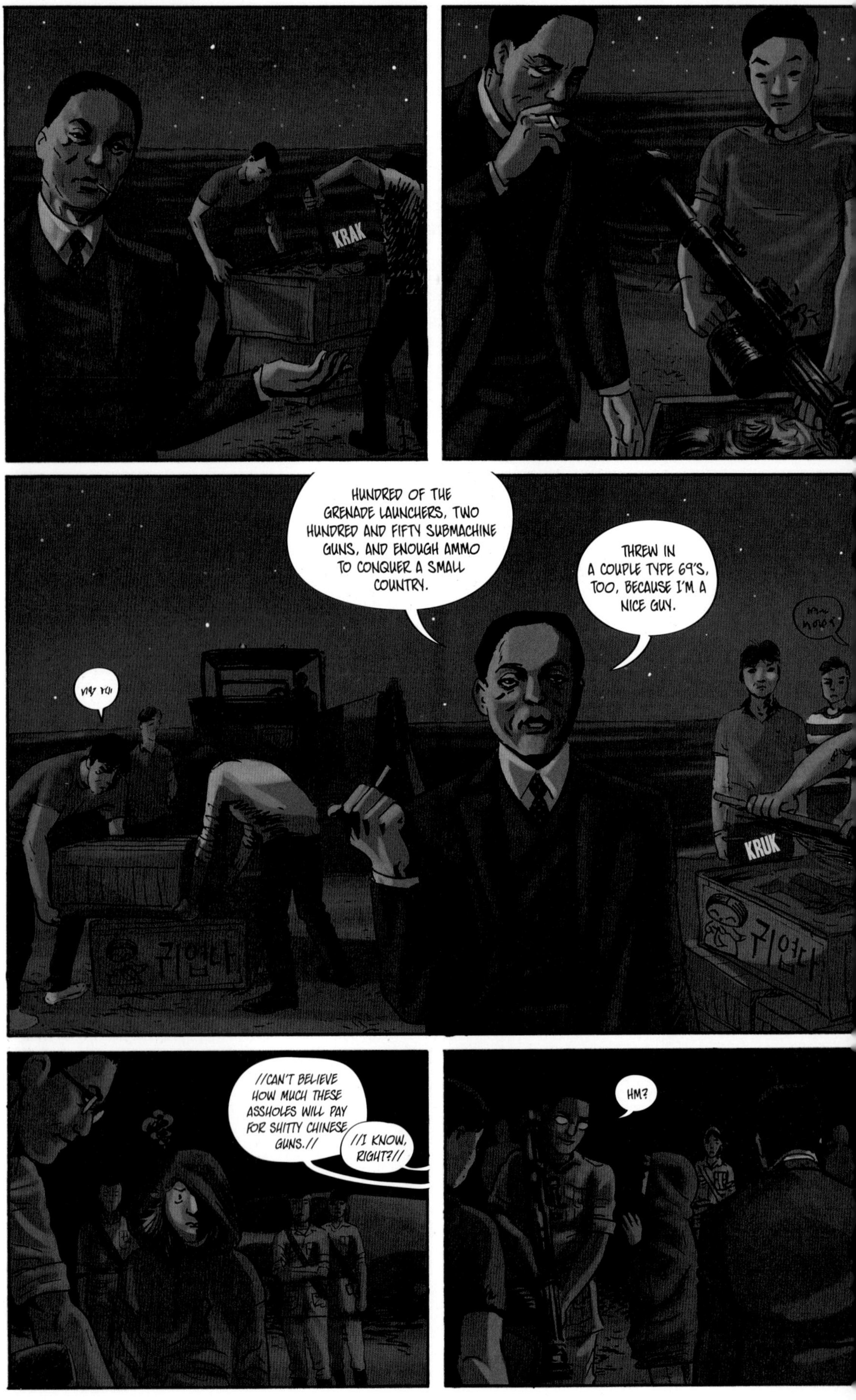
KRAK
HUNDRED OF THE GRENADE LAUNCHERS, TWO HUNDRED AND FIFTY SUBMACHINE GUNS, AND ENOUGH AMMO TO CONQUER A SMALL COUNTRY.
THREW IN A COUPLE TYPE 69'S, TOO, BECAUSE I'M A NICE GUY.
KRUK
//CAN'T BELIEVE HOW MUCH THESE ASSHOLES WILL PAY FOR SHITTY CHINESE GUNS.//
//I KNOW, RIGHT?//
HM?

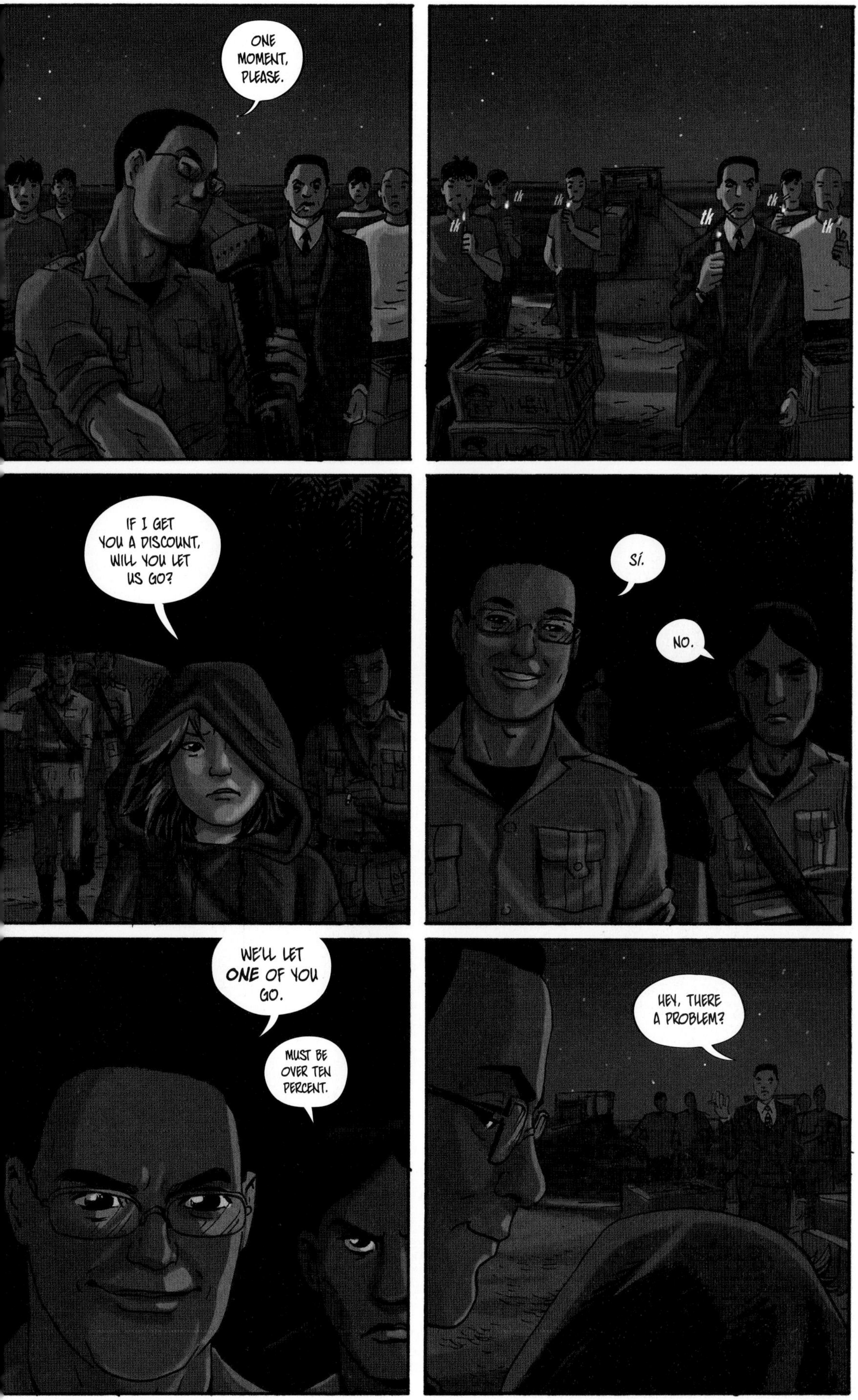
ONE MOMENT, PLEASE.
tk
tk
tk
tk
tk
tk
IF I GET YOU A DISCOUNT, WILL YOU LET US GO?
SÍ.
NO.
WE'LL LET **ONE** OF YOU GO.
MUST BE OVER TEN PERCENT.
HEY, THERE A PROBLEM?

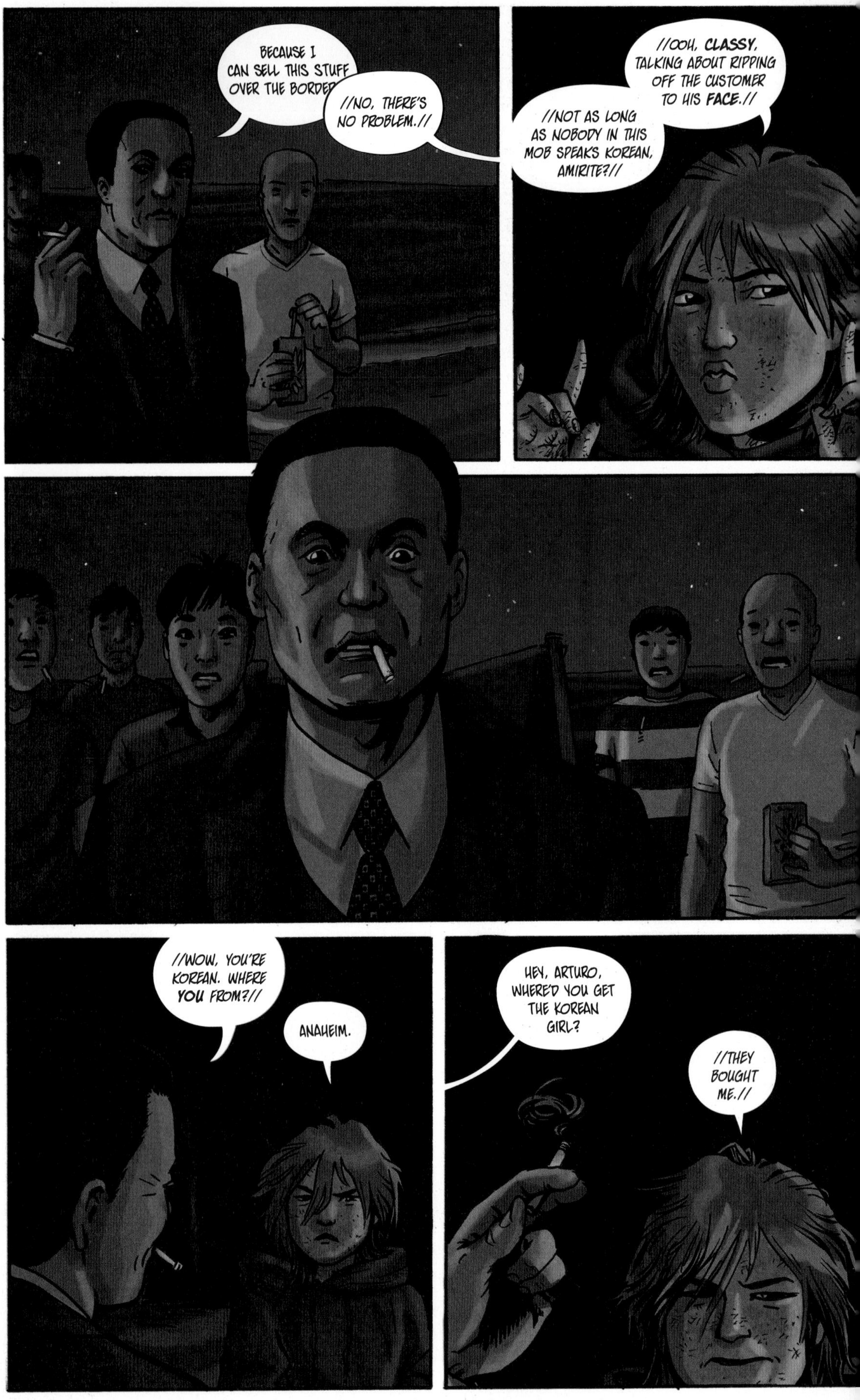
BECAUSE I CAN SELL THIS STUFF OVER THE BORDER
//NO, THERE'S NO PROBLEM.//
//NOT AS LONG AS NOBODY IN THIS MOB SPEAKS KOREAN, AMIRITE?//
//OOH, **CLASSY**, TALKING ABOUT RIPPING OFF THE CUSTOMER TO HIS **FACE**.//
//WOW, YOU'RE KOREAN. WHERE **YOU** FROM?//
ANAHEIM.
HEY, ARTURO, WHERE'D YOU GET THE KOREAN GIRL?
//THEY BOUGHT ME.//

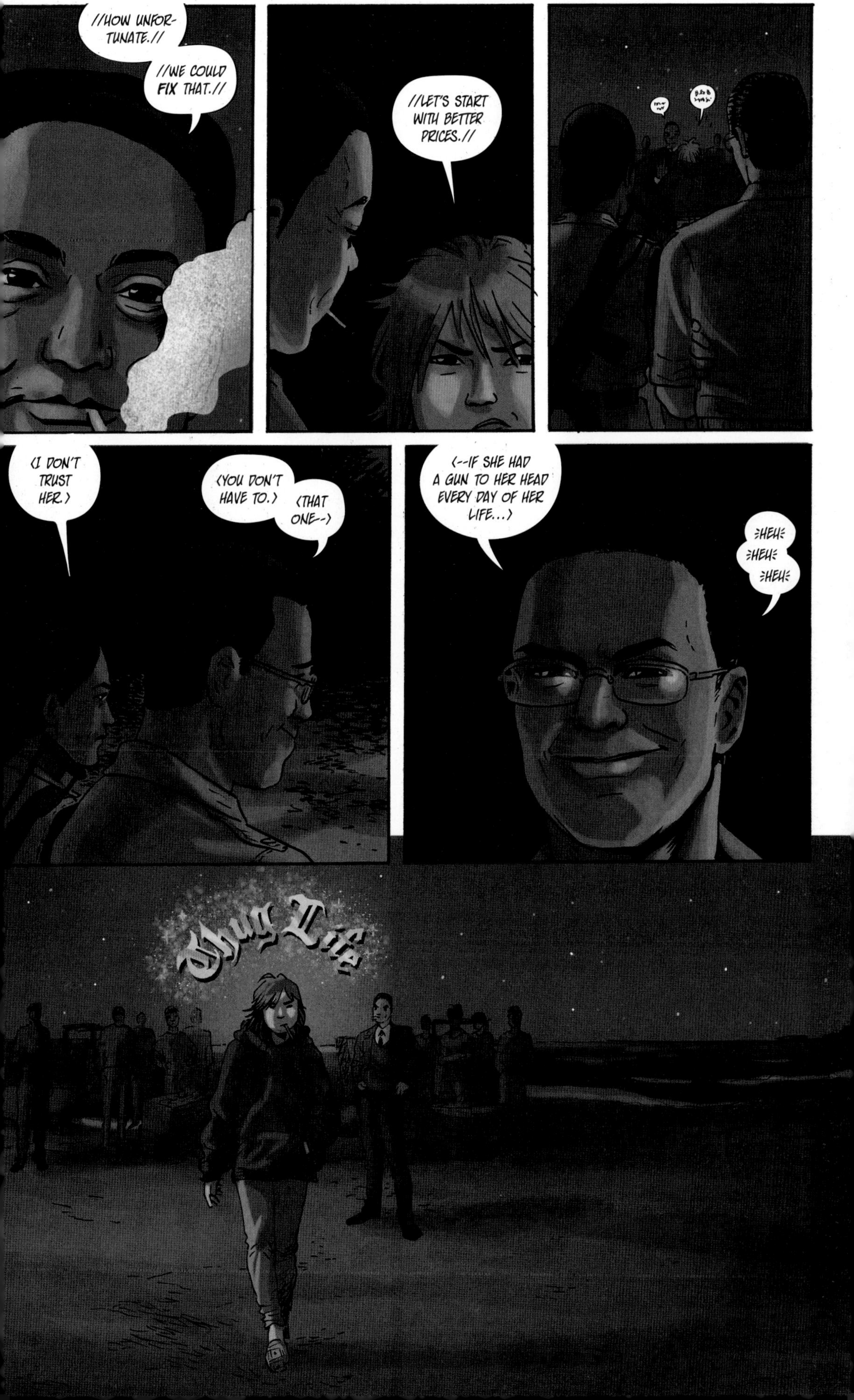
//HOW UNFOR-TUNATE.//
//WE COULD FIX THAT.//
//LET'S START WITH BETTER PRICES.//
‹I DON'T TRUST HER.›
‹YOU DON'T HAVE TO.›
‹THAT ONE--›
‹--IF SHE HAD A GUN TO HER HEAD EVERY DAY OF HER LIFE...›
HEH
HEH
HEH
Thug Life

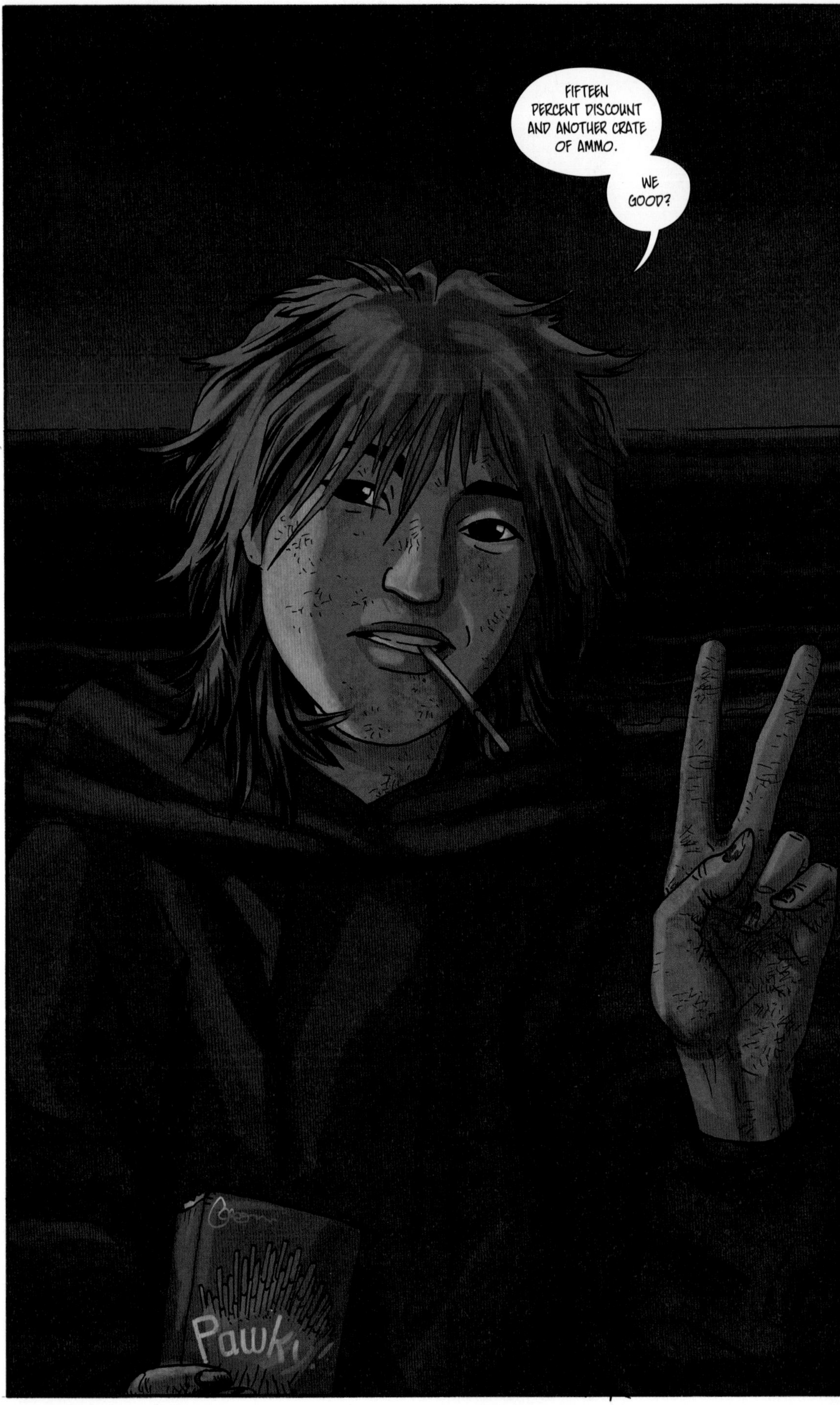
FIFTEEN PERCENT DISCOUNT AND ANOTHER CRATE OF AMMO.
WE GOOD?
Pawki

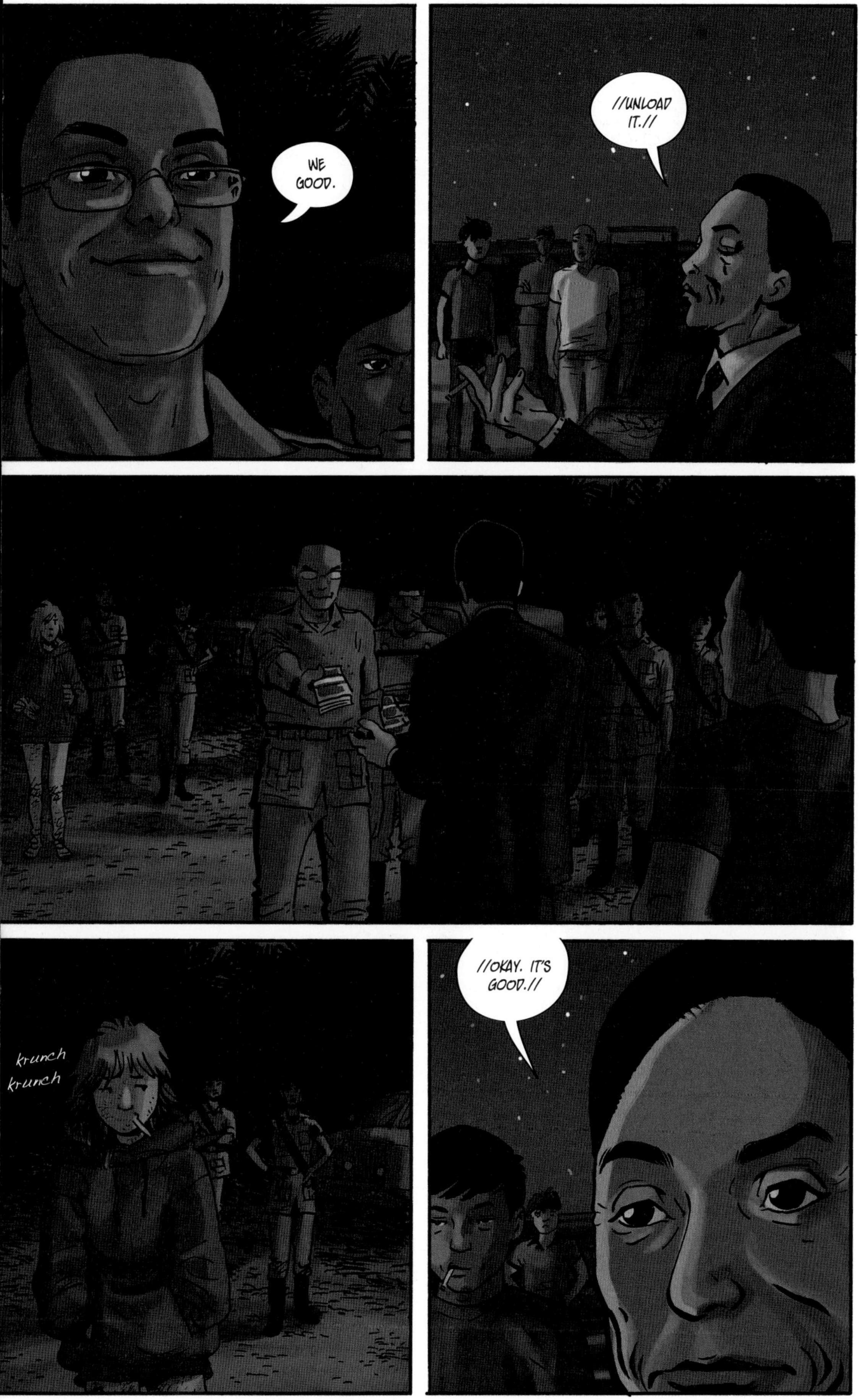
WE GOOD.
//UNLOAD IT.//
krunch
krunch
//OKAY. IT'S GOOD.//

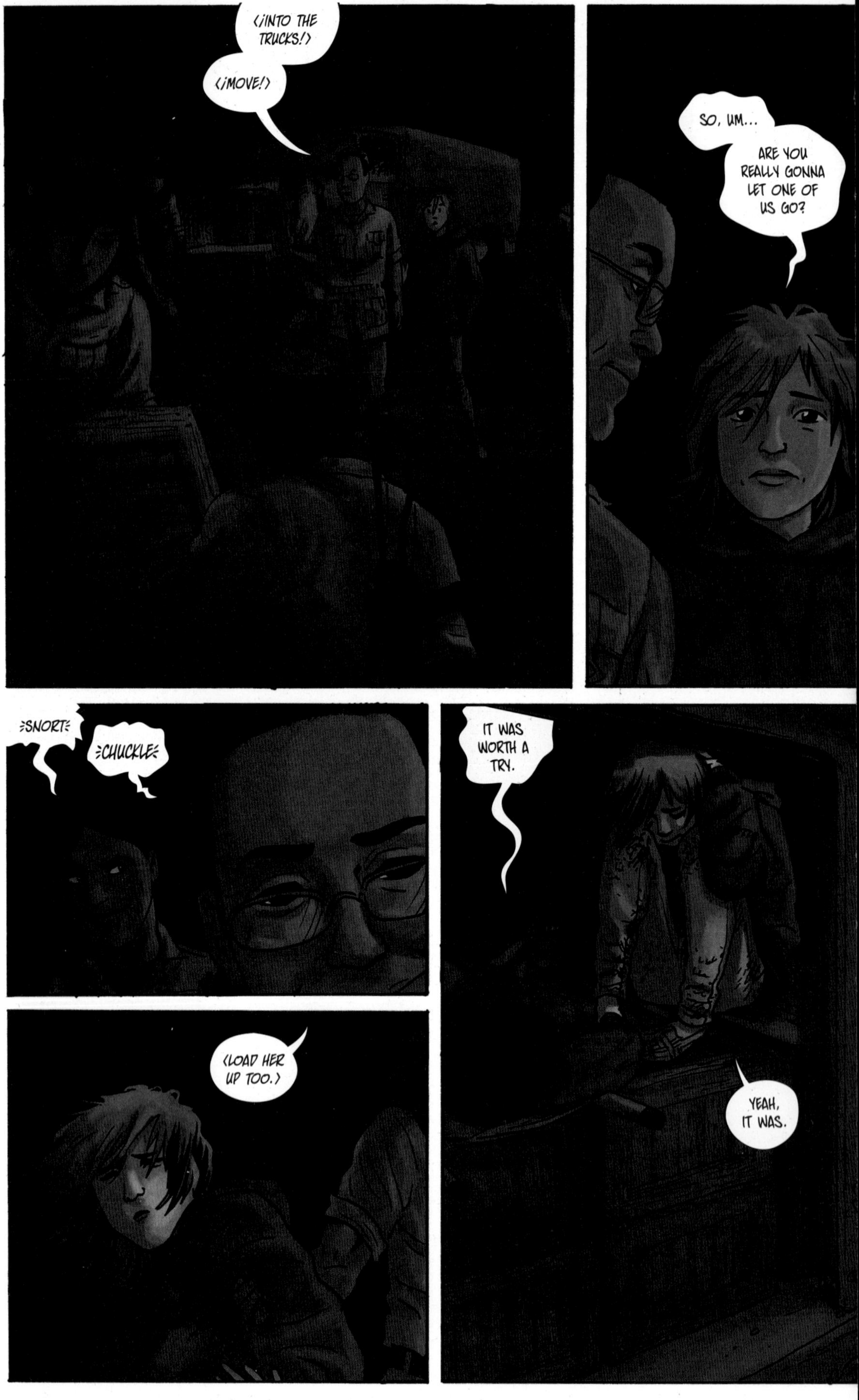
‹¡INTO THE TRUCKS!›
‹¡MOVE!›
SO, UM...
ARE YOU REALLY GONNA LET ONE OF US GO?
SNORT
CHUCKLE
IT WAS WORTH A TRY.
YEAH, IT WAS.
‹LOAD HER UP TOO.›

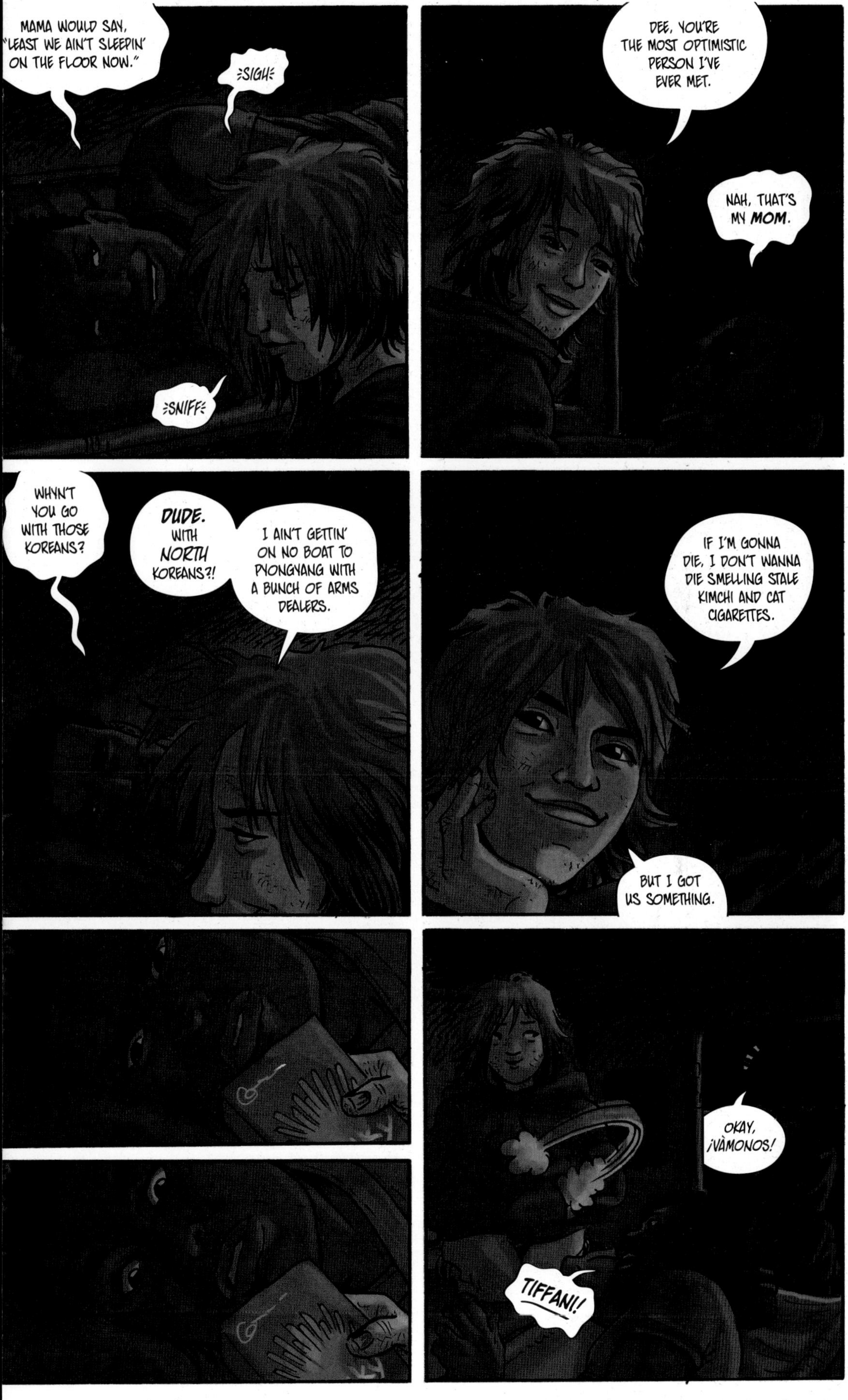
MAMA WOULD SAY, "LEAST WE AIN'T SLEEPIN' ON THE FLOOR NOW."
SIGH
SNIFF
DEE, YOU'RE THE MOST OPTIMISTIC PERSON I'VE EVER MET.
NAH, THAT'S MY **MOM**.
WHYN'T YOU GO WITH THOSE KOREANS?
DUDE. WITH NORTH KOREANS?!
I AIN'T GETTIN' ON NO BOAT TO PYONGYANG WITH A BUNCH OF ARMS DEALERS.
IF I'M GONNA DIE, I DON'T WANNA DIE SMELLING STALE KIMCHI AND CAT CIGARETTES.
BUT I GOT US SOMETHING.
OKAY, ¡VÀMONOS!
TIFFANI!

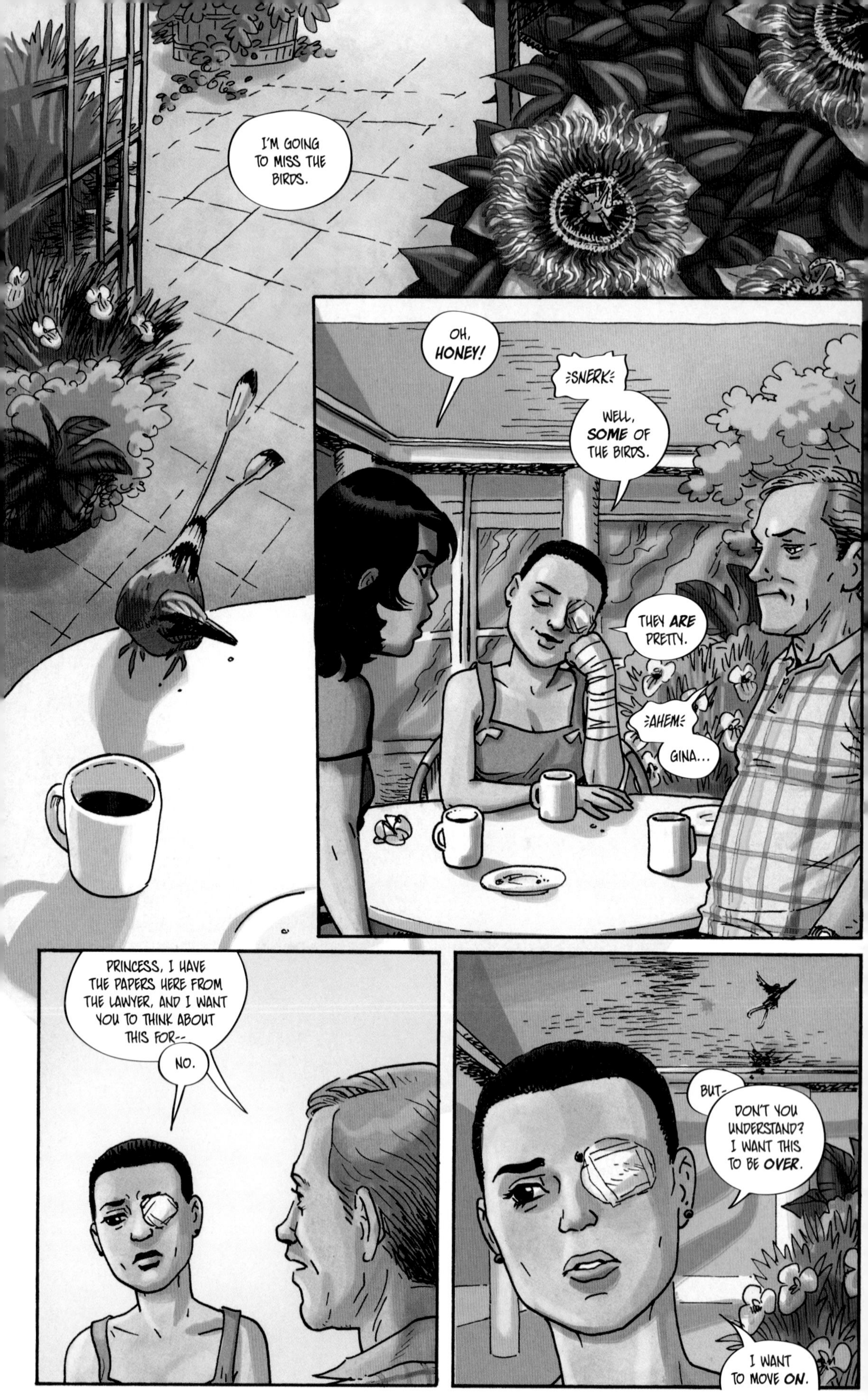

I'M GOING TO MISS THE BIRDS.
OH, HONEY!
SNERK
WELL, SOME OF THE BIRDS.
THEY ARE PRETTY.
AHEM
GINA...
PRINCESS, I HAVE THE PAPERS HERE FROM THE LAWYER, AND I WANT YOU TO THINK ABOUT THIS FOR--
NO.
BUT-
DON'T YOU UNDERSTAND? I WANT THIS TO BE OVER.
I WANT TO MOVE ON.

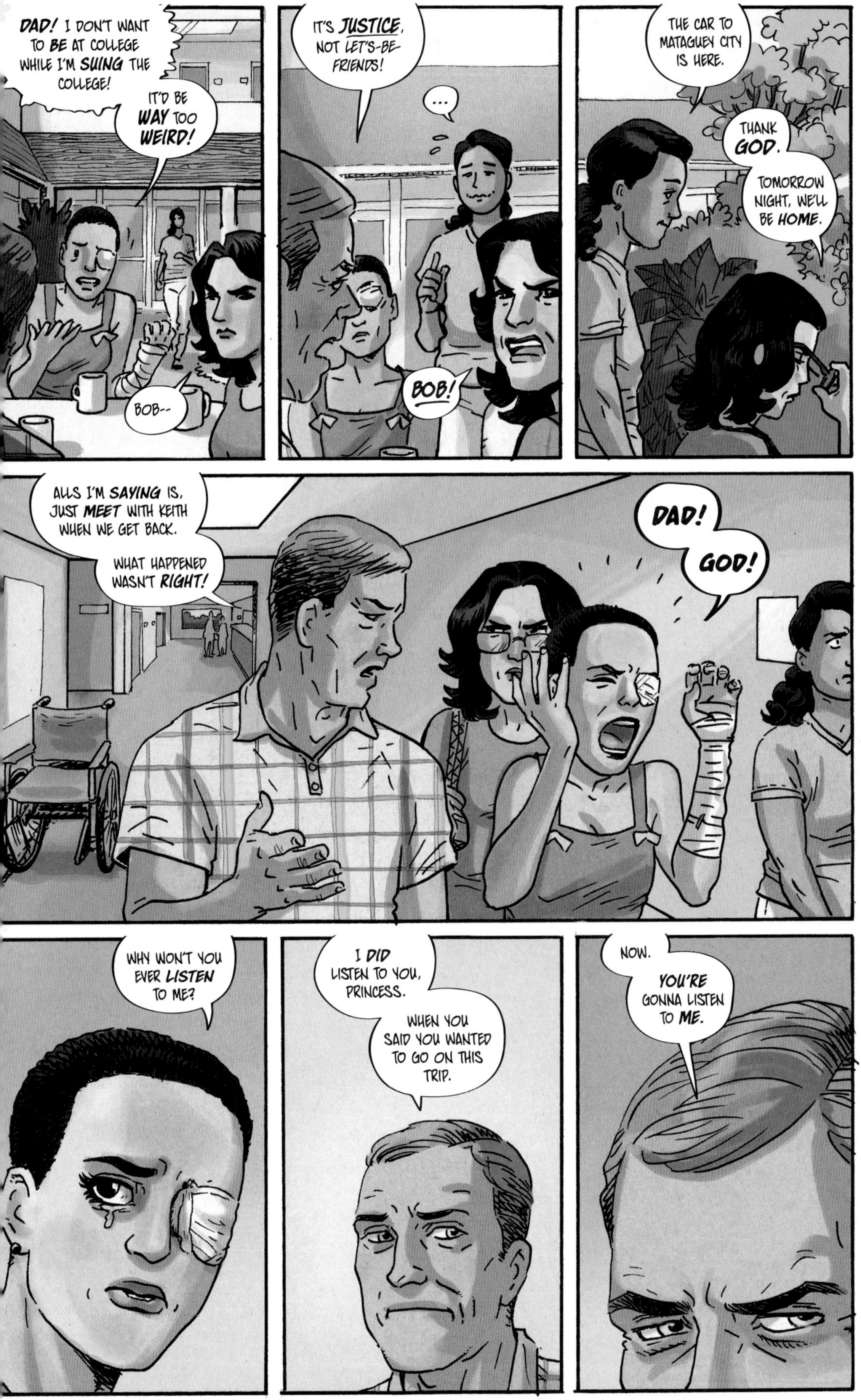
DAD! I DON'T WANT TO BE AT COLLEGE WHILE I'M SUING THE COLLEGE!
IT'D BE WAY TOO WEIRD!
BOB--
IT'S JUSTICE, NOT LET'S-BE-FRIENDS!
...
BOB!
THE CAR TO MATAGUEY CITY IS HERE.
THANK GOD.
TOMORROW NIGHT, WE'LL BE HOME.
ALLS I'M SAYING IS, JUST MEET WITH KEITH WHEN WE GET BACK.
WHAT HAPPENED WASN'T RIGHT!
DAD!
GOD!
WHY WON'T YOU EVER LISTEN TO ME?
I DID LISTEN TO YOU, PRINCESS.
WHEN YOU SAID YOU WANTED TO GO ON THIS TRIP.
NOW.
YOU'RE GONNA LISTEN TO ME.

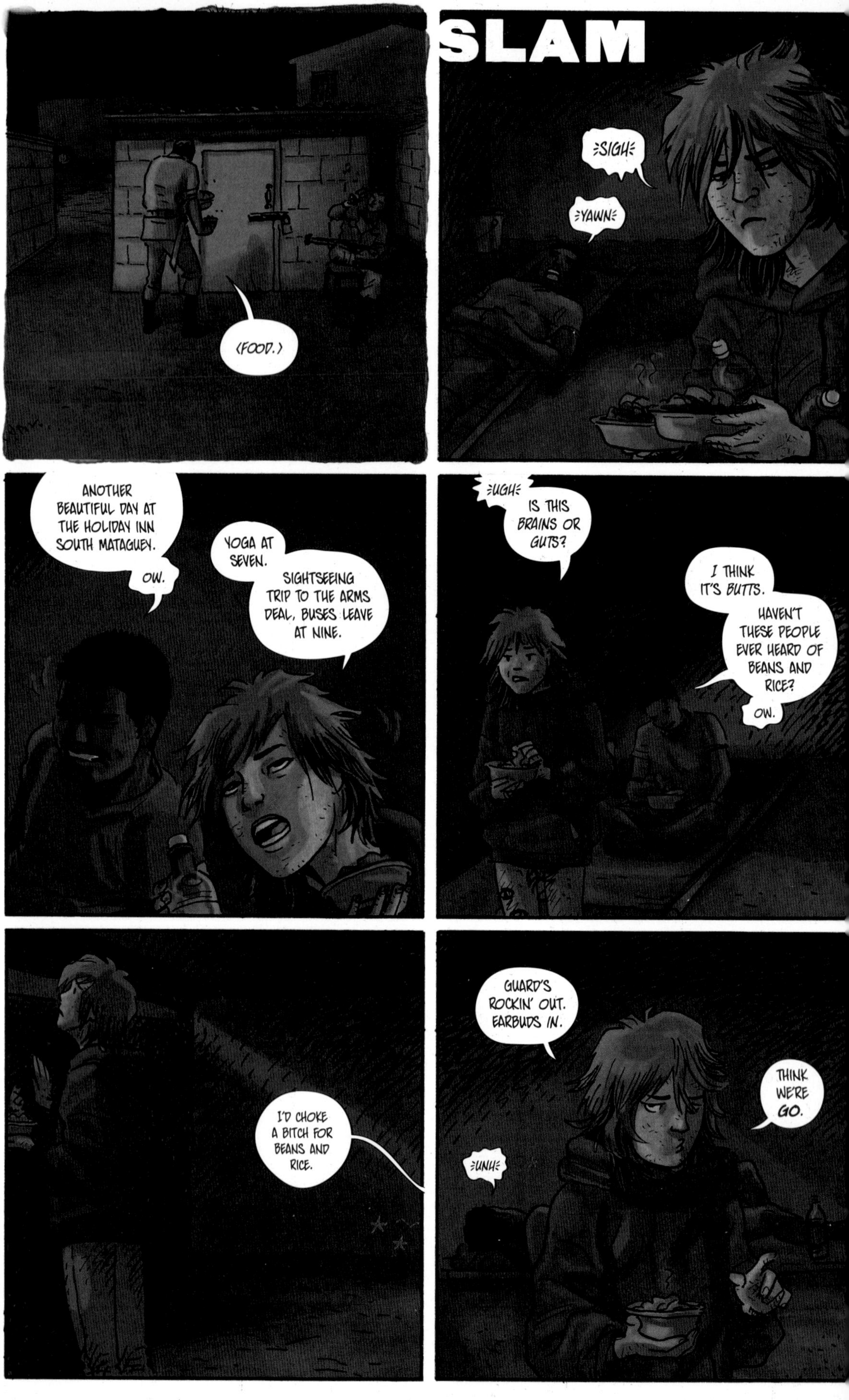
SLAM
(FOOD.)
SIGH
YAWN
ANOTHER BEAUTIFUL DAY AT THE HOLIDAY INN SOUTH MATAGUEY.
OW.
YOGA AT SEVEN.
SIGHTSEEING TRIP TO THE ARMS DEAL, BUSES LEAVE AT NINE.
UGH
IS THIS BRAINS OR GUTS?
I THINK IT'S BUTTS.
HAVEN'T THESE PEOPLE EVER HEARD OF BEANS AND RICE?
OW.
I'D CHOKE A BITCH FOR BEANS AND RICE.
GUARD'S ROCKIN' OUT. EARBUDS IN.
UNH
THINK WE'RE GO.

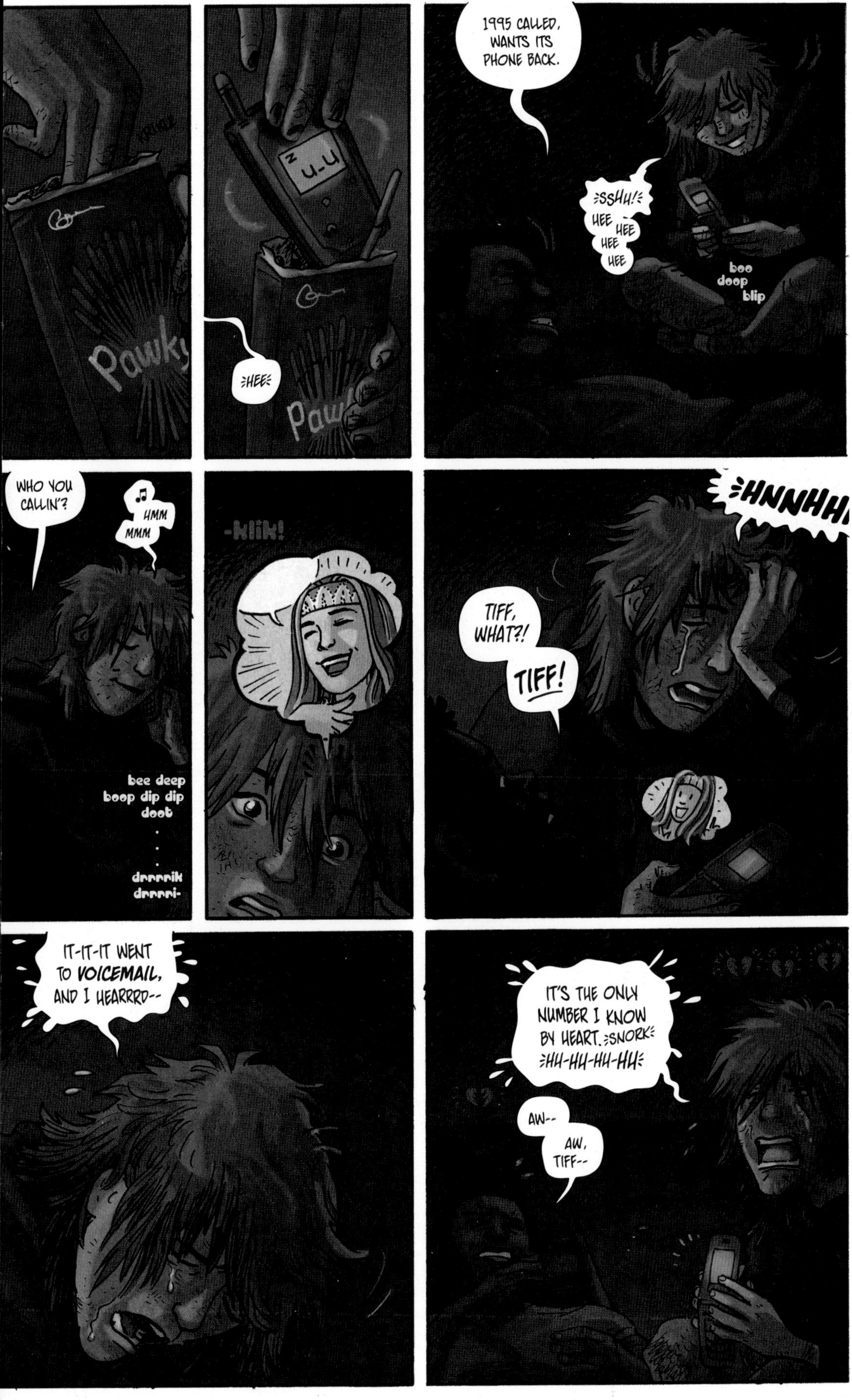

Pawky
Pawky
u-u
HEE
1995 CALLED, WANTS ITS PHONE BACK.
SSHH!
HEE HEE HEE HEE
boo deep blip
WHO YOU CALLIN'?
HMM MMM
bee deep boop dip dip doot
. . .
drrrrik drrrri-
-klik!
HNNHH
TIFF, WHAT?!
TIFF!
IT-IT-IT WENT TO VOICEMAIL, AND I HEARRRD--
IT'S THE ONLY NUMBER I KNOW BY HEART. SNORK
HU-HU-HU-HU
AW--
AW, TIFF--

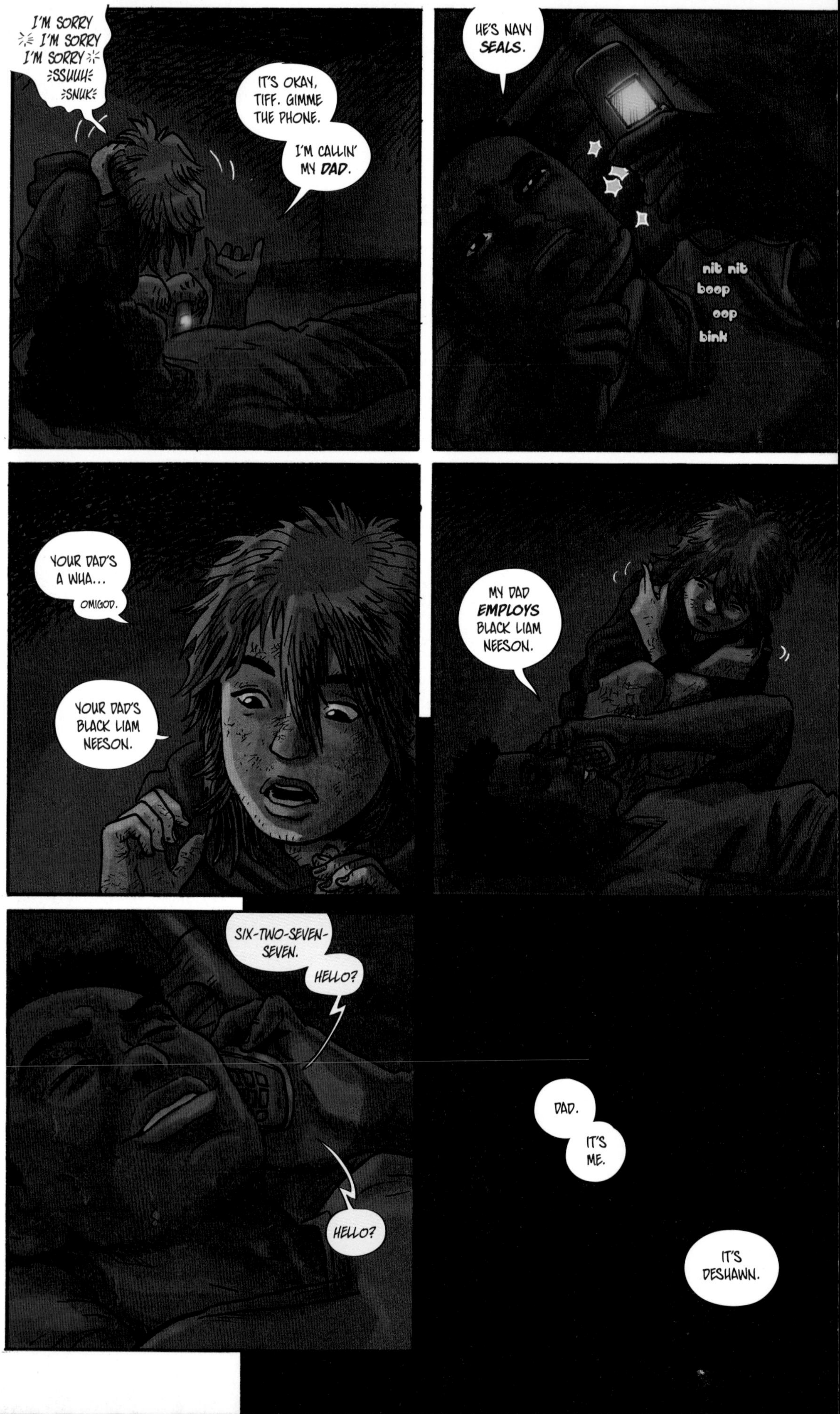
I'M SORRY I'M SORRY I'M SORRY SSUUH SNUK
IT'S OKAY, TIFF. GIMME THE PHONE.
I'M CALLIN' MY DAD.
HE'S NAVY SEALS.
nit nit
boop
oop
bink
YOUR DAD'S A WHA...
OMIGOD.
YOUR DAD'S BLACK LIAM NEESON.
MY DAD EMPLOYS BLACK LIAM NEESON.
SIX-TWO-SEVEN-SEVEN.
HELLO?
HELLO?
DAD.
IT'S ME.
IT'S DESHAWN.

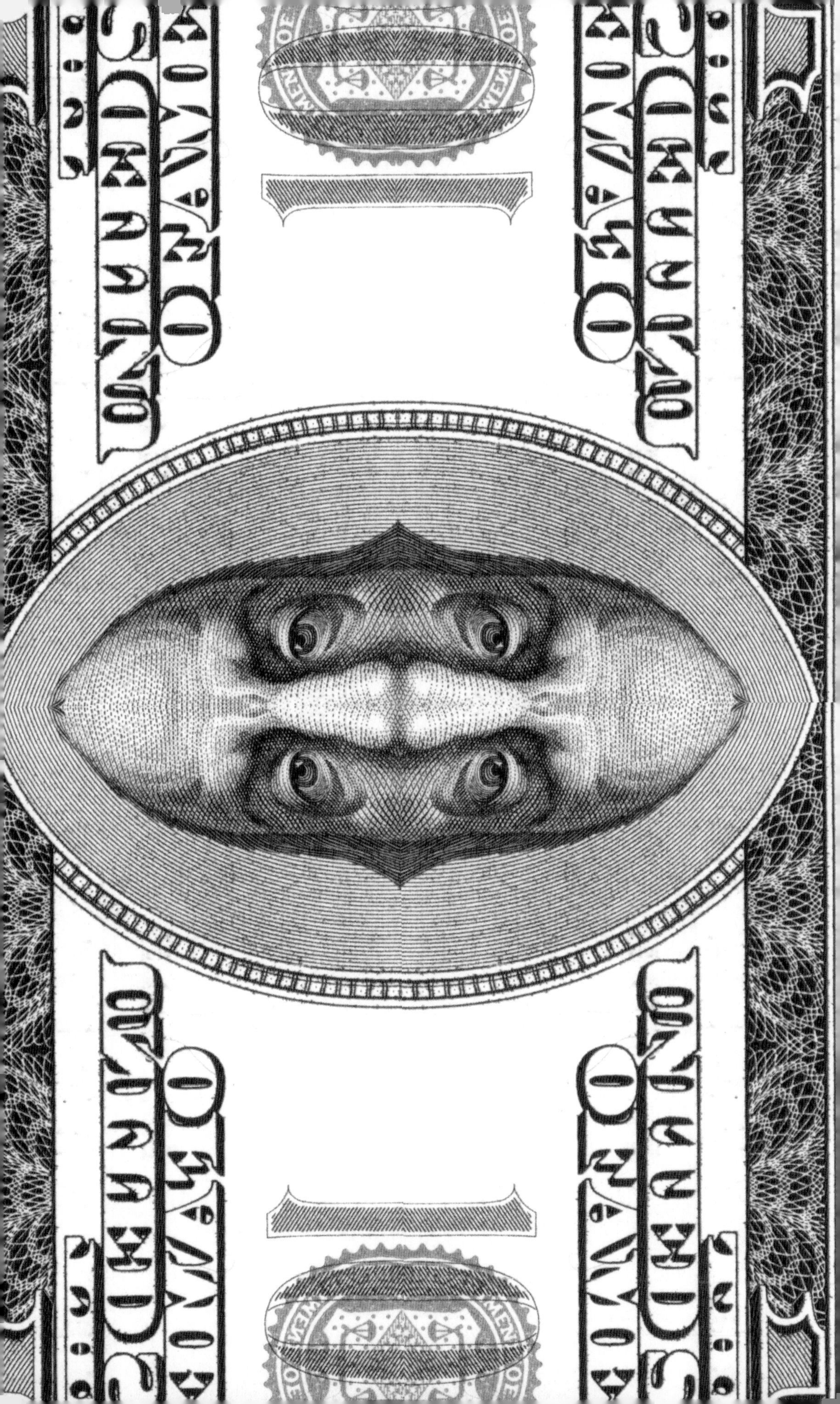
ONE HUNDRED DOLLARS

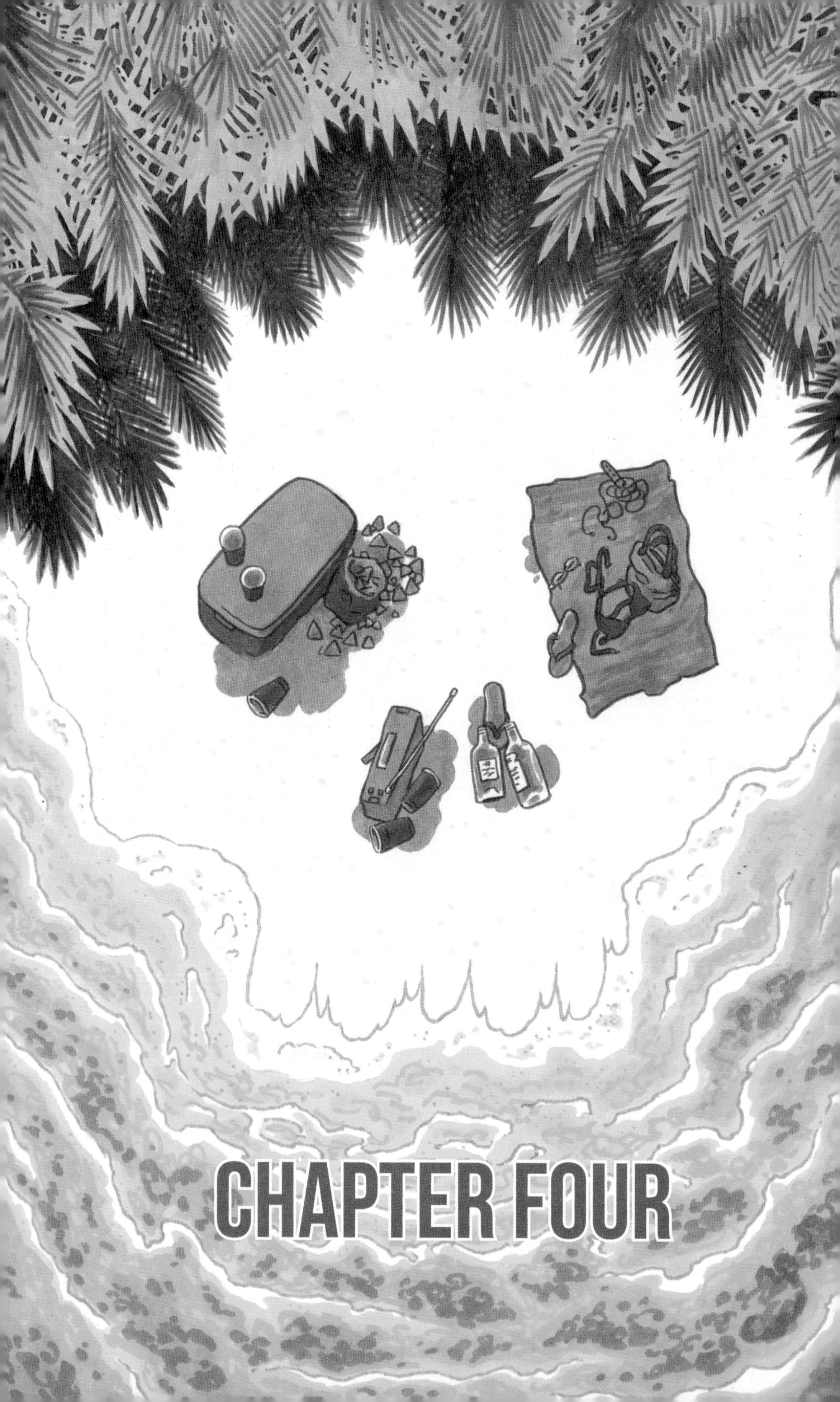

CHAPTER FOUR

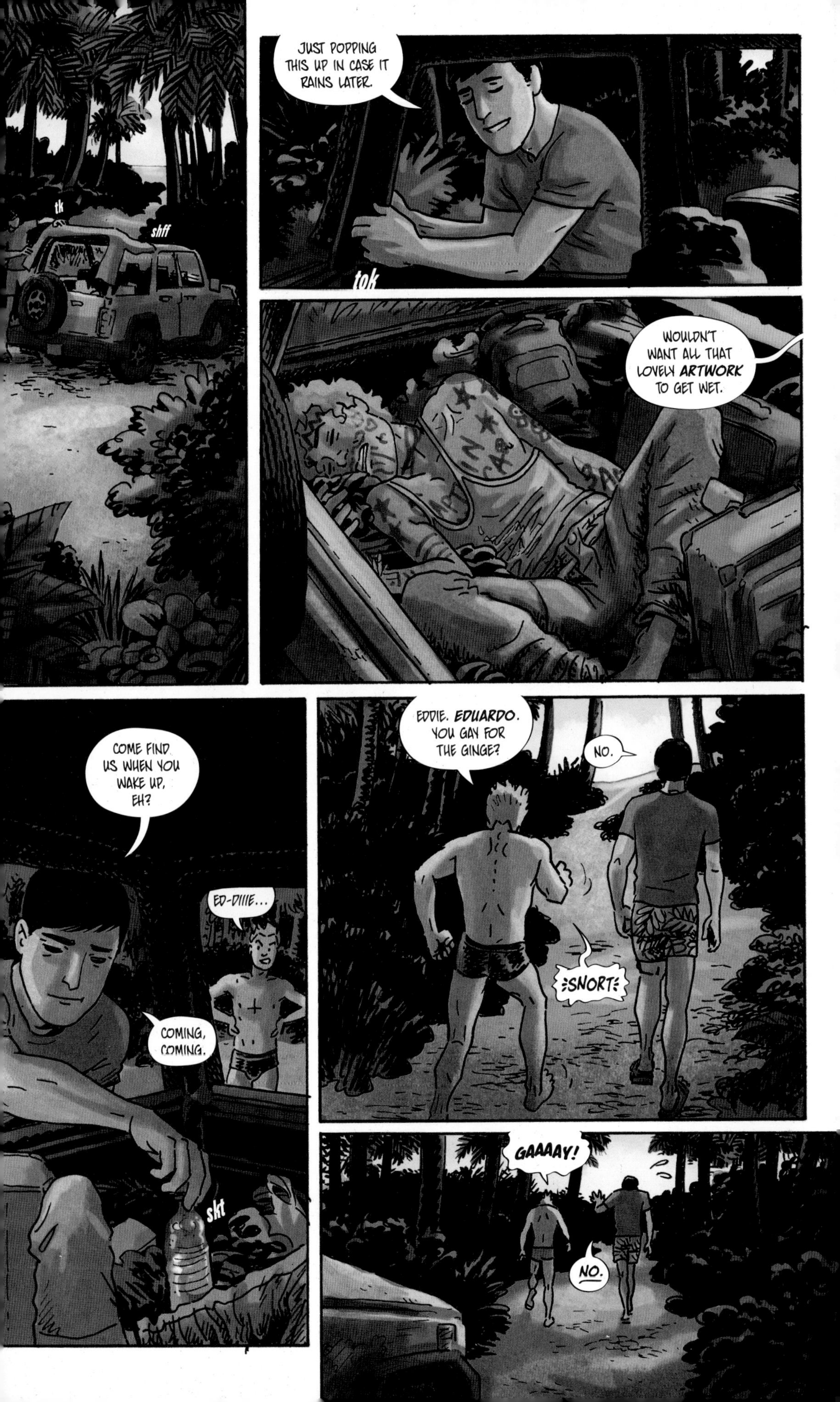

tk
shff
JUST POPPING THIS UP IN CASE IT RAINS LATER.
tok
WOULDN'T WANT ALL THAT LOVELY ARTWORK TO GET WET.
COME FIND US WHEN YOU WAKE UP, EH?
ED-DIIIE...
COMING, COMING.
skt
EDDIE. EDUARDO. YOU GAY FOR THE GINGE?
NO.
SNORT
GAAAAY!
NO.

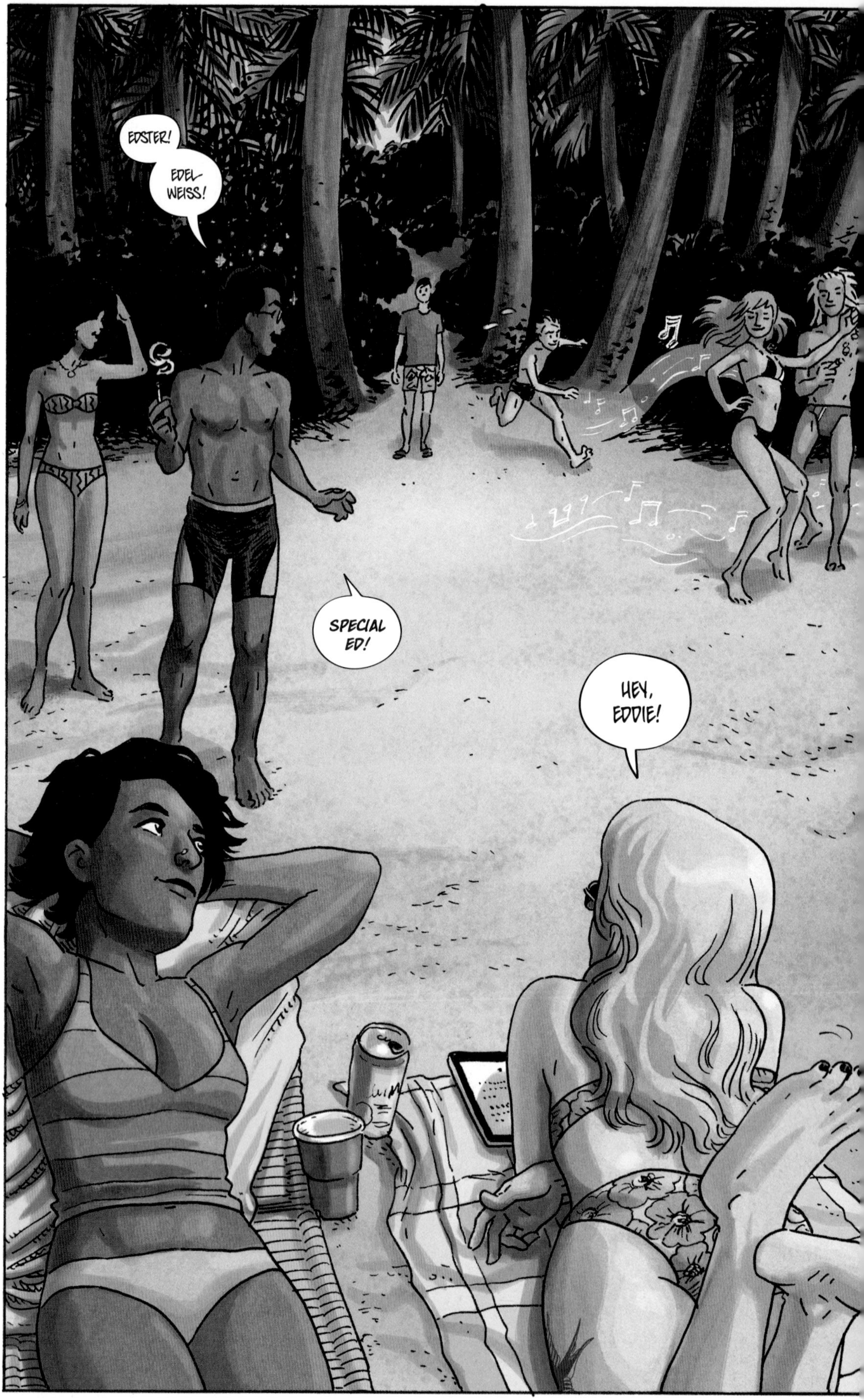
EDSTER!
EDEL-WEISS!
SPECIAL ED!
HEY, EDDIE!

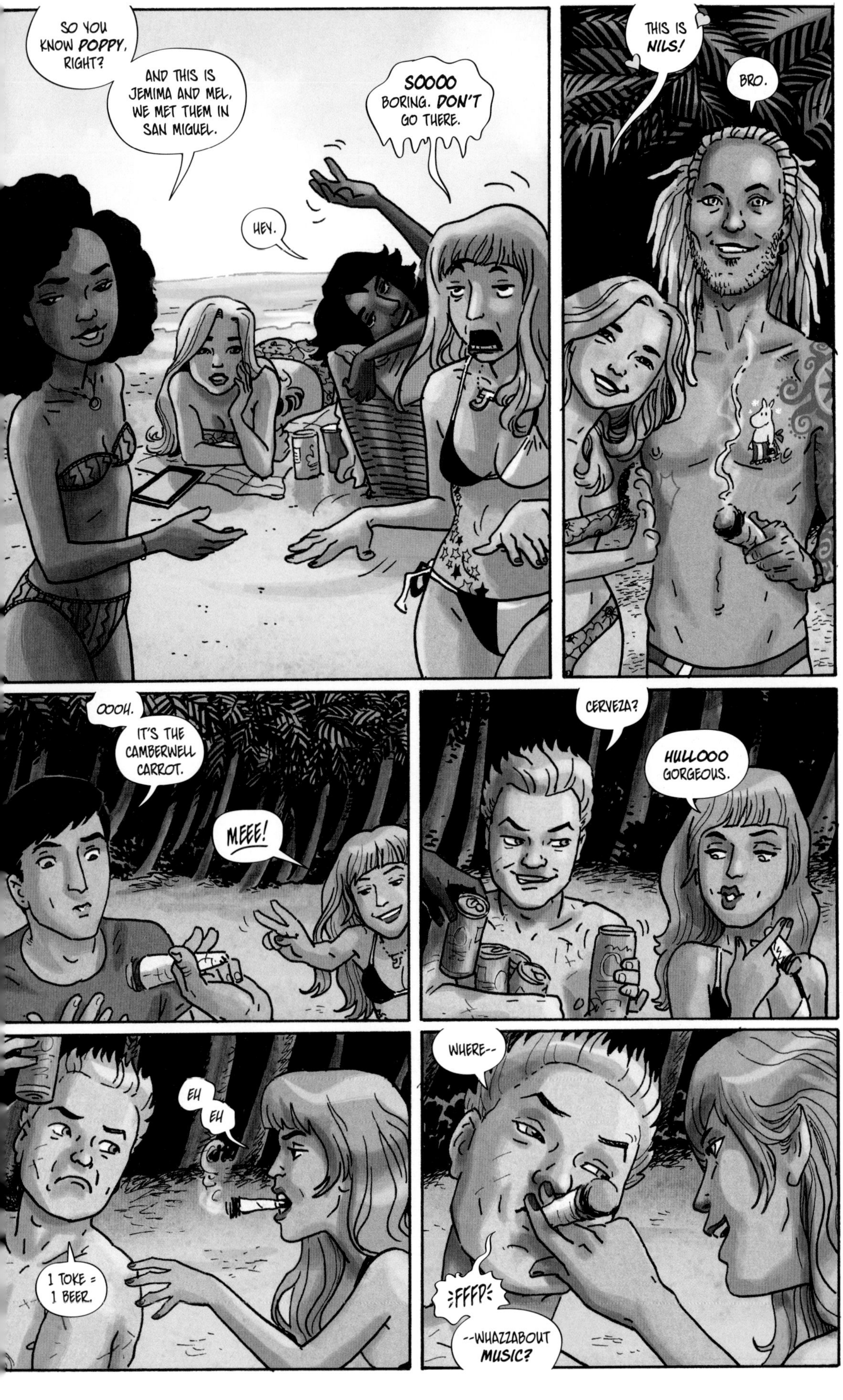
SO YOU KNOW POPPY, RIGHT?
AND THIS IS JEMIMA AND MEL, WE MET THEM IN SAN MIGUEL.
HEY.
SOOOO BORING. DON'T GO THERE.
THIS IS NILS!
BRO.
OOOH.
IT'S THE CAMBERWELL CARROT.
MEEE!
CERVEZA?
HULLOOO GORGEOUS.
EH
EH
1 TOKE = 1 BEER.
WHERE--
FFFP
--WHAZZABOUT MUSIC?

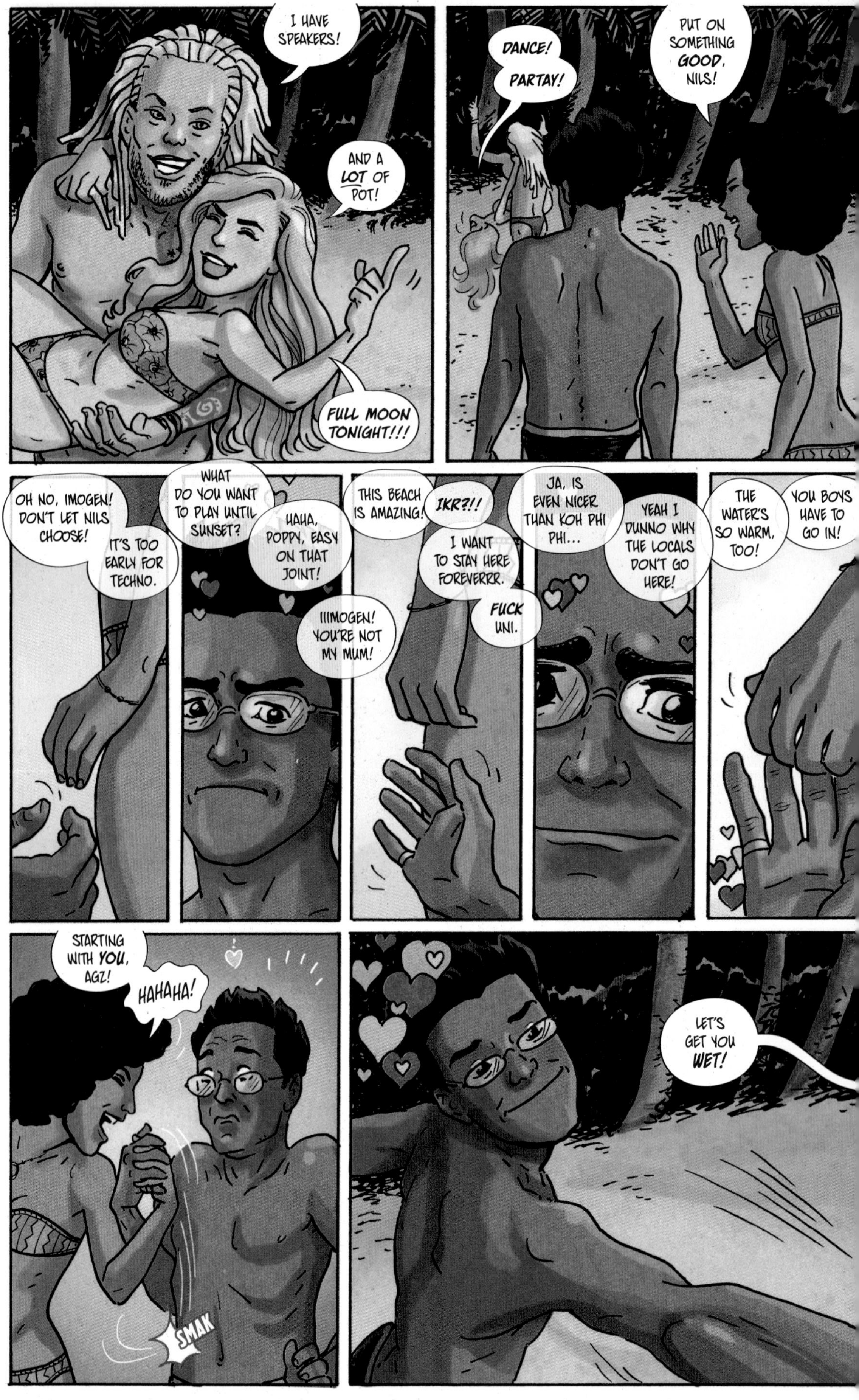
I HAVE SPEAKERS!
AND A LOT OF POT!
FULL MOON TONIGHT!!!
DANCE!
PARTAY!
PUT ON SOMETHING GOOD, NILS!
OH NO, IMOGEN! DON'T LET NILS CHOOSE!
IT'S TOO EARLY FOR TECHNO.
WHAT DO YOU WANT TO PLAY UNTIL SUNSET?
HAHA, POPPY, EASY ON THAT JOINT!
IIIMOGEN! YOU'RE NOT MY MUM!
THIS BEACH IS AMAZING!
IKR?!!
I WANT TO STAY HERE FOREVERRR.
FUCK UNI.
JA, IS EVEN NICER THAN KOH PHI PHI...
YEAH I DUNNO WHY THE LOCALS DON'T GO HERE!
THE WATER'S SO WARM, TOO!
YOU BOYS HAVE TO GO IN!
STARTING WITH YOU, AGZ!
HAHAHA!
SMAK
LET'S GET YOU WET!

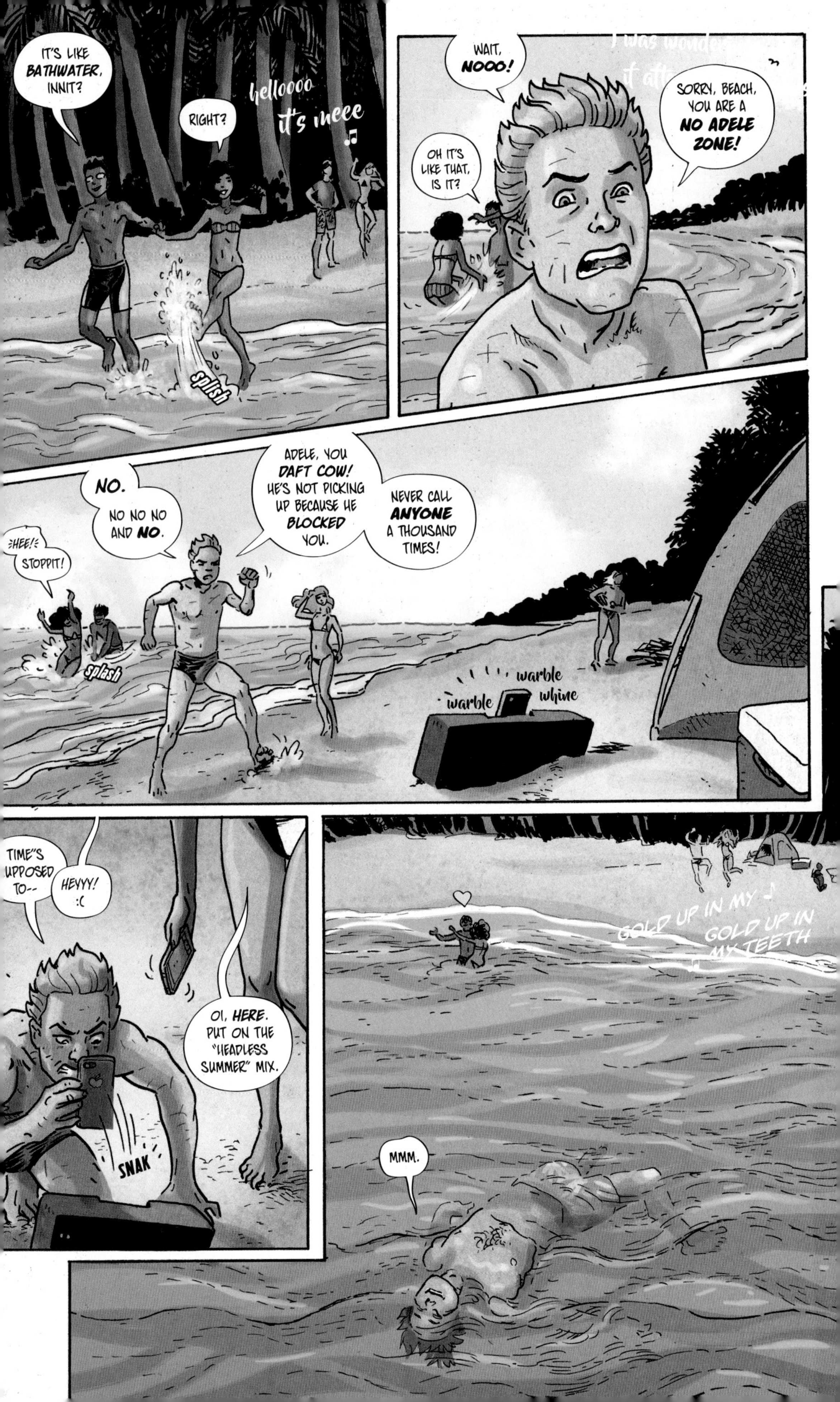

IT'S LIKE BATHWATER, INNIT?
RIGHT?
hellоooo
it's meee ♪
WAIT, NOOO!
OH IT'S LIKE THAT, IS IT?
SORRY, BEACH, YOU ARE A NO ADELE ZONE!
NO.
NO NO NO AND NO.
ADELE, YOU DAFT COW! HE'S NOT PICKING UP BECAUSE HE BLOCKED YOU.
NEVER CALL ANYONE A THOUSAND TIMES!
HEE! STOPPIT!
splash
warble
warble
whine
TIME'S UPPOSED TO--
HEYYY! :(
OI, HERE. PUT ON THE "HEADLESS SUMMER" MIX.
SNAK
GOLD UP IN MY ♪
GOLD UP IN MY TEETH
MMM.

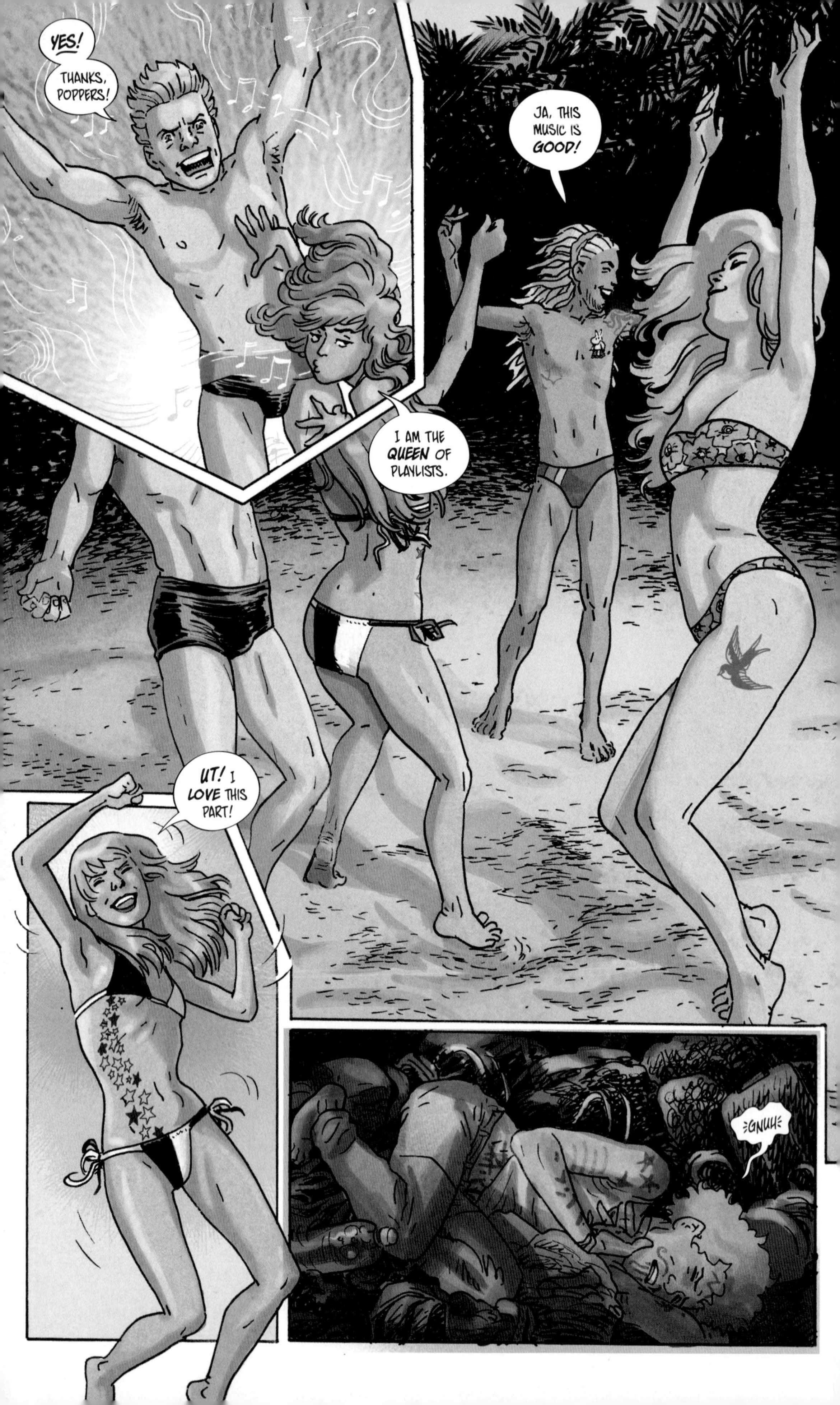
YES!
THANKS, POPPERS!
JA, THIS MUSIC IS GOOD!
I AM THE QUEEN OF PLAYLISTS.
UT! I LOVE THIS PART!
GNUH

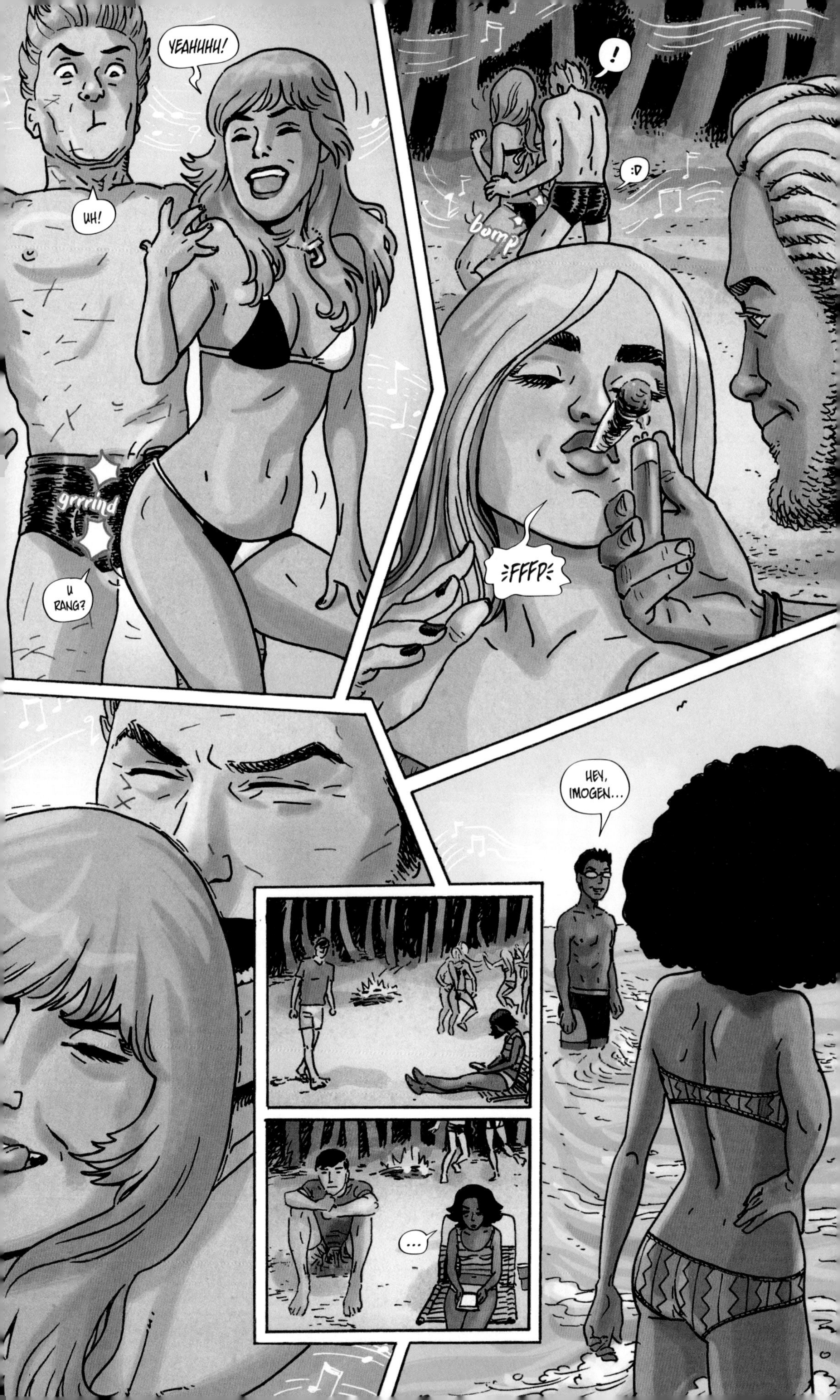
YEAHHHH!
UH!
grrrind
U RANG?
!
:D
bump
FFFP
HEY, IMOGEN...
...

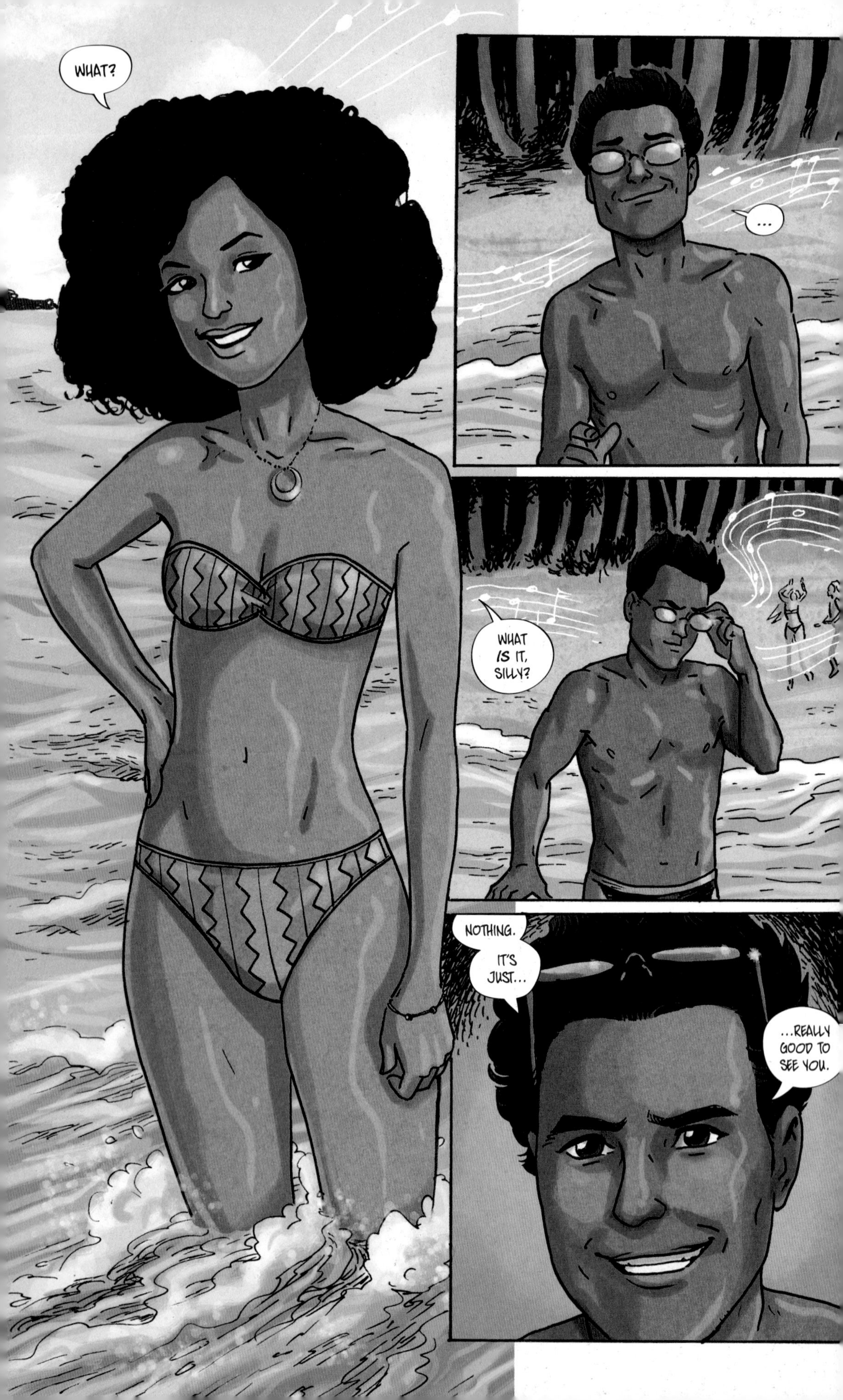
WHAT?
...
WHAT *IS* IT, SILLY?
NOTHING.
IT'S JUST...
...REALLY GOOD TO SEE YOU.

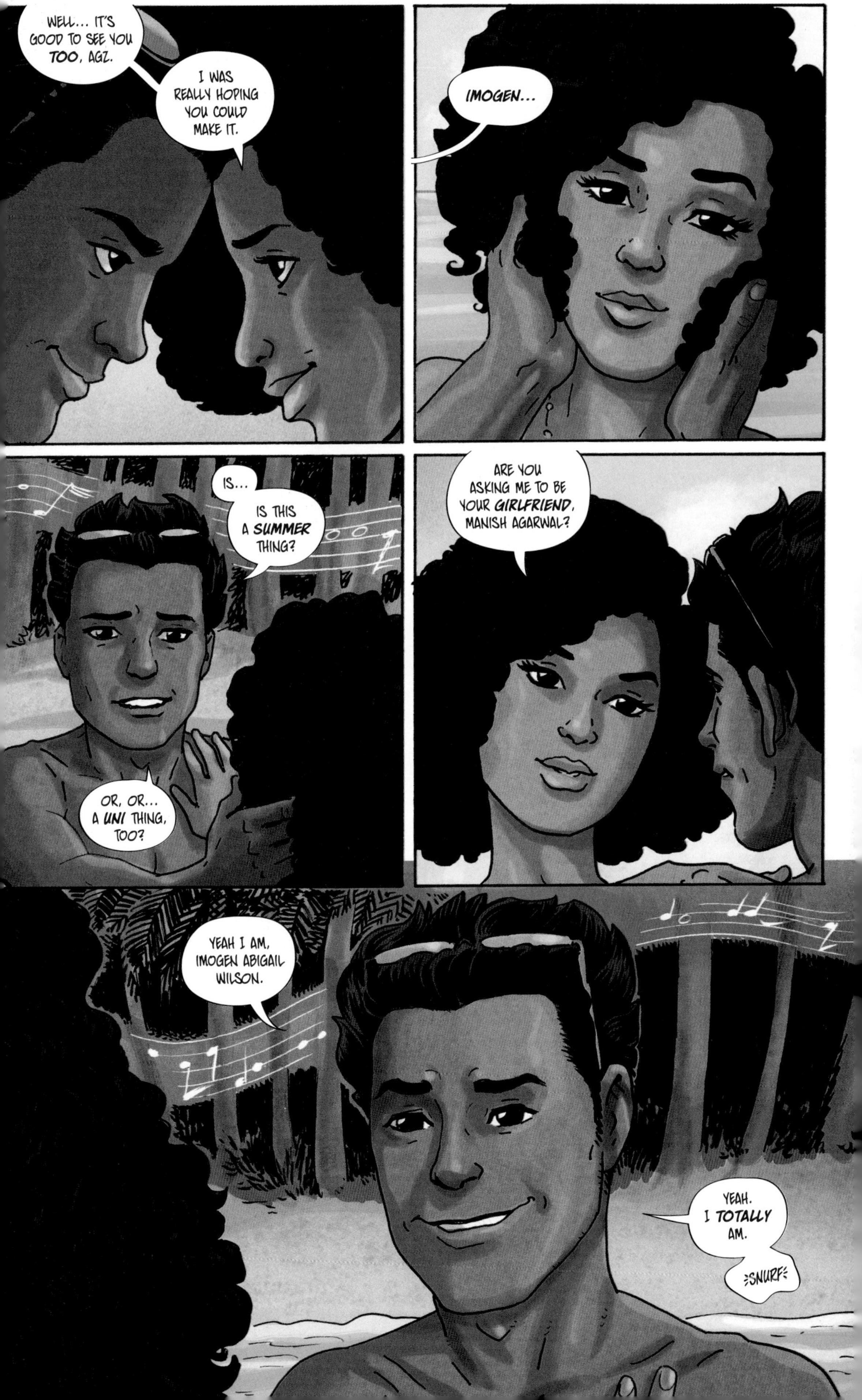
WELL... IT'S GOOD TO SEE YOU TOO, AGZ.
I WAS REALLY HOPING YOU COULD MAKE IT.
IMOGEN...
IS...
IS THIS A SUMMER THING?
OR, OR... A UNI THING, TOO?
ARE YOU ASKING ME TO BE YOUR GIRLFRIEND, MANISH AGARWAL?
YEAH I AM, IMOGEN ABIGAIL WILSON.
YEAH. I TOTALLY AM.
SNURF

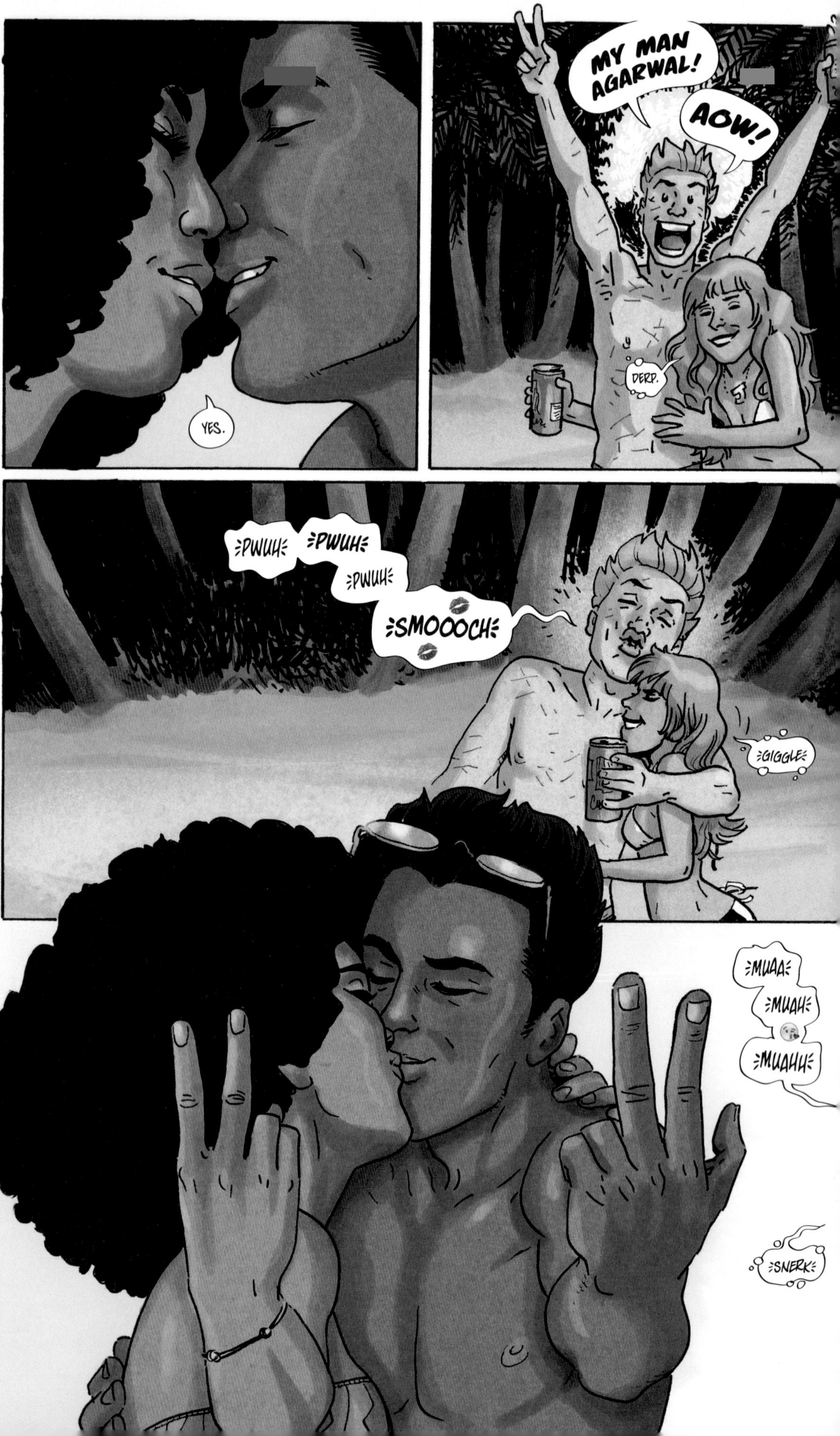
YES.
MY MAN AGARWAL!
AOW!
DERP.
PWUH
PWUH
PWUH
SMOOOCH
GIGGLE
MUAA
MUAH
MUAHH
SNERK

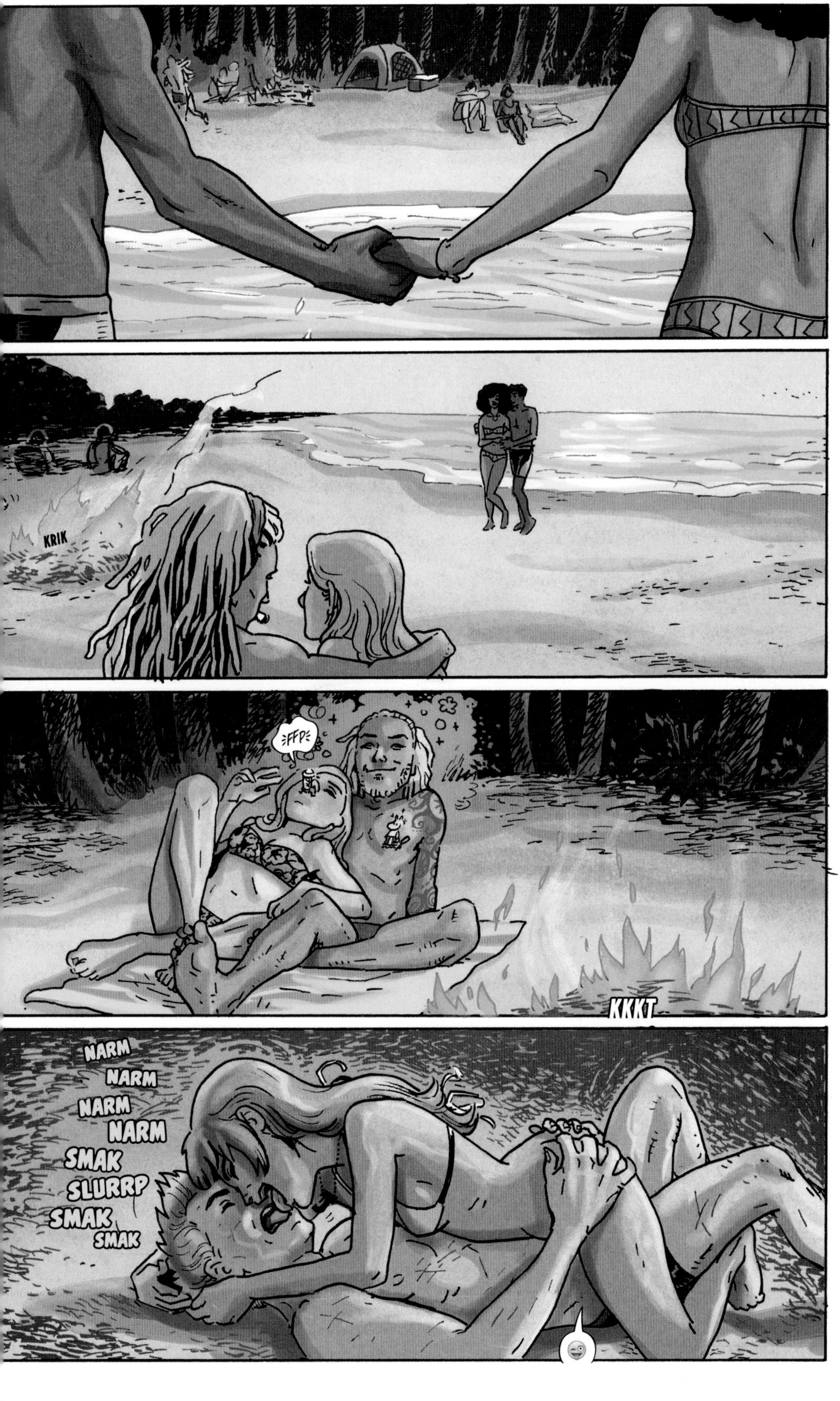
KRIK
FFP
KKKT
NARM
NARM
NARM
NARM
SMAK
SLURRP
SMAK
SMAK

NNH
ARMF
≈SIGH≈
ER... DO YOU WANT--
I'M GAY.
--ANOTHER BEER?
OH!
UM, YEAH. THANKS.
'KAY.
tink

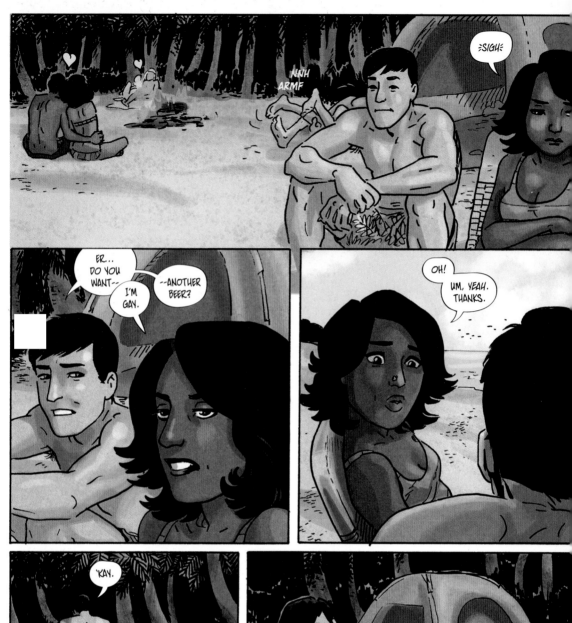

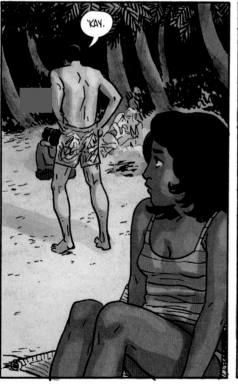

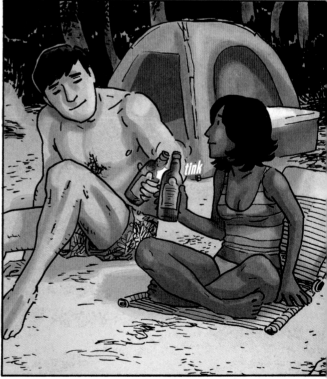

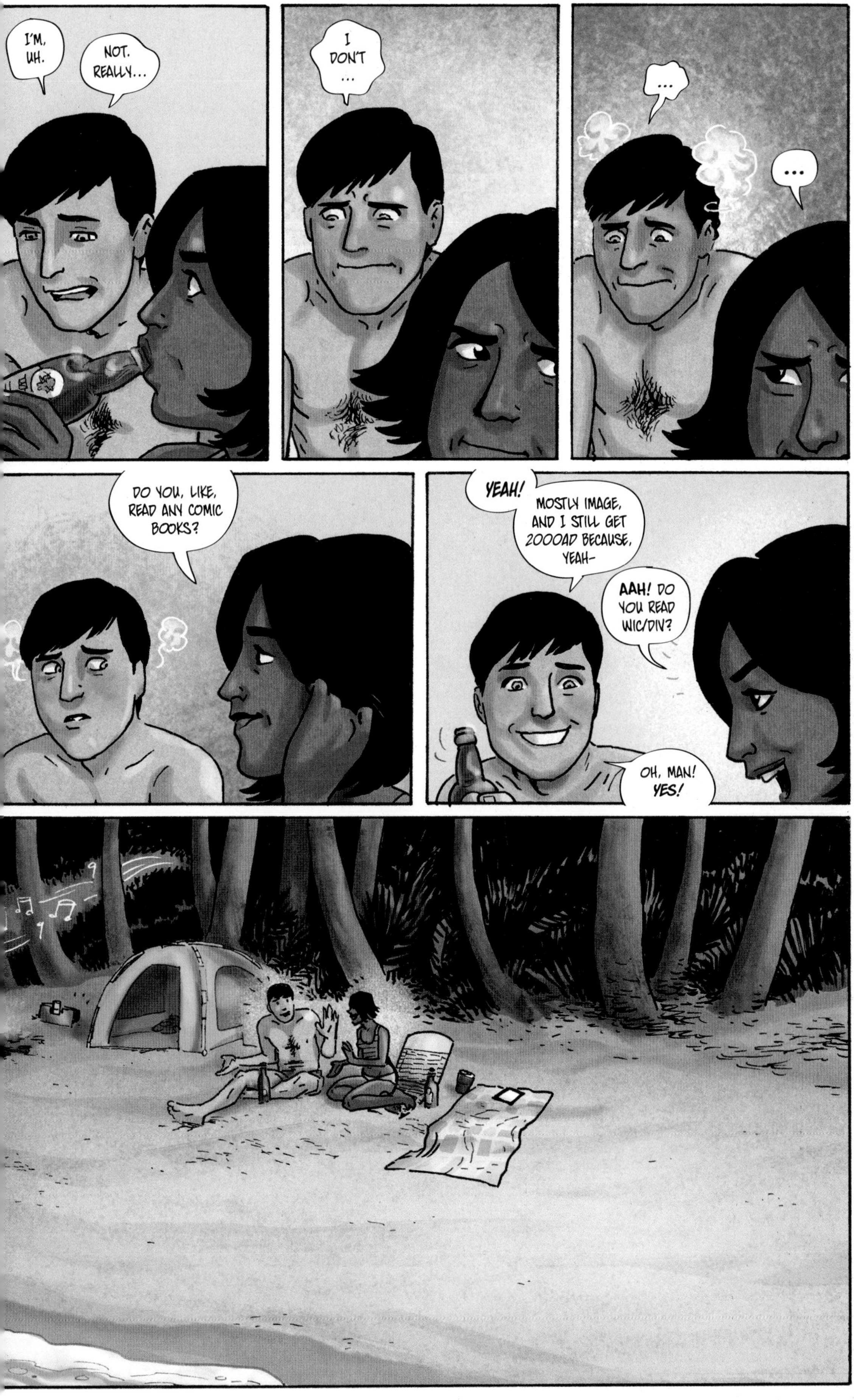

I'M, UH.
NOT. REALLY...
I DON'T ...
...
...
DO YOU, LIKE, READ ANY COMIC BOOKS?
YEAH!
MOSTLY IMAGE, AND I STILL GET 2000AD BECAUSE, YEAH-
AAH! DO YOU READ WIC/DIV?
OH, MAN! YES!

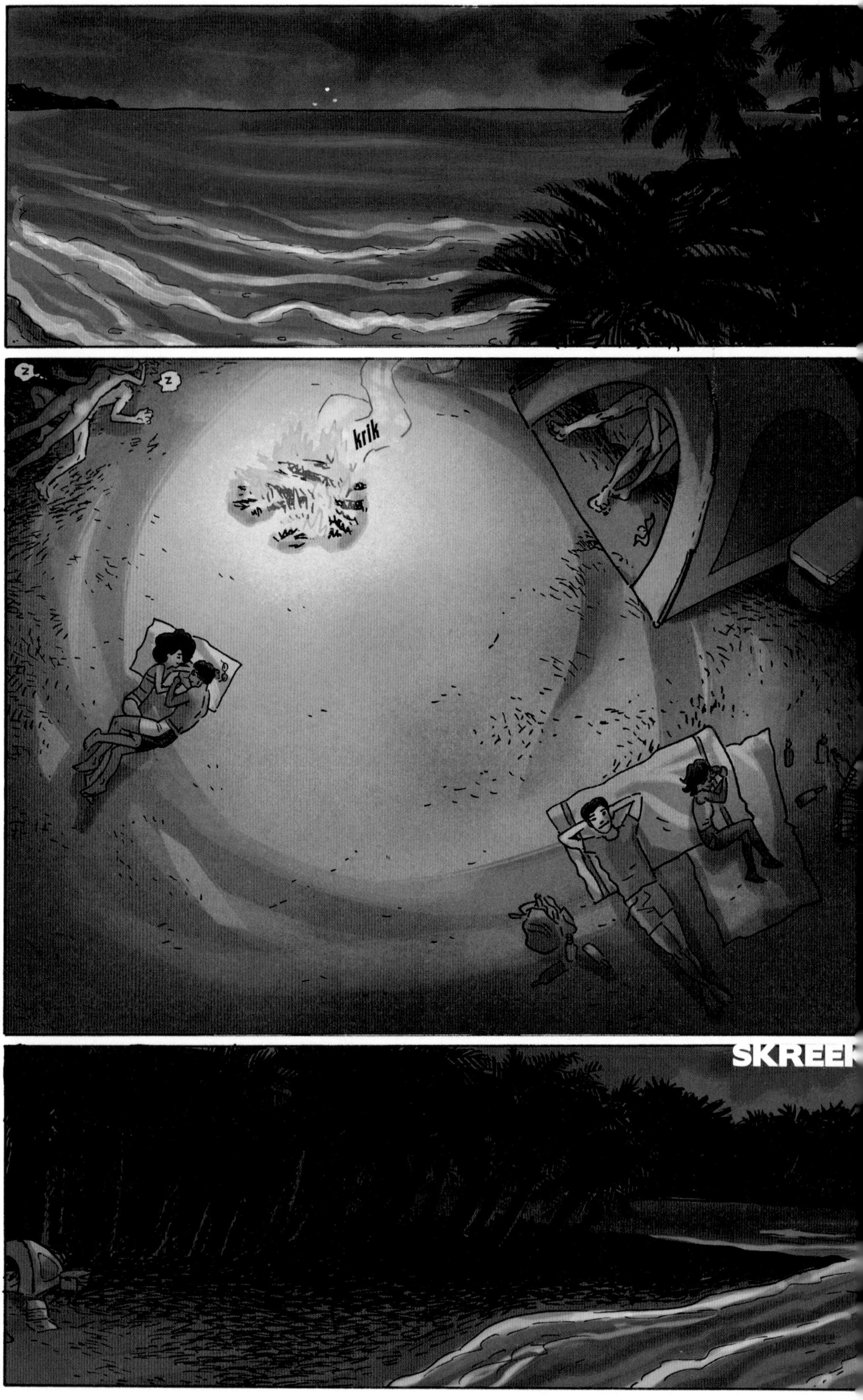
Z
Z
krik
SKREE

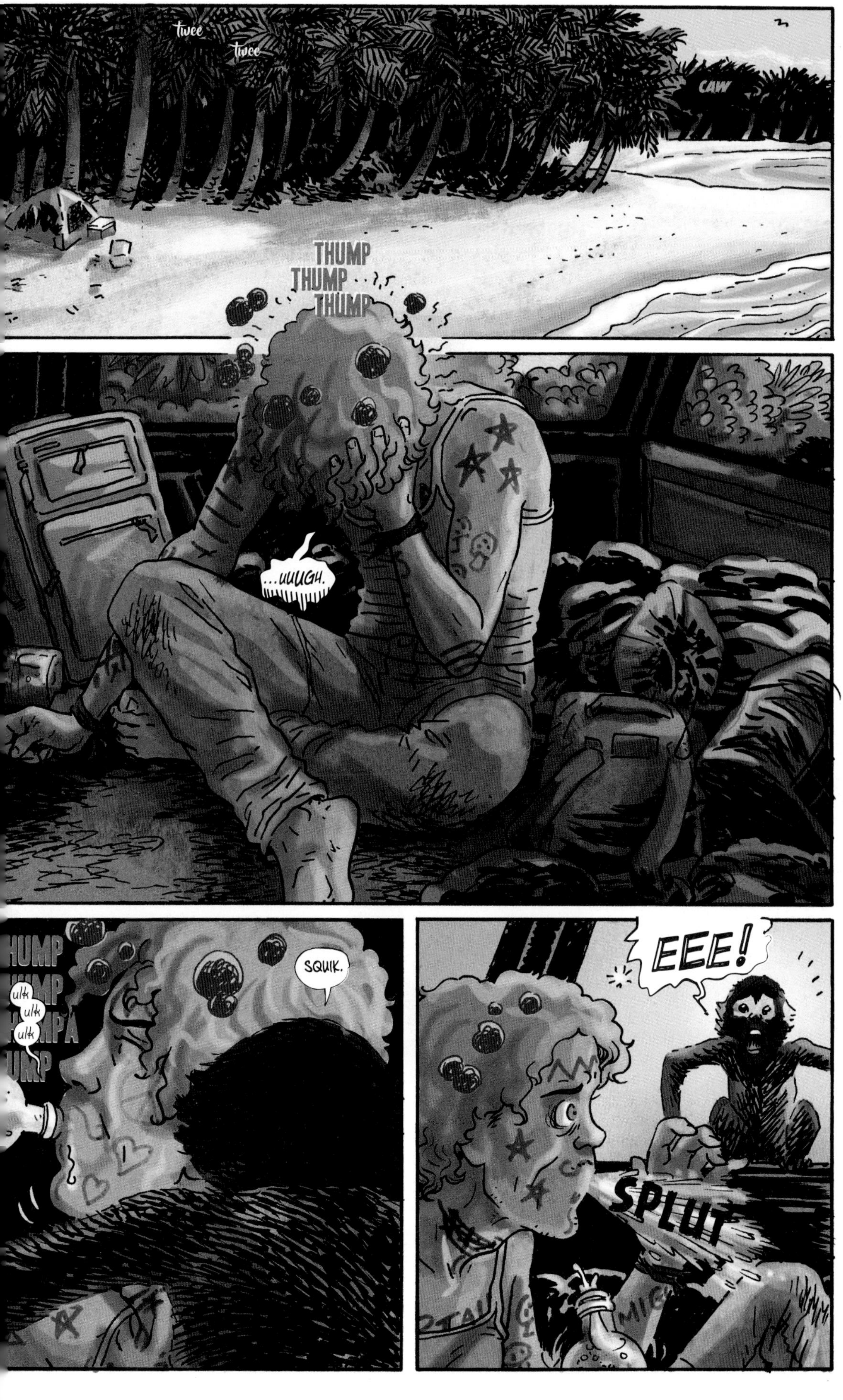
twee
twee
CAW
THUMP
THUMP
THUMP
...UUUGH.
SQUIK.
ulk
ulk
ulk
EEE!
SPLUT

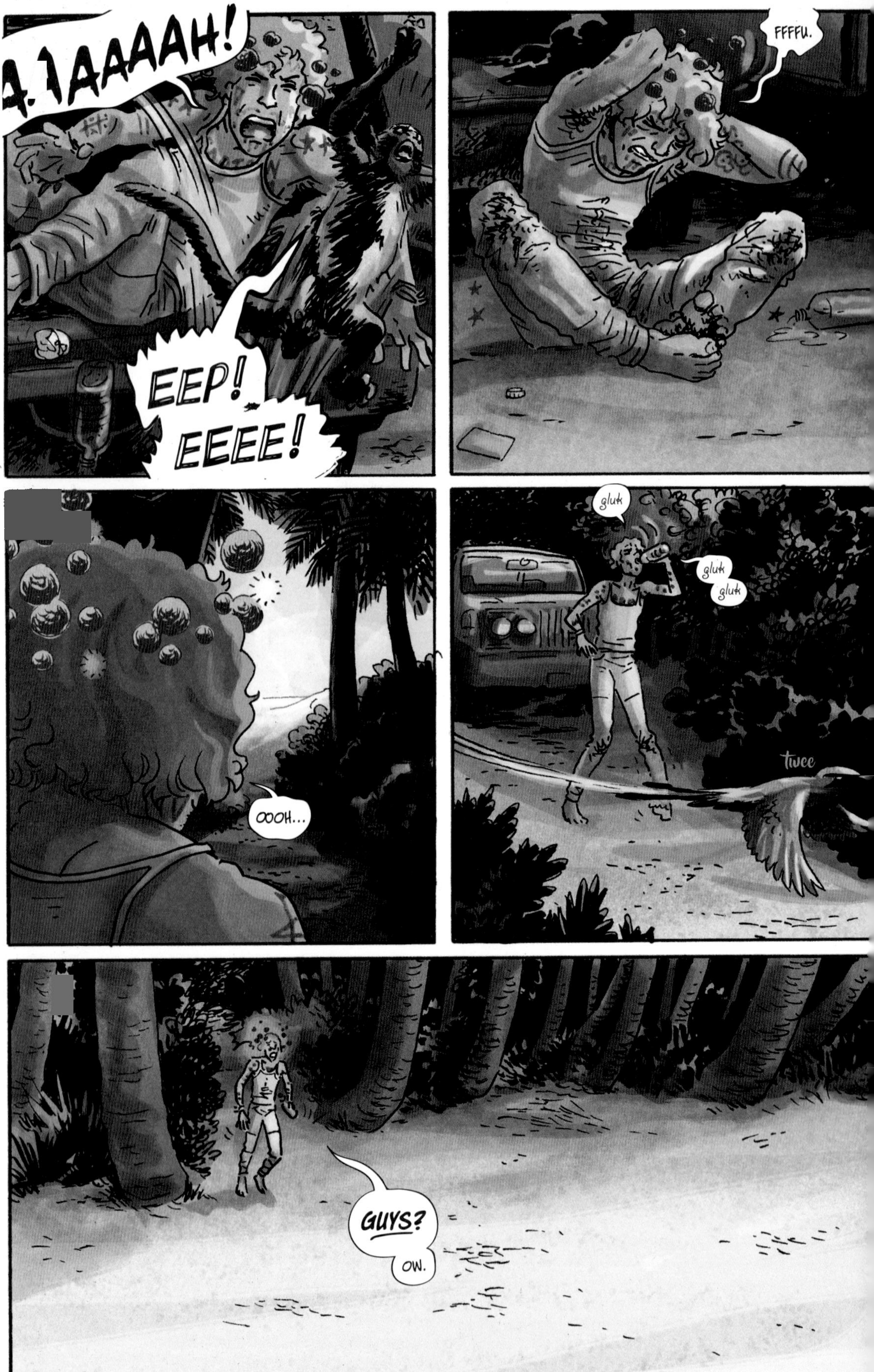
AAAAAAH!
EEP! EEEE!
FFFFU.
OOOH...
gluk
gluk
gluk
twee
GUYS?
OW.

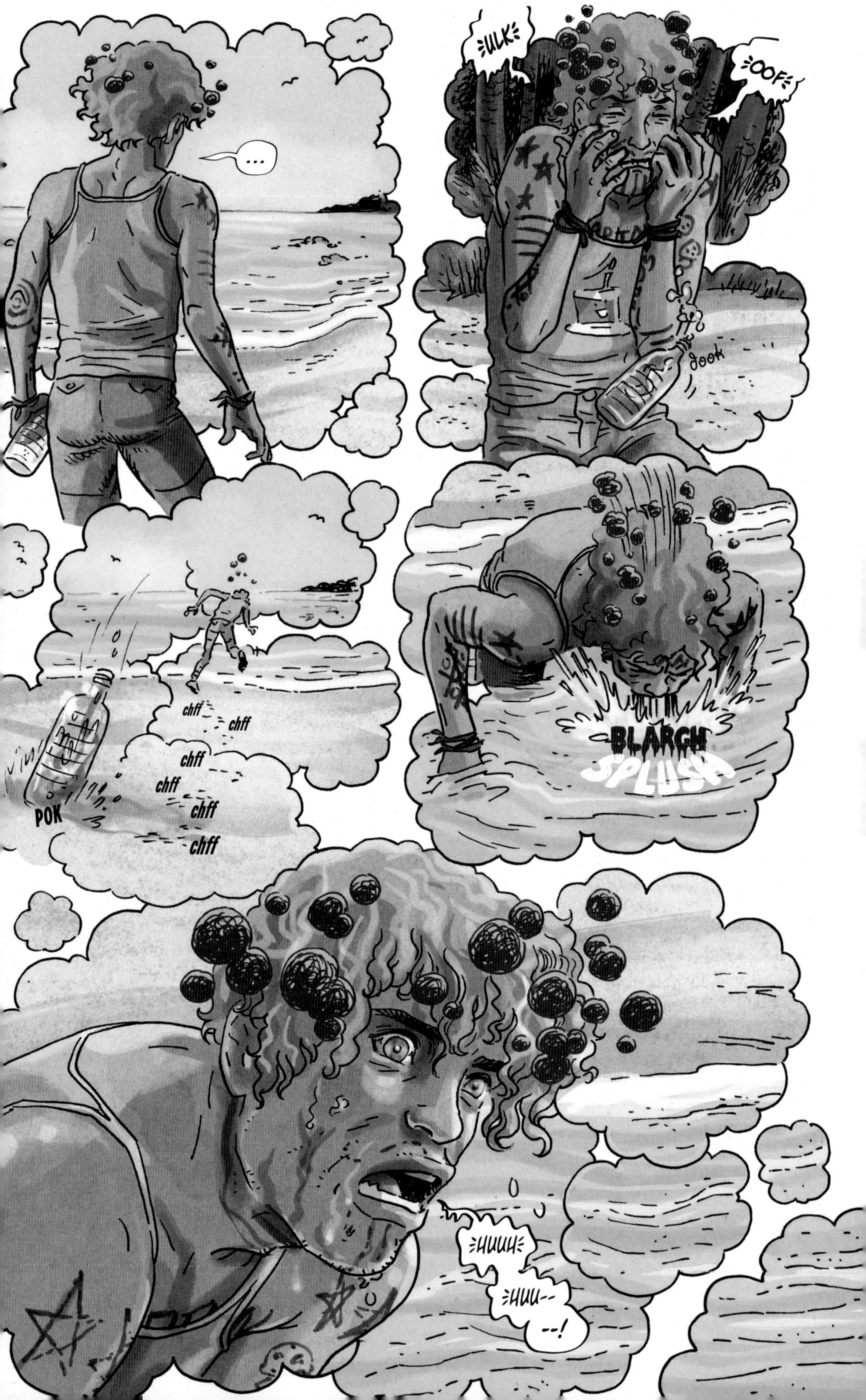
...
ULK
OOF
dook
POK
chff
chff
chff
chff
chff
chff
BLARGH
SPLUSH
HUUH
HUU--
--!

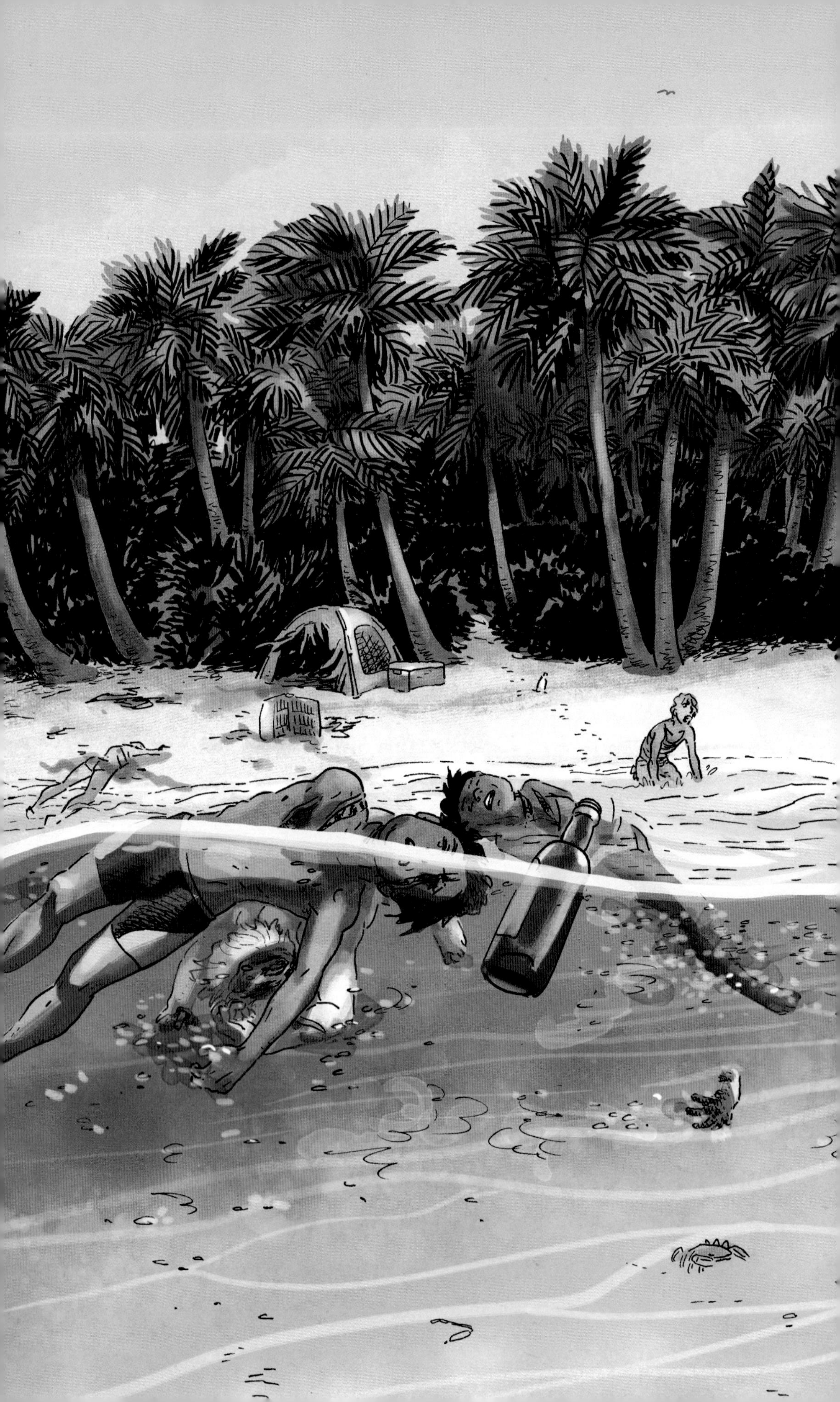

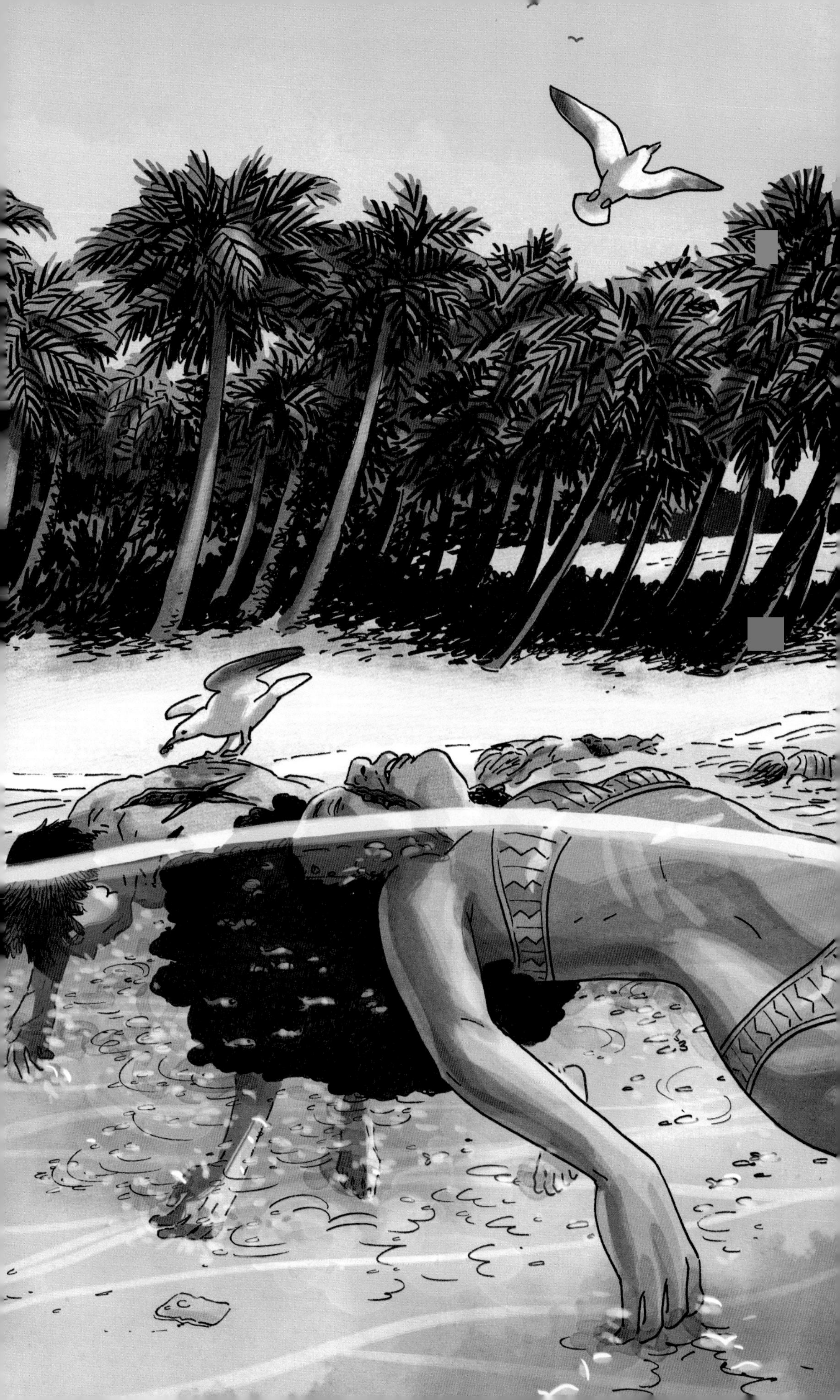

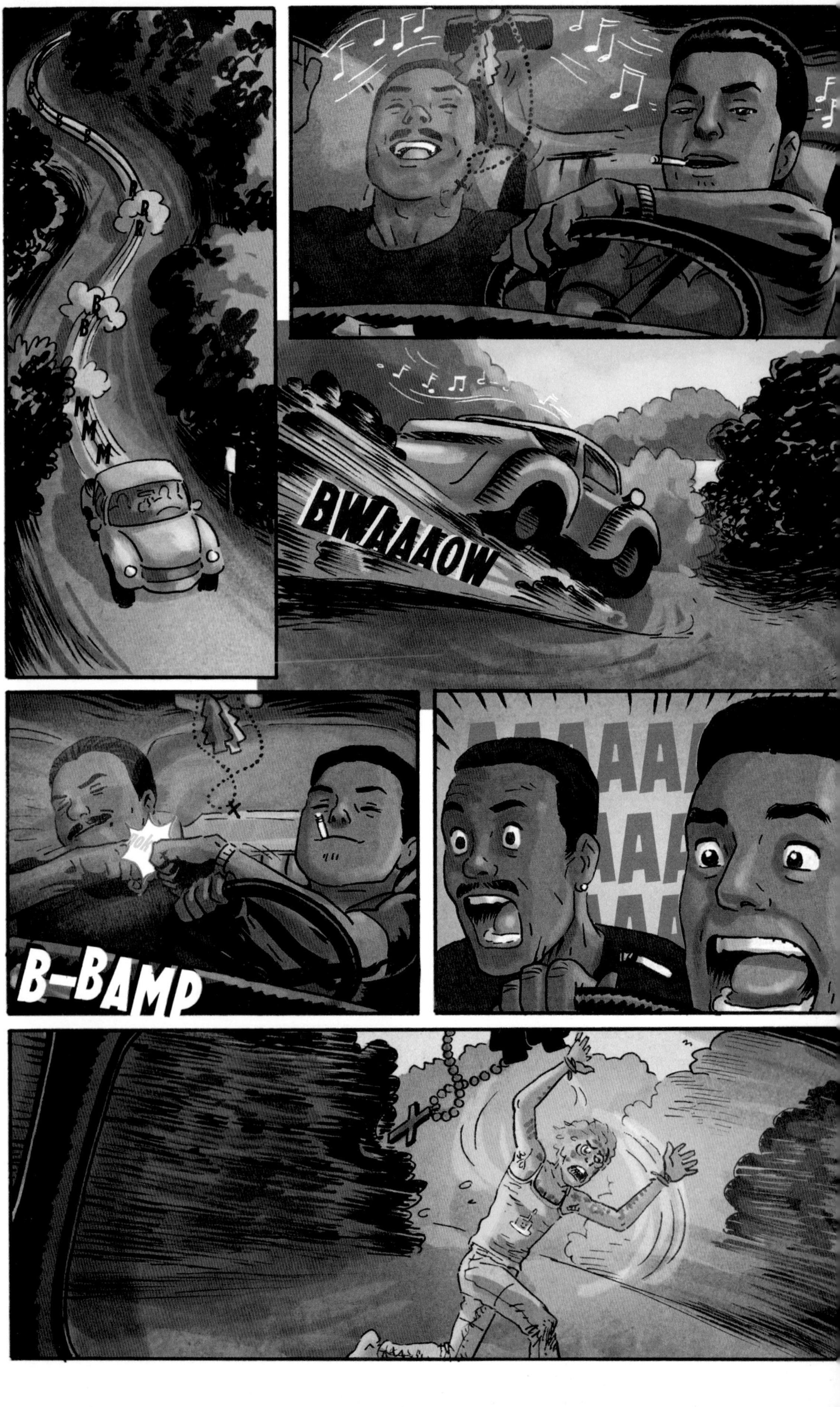

BWAAAAOW
B-BAMP

THEY FOUND ANOTHER ONE OF YOUR KIDS, HARRY.

IN ZANCUDO PROVINCE.

WHAT??

WHAT THE *HELL* IS HE DOING IN THE MIDDLE OF THE *JUNGLE?!*

THAT'S *HUNDREDS* OF MILES *IN THE WRONG DIRECTION* FROM THE CRASH SITE!

I DUNNO, HARRY. *KIDS.*

=HUUUUHHH=

FLIP YOU FOR WHO SCHLEPS OUT TO MOSQUITOVILLE TO GET HIM.

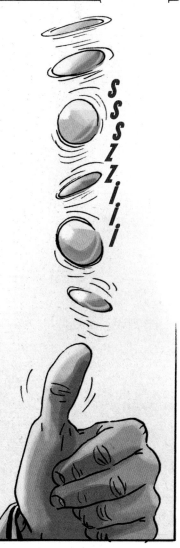

SSSZZiii

OKAY.

WHOEVER STAYS BEHIND GETS TO CALL THE PARENTS.

DEAL.

HEADS I WIN, TAILS YOU LOSE?

FINE.

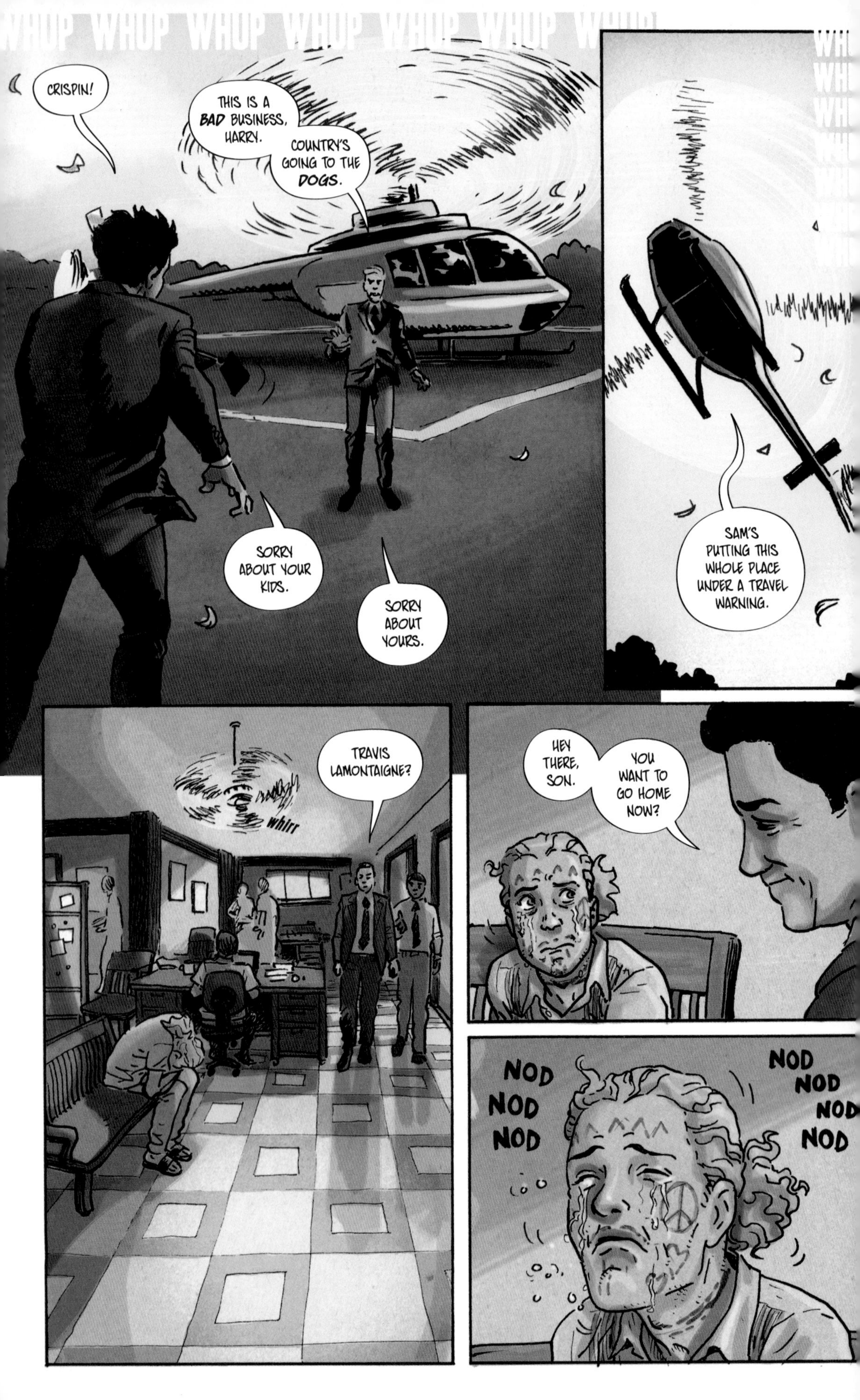
WHUP WHUP WHUP WHUP WHUP WHUP WHUP
CRISPIN!
THIS IS A BAD BUSINESS, HARRY.
COUNTRY'S GOING TO THE DOGS.
SORRY ABOUT YOUR KIDS.
SORRY ABOUT YOURS.
SAM'S PUTTING THIS WHOLE PLACE UNDER A TRAVEL WARNING.
whirr
TRAVIS LAMONTAIGNE?
HEY THERE, SON.
YOU WANT TO GO HOME NOW?
NOD NOD NOD
NOD NOD NOD NOD

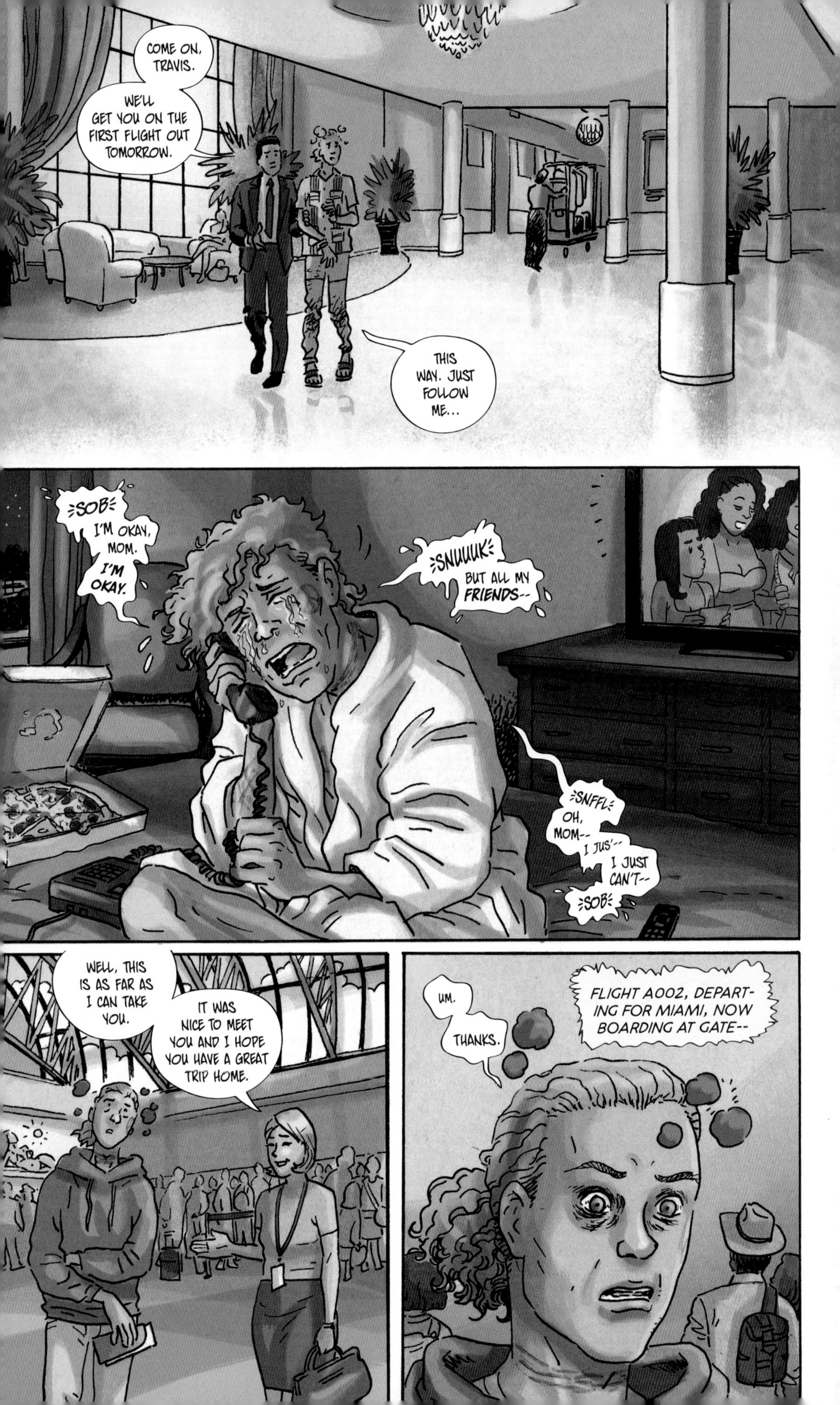
COME ON, TRAVIS.
WE'LL GET YOU ON THE FIRST FLIGHT OUT TOMORROW.
THIS WAY. JUST FOLLOW ME...
SOB I'M OKAY, MOM. I'M OKAY.
SNUUUK BUT ALL MY FRIENDS--
SNFFL OH, MOM-- I JUS'-- I JUST CAN'T-- SOB
WELL, THIS IS AS FAR AS I CAN TAKE YOU.
IT WAS NICE TO MEET YOU AND I HOPE YOU HAVE A GREAT TRIP HOME.
UM.
THANKS.
FLIGHT A002, DEPARTING FOR MIAMI, NOW BOARDING AT GATE--

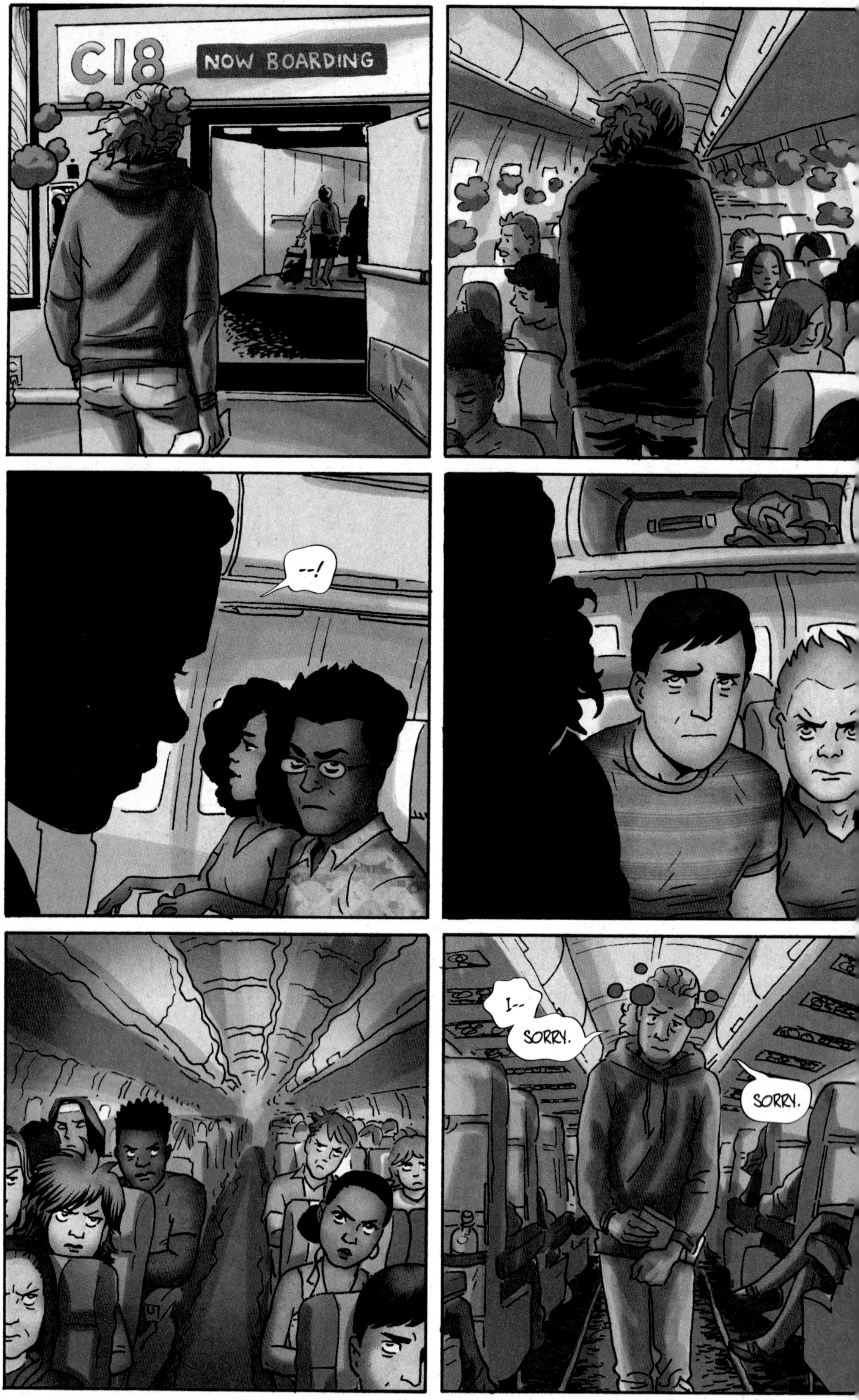
C18
NOW BOARDING
--!
I--
SORRY.
SORRY.

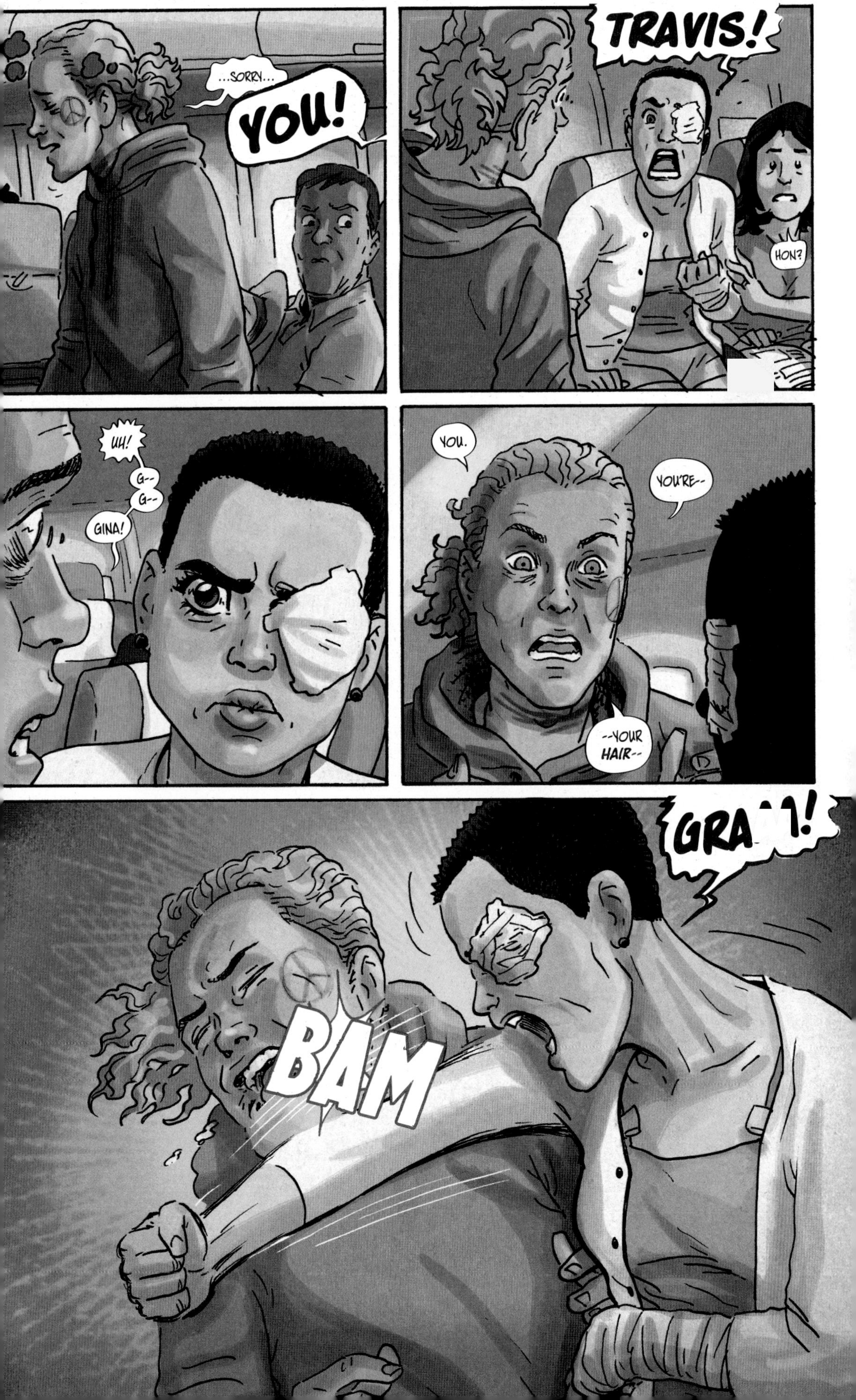

...SORRY...
YOU!
TRAVIS!
HON?
UH!
G--
G--
GINA!
YOU.
YOU'RE--
--YOUR HAIR--
GRA
BAM

CHAPTER FIVE

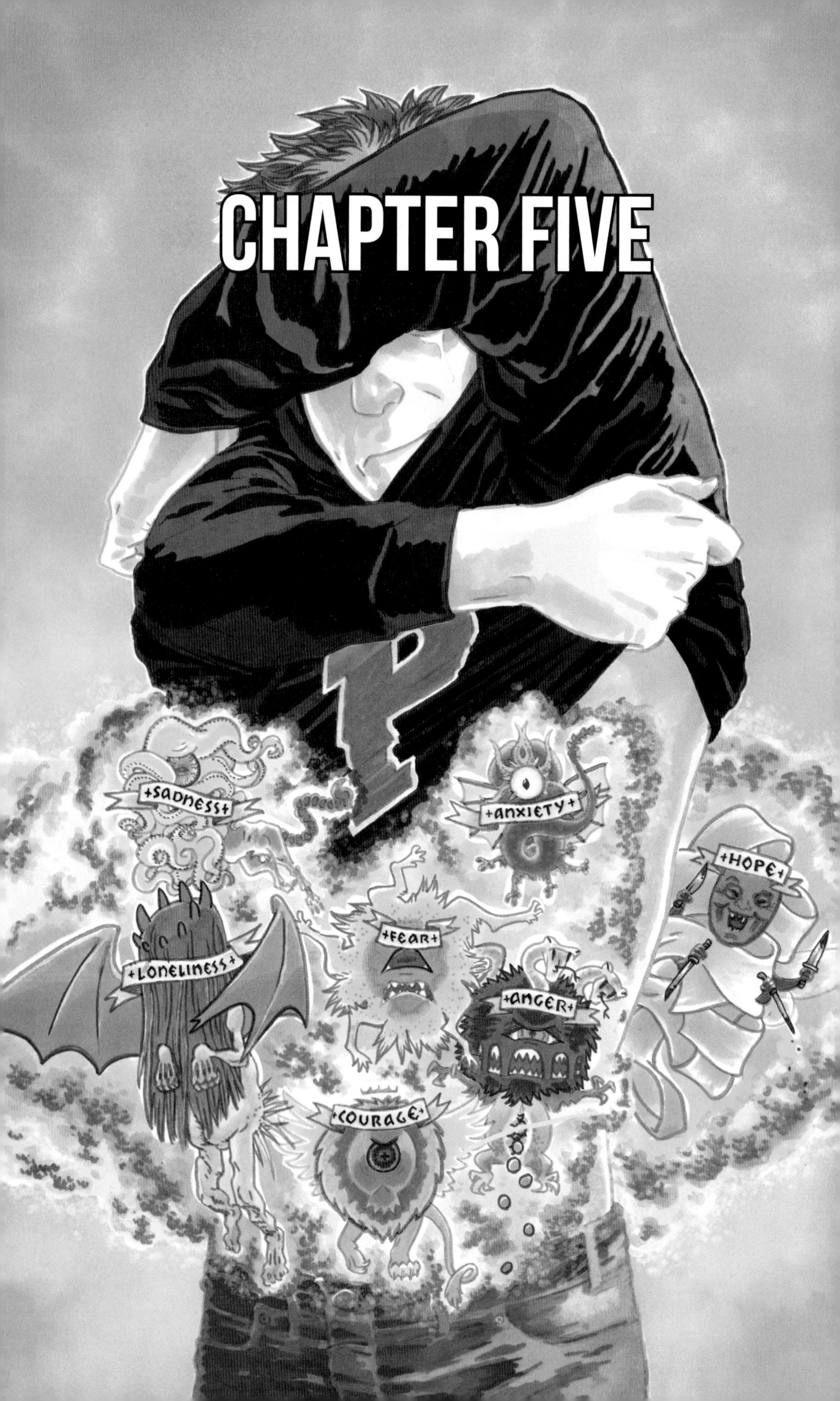

+SADNESS+
+ANXIETY+
+HOPE+
+FEAR+
+LONELINESS+
+ANGER+
+COURAGE+

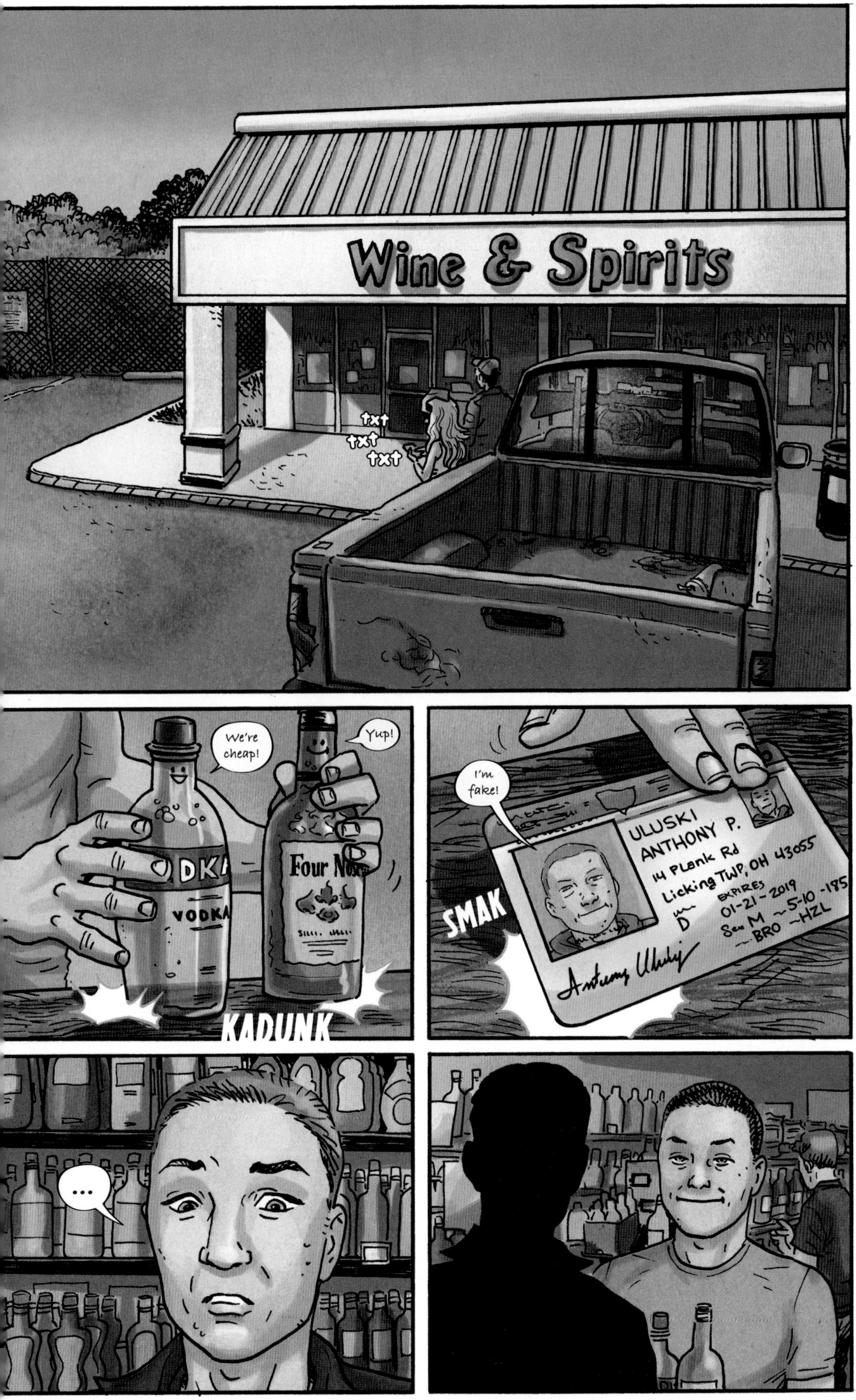
Wine & Spirits
txt
txt
txt
We're cheap!
Yup!
VODKA
Four Noses
KADUNK
I'm fake!
ULUSKI
ANTHONY P.
14 Plank Rd
Licking TWP, OH 43055
EXPIRES
01-21-2019
SMAK
...

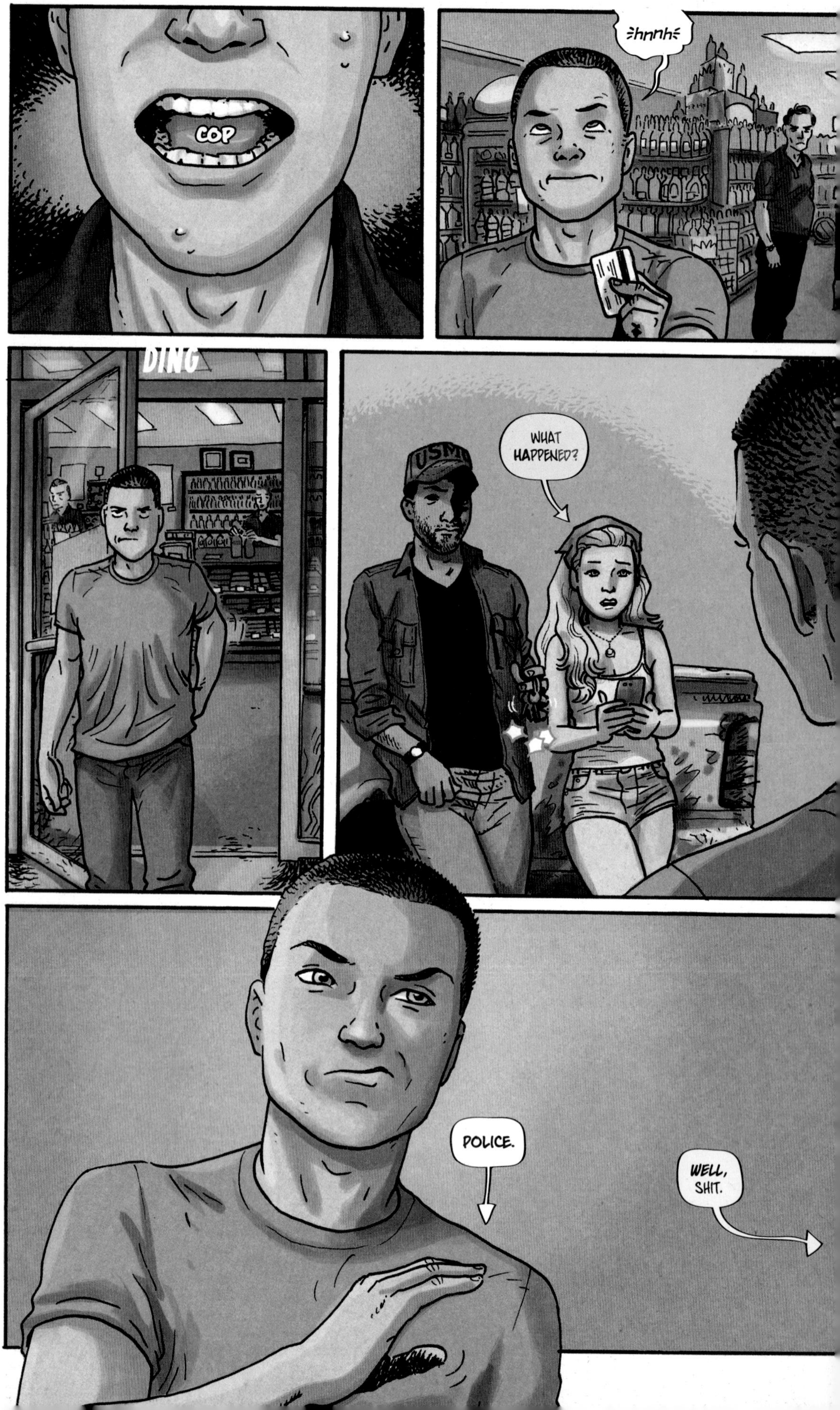
COP
hnnh
DING
WHAT HAPPENED?
POLICE.
WELL, SHIT.

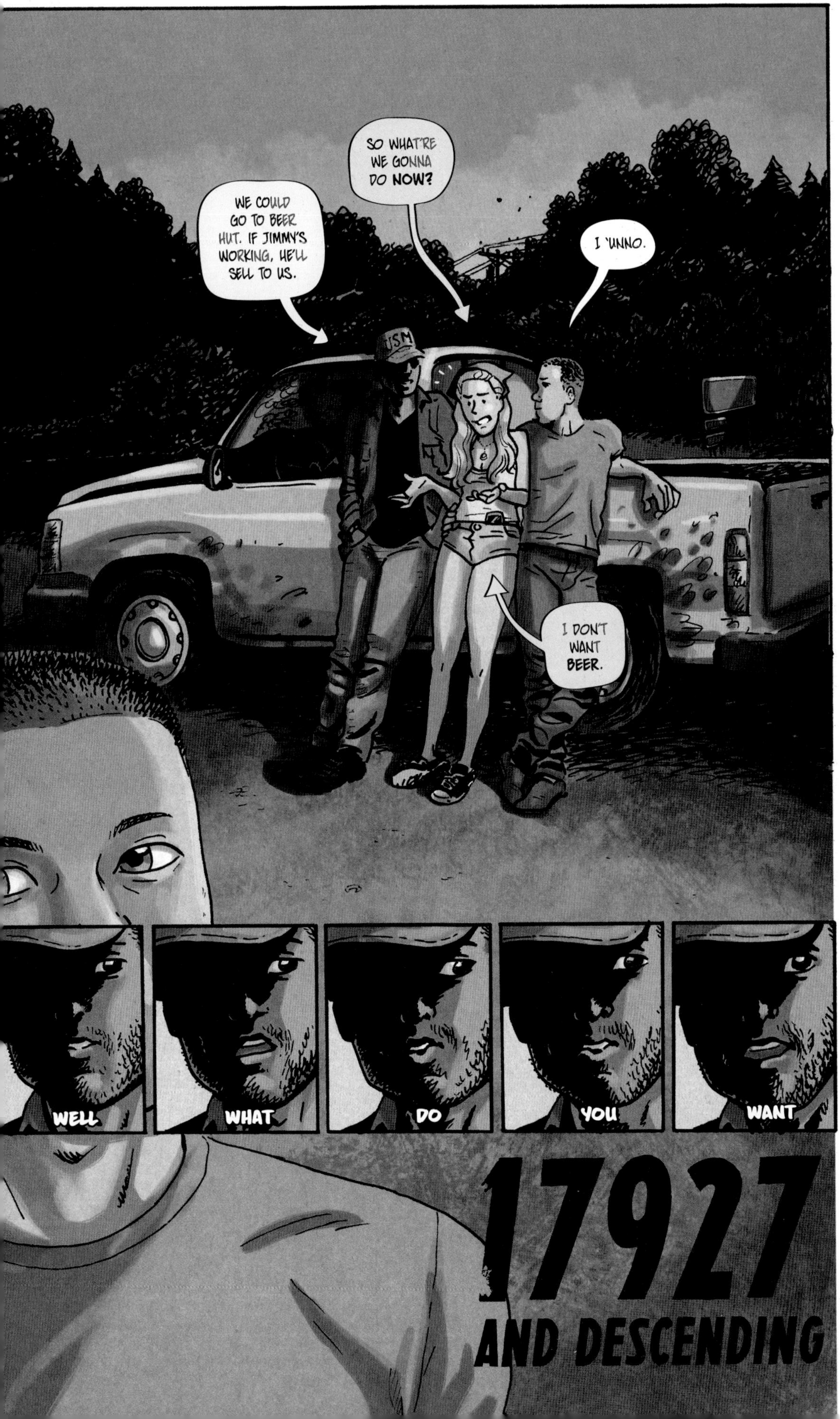
SO WHAT'RE WE GONNA DO NOW?
WE COULD GO TO BEER HUT. IF JIMMY'S WORKING, HE'LL SELL TO US.
I 'UNNO.
I DON'T WANT BEER.
WELL
WHAT
DO
YOU
WANT
17927
AND DESCENDING

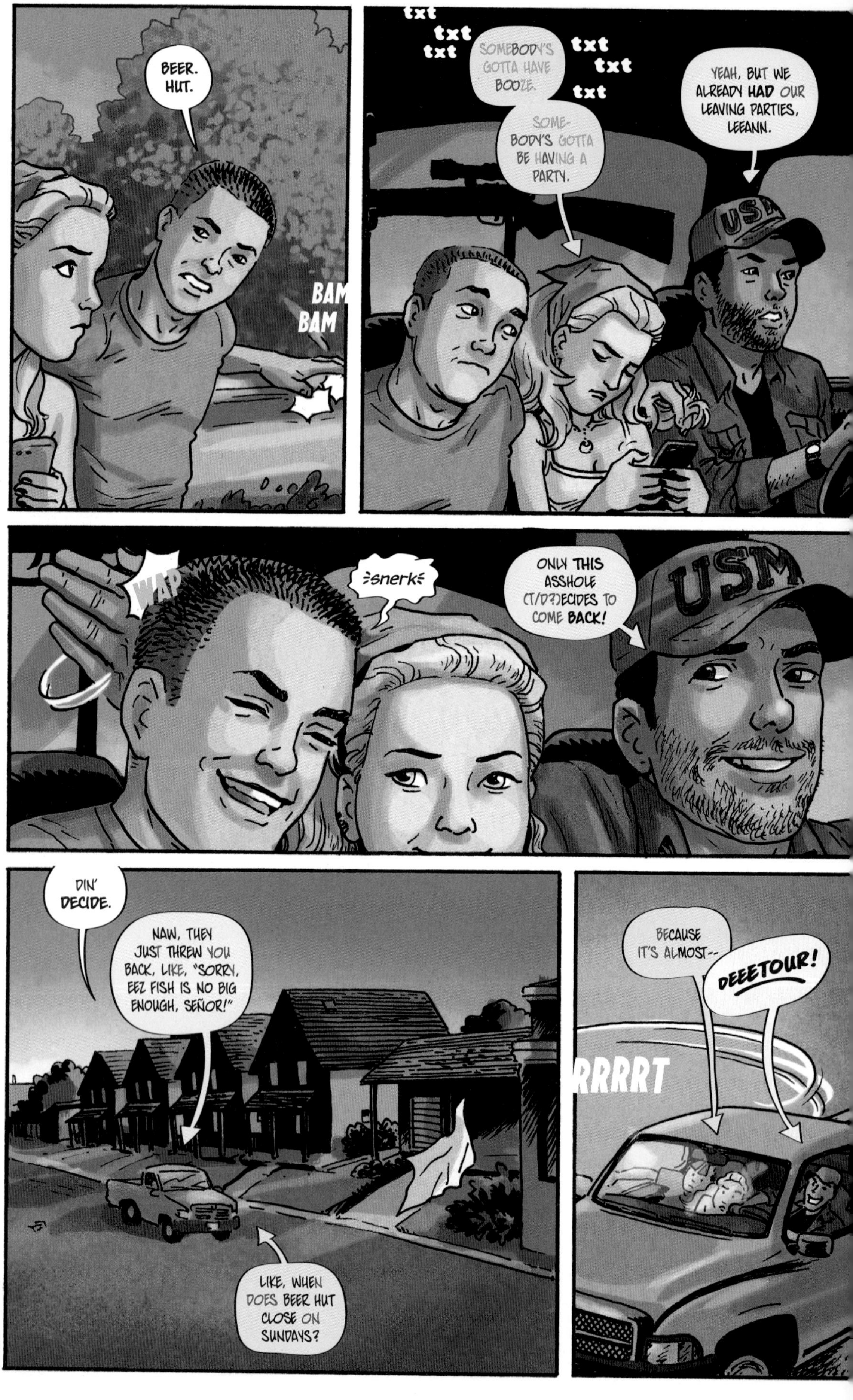
BEER. HUT.
BAM BAM
txt txt txt
SOMEBODY'S GOTTA HAVE BOOZE.
SOME-BODY'S GOTTA BE HAVING A PARTY.
txt txt txt
YEAH, BUT WE ALREADY HAD OUR LEAVING PARTIES, LEEANN.
WAP
snerk
ONLY THIS ASSHOLE (T/D?)ECIDES TO COME BACK!
DIN' DECIDE.
NAW, THEY JUST THREW YOU BACK, LIKE, "SORRY, EEZ FISH IS NO BIG ENOUGH, SEÑOR!"
LIKE, WHEN DOES BEER HUT CLOSE ON SUNDAYS?
BECAUSE IT'S ALMOST--
DEEETOUR!
RRRRT

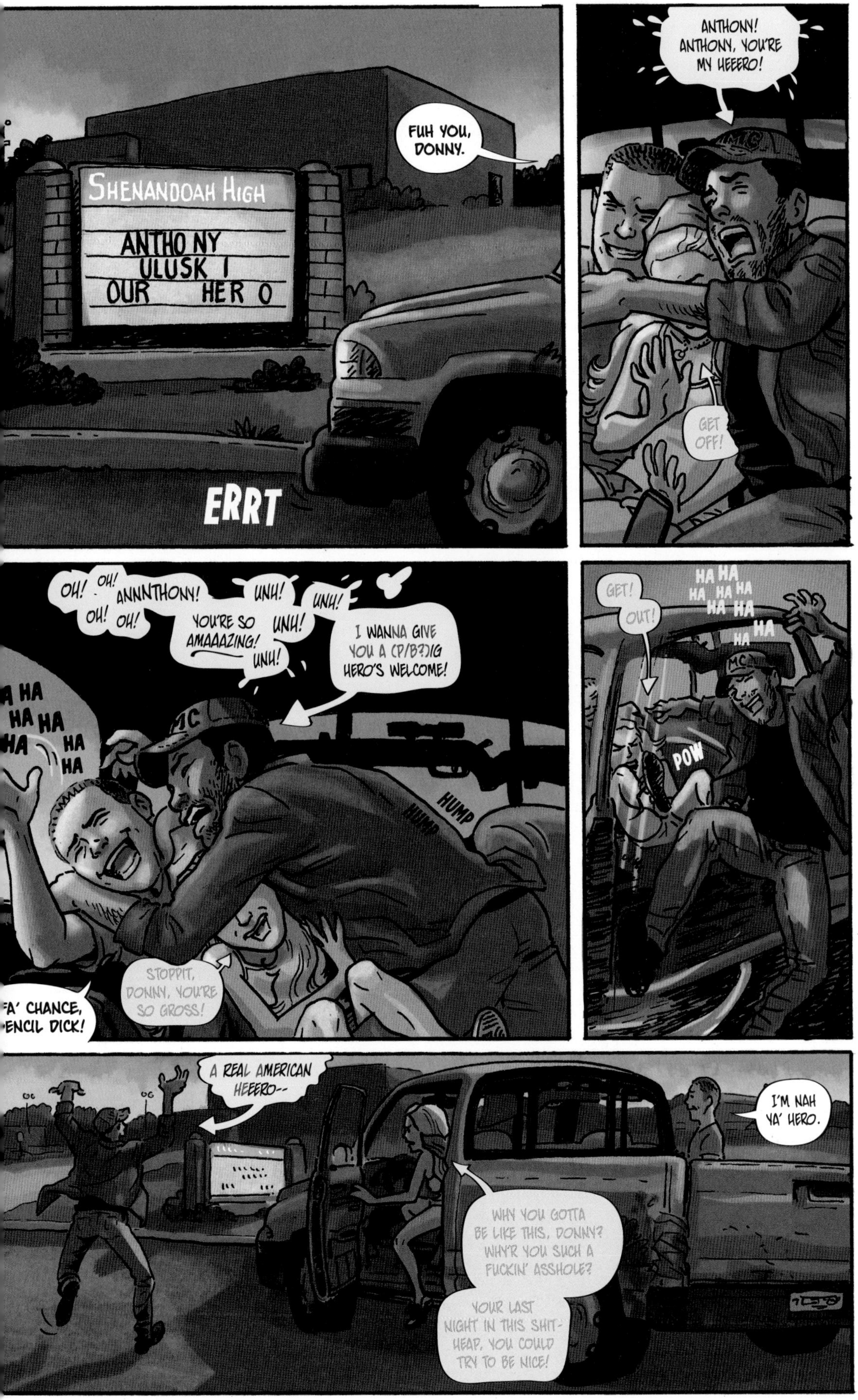

SHENANDOAH HIGH
ANTHO NY ULUSK I OUR HER O
FUH YOU, DONNY.
ERRT
ANTHONY! ANTHONY, YOU'RE MY HEEERO!
GET OFF!
OH! OH! ANNNTHONY! OH! OH!
UNH! YOU'RE SO AMAAAZING! UNH! UNH! UNH!
I WANNA GIVE YOU A (P/B?)IG HERO'S WELCOME!
A HA HA HA HA HA HA HA
HUMP HUMP
'A' CHANCE, ENCIL DICK!
STOPPIT, DONNY, YOU'RE SO GROSS!
GET! OUT!
HA HA HA HA HA HA HA HA HA
POW
A REAL AMERICAN HEEERO--
I'M NAH YA' HERO.
WHY YOU GOTTA BE LIKE THIS, DONNY? WHY'R YOU SUCH A FUCKIN' ASSHOLE?
YOUR LAST NIGHT IN THIS SHIT-HEAP, YOU COULD TRY TO BE NICE!

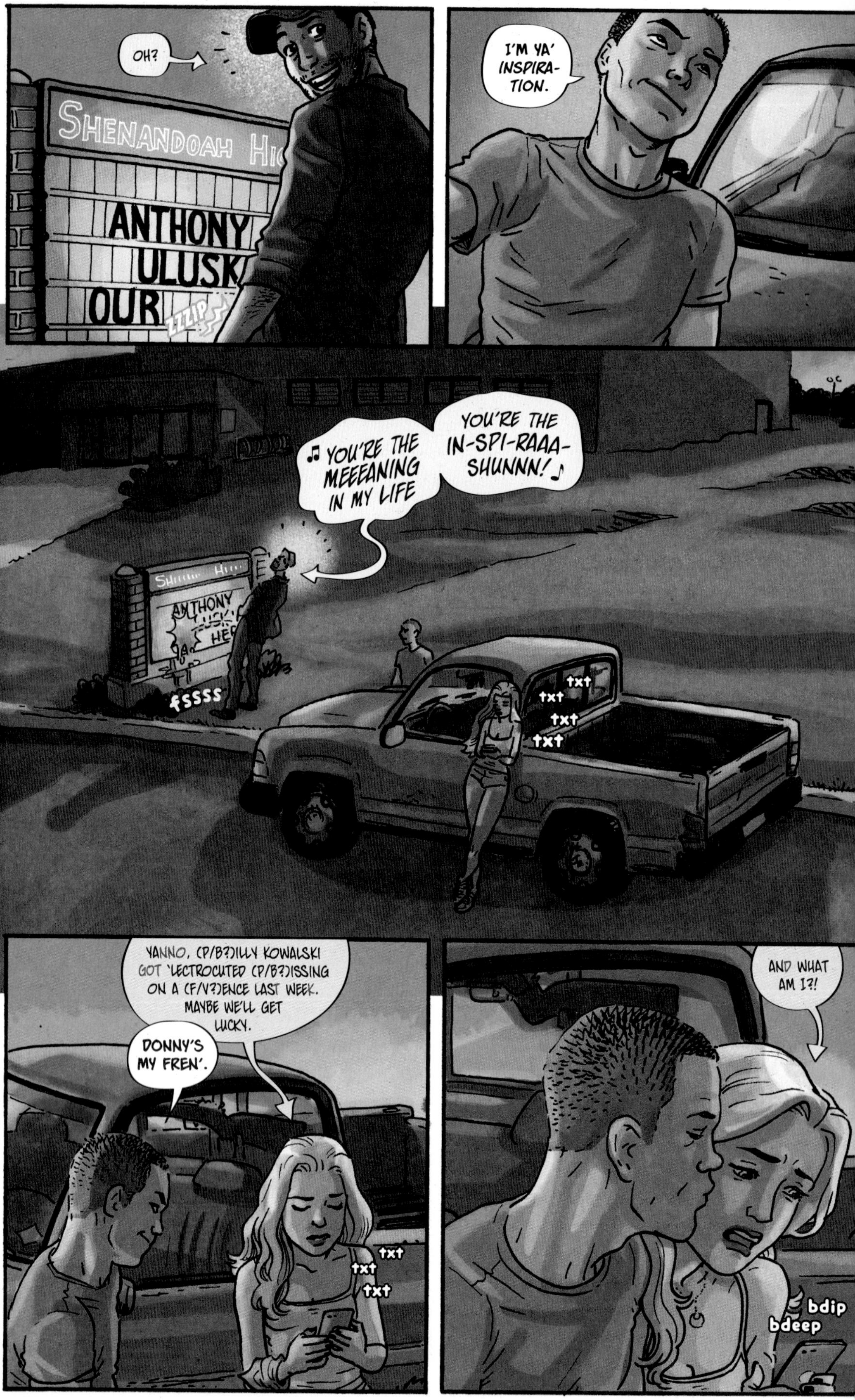
OH?
SHENANDOAH HI
ANTHONY
ULUSK
OUR
ZZZIP
I'M YA' INSPIRA-TION.
♫ YOU'RE THE MEEEANING IN MY LIFE
YOU'RE THE IN-SPI-RAAA-SHUNNN! ♪
ANTHONY
FSSSS
txt
txt
txt
txt
YANNO, (P/B?)ILLY KOWALSKI GOT 'LECTROCUTED (P/B?)ISSING ON A (F/V?)ENCE LAST WEEK. MAYBE WE'LL GET LUCKY.
DONNY'S MY FREN'.
txt
txt
txt
AND WHAT AM I?!
bdip
bdeep

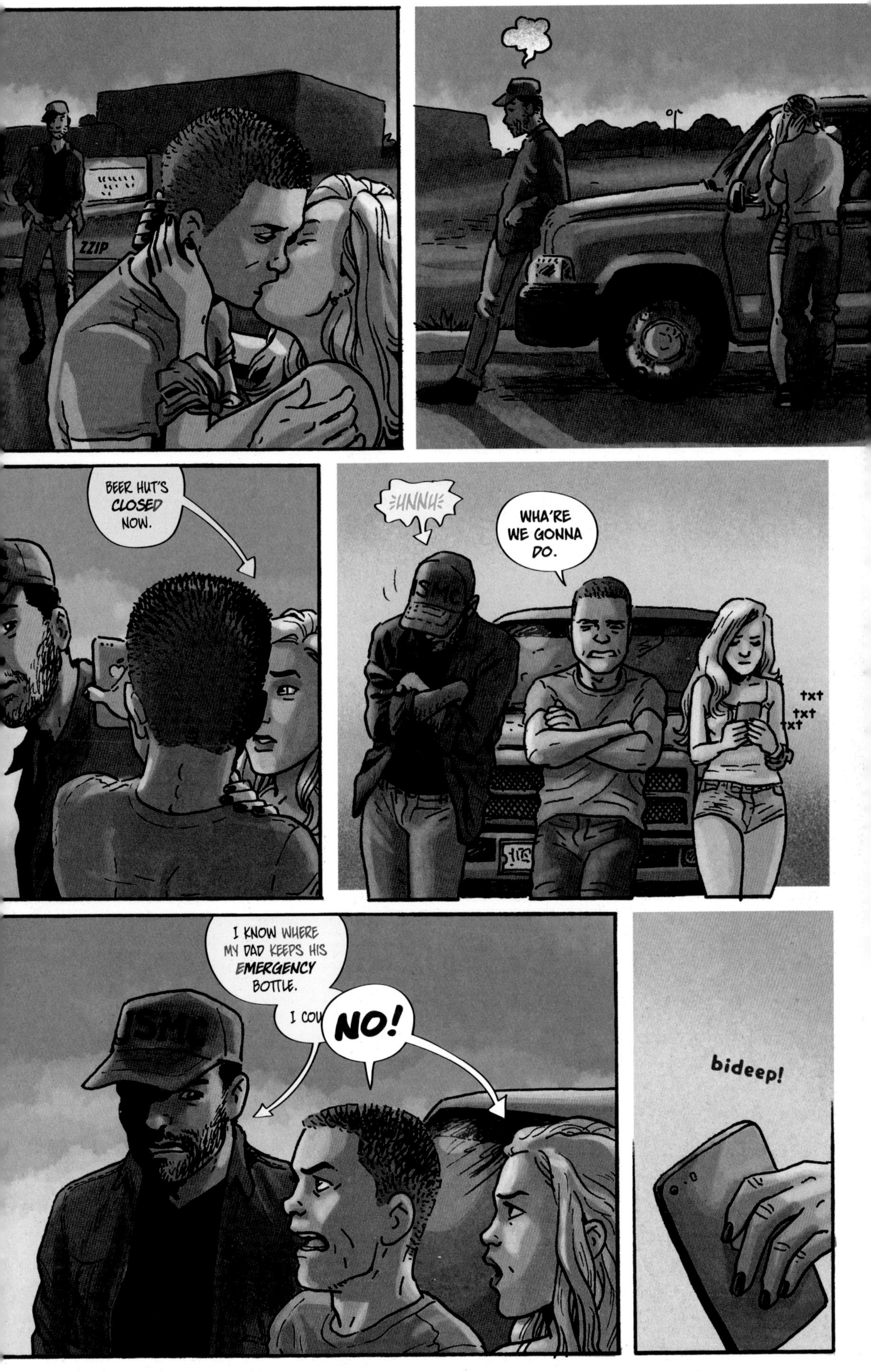
ZZIP
BEER HUT'S CLOSED NOW.
HNNH
WHA'RE WE GONNA DO.
txt
txt
txt
I KNOW WHERE MY DAD KEEPS HIS EMERGENCY BOTTLE.
I COU
NO!
bideep!

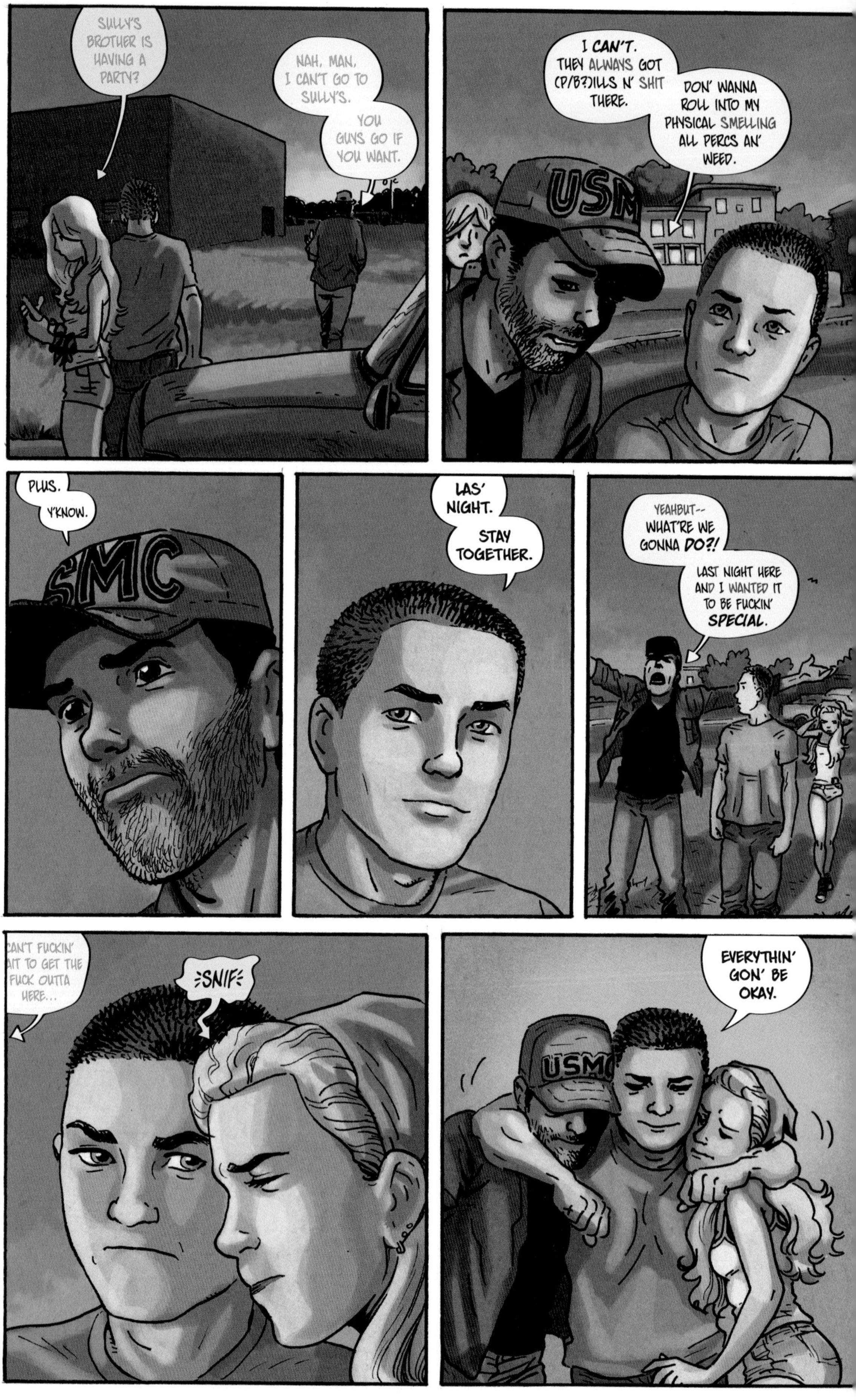
SULLY'S BROTHER IS HAVING A PARTY?
NAH, MAN, I CAN'T GO TO SULLY'S.
YOU GUYS GO IF YOU WANT.
I CAN'T. THEY ALWAYS GOT (P/B?)ILLS N' SHIT THERE.
DON' WANNA ROLL INTO MY PHYSICAL SMELLING ALL PERCS AN' WEED.
USMC
PLUS.
Y'KNOW.
SMC
LAS' NIGHT.
STAY TOGETHER.
YEAHBUT-- WHAT'RE WE GONNA DO?!
LAST NIGHT HERE AND I WANTED IT TO BE FUCKIN' SPECIAL.
CAN'T FUCKIN' AIT TO GET THE FUCK OUTTA HERE...
SNIF
EVERYTHIN' GON' BE OKAY.
USMC

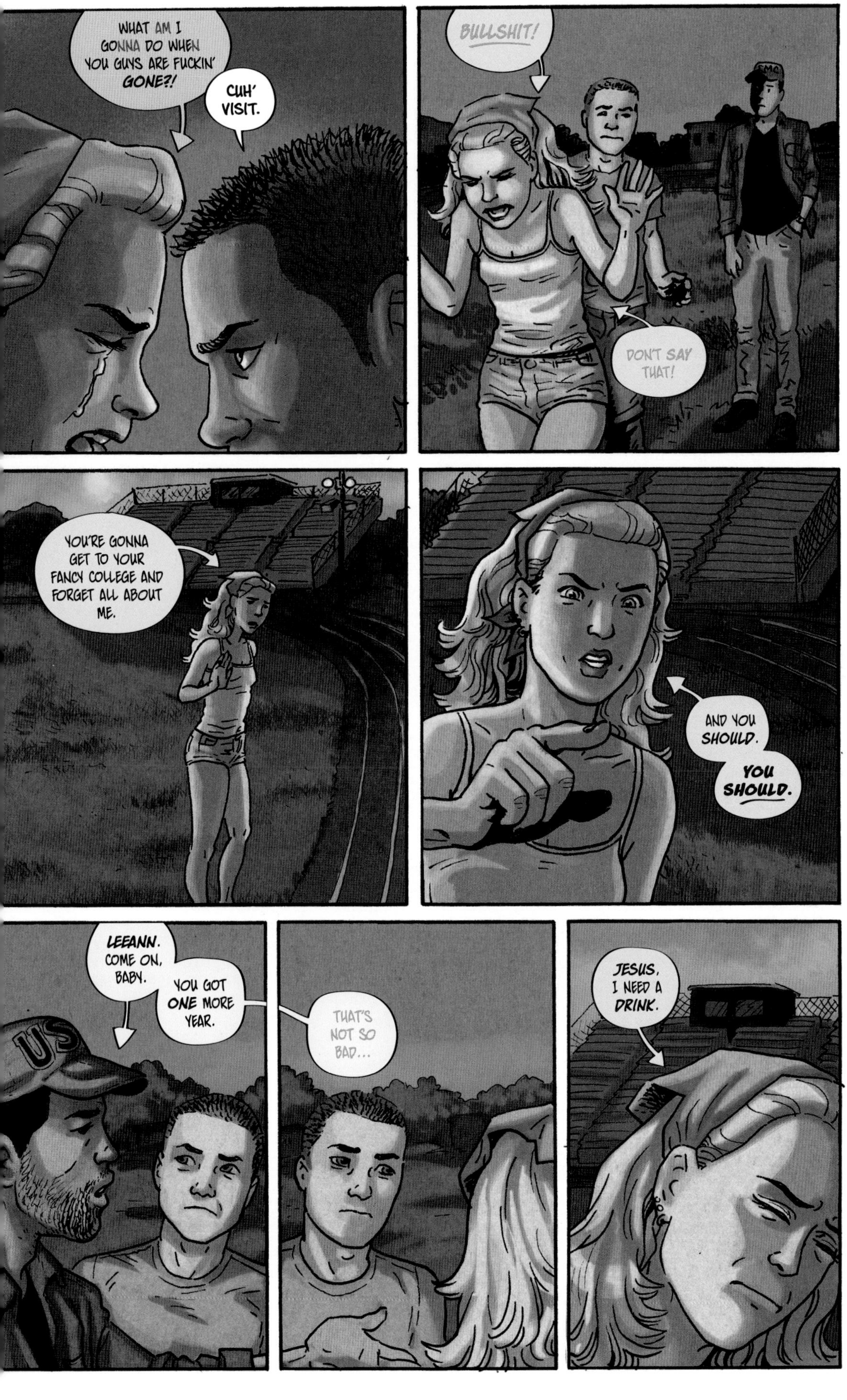
WHAT AM I GONNA DO WHEN YOU GUYS ARE FUCKIN' GONE?!
CUH' VISIT.
BULLSHIT!
DON'T SAY THAT!
YOU'RE GONNA GET TO YOUR FANCY COLLEGE AND FORGET ALL ABOUT ME.
AND YOU SHOULD.
YOU SHOULD.
LEEANN. COME ON, BABY.
YOU GOT ONE MORE YEAR.
THAT'S NOT SO BAD...
JESUS, I NEED A DRINK.

KEYS, DONNY.

GOING TO MY MOM'S.

YOU BOYS DISTRACT HER.

ANTHONY ULUSK OUR HE

RRRT   RRRT

txt
txt
txt
fweesh

txt
txt
fweesh

txt
txt
fweesh

txt
txt
fweesh

txt
txt
fweesh

txt txt
fweesh

txt
txt
txt
txt
txt
txt
txt
txt
txt
txt
txt
fweesh

txt
txt
fweesh

txt
txt txt
txt

bdeep   bding
bdeep

bding
bdeep

bding
bdeep
bding
bdeep

bdeep
bding

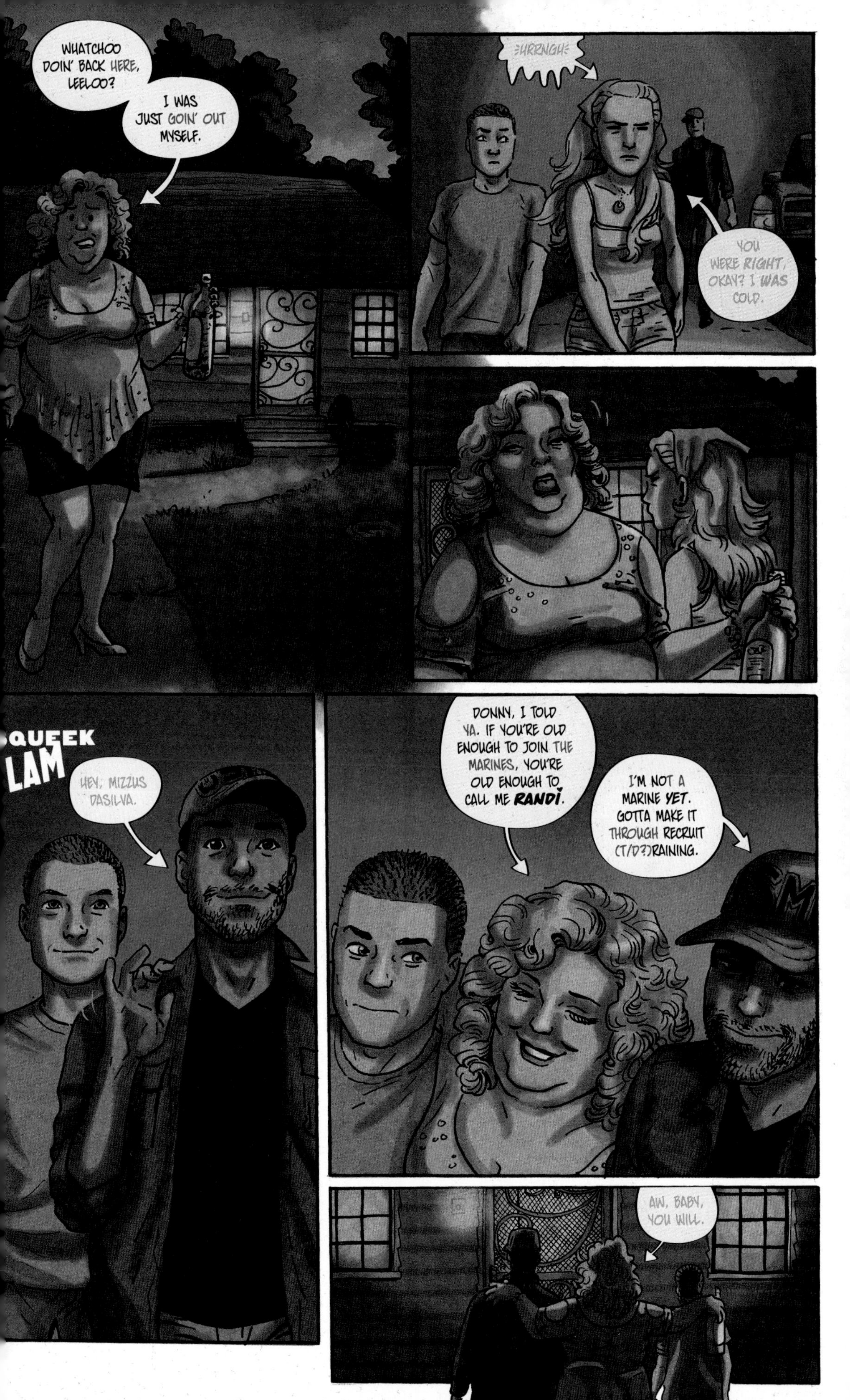
WHATCHOO DOIN' BACK HERE, LEELOO?
I WAS JUST GOIN' OUT MYSELF.
HURRNGH
YOU WERE RIGHT, OKAY? I WAS COLD.
QUEEK
LAM
HEY, MIZZUS DASILVA.
DONNY, I TOLD YA. IF YOU'RE OLD ENOUGH TO JOIN THE MARINES, YOU'RE OLD ENOUGH TO CALL ME RANDI.
I'M NOT A MARINE YET. GOTTA MAKE IT THROUGH RECRUIT (T/D?)RAINING.
AW, BABY, YOU WILL.

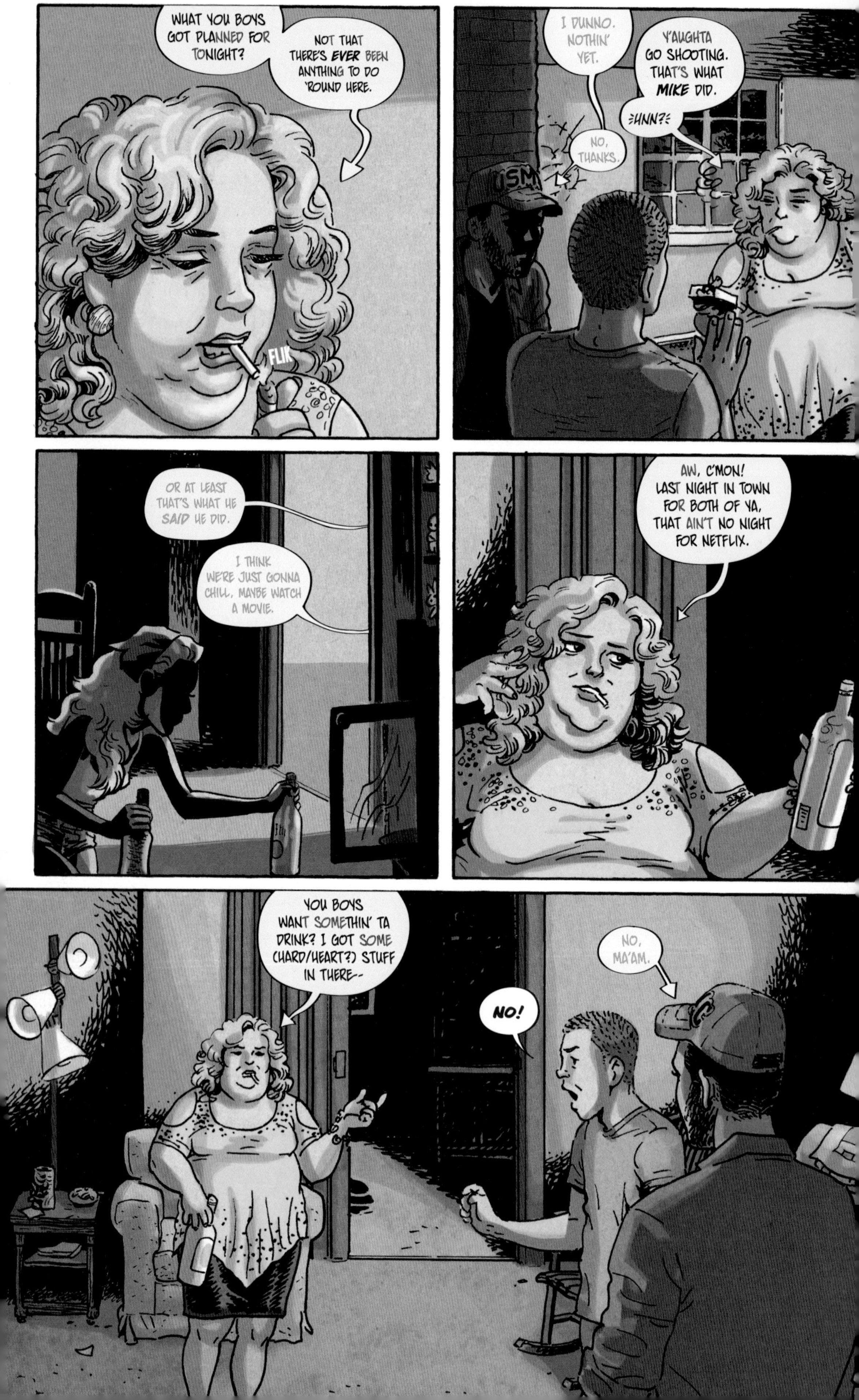
WHAT YOU BOYS GOT PLANNED FOR TONIGHT?
NOT THAT THERE'S EVER BEEN ANYTHING TO DO 'ROUND HERE.
FLIK
I DUNNO. NOTHIN' YET.
Y'AUGHTA GO SHOOTING. THAT'S WHAT MIKE DID.
UNN?
NO, THANKS.
USM
OR AT LEAST THAT'S WHAT HE SAID HE DID.
I THINK WE'RE JUST GONNA CHILL, MAYBE WATCH A MOVIE.
AW, C'MON! LAST NIGHT IN TOWN FOR BOTH OF YA, THAT AIN'T NO NIGHT FOR NETFLIX.
YOU BOYS WANT SOMETHIN' TA DRINK? I GOT SOME (HARD/HEART?) STUFF IN THERE--
NO!
NO, MA'AM.

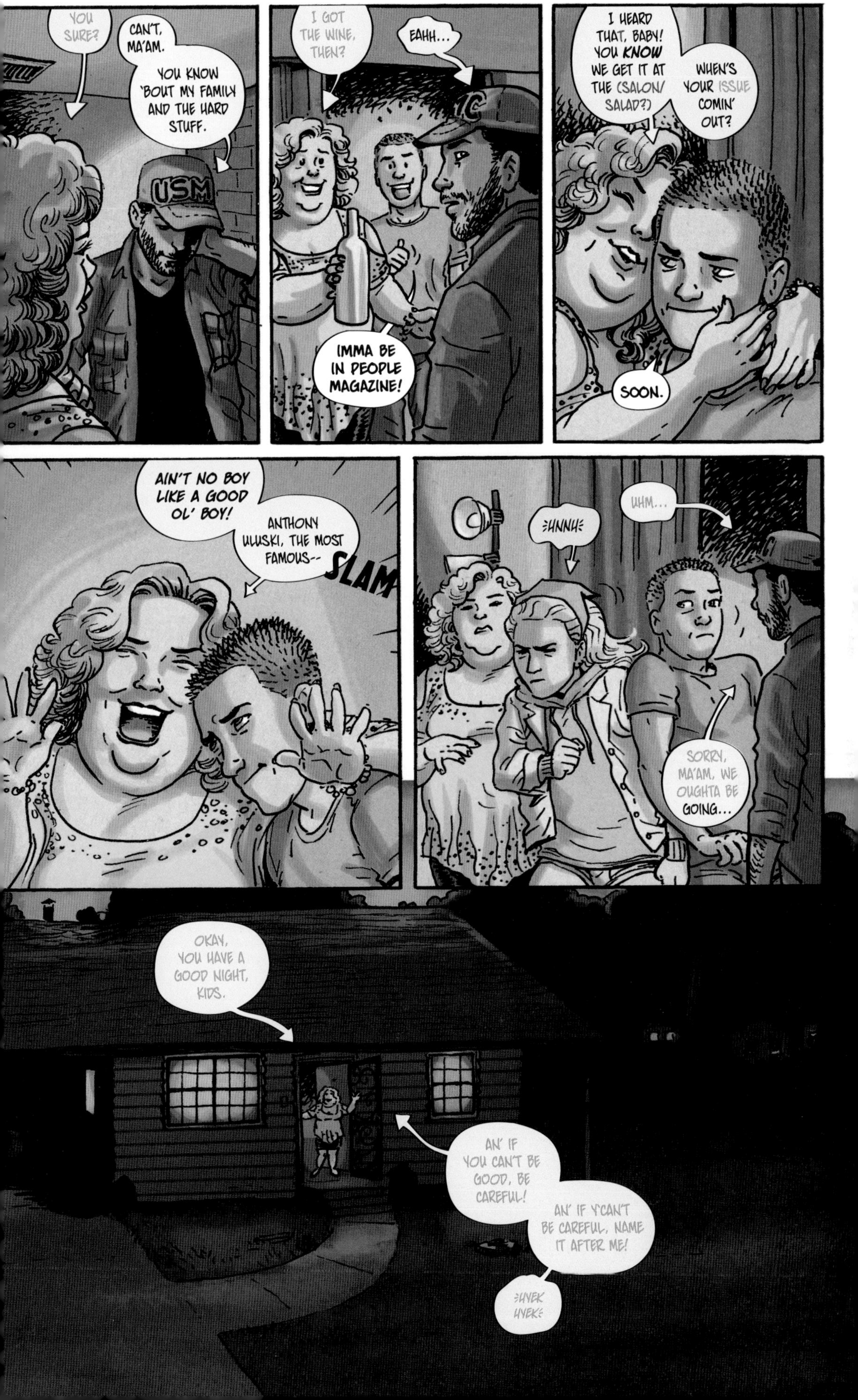
YOU SURE?
CAN'T, MA'AM.
YOU KNOW 'BOUT MY FAMILY AND THE HARD STUFF.
I GOT THE WINE, THEN?
EAHH...
IMMA BE IN PEOPLE MAGAZINE!
I HEARD THAT, BABY! YOU **KNOW** WE GET IT AT THE (SALON/ SALAD?)
WHEN'S YOUR ISSUE COMIN' OUT?
SOON.
AIN'T NO BOY LIKE A GOOD OL' BOY!
ANTHONY ULUSKI, THE MOST FAMOUS--
SLAM
UHNNH
UHM...
SORRY, MA'AM, WE OUGHTA BE GOING...
OKAY, YOU HAVE A GOOD NIGHT, KIDS.
AN' IF YOU CAN'T BE GOOD, BE CAREFUL!
AN' IF Y'CAN'T BE CAREFUL, NAME IT AFTER ME!
HYEK HYEK

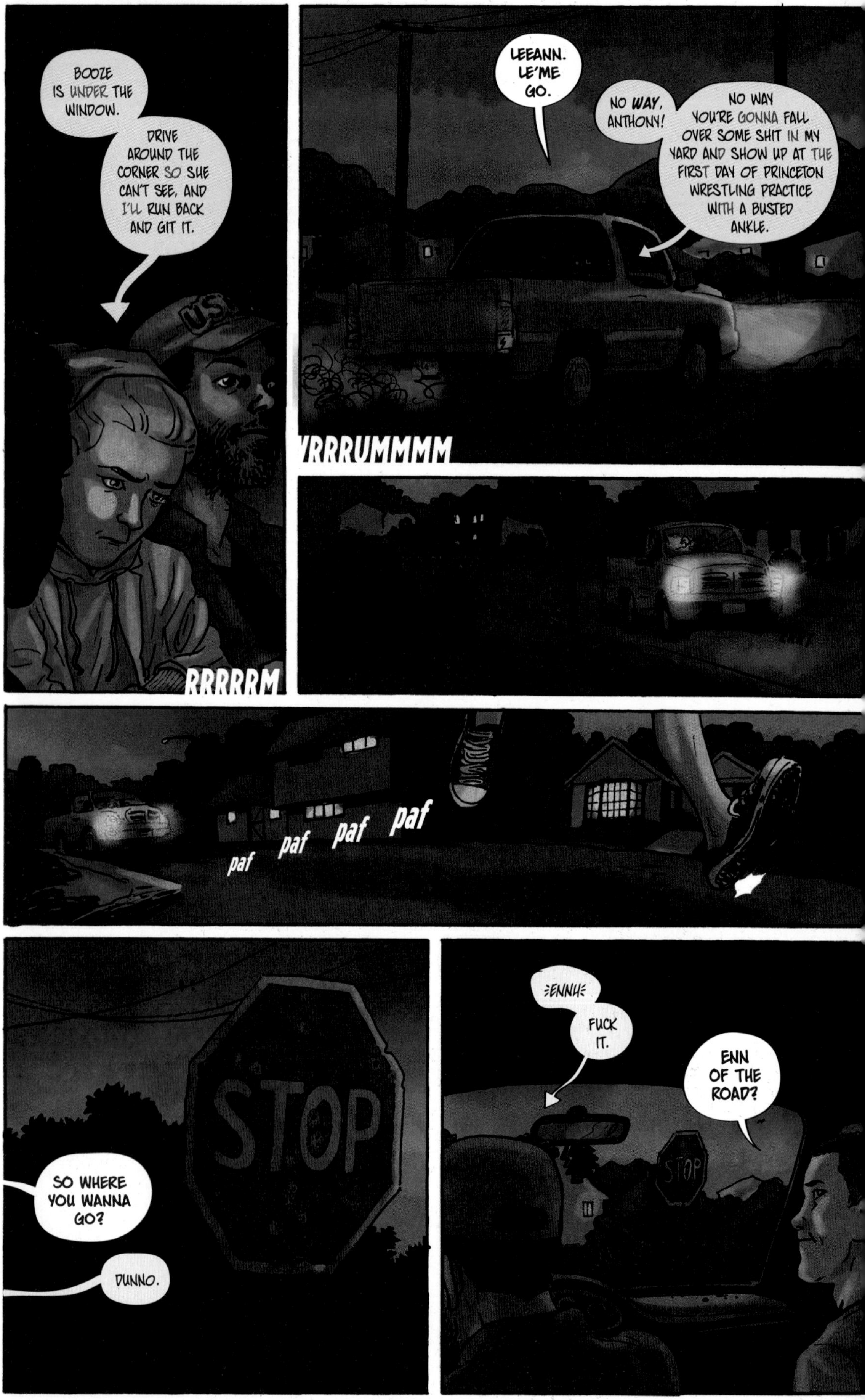
BOOZE IS UNDER THE WINDOW.
DRIVE AROUND THE CORNER SO SHE CAN'T SEE, AND I'LL RUN BACK AND GIT IT.
RRRRRM
LEEANN. LE'ME GO.
NO WAY, ANTHONY!
NO WAY YOU'RE GONNA FALL OVER SOME SHIT IN MY YARD AND SHOW UP AT THE FIRST DAY OF PRINCETON WRESTLING PRACTICE WITH A BUSTED ANKLE.
VRRRUMMMM
paf paf paf paf
STOP
SO WHERE YOU WANNA GO?
DUNNO.
ENNH
FUCK IT.
ENN OF THE ROAD?
STOP

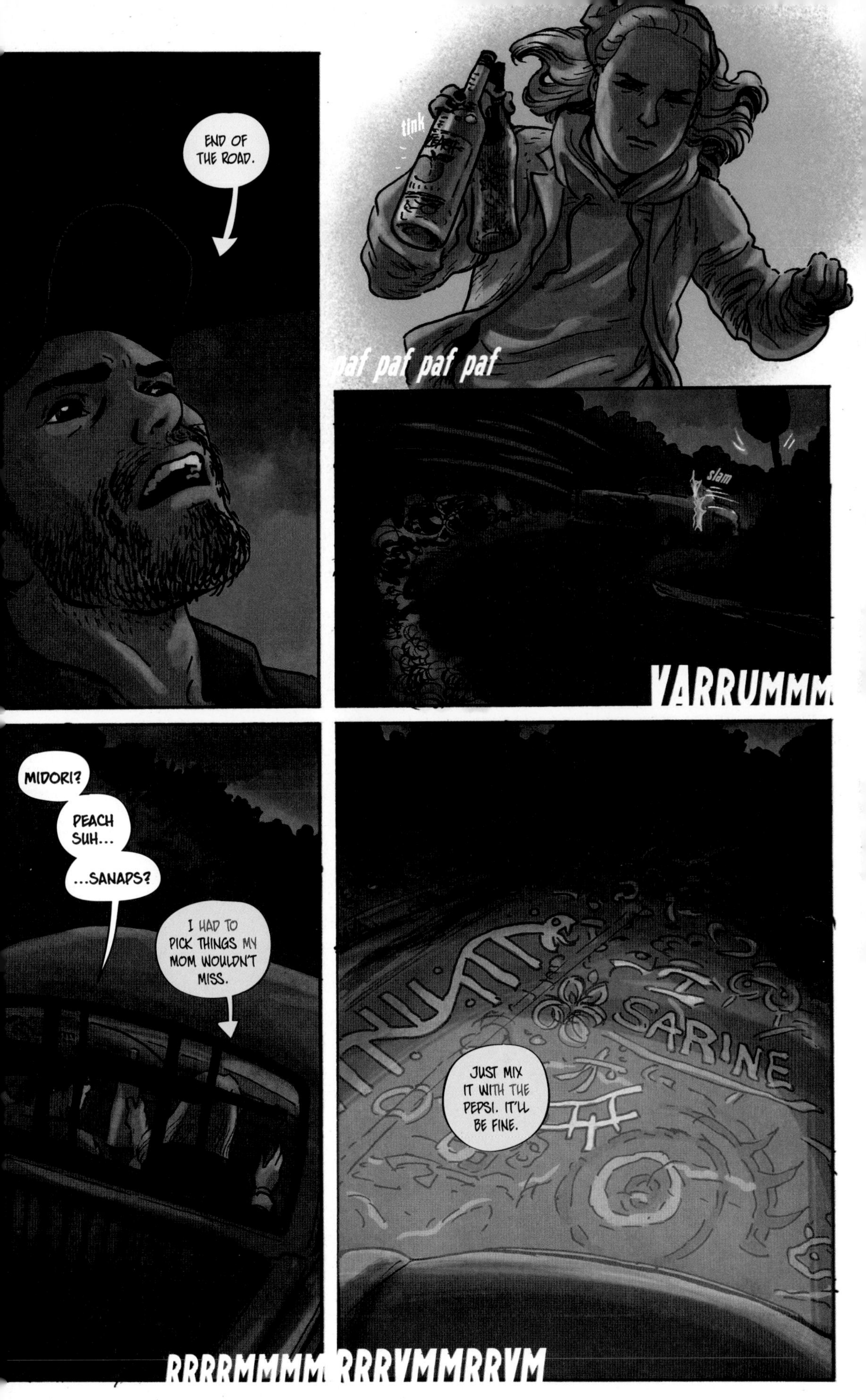
END OF THE ROAD.
tink
paf paf paf paf
slam
VARRUMMM
MIDORI?
PEACH SUH...
...SANAPS?
I HAD TO PICK THINGS MY MOM WOULDN'T MISS.
SARINE
JUST MIX IT WITH THE PEPSI. IT'LL BE FINE.
RRRRMMMM RRRVMMRRVM

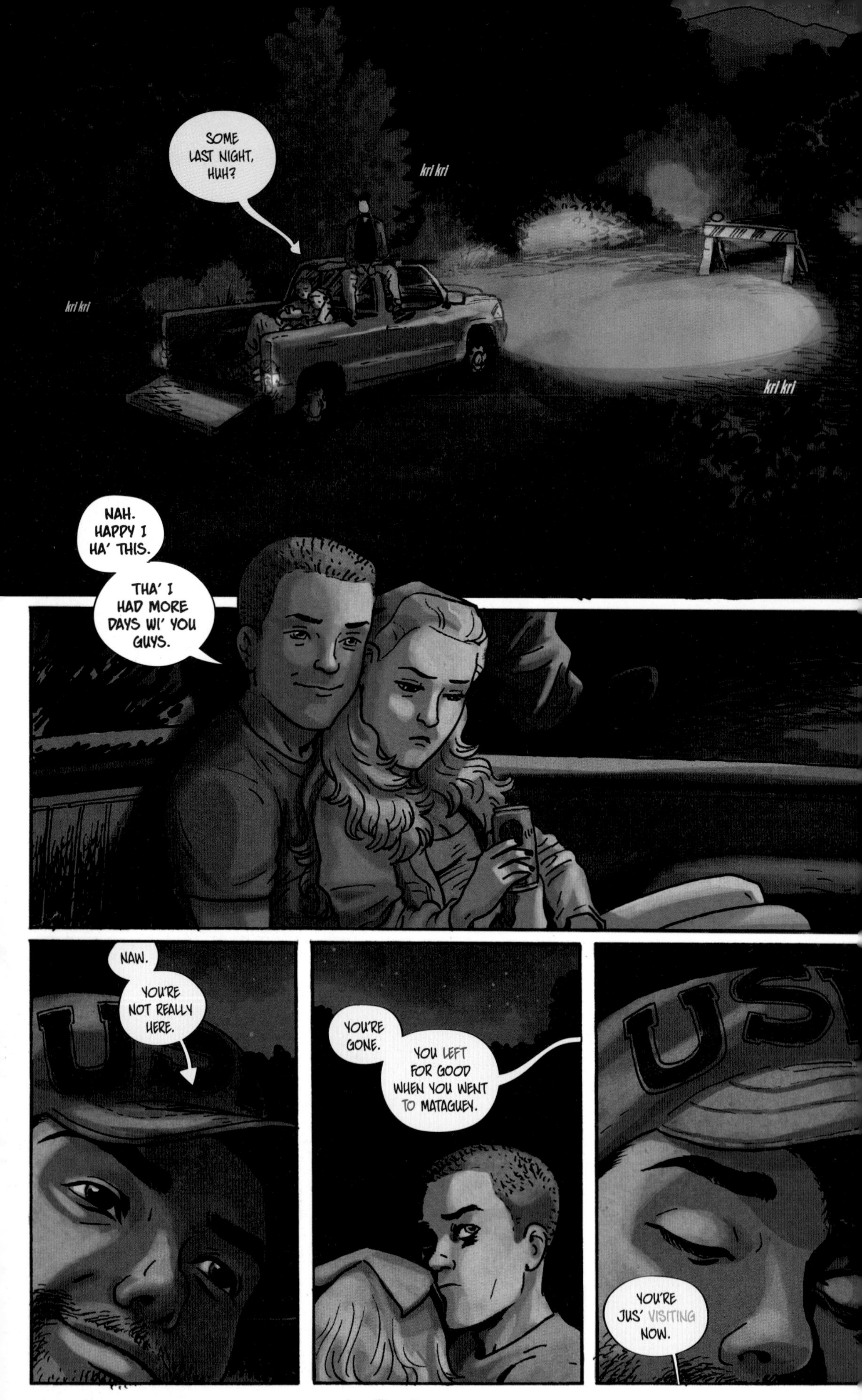
SOME LAST NIGHT, HUH?
kri kri
kri kri
kri kri
NAH. HAPPY I HA' THIS.
THA' I HAD MORE DAYS WI' YOU GUYS.
NAW.
YOU'RE NOT REALLY HERE.
YOU'RE GONE.
YOU LEFT FOR GOOD WHEN YOU WENT TO MATAGUEY.
YOU'RE JUS' VISITING NOW.

NAH' FAIR! YOU'RE GOIN' PISSBURGH TOMORROW, JOIN TH' MARINES!

I AIN'T GONNA MAKE IT, ANTHONY.

WHA'.

THEY GOT AN *EXAM.*

BEFORE I EVEN *GET* TO *BOOT* CAMP.

I'LL GO WI' YOU TO PISSBURGH.

GOD. NO. GO TO FUCKING *PRINCETON.* SHOW UP FOR PRACTICE.

I'LL GO WI' YOU.

NO!

I FUCK IT UP, YOU THINK I WANT ANYBODY THERE TO *SEE* IT?

ESPECIALLY YOU.

gluk

HEYYY DONNNY...

slish

krl krl

krl krl

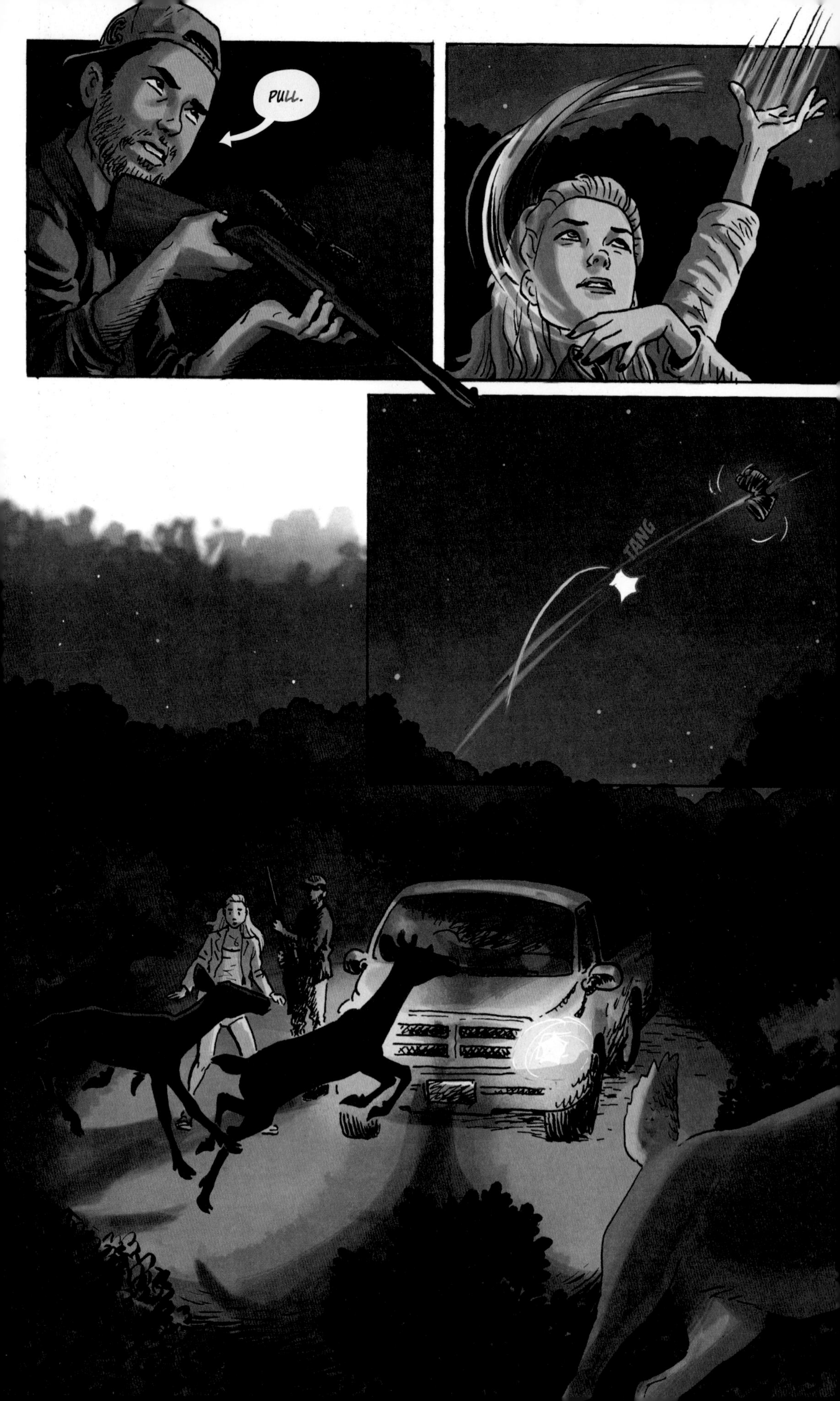
PULL.
TANG

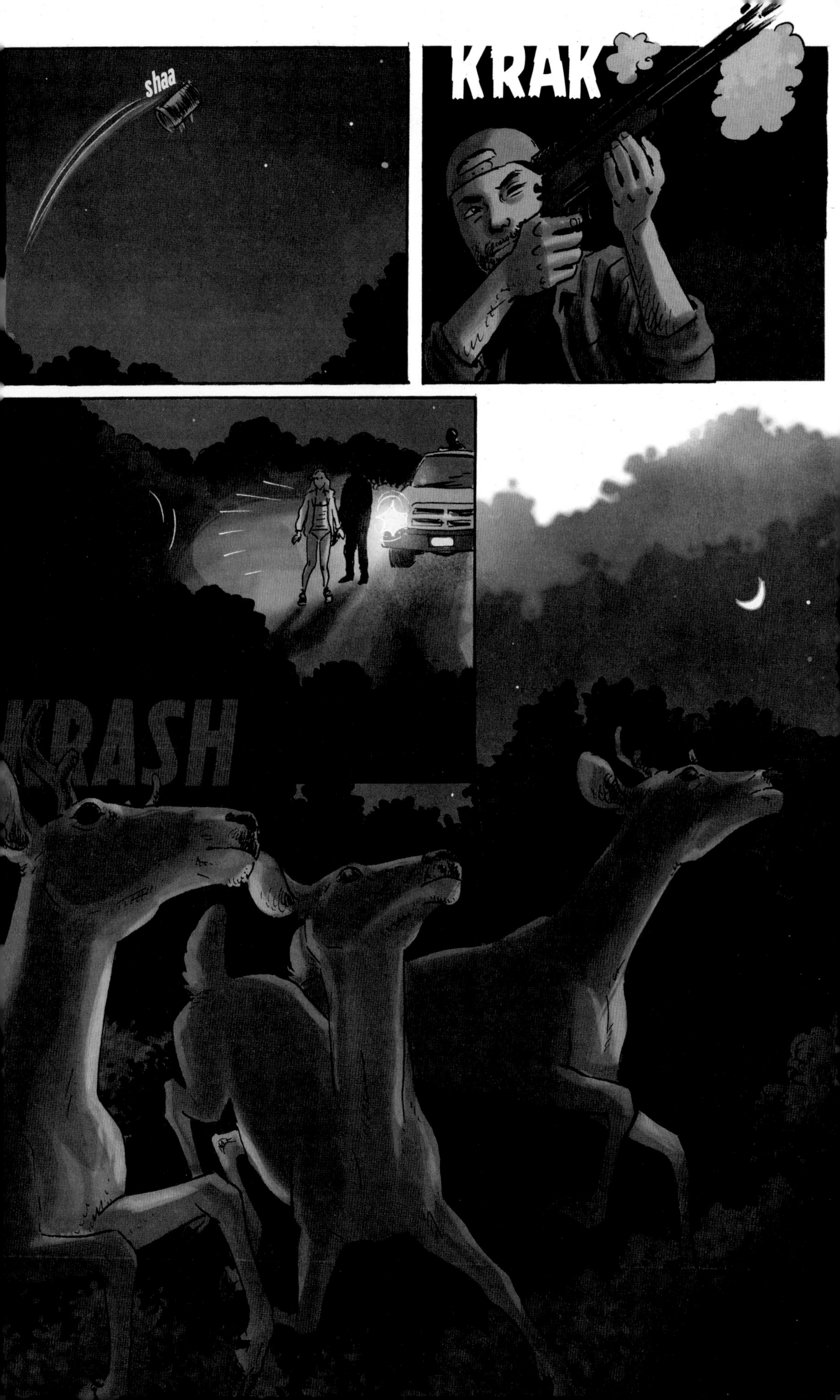
shaa
KRAK
KRASH

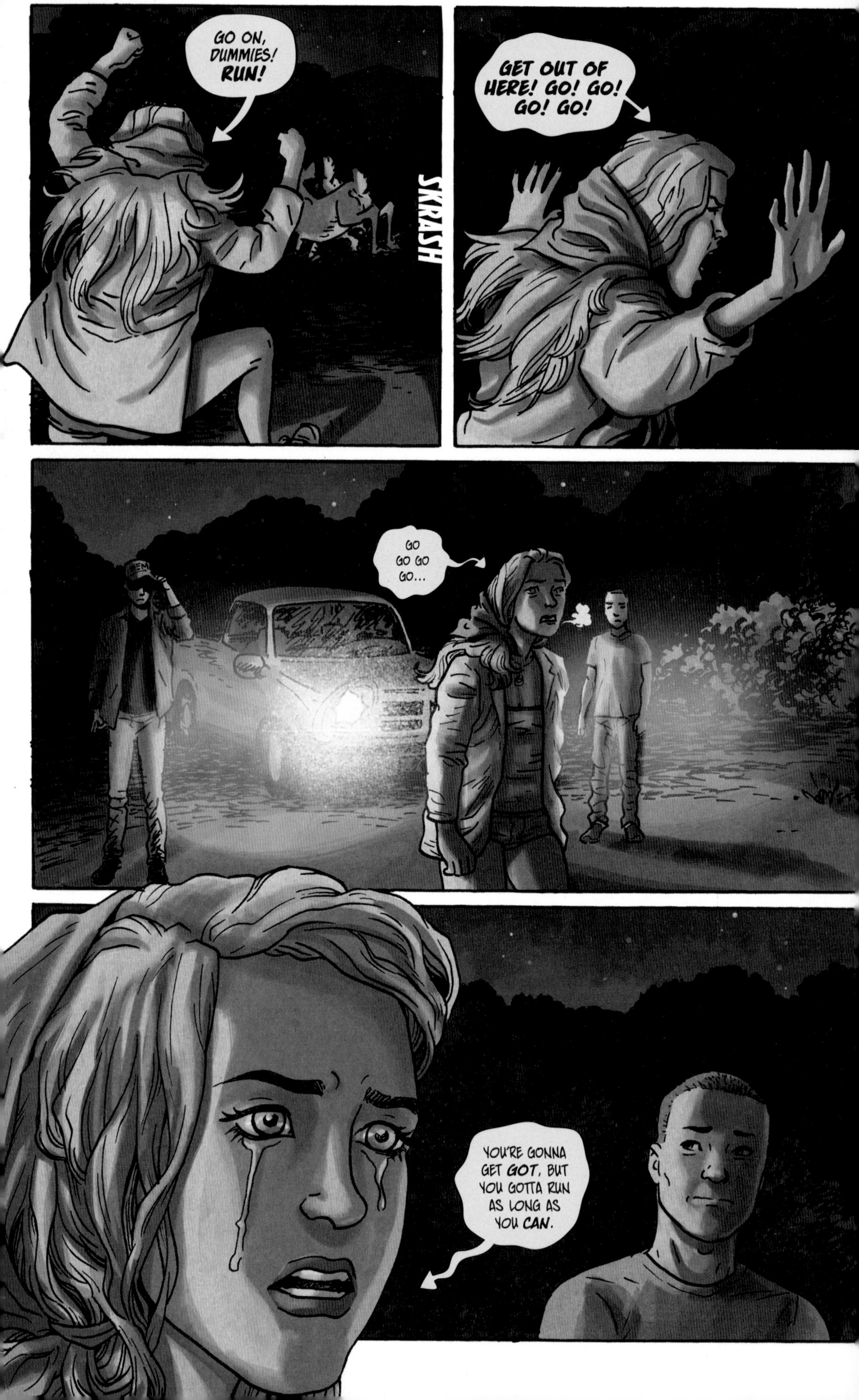
GO ON, DUMMIES! RUN!
SKRASH
GET OUT OF HERE! GO! GO! GO! GO!
GO GO GO GO...
YOU'RE GONNA GET GOT, BUT YOU GOTTA RUN AS LONG AS YOU CAN.

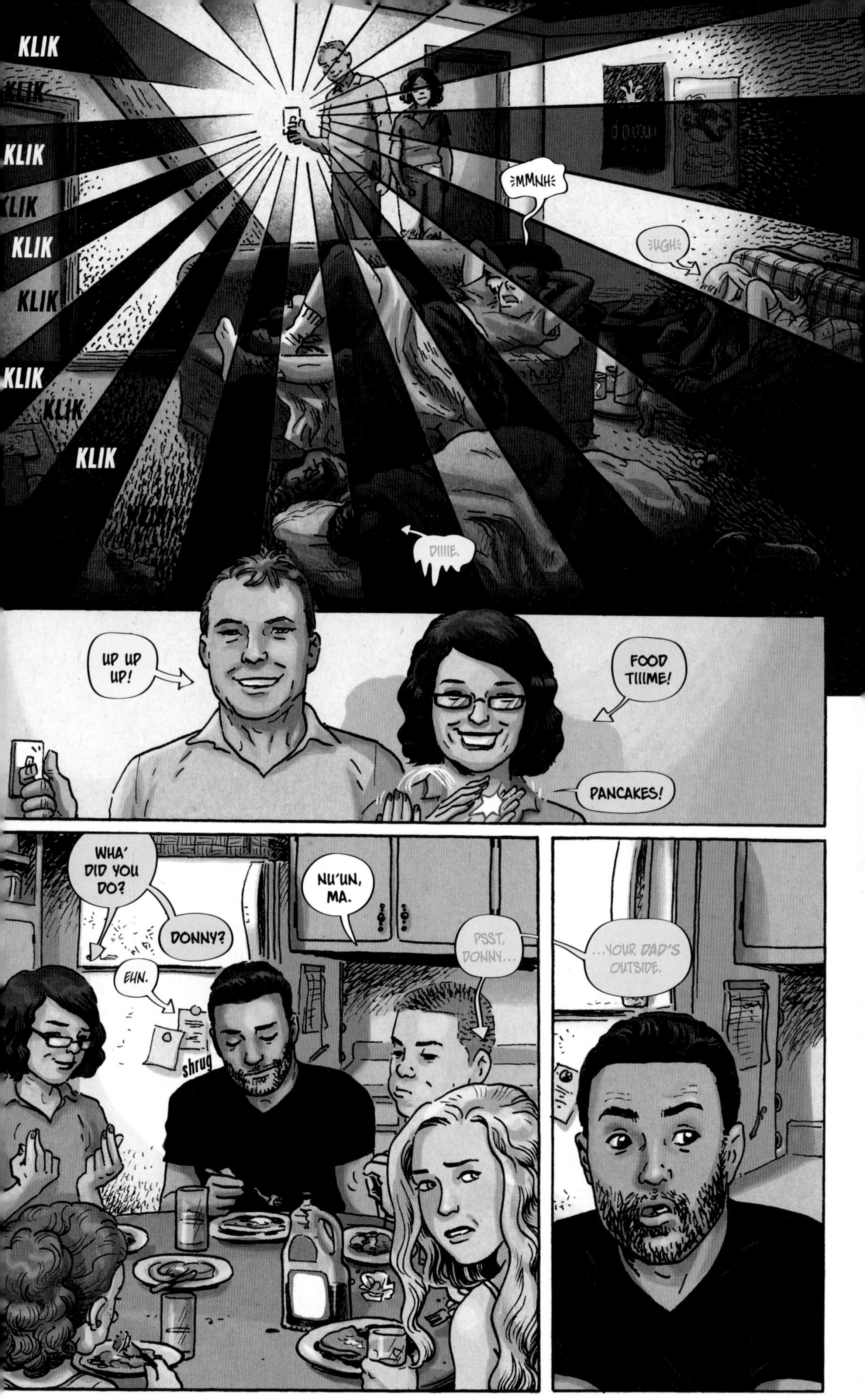

KLIK
KLIK
KLIK
KLIK
KLIK
KLIK
KLIK
KLIK
KLIK
MMNH
UGH
DIIIIE.
UP UP UP!
FOOD TIIIME!
PANCAKES!
WHA' DID YOU DO?
DONNY?
EHN.
shrug
NU'UN, MA.
PSST, DONNY...
...YOUR DAD'S OUTSIDE.

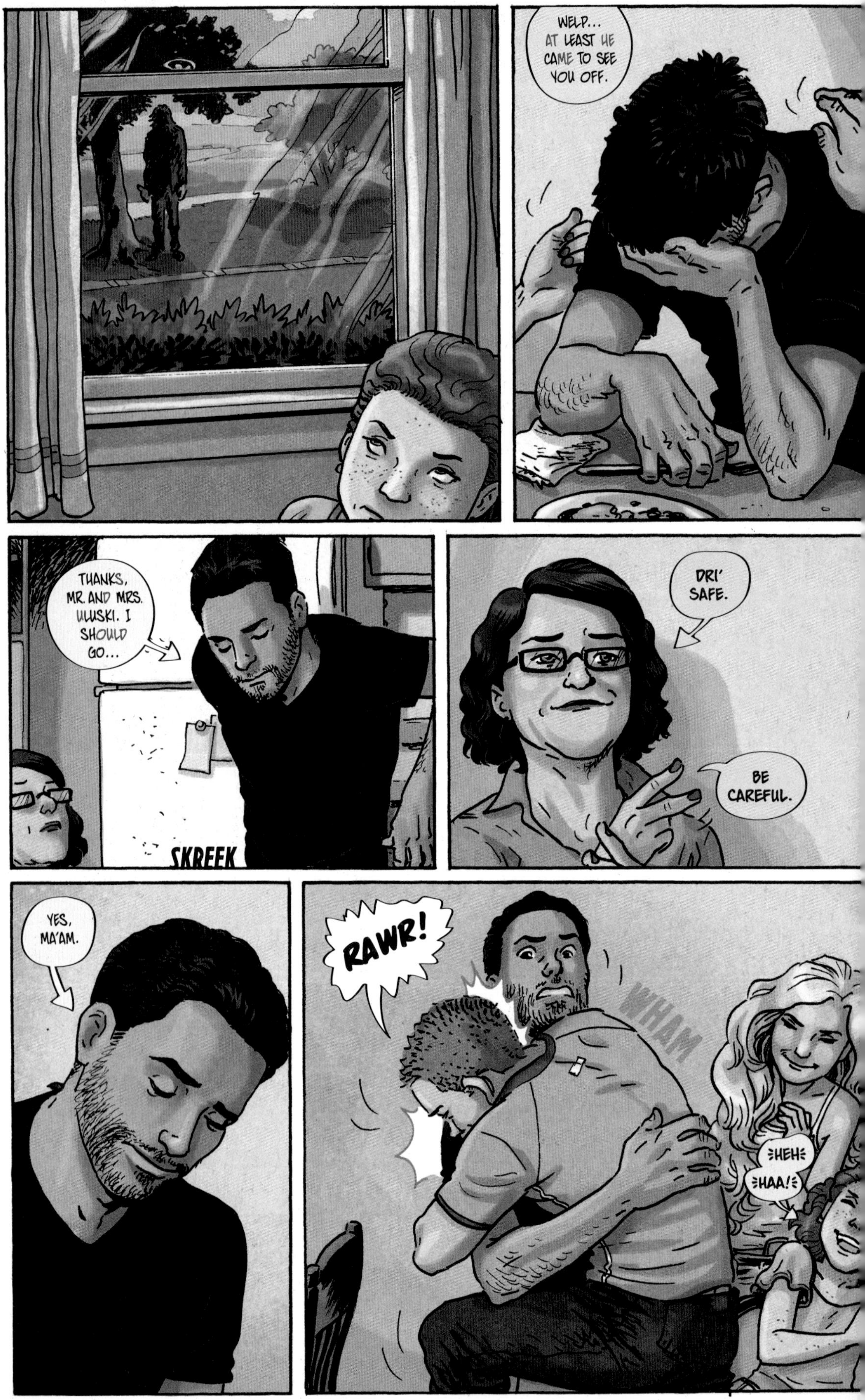
WELP... AT LEAST HE CAME TO SEE YOU OFF.
THANKS, MR. AND MRS. ULUSKI. I SHOULD GO...
SKREEK
DRI' SAFE.
BE CAREFUL.
YES, MA'AM.
RAWR!
WHAM
HEH
HAA!

MARINE.

LOSER.

WAP

NUH-UH.

WINNERS.

BOTH OF US.

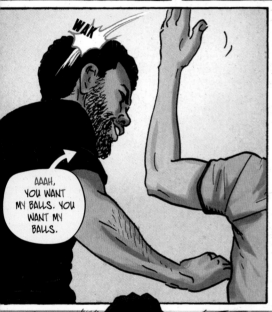

WAK

AAAH, YOU WANT MY BALLS. YOU WANT MY BALLS.

YOU'RE A BUTT, DONNY!

BYE!

GOOD LUCK!

VRRRRM

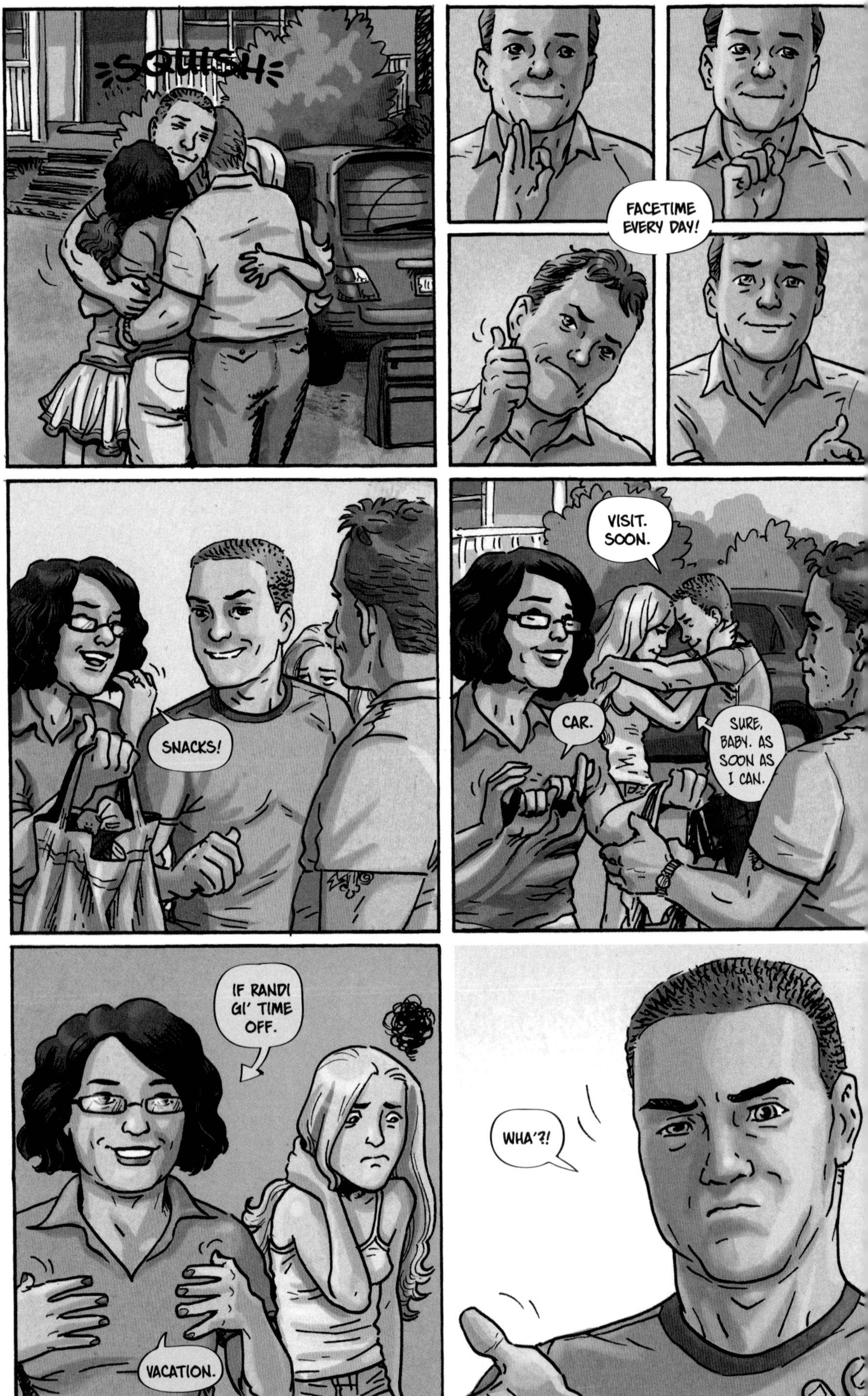
SQUISH
FACETIME EVERY DAY!
SNACKS!
VISIT. SOON.
CAR.
SURE, BABY. AS SOON AS I CAN.
IF RANDI GI' TIME OFF.
VACATION.
WHA'?!

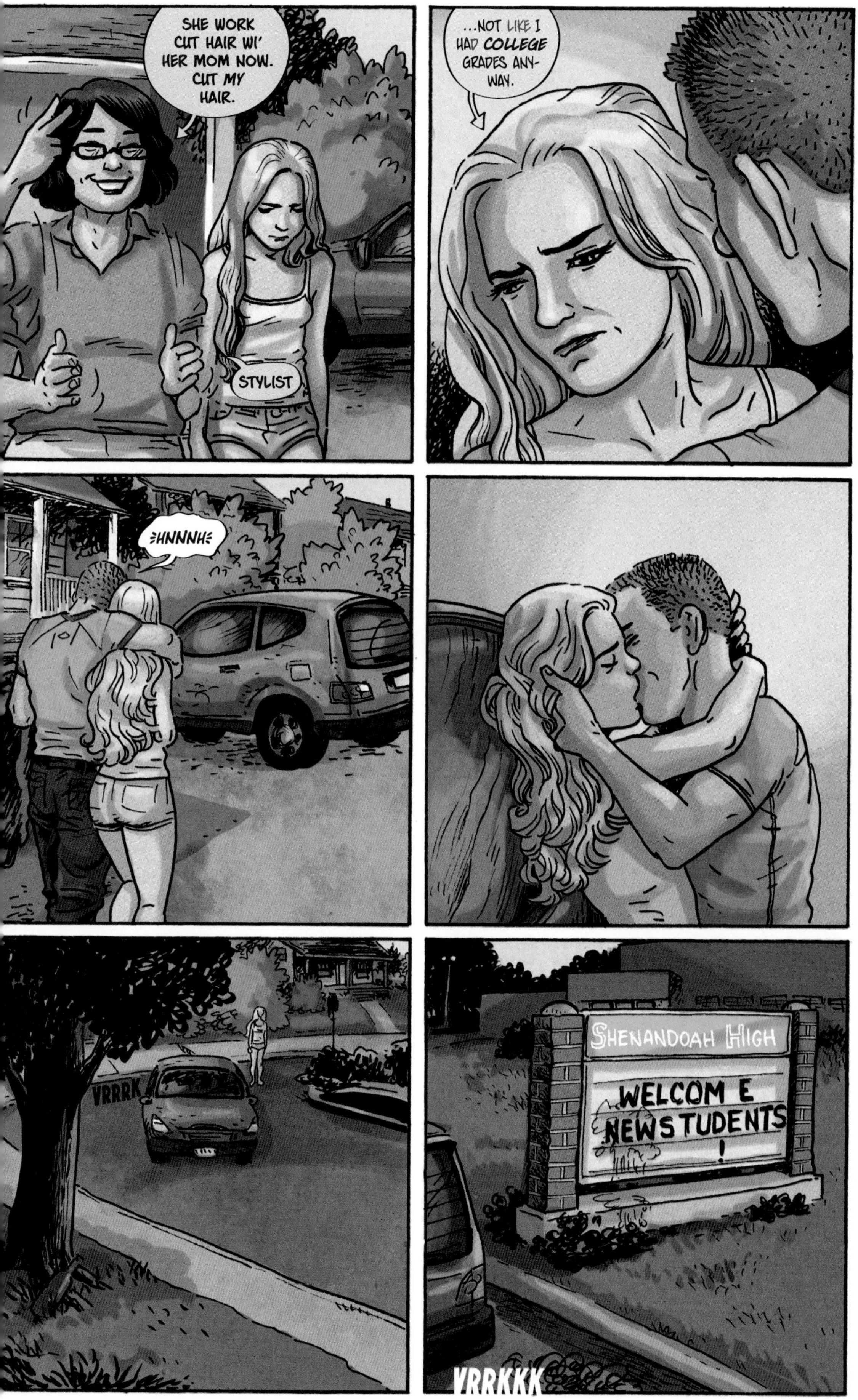
SHE WORK CUT HAIR WI' HER MOM NOW. CUT MY HAIR.
STYLIST
...NOT LIKE I HAD COLLEGE GRADES ANY-WAY.
HNNNH
VRRRK
SHENANDOAH HIGH
WELCOM E NEWS TUDENTS !
VRRKKK

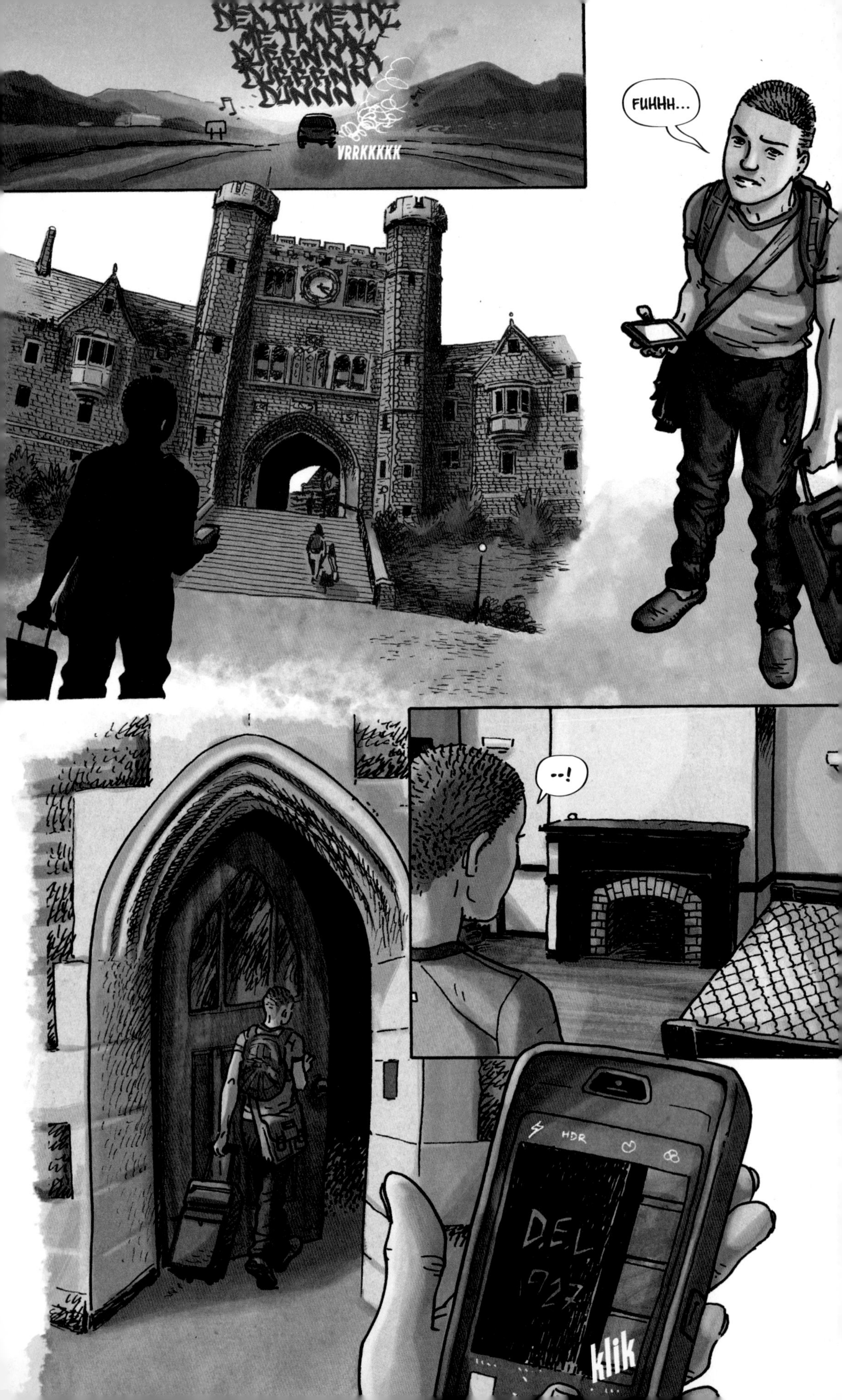
VRRKKKKK
FUHHH...
--!
HDR
klik

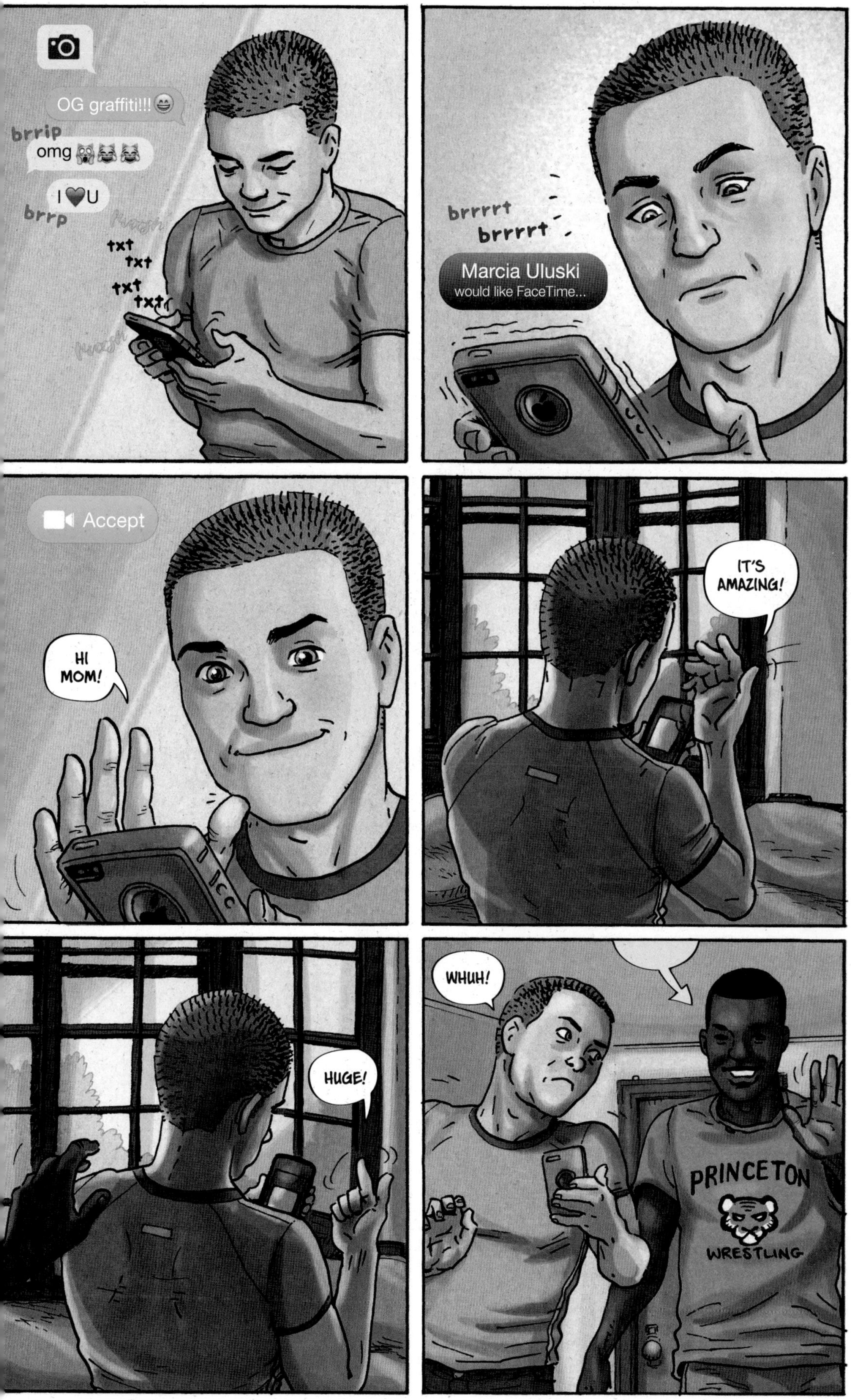

OG graffiti!!!
brrip
omg
I ♥ U
brrp
txt
txt
txt
txt
brrrrt
brrrrt
Marcia Uluski
would like FaceTime...
Accept
HI MOM!
IT'S AMAZING!
HUGE!
WHUH!
PRINCETON
WRESTLING

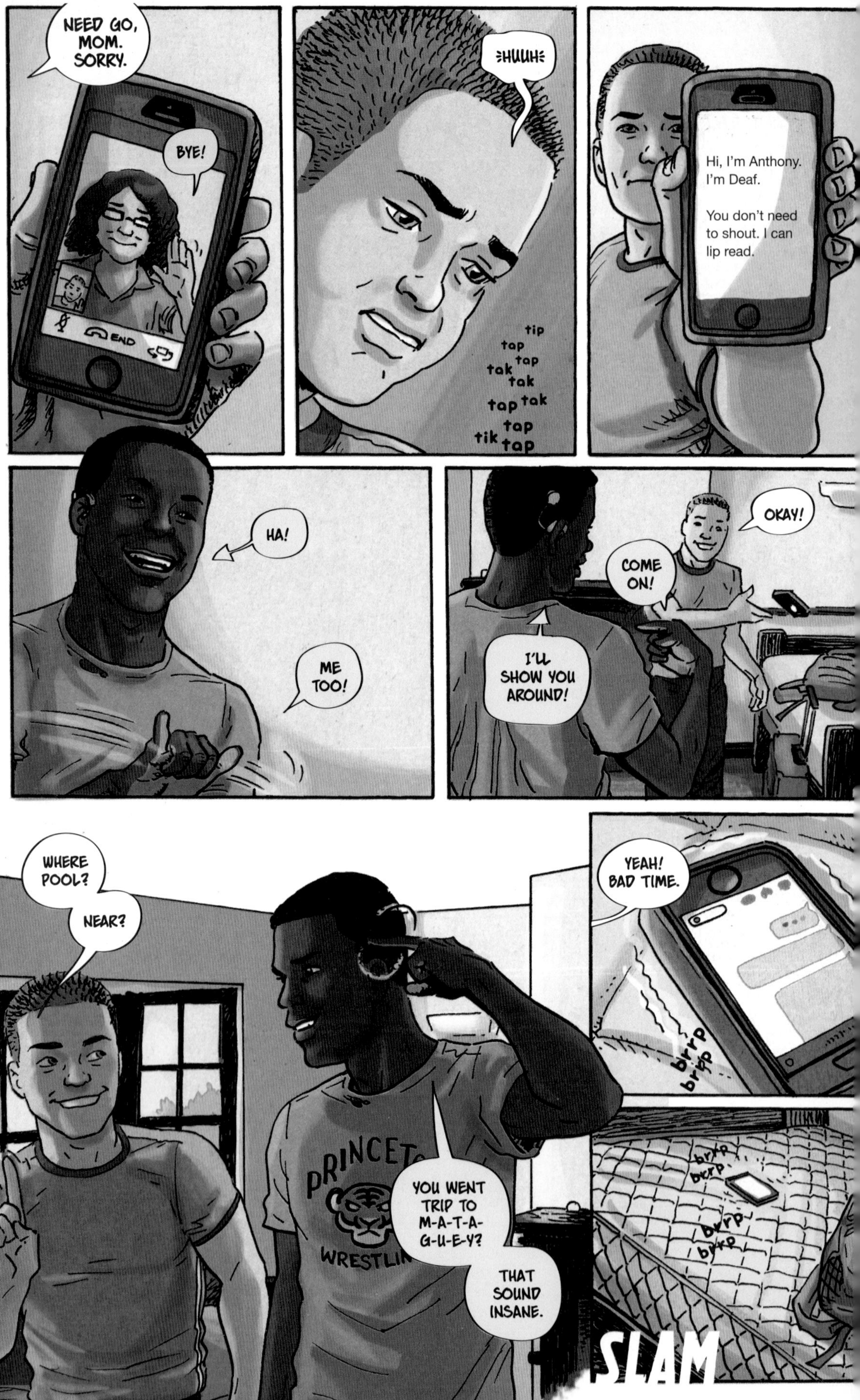
NEED GO, MOM. SORRY.
BYE!
END
HUUH
tip tap tap tak tak tap tak tik tap tap
Hi, I'm Anthony. I'm Deaf.
You don't need to shout. I can lip read.
HA!
ME TOO!
OKAY!
COME ON!
I'LL SHOW YOU AROUND!
WHERE POOL?
NEAR?
YOU WENT TRIP TO M-A-T-A-G-U-E-Y?
THAT SOUND INSANE.
YEAH! BAD TIME.
brrp brrp
brrp brrp
brrp brrp
SLAM